MW00614710

Cover Design--Cat Imb
Photographer. E. Vallejo
Formatting - Garnet Christie
Editing: Illuminate Editing Services

ISBN Print—978-1-7378243-9-8

fragments of you

GARNET CHRISTIE

From the Author.

Just a warning that Bentley and Nora are flawed. They're real. They don't always deal with their issues like they are supposed to—kind of like us sometimes. I could write about these characters who are tough as nails and deal with problems head on, but I don't like to write about perfect people. My heart thrives on writing about hearts who are at the weakest points of their life. I love writing about the one's who are wounded, who are scared to try again, and sometimes even try to tuck away the pain and forget it even happened to start with.

I can't promise you continous happy story with these two, but I can promise you a sweet ending if you're willing to stick around. Bentley is a mess, and Nora can doubt herself. But then again they are only human. What matter's is how they mature in the end and become the people they should have been from the start. I hope you see that as you go through love story.

This story is intended for readers 18+
Content includes frequent, strong language, graphic adult sexual scenes, and mentions of cheating.

Dedication

To anyone thinking you're not enough—that is a lie. You are always enough.

Chapter 1

Bentley

The vibration of my phone stirs me. I open my eyes and blink at the ceiling, willing the sleep away. My nose curls up at an overpowering floral scent. It smells like shit, and I hate it. There's a soft moan while my cell continues to buzz, and I look to my right—to the stranger in my bed.

A frown crinkles my forehead. *What was her name again?* Fuck. I can't remember, and it's not from drinking. Honestly, I rarely remember the name of any girl I take for a ride.

And man was this one a ride.

But now, she's bugging me with her snoring and fake rose smell. However, I won't be a douche. At least not a total one. I decide to give her the usual ten minutes before I wake her and send her home.

After straining for my phone, I check the screen. A missed call from Nora. That short, sweet name strikes warmth in my chest, and even though I'm itching to call her back, that seems rude to do to Nora when someone else is still in my bed. I'm clicking the screen off when her name pops up again, this time with a text message.

Hey. That movie we wanted to catch is still out. You up for going this afternoon?

Hell yeah. She doesn't know it, but I'm always down for seeing her.

A long tan arm flings across my chest, and I lurch.

Time to leave.

Looks like I'll be breaking my own ten-minute rule as I give the girl's arm a jostle.

"Hey, sweetheart."

She moans and sighs.

"Rise and shine."

"Hmmm?" Her head lifts up. Long nails that scraped down my back all night grasp at the snarly strands of hair covering her eyes. "What is it?"

I resist the urge to grimace. *Not so cute in the morning.* Then again, they never are. Not with the mascara lines streaming down their eyes and the smeared lipstick that leaves my pillows stained.

"I'm sorry." I kick the sheet off me and move out of bed, pretending I'm in a hurry. "Hate to do this to you, but I have to go."

"Go?" She sounds pissed while clutching the sheet, struggling to sit up. The scowl on her face tells me I'm right. "I don't even get a coffee? You might have warned me before letting me stay."

"It's not that, sweetheart." I grab my phone off the nightstand. "I just found out my Grandma's in the hospital. It's really sudden."

Her mouth falls open and long fingers slap over her lips. "Oh. Oh, I'm so sorry." She starts to scramble for her clothes. "I'll get out of your hair. Let me, uhh—"

"No worries. Sorry I won't be able to see you out." Turning for the bathroom, I hide my smile. *Works every time.* And she can't get mad. No woman with half a heart would be upset with a dude checking in on his sick Granny. Also, she won't get hurt. *Double win.* It's my usual golden ticket. "I'm gonna shower."

"Sure." She's finally standing and throwing on her bra. "Thanks for a great night." She smiles, and I see the dimples pop out. I'm pretty sure that's why I picked her last night. She has those dimples, just like…

Fuck… shut up. Shut up.

I nod. "You too."

"I hope everything works out with your Grandma."

"I'm sure it will," I wink. "Be safe on your way home."

"Thanks."

I shut the door, start the waterd wait.

I slowly count to ten, then hear her leave—the usual amount of time it takes for them to scramble and head out.

I'm peeling out of my briefs when my phone goes off again. The name popping up will never be one I brush off, and I take the call, bringing the phone to my ear. "Hey, Dad."

"Bentley." There's a warning undercurrent residing in his dark tone.

Shit. My stomach rolls inside. "Okay." I turn off the shower, opting to stand bare ass naked in the bathroom, hoping my Dad won't be too long. "What happened? What did I do?"

"Gracie's birthday."

"Damn it." I slap a palm across my face and squeeze my eyes shut. "I forgot to call." Yesterday was my little sister's birthday, and that mini princess thinks I'm a superhero. "Dad—"

"She cried."

"Fuck." Guilt needles away at me. I hate it when women cry. There isn't a sadder sight in the world, so I always try to avoid the occurrence. And Gracie is only eleven. *Some brother I am.*

"Son, you've got to *do* better. At least call when you say you will."

"Yeah. I know. I'm really sorry," I sigh. "Is she okay?"

"I think so. Your Mom took her and some friends to the roller rink a while ago."

I chuckle. "She's still into that?"

"Ever since you taught her, yes."

Smiling, I envision her with those wild brown curls fluttering behind as she races around the rink.

My dad clears his throat, and that sound gives me a clue where this is heading. "What were you doing last night anyway?"

Shit. Why does he always do this? "I was working late." The lie is bitter on my tongue, but it's better than admitting I was fucking a girl whose face blends in with everyone else's.

"Sure, Bentley." His voice is harsh and sarcastic. "I don't know when you're going to see how empty it is dragging home another girl every night, but I'm telling you now that this lifestyle you're livin—"

I groan and don't care if he hears it. "Hey, can I call you back? Work is ringing me." I'll be damned if I start my day off with another lecture. I've had enough to last a lifetime.

He pauses, then sighs. "We love you. Call later if you can."

"Thanks, Dad." Ruffling the top of my hair, I half smile. Lectures and all, my old man never ends a phone call on a bitter note, and he's open with his affection for his kids. Always has been. I'm lucky. That's the real reason why I never hesitate to pick up. "I love you guys too. Give Mom a kiss. Tell Gracie I'll call her tonight." *And this time, I will.*

"Okay."

The call ends, and my shoulders weigh down.

"Damn." I really am a shit brother, but I promise to do better tonight. Living over a thousand miles away doesn't give me an excuse, plus I'll be free tonight since I blew off so much steam the night before.

Right, Nora. That's the real reason why I'm in here. I turn on the shower again and go forward with my original plans.

I step in and let the water pulsate against my raw shoulder blades and back. That wild thing last night really tore me up, and maybe I'm being a pussy, but the shower right now hurts like hell. *No more acrylic nail girls.* I've told myself that before, but it seems like I always forget when in the moment. But this time *is* the last time. The carnage they do to my skin is making them not worth it anymore. Either that or I need to dial down my skills.

For now, I accept the sting.

My mess up with Gracie drains away, as does the fake scent of flowers that made me want to hurl. All the problems wash down the drain, but something else pops in my head.

I sigh in contentment. All I can think about as the water cascades over me is Nora's familiar scent that will soon surround me. It's a smell I'll enjoy. Well… more like drown in.

I don't know what the fuck that intoxicating smell is, but it wrecks me every time I'm near it.

Raking my fingers through my hair, I take a deep breath and squeeze my eyes shut. *Damn.*

The scenario is already playing out. We'll be in the theater, fighting over who's eaten the most popcorn, but the whole damn time, I'll be daydreaming about having that scent forever in my bed, all while knowing it shouldn't happen.

Dad's right. Bringing home a new girl isn't always the most fulfilling thing, but hey, it's fun. And while I want to have *fun* with Nora, I can never bring myself to do it. *She's off-limits*—I remind myself for the millionth time.

Because she's so steady—the exact opposite of who I am now.

Years ago, this wasn't the case. I wasn't always fast and short-lived, but life has a way of destroying the parts of you you'd never expect, and that's that. As for Nora, I don't want to be the one that throws her into the same cycle I'm in now.

I used to be like her, but not anymore.

There's never a rotation of guys. They stay for months on end, and her breaks in between are even longer. Her demeanor remains consistent. It makes her stable—the exact kind I don't fuck around with.

That's how you get into trouble and break hearts in the process.

Still, I think of those deep brown eyes of hers, round and wide, wishing I could stare into them while I—

"Fuck."

I shake away the thought and begin rinsing my hair.

Control, Bentley… fuck.

For once, I have a female friend who's easy to be with, and to hell with me if I'm about to mess that up.

It's the one thing I can never let happen. Not now, not ever.

Whatever it takes. I lean against the cold tiles while steam floats around me. I vow to keep her safe, always.

And despite the liar I am, that's the damn truth.

Fragments of You

Chapter 2

Nora

"And things are still okay in Colorado?" The voice of my older sister, Carly, blares over the speaker while I sit in my car. "We all miss you, you know." I can hear the guilt she's trying to lace into the statement. "I still don't know why you're there."

"Car, we've been through this." I tap the back of my skull against the headrest twice. "I like it here. You guys enjoy Florida and all those sugary beaches. I'm staying here, sticking with my job, and making sure sand doesn't get into every item I own."

"Mmm-hmm." She pauses for a moment. "You know, I saw an article the other day that said Pharmacists have a shorter life span."

"Car…" A puff of air trails out slowly. "First off, I doubt you read that. Secondly, shut up. I'm not under enough pressure to die of a stroke." A touch of anxiety swirls in my chest.

She still doesn't know I'm only working part-time. They'd freak if they knew my hours had been cut.

"Well, just saying you should be with your family. Mom and Dad aren't getting any younger. Plus, maybe you could find a different job out here, even if it's not at a pharmacy."

"Silly." I scrunch my nose, feigning a playful tone. "You *do* realize how long I had to go to school for this, don't you?"

"Eight years," we say in unison.

"All that wasted time," she bites out.

And the money. Tons of money lost pursuing my dream job in my dream State. "I don't want a career change."

"What?" Her voice goes dead. "Is bartending in short shorts beneath you or something?"

Me in shorts, no way. I cock my brow. "Possibly."

"Just sayin'." She's sneering right now—I can just see it. "During the winter months, I make bank as the old-timers fly south. People like spending while vacationing."

"Yeah, well, I make *bank* all the time thanks to a steady job." My teeth grit at the lie dripping off my tongue.

"Oh, whatever." She smacks her lips twice over the phone. "You're at least coming home for Christmas, right?"

I don't answer. There's a sight about ten feet away that's making a slow stride through the parking lot. A beautiful, gorgeous sight that always leaves my throat dry and my heart racing. *Bentley.* I can hardly breathe when watching him. *So, so perfect.* But sadly, not mine.

"Nora?" Carly's voice cracks through my daze.

"Bentley's here, and I have to go. Sorry, Car." My gaze stays pinpointed to Bentley. There's no way I'm missing a free chance to ogle since I have to hide it most of the time.

"Oh, the fuck-boy."

"Carly…" Telling her I found out Bentley is a bed hopper was a mistake.

"You're not sleeping with him, are you? Because that's how you get hurt."

"Pffff…no." For some reason, her words make a sting seep into my heart.

"Nora…" Her voice spikes with a warning. "I've seen pictures of him. He's sexy as all hell, so how are you *not* shagging him?"

"He's short." I snort through my nose. Taller than me, but still short for a guy. Not that it matters—*he's* all that matters to me.

"Which doesn't sound like it matters. Not with the stories

you told—"

"Please, I'm not banging him, and I have to go." *Why did I say anything?* I grab my keys and prepare to turn off my car. "Tell Mom and Dad hi. Love ya."

"Nor—"

Killing the ignition, I climb out and rub my clammy palms together. It's bad enough I have to *pretend* I'm devoid of attraction for the guy I've been obsessing over for two years. Does the idea of sex with him have to be rubbed in my face too? I can't catch a break.

I cross the parking lot, catching up to Bentley, and he turns around before I'm even halfway.

"Hey, sunshine." He winks with a smile, and butterflies unleash in my stomach. "You look lovely today."

The familiar greeting weakens my knees. They wobble just a hair, and God, those eyes don't help me—light Grecian blue, soul-piercing, and a total knee buckler against his sun-tan. I hike my purse strap higher on my shoulder, trying not to stare too long, ignoring the hard beats of my pulse in my neck.

"You made it." I hope my smile isn't too tight.

"Why wouldn't I?" He rumples a hand through the top of his short spiky hair, and once again, the sandy brown arrangement stays in place. I give full credit to the hair gel. It must be more like super glue. He flicks his eyes down at me, and the corner of his lip quirks up. "You know I've wanted to see this one for a while. Also, I wanted to see you again too."

"Yeah." I gaze down at the ground as my cheeks flush, brushing the comment aside.

He's only teasing.

That I'm certain of since we were supposed to see this movie last night, but he never called. *I wonder if he was with someone.* Swallowing past the lump in my throat, I flick a piece of hair off my shoulder. "I've wanted to see this movie too."

"Not me?" He gawks, mouth wide open. "Shame on you."

"Oh, stop." I poke at his buff shoulder. "You know I never mind seeing you."

"Ah. Yes." He slings his arms around my shoulder for a quick side hug. "That's better."

The sensation hitting me is bittersweet. Over the course of our relationship, I've pieced together that the only time our plans don't work out is when he's busy with another girl. I don't ask names, and I don't dare ask questions, but I'd be dumb to assume otherwise. I've heard and seen too much. Whenever someone new comes around, he's a ghost.

He shuffles sideways towards me and bumps me with his elbow. "That's not the face I like to see. Smile."

"Sorry." I hold my head up high and add some bounce to my step, shoving the forlorn thought away. "This week was long, but I'll pull through."

His eternal smile fades for a moment as his lips pull down. "Is it because of work? Is the puppy-hater still giving you problems?"

I giggle. "My boss *never* said she hated puppies—"

"No," his face beams with a wide grin, "but she did say puppies aren't cute, and that's not right. No wonder she's such a bit—witch."

I choke on a laugh. "Oh man, thanks for sparing me the bad language." He reaches for the door handle, and I waggle my brows. "You know, with my virgin ears and all."

He shakes his head and fake scowls, holding the door wide for me. "Get inside, miss."

I bite back a chuckle and obey. "I'll get the tickets," I say, past my shoulder. "How about you grab the snacks?"

He winks, "You betcha."

Strolling to the ticket counter, I pay. Tightened purse strings still won't turn me into a freeloader, even though Bentley could buy both. His job pays well.

He turns to face me as I wind around to the concession counter, tickets in hand.

"Here's the popcorn. You want a red slushy?"

"You know me so well." Too well, to be honest.

"Like a book, sweetheart." The words drop a heaviness between my thighs. "Bet I could even pick out the candy you would order."

"Yeah, well, I could say the same." I reach out for the popcorn, only for him to withdraw the red and white paper sack.

He cocks up a brow. "Don't load it up with too much butter."

"Shut up." I snag it from his clutch and strut away, my nose in the air. "That's the best part."

"You'll make me fat," he hollers from over his shoulder.

Rolling my eyes, I'm deciding to douse it with as much butter as I want. *Fat. Whatever.*

I've been blessed to see him shirtless at the pool. Not only is his frame naturally thin, prone to fighting extra poundage, but he's a machine. He lifts, runs, boxes, plays soccer, tennis, bicycles… he does it all. Not to mention his hoop-skills. Every time I've watched him play, each throw is a swish. If anything, he needs the extra calories, which is why I'm still adding butter when he joins me.

"Holy crap, Nora." He slams down the drinks, forces my thumb off the button, and grabs the bag. "I'll have to eat protein bars for a week."

"Don't be a diva." I dig my fingers in the bag, grabbing a greasy handful. After eating it, I hold up my hand, showing off all the butter, and moan. "Mmmm."

His face scrunches up. "Show some consideration."

My eyes narrow. "Maybe if you fatten up, you'll look better."

"Oh, I think you need some glasses." He swaggers back and gestures at his trim physique. "Trust me when I say that *no one* complains about this."

Well duh. Of course not, but it's hardly the thing to say. Flirting with him always proves to make things awkward for us weeks later. Bentley always ends up pulling back and avoiding me for a while.

"Which is why you have me," I retort, keeping my eyes from crawling over every inch of his delicious body. Especially the pecs his Henley shirt stretches to accommodate, which leaves nothing to my imagination. "Someone has to be honest with you."

He barks out a laugh, and I brush past him with a smirk plastered on my face. But the whole time, my heart thunks in my chest, revving up in pace when he catches me in the hall.

All I can think about is touching and feeling every freaking inch of him—shirtless, with the zing of his cologne surrounding me. The thought passes through my head every time we're together.

Sweet Moses. The things I'd do to him.

I drown in indecency when his fingers tousle in my ponytail. "You missed a spot."

Craning to glance behind my shoulder, I see him barrel wrapping a strand of hair around his index finger.

"Actually, you always miss this spot." His eyes squint like he's studying it. "You curl it, don't you?"

"No," I purse my lips. "My hair is naturally wavy." I examine the straighter lock he's just played with. "I guess not all of it is, though. I'll curl that part next time."

"Don't." He smiles wide. "Sometimes, that's the only way I find you in a crowd."

My nose wrinkles with the tease. "Like you *ever* try to find me in a crowd."

"Oh," he bumps his shoulder into mine, "You have no idea." He steps out, taking the lead to open the theater door for me.

"Whatever." Sliding past, I keep my head down, positively blushing over the interaction.

I'm not in a much better state as the credits roll two hours later.

"What did ya think?"

I shrug, trying to ignore his arm that's rubbed against mine the whole dang movie. It's another reason why my thoughts have been on a rampage this afternoon. "There were too many car chases."

"Eh." He stretches out his neck. "At least the girl was hot."

I snort through my nose, "No comment."

The chuckle that pours out of him, warm and gentle, floats right into my chest, and I go fuzzy inside. Chewing on my lower lip, I desperately try to regain some control of my head space as my cheeks and neck burn. I'm usually much more composed when it comes to dealing with Bentley.

The last two years have eaten away at my resolve.

"Hey." Bentley nudges me, and reality floods back. "Where

were all your commentaries during the film? You've been so quiet today." He angles in the seat and faces me better. "Are you sure you're okay? Anything you want to talk about or say?"

I'm freaking crazy about you. "No." I shake my head. "I think I just needed to get out and have some fun."

"Fun, huh?" Those unreal eyes light up with a glow. "Well, I can give you that." He looks at his phone. "It's still early. You want some ice cream?"

Man, if he doesn't know the way to my heart—my mouth is already drooling. "I'll never say no to ice cream."

"Awesome." He reaches out and taps the tip of my nose with his finger. It's a gesture that never fails to unleash a swirl in my stomach, this time being no exception. "And if you're still not happy, we can go get hibachi."

"Really?" My brows hit my hairline.

"Really." He stands and extends his hand out to help me up. "Let's give you a good time before Monday starts."

Excitement rings so high in my blood, I'm leaping out of my seat.

We walk out of the theater, and I have a huge stupid grin on my face. *I get him all to myself.* It means I'm assured of a night of laughter, easy conversation, and a sweet drumming of arousal flooding through me as I sit across and stare into his eyes. Being around him feels like I'm with my other half, but I can't tell him that. *He'll freak.* I've learned the hard way to keep my emotions concerning Bentley to myself, so now I just take what I can get.

The sting of being forgotten last night is lessening in my chest when his phone goes off.

He checks the caller ID and smirks before answering, "Hey, hey."

That bright enthusiasm. It never gets old and always makes my stomach flutter. But the sensation crashes and dies when I hear a girl's voice answering back. I can't make out a word she's saying, but the laugh Bentley responds with releases a wave of nausea through my core. *No. No. No.*

He laughs again. "Okay, sweetheart, calm it down."

Sweetheart. It's an arrow of pain and jealousy through my chest, and the sharp ache rippling deep inside almost makes me bow over.

"Give me a moment and I'll be over to help."

No. I stare blankly at the gray sidewalk.

"No. Oh, uh no. I'm just with a friend. I'll be right over."

My body and shoulders deflate at that word. *Friend.* We should be more, but I'm quick to toss my head back when he ends his call and rests his hand on my shoulders.

"Hey, I hate to do this, but someone needs my help."

"Oh no. I understand." It takes all my strength to control the tremble residing in my voice. "Ice cream isn't even a big deal." The words plow into my stomach, eating through the organ until a pit of emptiness takes over.

"Thanks." His smile is soft as he tucks a wayward strand behind my ear. "You're amazing, you know that?" He backs up, yanking his car keys out of his pocket. "I'll call you tomorrow, and we'll do dinner. Okay?"

I stumble back a step. "Yeah, sure." My voice quakes this time.

But he doesn't notice because he's already gone—trotting across the lot, waving his arm wildly in the air as his final goodbye.

A deadness washes over me when his car pulls out the parking lot, and I feel a warm sensation hitting the corners of my eyes.

I've lost him to another woman yet again, and my previous experiences warn me that he isn't going to call tomorrow. I'm going to sit in disappointment like I do every time he fails to come through.

And, it turns out I'm right.

Because as Sunday evening comes and goes, I'm left staring at my phone. A phone that's been silent all evening. And I'm, yet again, left wondering why I never seem to be enough.

Chapter 3

Bentley

"Hey, man," Rich yells from the kitchen. "Want another?"

"Nah, I'm good." Too much beer and I'll get a gut, like Dad. Hell no. I try to enjoy the game on TV, but it rarely ever happens. Playing is better than watching.

"By the way," Rich returns, beer and chips in hand, "Joy told me she called you the other day."

"Yeah." I recline further into the couch. "I was leaving the theater with a friend." *Friend* is a cover word. My urge to flirt with her makes her more, but she'll never be anything I touch.

"What'd Joy want? She called me first, but I never answered."

I shake my head. "There was a spider in her shower."

He laughs through a mouth full of chips, spewing crumbs. "God, my cousin is so annoying."

"What's so wrong with that?" While reaching for my water, my eyes flick to the game. "My mom is terrified of them. I always killed them for her when I lived at home." I shoot him de-eye glance of annoyance after he sits. "Why didn't you answer?"

"Dude! This brunette was here. That tight thing was loaded with positions. How do you break that up to take a call?"

"You don't."

He grunts. That's his sound of agreement. After that, we both go silent.

Rich and I hang out all the time, and while I'm not into watching games, it's a small sacrifice for someone I can chat with. Parties, women, games, and work—it's all we talk about. Sometimes he gets a wild hair up his ass and joins me at the gym, but that never lasts. He's trim enough but can't walk up a flight of stairs without bitching. I can't understand how he lasts in bed, at least not with the way he brags about his abilities. I peg him down for one round, max.

"By the way," he asks, "How was your trick the other night from my party? I don't know who she was, but that thing had everyone hot and bothered."

Shrugging, I prop my hands on the top of my head, interlocking my fingers. "She was alright."

"Alright?" He sits upright. "Dude, that girl was hot as fuck. How can you just say alright?"

I give him my first chuckle of the night. "I don't know. She was just alright."

He waves his hands in the air, searching for more answers.

"Whatya want me to say? It was like all the other times. She screamed and tore my back to shit till *I* screamed."

A roaring laughter tears from his throat. "You're such a pussy."

"I know." Fuck my admittance—actually, fuck tonight.

Everything feels wrong. Tonight, here, with no one meaningful beside me, Dad's words are hitting hard.

"I don't know." I shoot a glazy stare at the TV with a weak thunk occurring in my chest. "Maybe all this sleeping around stuff isn't worth it."

"Someone's been talking to their Dad again."

"He did ring. I forgot to call my sister for her birthday."

He grunts again. "See. That's why you shouldn't talk to him."

A sigh works out of me as I scrub over the top of my hair.

"That's what you do, Rich. That's not me." He laughs in that condescending way, and my blood pressure rises. "I happen to love my family. Lectures included." And why wouldn't I? My family is great. I'm the only fuck up in it.

"Whatever, man, suit yourself. All I know is I wouldn't let my Dad tell me off for forgetting to call on a lame-ass birthday."

My brows snap together. "My sister is eleven, dick face. Have a heart. Plus, she loves me."

He snorts hard through his nose. "Don't know why. You're a filthy bastard."

The insult has me slouching into the couch. "Yeah, I am." I try to loosen my tense body and chill out, but I can't.

Screw this. It's time to go home.

I stand. "Listen, I'm gonna call it early. Today blew." It didn't, but I want an out. The foul stick up my ass tonight leaves me in zero mood for attacks.

"Yeah, sure." His eyes never leave the set. "I'm having a party Friday. Come ready for some pussy. Justin is inviting a shit ton of sorority girls."

My face deadens, and I shake my head. He talks about sex like he's fifteen. I like sex too, but fuck. *He's vulgar.* Which is why I haven't told him about my older sister, Lena. One sight of her, and he'd be urging us on the next plane ride home just to nail her—fuck no.

He'll never get near someone I respect or love.

"Yeah, sure." I wave on the way out.

My shoulders hunker down while absorbing the cold. I push out a frosty breath and leave the condo entrance, heading for my car.

Looking at the stars, I admire their spark. *A blanket of twinkles in a dark sea.* That's how Mom always describes them. Half of me wishes I had someone to admire the view with, but there's no one. I shove my hands in my pocket, and my fingertips graze my cell phone—after pulling it out, I stare at it and pause.

A beat later, I think of two vibrant brown eyes and a head-full of grippable chestnut hair. *Nora.* She's bright, much like the stars above. *Forgiving too.* A frown takes over.

I abandoned her on Saturday, then left her high and dry

Sunday. I've done this to her before, and if that doesn't make me a dick, then I don't know what does. I only flaked out because I was weak—consumed with thoughts better left untold. Ones of wanting her scent in my nostrils while she's in my bed, chanting my name. The temptation was too much, so I ditched her... again.

Each time I let her down, I expect the chew-out session I deserve. It never happens—something I'm still not sure if I'm happy or upset about. It makes me feel like I'm less to her than she lets on, but I'm not going to lose her by fucking things up with complicated shit.

But tonight, I need her. Alone, cold, and disgruntled for whatever reason, I need that spark so bad each pump of blood makes my veins ache. After a few seconds of the uncomfortable sensation, I cave and send her a text.

Hey, sunshine. What's going on tonight?

She usually answers soon. I hope that's the case tonight. Finishing the walk to my car, I know I'm heading straight under the covers tonight.

My body is ready to sleep in an empty bed. No nameless faces, no screaming of any high-pitched voices. Just me.

I'm only about a block from Rich's house when my phone rings, and the name of my sister, Lena, flashes back at me.

"Hey, stupid," I say with a smirk.

"Hey, butt face." She whips her response out like a switchblade.

We both laugh, loving our childhood insults now that we're older.

"Catch you at a good time?"

"Yeah." I zip around a corner and stop at a light, my finger tapping on the wheel. "What's going on?"

"Whole big load of nothing. I just wanted to make sure you're still alive over there." I hear the sly jab in her voice. "Glad I caught you when you're *ahem*, free."

"That's a low blow." I squint down at the display but can't stop the smile. "I hate you."

"Oh, yeah…" A laugh slips out. "I know." The tone of her voice drops, and she clears her throat. "By the way, thanks for calling Gracie the other night. She wouldn't stop talking about it."

"No problem." Calling can't erase the guilt that still eats a hole in my chest when thinking about it. "Only wish I hadn't forgotten the first time." The light changes, and I go.

A shift happens, and I feel a weight settle in the pause. My fingers tighten around the wheel because now I suspect Lena did call for a reason. I just have to wait to hear what it is.

"Are you still planning on coming home in a few weeks?"

I furrow my brows. She usually follows up Dad's lectures on morality, only she's not as hardcore. My head cocks at the unexpected question. "I was thinking about it, yeah." I stop at another light.

"Wait." The word barks out fast and hurried. "Just. Uh… wait. Maybe another month or something."

"Uhhh… Okay," I say slowly. "Any reason why?"

"*She's* back."

I freeze—can't even blink. The world drops away into the blackest hole known to man.

A car behind me beeps.

"Shit." The light is green. My car lurches when I step on the gas, my knuckles white on the wheel as my throat clogs. "How do you know?" The question is so thick I almost choke on it.

"I saw her when I took Gracie for ice cream," she huffs, her tone tense. "Fucking bitch had the nerve to stop me and ask how you were doing. Even said she missed you."

A blow hollows out my chest, sending parts of my heart through my body. *Ivy misses me?* I lurch back to life at Lena's growl.

"I swear to God, Bent, if Gracie hadn't been there, I would have scratched the bitch's eyes out and tied her to the first bus out of town."

Pulling into my driveway, I'm only half alive. But I know I'm not alone when Lena and I sigh at the same time. I slam my back into the leather seat, desperate for another sensation besides that of the past sweeping me away—of this pain that's cutting so deep, tears are at the corners of my eyes.

"That's why I'm telling you to wait, Bentley. I don't know how long she'll be here, but I can sure as hell find out, then I'll call you when she leaves. Copperslane is only so big."

I rub at my eyes, hoping the torment swirling in my ribcage will fuck off and die.

My home, Copperslane Washington, is a posh small town with a big city vibe. Too bad the charm it once had to me is now overcrowded with grief. The place fucking sucks, and I left after Ivy tore my soul to shreds. I got tired of everyone knowing my business and giving me the same old, damn pity stares. Fuck that.

"Or come down and confront her. You know, make her feel like the cheating bitch she is."

Fuck. I think my chest is going to cave from the weight crushing down on it. My eyes squeeze shut. "I can't see her, Lena."

"I didn't think so. I mean not after everything she did." Her tone softens.

My throat dries up, and my hands shake. *Why did I have to hear about her tonight?*

"Bent…" Lena's voice is even softer now. "You know it's okay? If you have something to get off your chest, you can tell me. I won't tell Mom or Dad."

I take a deep inhale. "I want to be there, but… fuck." My cheeks puff out while blowing out stale air. "If I *saw* her, I think it'd be the end of my sanity." My voice breaks at the end, just like my heart is doing.

"Damn it." I hear her sniffle. "You're still not over it all."

"I thought I was." My head drops. "But now? Shit." I stop a tear. *Fuck me if I cry over her again.* Alone in my car or not, I'm going to have some dignity over this.

"Hey, not being over it is understandable, no matter how long it's been. Either way, I'm glad I warned you since I wasn't sure at first."

I nod slowly. "Me too." Man, seeing Ivy would have been a huge cluster-fuck of my brain. *Thank God for Lena.* The trip home will definitely have to wait. I hope Gracie won't be too sad about that. "Call me when she leaves.I'll visit after."

"Count on it. And if I gouge her eyes out, I'll be sure it ends up on Snapchat for you."

That makes me laugh, even if the sound is mingled with a half cry. "Just stay out of trouble. She's not worth it."

"Ha. For you, she is. Don't think about her and get some sleep. Love ya, butt head."

"Back at ya, stupid."

The call ends. I sit there for I don't know how long. I'm empty, drained—like I want to sleep but can't—like I want to find a girl and fuck out the throb lashing through me, but I can't do that either. Instead, I sit there for far too long and absorb nothing.

I don't talk about Ivy much. Hell, I try to think about her even less, but in moments like this, where everything is blown back in my face, and the pain is cut wide open again, all I possess is the ability to do nothing.

When I climb out of the car and go inside, I notice several hours have passed. *Shit.* I should be asleep. Work will be a bitch if I don't head for bed right now. But shut-eye doesn't come easy.

Actually, it doesn't come at all.

In the dark, I open my eyes and rehash the evening.

Rich, gross beer, TV, women talk, Nora…

Nora. My body strains for a breath, maybe it's my weakened state, but she's all I want.

She never texted me back, and her absence is making the pain in my chest fester. *I need her.* And that demand has me clutching for the phone at two in the morning.

I've called her late before, so I know she won't mind. Besides, this isn't just any phone call. It's an emergency, one my body seems to sense as my fingers tremble while I pull her number up on speed dial. Thank goodness her name is at the top.

I already know talking to her won't be enough. A rough swallow rushes down my throat. *I'm asking her out to dinner tomorrow.* It's not right, but I need something to seal the wound gashing away at me.

Nora can do that—*does* that, even though she doesn't know it. She's the perpetual sweet calm to the storms I face.

The phone rings. It rings a few times, and at first, my heart tightens. *What if she won't answer?* I hate that thought because damn, do I need to hear that voice of hers.

Then the ringing stops.

"Hello?"

The world stills. She's answered when I've needed her the most… like always. One sound of that voice is like honey to my soul, and the pain of Ivy starts to balm-over. I smile.

"Hey, sunshine."

Chapter 4

Nora

The teal sheets of my bedding are twisting around me like a tornado as I check the clock, grumbling at the ungodly hour. It's two A.M. Sleep is eluding me. It's getting more frequent, and I'm chalking it up to my unsteady job hours. I don't work tomorrow, and the anxiety of knowing I'll be on my own all day, isolated, while other people are striving ahead, makes it impossible for me to rest.

"Damn it."

I'm throwing back the sheets, contemplating another glass of warm milk, when my cell phone goes off.

Only one person calls at this hour.

Bentley. Butterflies erupt, knowing it's him. It doesn't happen every night, but sometimes he can't sleep either. I end up answering before the third ring.

"Hello?"

"Hey, sunshine."

A manic thump pounds against my ribs, and I smile. "Hi." My voice is so sugary sweet I should be throwing up.

"There she is." Bentley's voice is bright despite the dark our. "You didn't answer my text earlier, so I got worried. Everything good?"

"Did I not?" I blink a few times. "I thought I texted you back right away." *Not true.* I saw his text but was still a little wounded and scared to answer after he ditched me.

"Trust me, you didn't." There's a silent beat. "I know because I was disappointed. I've been waiting all night to hear from you."

A warmth floods between my thighs, the combination of his words and voice making me squirm under my sheets. I combat the reaction with a giggle. "So you thought *this* would be a good time to call?"

"Anytime's a good time to call you. Especially when I can't sleep."

I bite down on my lip, relishing that when he struggles, it's me he comes to—and that part of our relationship is the best. When we're hurting, tired, or sad, we turn to one another. No strings attached, no messy "I helped you, you helped me." Just two people who stumble and pick each other up when life hits us a little harder than usual.

"What did you do today? Tell me everything." His voice is gentle and warm.

Everything. My brows furrow. "I'm afraid there's not much good to speak of. Work is a bitch, and I cried."

"Cried?" His voice softens. "Aw, Nora. Who would dare make you cry? Tell me who I need to chew out."

"No, that's not it. One of our older customers passed away." I steady my voice, the sting popping up all over again. "He was my favorite. He always brought cookies and gave me my own plate. Mine always had extra chocolate chips." I sniffle.

"Sweetheart, I'm sorry. Why didn't you call me? I would have brought you a soda or maybe a bar of chocolate. Something to buck you up."

"Oh, no." I pat the dampness from my eyes, a smile breaking across my mouth at how thoughtful Bentley is. A friendly reminder that underneath his occasional dropouts, he's a man capable of the kindest acts. "You wouldn't have had to do anything like that."

"I would have, though, for you." The words are soft, flowing into my ear. "If I knew you were upset, I'd do just about anything to make you feel better. You mean a lot to me, Nora."

My heart kicks into overdrive, the room floating around me. Knowing I mean something to him nourishes my soul in all the right ways. My thoughts are so thick, I barely notice the silence and jolt to life at the sound of his voice.

"However, I'm glad you're only telling me about this guy now. I didn't realize I had competition."

A chuckle slides out of me—it stops my tears with a weight flying out of my chest.

"That's the sound I like to hear." A smile plays heavily in his voice. "Enough with all that sad stuff, huh?"

I nod. "Thanks, Bentley."

"Anytime, sunshine."

"Anyway, enough about me." I shake the thought of my afternoon away, sinking a little under the covers. "What's new with you? How was work?"

"Oh, man," he sighs. "I ended up saving our company close to ten grand today on a bad investment."

"Why am I not surprised." Bentley is a financial genius. "I know that's why they pay you well."

"It is." He snorts. "Now, if the CEO would let me do my damn job and talk to me before it's almost too late. Ahh." He breathes hard into the phone. "But he's a micro manager, so I suppose he can't help it."

"You're right—he can't help it." I stifle a yawn, fatigue winding through my legs and arms. "He's always been like that, and you're always having that problem. I doubt it will change."

"Yeah, I know, but one can hope, huh?"

"There you are, finding the silver lining again." I rub at the sleep taking over my eyes. "Does stuff like that ever make you want to leave or find something better?"

"Hmm. Maybe. The pay makes it worth the trouble, but aspirations are always nice. I might aim for a different employer someday."

"Like who?" I shimmy under the sheets till I'm chin-deep. "What would be the ultimate dream job?"

He pauses. "I know one pal who's a financial manager for

Apple. I think that would be cool."

I grimace. "A huge entity? That sounds stressful."

"Well—"

A smile creeps over my mouth, "But I also know you're smart and collected enough to handle something like that, so I know you'd be good."

"Damn…" His voice perks up, and he sighs. "I love it when you say things like that. You sure do know how to make a man feel good," he chuckles softly. "Whoever catches you will have a lifetime of compliments."

The praise shoots straight into my heart, daring me to melt. I push out a soft *thank you* and get lost in the tone of his voice as he carries on the conversation. During the day, he's more jovial, but in the midnight hours, I feel like he hides nothing from me. He lays it all out.

Big and small.

From the new protein shake he's trying out to his sister being a cute little weirdo with her K-pop phase, or a potential house he might buy, and the 5k he's thinking about being in—I listen to every word, soaking in the pieces of Bentley. I wonder if he's showing this to anyone else. Because when I hear him like this, open and free, it makes me think I'm special.

That is until I doze off.

"Nora?"

I stir. "Hmm. What?"

"You fell asleep on me. And right when I told you about the new flavor that I meal-prep my chicken with." He *tsks*. "How dare you?"

"Sorry, but you lost me at teriyaki." I rub my eyes, noticing the silence on the line, and I envision his face. *I know exactly what he's doing.* He's scowling. "And don't look at me like that."

"Like what?"

"Like I've sinned against everything Godly."

He laughs full-out. "Got me pegged that well, huh? I *was* scowling."

I giggle. "Called it." *Like always.*

"What are you doing for dinner tomorrow?"

I groan. "Nothing. The evil witch has barred me from the

pharmacy. I have time off. Bentley—"

"Hey, it will work out." I hear that happy glimmer in his voice again, and my eyes droop closed. "How 'bouts we meet tomorrow for sushi… my treat?"

"That sounds good."

"Great. Bring your smile. That's the only way I'm eating with you."

"Hmm-mmm." My eyes roll. "Whatever."

"Night. See you tomorrow. Don't be late."

He hangs up, and I place my phone down.

Don't be late.

I know I won't be. All I'm hoping is that he'll actually show up. Because with Bentley, I always feel like I'm living for that crapshoot high. So, so elusive, yet so thrilling when I hit the jackpot of his isolated time.

The next afternoon, steam and bubbles engulf me, and I tip my head back, letting water from the hot tub kiss my nape. "You're never going to get me out of here, you know," I smirk at my friend Tessa, my bestie from our university days, as she gulps down the remaining wine in her glass. We've decided to meet up and chill for a moment after her work day. I smile, then gaze out again at the spectacular mountain view from her balcony.

"Fine by me." Her silvery voice draws my eyes back to her. "Like I ever have any visitors."

Tessa. Our bond is one I never thought would happen. By the time I got into CU in Colorado, Tessa had already established herself as the brooding badass girl. She didn't hang out with anyone and never smiled. Sure, she'd pop around to a party here or there, although we never knew why—and no one dared approach her while she sulked in the corners with her hollow gray eyes and black hair.

For a while, she terrified me due to that mean-streak look. But that changed when I tried to leave a party after being haggled by a creep. He grabbed me, trying to force a kiss. When I did a less than adequate job of defending myself, it was Tessa who came up from behind, tapped the dude on the shoulder, then kicked him in the crotch.

At first, she claimed she only did it because she felt sorry for me, but after hanging out at my dorm that night, I discovered she was lonely. A rich kid whose parents didn't give a crap. She lacked the social skills to connect with people. We ended up clicking after that evening, rented a house soon after to finish college, and have been inseparable since.

She slips further into the water and closes her eyes. "I mean it, Nor, you should move in with me. It could be like the old days."

"You mean like before you dropped out of college?" I try to make the reminder a gentle poke. Years later, and I'm still not letting that go. I keep hoping she'll go back and finish her degree. She was so close to graduating with honors. It kills me to know she gave up on herself. Occasionally I encourage her to finish, praying it will respark the passion I once saw.

"Don't go there." She opens one eye to peer at me. "You would have done the same if your parents didn't give one iota." Her one eye seals shut. "Besides, I still got the job I wanted. I'm helping deaf kids like I always dreamed of, and I didn't need a degree. Money and tenacity were enough." A yawn slips out of her. "Anyway, you can have the room on the top floor, the one that has the bathroom with the sweet whirlpool tub. I hate baths." She scrunches up part of her lip and gags. "Even this is too much. I'm roasting here."

My situation at work hits me, making my shoulders deflate. "Ugh. I might have to if Laura doesn't give me back my hours. The way things are, I don't think I'll be able to afford my apartment after a while. I didn't even work today."

"That woman is such a wench." She takes a moment to secure her luscious midnight locks with an overstretched hair tie. "Just find someplace else already. There are other pharmacies, I'm sure. Maybe one with a hot young dude or a sweet old man at the helm."

"It's not that simple." I stare blankly at the water, wiggling my toes through the tiny bubbles. "I'm under contract there,

Tess."

"So?" she shrugs. "Break it."

"I took a sign-on bonus when starting there. If I quit, I'll have to pay all of it back."

She lurches upright. Her naturally down-turned eyes widen, and she angles her head. "You never told me this."

"That's because it's a pretty standard thing to do. At least for a chain pharmacy." I reach for my wine, suddenly needing a relaxing taste. "As it is, I've spent the bonus and can't afford to pay it back."

She frowns. "So you're stuck? Basically reduced to being their slave even though the manager is a bitch?"

I nod. "Me and two others still haven't worked there long enough to leave." A weak smile creeps across my lips. "At least I'm not alone."

"I suppose that's one way to approach things. How do your folks feel about their baby being mistreated?"

"Oh gosh." I chew the inside of my cheek. "I haven't told them." My lips pinch together when her brows shoot up. "Dad would be so upset—especially since he didn't want me in this line of work to begin with. I think he'd probably come here himself, chew that woman's ass out, then drag me home."

"Hey, I'd take it." That familiar fiery gaze of hers dims. She shoots a bored droopy expression to the vast Colorado view. "It beats having folks who think money is a substitute for time and love."

My heart weighs down with that pitiful look flashing across her face. "Have they still not visited you since two years ago?"

"Oh," her eyes roll, "Of course not. They sent a big fat check, however. Like that means anything." She smacks her palm onto the water's surface and scowls. "Talk to me about something else."

"Uhhh… The wine you picked out tonight is perfect."

She tosses her head back and laughs deeply. "Damn, you're bad on your feet."

"Unless I'm pissed."

"Which is never." She props her hands behind her head and relaxes. "You're more likely to get your feelings hurt than getting pissed."

"True. But—"

The alert on my cell phone cuts off my words. Tilting my head back to see who it's from, my heart knots with excitement. It's from Bentley.

See ya soon.

We're still on. I clamp down on my lip to contain an excited outburst.

"Go ahead. Get that squeal out and answer your unrequited love before you explode," Tessa says.

I snap my attention to her, a touch of frustration bubbling in my veins. "How did you know it's Bentley?"

"Those peepers of yours only light up like that when it's him," she snorts. "I doubt Henry Cavill could get the same reaction if he offered to serve you breakfast, naked."

I duck my head and snicker, but it's short-lived.

"Not that Bentley deserves that attention." Her voice is flat. "You really should put that sucker in his place."

"Tess—"

"Or for all that is sane, at least ask him out. I bet you had a chance when we hung out at Rich's house the other week." She rolls her eyes. "You two were shoved in a corner, talking for a lifetime. Why didn't you?"

The aggravation reaches a full boil, and I grunt, rolling through the water till I hit the back of the hot tub. A splash occurs, and my nape is now drenched—too bad it doesn't cool me off. "I've already told you, I *can't* do that."

"Hmm." She picks up her wine glass and stares at it, squinting, almost like she's willing more liquid to appear. "You've told me why once, but humor me again."

My brows scrunch. "Why?"

"Because I'm hoping when you repeat it, you'll hear how silly you sound."

I scrunch up my nose. "That's not funny."

Her head tilts in a dismissive shrug. "Wasn't intending it to be. Now spill."

"He just… I don't know. It's like he wants me but doesn't."
My fist clenches as I try to ignore her bored nod. "He'll ask me
out, but every time I think we're about to have a real date, he
usually ditches our plans."

"And you never bother to ask why or give him shit about
it?" She folds her arms across her chest under the water and
skirts up a brow. "Really, Nor. That's pathetic."

Pathetic. I sputter out a hot breath—one loaded with hurt.
"Well, what do you expect me to do?"

"Stick to your guns and act like the self-respecting girl I
know you are." She holds up a hand when I try to speak. "Letting him talk and see you when it's convenient for him isn't doing you any favors. Stand up and put the little cock-runner in
his place."

A pause takes hold, and my gaze drops to the water. A familiar pain forms across my chest, and I place my hand there.
"But if it drives him away—"

She flips her hand. "So what?"

"Tess." My shoulders tighten. "Regardless of what you
think, Bentley is important to me."

Her brow wrinkles, painting a look of doubt on her face.

"I mean it. Being around him is easy, fun, and something
I'm excited about." I chew on the inside of my cheek, wishing
Tess could understand. "Plus, we can read each other's thoughts,
and I enjoy that connection."

"Oh," she nods, "There is no doubt you two have chem-
istry." I watch her eyes widen for a moment. "I mean, damn.
Watching you two together is like seeing a fireworks show going
bonkers. You two just click. We all see it."

"Everybody but him," I mumble, shoulders going flat.

"I doubt that," she spits out. "Unless your Bentley is blind-
er than my grandpa, he sees it too."

"Then why does he always blow me off?" A bitter hole
punches through my chest, and my lips press against each other.
"If he can feel this, then why does he give me all the right signals
but never follows through?"

"That's something you'll have to ask him," she says softly,

"But you won't."

I frown, my heart so heavy it's sinking into my toes. "Losing him would be awful." My voice cracks. "I know you think I'm stupid for never confronting him, Tess, but if I drove him away... I'd rather own a fragment of his friendship and company, no matter how small, than to never see him again."

"Well then, suit yourself." One of her creamy shoulders pulls up. "It's *your* heart that you're putting through the wringer. No one else's."

"Gee, thanks." I'm trying to steel my tone, but I can hear the hurt seeping out of me like a fever. Admitting Bentley's dismissiveness and that he'll never be mine hurts like hell.

"Oh, by the way—" her voice perks up.

I catch her smiling. My eyes droop, and I shake my head. "I know you're trying to change the subject, but what?"

"—My brother is coming to visit soon."

"Trevor?"

"I only have one, so who else, silly?" She takes her wine glass and playfully skims the base of it on the water. "He's still single, you know."

My eyes go skyward. "Tess, stop—"

"And rich, and according to rumors through the grapevine, hot as fuck."

Tessa's not lying. Trevor Stevenson, Tessa's older brother, is totally drool-worthy with his silken wavy hair, silver eyes, and high cheekbones.

"He is—" saying 'hot' to Tess's face feels so weird, "—nice looking." The words drag out slowly.

"Liar." She stands, water running off her flat frame in droves. "You think he's sexy too, and I guess he is since he resembles me."

I bark out a laugh.

"See if you can snag him while he's here," she says, stepping out and reaching for a towel.

My face balls up. "Isn't that weird? Setting me on your brother?"

"No. You know me. Other girls... myself... ehh... we just don't get on. I think you're the only one I could handle as my sister." Her thin fingers grip tighter around the towel, securing it to her shoulders. "Someone's eventually going to snag that idiot, so try and let it be you."

Any rebuttal I have washes away as she slinks inside.

I sit there for a long while, alone, soaking in the mixture of the nippy air and the steam swirling around me. Tilting my head back, I relax.

Trevor. Tall, muscular, witty. A little bit softer tongued than his sister. Hot, to be sure, but no Bentley.

Bentley. A sigh slips out. Just that name heats my blood. *But am I being stupid?*

Maybe Tess is right, and Trevor is a more available option. First, though, I have to find out if he'd even be interested in me.

Lost in a pool of thoughts, I slink deeper into nothing, allowing myself to soak until I curl like a prune, and there's no time left to spare for dinner.

Tess is already crashed out on her sofa, sleeping to a Disney movie like always. I figure it's for the better. She doesn't need to know I'm meeting up with Bentley.

Once the front door is closed behind me, I whip out my cell phone and send him a text.

On my way!

His reply of telling me that he can't wait to see me is instant. I'm not even off the porch.

Awesome. Can't wait.

I can't breathe. Not when my anticipation is drilling into me. I've landed big with my crapshoot tonight, and that high is so real. I drive off and head to the restaurant, letting all the butterflies and heart flutters render me sick. Once I get there, I'll work hard to tuck this feeling away and act normal.He's seeing me, and I'm not going to do anything to mess that up or scare him away.

I tap my finger rhythmically against the wheel when the sushi house comes into view. When I see his car, I take a deep breath, trying to remind myself.

A fragment of him is better than nothing.

Tessa would have a fit at the choice I've made. Once again, I won't say anything concerning him ditching me on Sunday, but she doesn't need to know that. No one needs to know that. I mean, Tess is right. It's my heart on the line, and if it thinks Bentley is worth these unpredictable highs, so be it.

I climb out of my car and head inside, thrilled to see the one thing I know will blow up in my face. I'll have to soothe my heart once this is over, when he doesn't call back again, but I don't care.

A girl has to take a chance, live a little—exploding land-mines of emotion and all.

Chapter 5

Bentley

Trying not to pace inside the restaurant while expecting Nora is not working out.

Idiot.

I should have just picked our booth because I know that's where she'll want to sit. She hates tables. But I want to see her walk in, to watch that bright smile flash on her face when she catches sight of me—the one that brings her dimples right to the forefront and makes my chest tighten.

I've opted to catch a view of that.

So now, I'm standing awkwardly, heat tingling on every inch of my skin, lightly bouncing on my toes. My blood is racing so quickly it feels like a first date.

Really, all outings with Nora feel like a first date. I don't let it show, but I'm always nervous as hell whenever we agree to meet.

Her sunshine never gets old.

My eyes are plastered to the white sign showing tonight's special when a rush shoots up my spine.

Feel her before I see her.

Every. Fucking. Time.

I glance over my right shoulder, and *wow*.

Nora looks so damn perfect tonight. I blink, taking in the vision that is her. Her petite frame causes my pulse to burn in my veins, and that long tousled hair begs my fingers to tug on it. Combined with the off-white sweater trying to slide off her shoulder, it makes me want to beeline for her and yank her tight into me—to feel her heart race in the same rhythm as mine.

She walks towards me, and I'm consumed by the thought of feeling that pert little body in my arms, convinced I'd give anything to dip my head in the crook of her long neck and trace kisses on that soft skin of hers. My blood spikes when I imagine skimming the swells and dips of her tits, feeling her waist and hips with my hands, and even my tongue.

Fuck. Easy boy.

I take a tight swallow, then try to breathe normally.

She sees me and smiles.

My heart hitches up in my throat, and my chest wants to collapse. The air around me stills.

"Hey, there." She beams, readjusting her purse.

"Hey, sunshine." Shit. I sound winded, because I am.

This sweet creature steals every inhale I'm trying to take.

"You're only a *little* bit late, so I guess I'll stay and let you eat with me." I'm speaking through the raspiness of my throat.

She scrunches her nose. "I think you're early."

That scent of hers—sweet, yet not, sweeps around me while she breezes past. My eyes beg to close and get lost in it, but something else is stopping me first—those eyes of her's.

Rich nutty eyes lock on mine as she gazes over her shoulder. "Any more crap from you, and I'll order Sake Bombs just to run up the bill."

I pocket my hands, the butterflies calming down thanks to her good humor. My mouth curls up when she picks *our* booth—the one to the far left on the very end. She always picks the last one, so no one sits behind her.

So predictable, so cute, so *her*.

I shrug out my jacket, tossing it in the seat. Smoothing out my button-up shirt, I swear her eyes rove me for a moment. It makes me smirk.

"Like what you see?" I pat my chest and plop into the side

across from her.

She squints. "I thought I saw a stain. Turns out that thing is just ugly."

"Mmm-hmm." Placing my elbows on the table, I lean forward. "And since when are horizontal stripes an eyesore?"

"Uhhh," her eyes dart around the room. When they settle on me again, she clamps down on her pouty lower lip and smiles. "Since I saw them on you."

She giggles at the end, and that light sound leaving her shoots right through my heart, and I end up giving her a stupid smile fit for junior high.

We stop our banter long enough to order our drinks and mains. When I go to restart the conversation, two wide eyes are staring at me intently.

I let them rest on me for a moment, enjoying the way her attention makes my head hum, then I turn my palms skyward and shrug. "What?"

"You look tired." She runs her long index finger on the tabletop, tracing small invisible circles. "Everything good with you?"

No. Ivy popping up in my hometown, meaningless nights spent with nameless faces, my shit friends who I'm failing to connect with… it's all catching up.

I recline into the padded seat and try to act relaxed, hoping for once she can't see into me. It's hard to explain it, but she's got this weird ability to know when I'm lying. "Well, I *was* up till three this morning talking to someone, if you recall. Plus, I still got up at six and went to the gym."

Her mouth falls open. "You still got up and worked out?"

I nod.

"You're insane." She shakes her head, then ducks, taking a quick sip of water. "Also, don't forget that you called me."

So far, so good. Seems I've succeeded in pulling the wool over her eyes this time.

"But that still doesn't explain why you look like you've got something on your mind."

Well, shit.

I'll have to lie harder. "Nora, trust me. Everything on my

end is good."

"Mmm-hmm." She folds her arms at the elbows, resting them on the table. "I think something else is up, but whatever." Her head jerks away, and she casts her attention across the restaurant, refusing to make eye contact.

Failed, again, Bentley.

It would also be nice to get some things off my chest, even if it's just cryptically. "Eh, it's really nothing." I rest my hands on the top of my hair the way I usually do, interlocking my fingers. "There's a buddy back home who's having it rough right now."

Her full attention lands on me and she leans forward, placing her hands in her lap. "Do tell."

"Nosey," I tease, but in the back of my head, I'm brainstorming, carefully plotting not to give too much of myself away. I don't talk about Ivy to anyone besides Lena. It hurts too damn much.

Tread carefully.

"Years back in high school, I had this pal. He dated a girl, and they made all these plans." I ignore the tingle in my throat when it tries to close. "The two love birds were supposed to go to college together, get married... ya know, have a sweet life, all that gross stuff." The recall is making my stomach turn. I hope she can't see the truth—that I was the other love bird, and my heart bled out. "Right before they graduated, he found out she slept with the town. There were even running jokes about her. My friend wasn't aware of them. She had the nickname 'easy Ivy'. I don't think there was a single dude in the town who hadn't been with her."

Her full pink lips fall open, and her face whitens. "Oh, that's—that's awful. Your poor friend."

Her tone makes my heart falter for a second.

My sweet Nora.

Those eyes of hers, rounding with sympathy, deliver a healing surge to the hole in my chest, and I feel it close—at least for the moment. "It tore him up real bad, but she moved." My fingers want to clench when I get to the next part, but I fight it. "He just found out she's visiting again, and he's having a hard time." I scrub over my face. "He's been calling all the time wanting to talk it out. So yeah, I'm beat."

Finished with my speech, I give her a weary smile, slinking further into my seat. The whole time I'm praying I've secured the blinders over her eyes. *Just this once... please.*

One corner of her mouth tugs up, and I wonder what it'd be like to taste those lips of hers.

I bet she tastes like sugar.

"You're such a good friend, Bentley. He's lucky to have you."

Fuck yeah... she'd be sugar.

Pure, unadulterated sugar against my mouth because the tone leaving her throat is intoxicating honey—sweet, smooth, and lovely. I become motionless, staring at her.

Ivy who?

I'm tempted to stretch across the table and steal a taste this instant, then drag her home with me and devour the rest of her so I can fix this need throbbing in my veins.

What the fuck am I doing?

I break eye contact before I blast our feel-good friendship to hell. Don't mess with someone who has it all together—the way I used to be—and leave an even bigger mess in the process.

Not gazing right at her allows the world to spin once more. Glancing across to an area filled with dining tables, I want to snort at the sight. Thank God there's a diversion.

"Something's caught your attention," she says. "What's so funny?"

Man, she's good. I return my gaze to her and cock my head. "How could you tell?"

"I just can. It's all in your eyes." She tugs down the sleeves of her sweater and waits for my response.

"Okay." I duck my head low and lower my voice. "Be subtle, but check out the dining area with the tables. Check out the far right one."

She scrunches her nose and slowly turns her head to glance across. Those slim shoulders of hers duck with a light giggle when she sees it.

A couple is seated in a corner, quietly conversing, and damn, it seems timid and awkward. Almost painful to watch.

"Whadya think," I jerk my chin their way. "First date?"

"Oh, yes." She faces me, and her eyes are bright like starlight. "Absolutely a first date, without question."

I muffle a laugh as the guy readjusts in his seat for the millionth time. "Look at how nervous he is."

She dares a fast glance. "What gives it away?"

I squint. "You're more observant than that."

"I'm still not a guy, though."

"Thank God," I wink.

We both laugh.

Something in my heart booms when Nora sits up straight and scoops hair off her shoulder. I see milky-smooth skin thanks to her sweater failing its job for coverage. I'm glued to the area—dazed.

"I bet you never get nervous."

Averting my eyes from the sight, I take a slow blink, lost at her meaning. "Nervous?"

"Yeah, first dates and all." She shrugs. "I bet you never get the jitters or anything like that."

I puff out my chest. "Oh, of course not." Liar. My stomach is fluttering so hard right now I'm shocked she can't hear it. I lean forward and prop an arm on the table, ignoring it all. "And what about you? Do you get anxious?"

"Depends on the person." She clamps down on her mouth and smiles.

"Say the person was me."

Fuck. Why did I say that?

I want to slap a hand over my mouth and beat my head against the table. Instead, I sit here, each limb tight as a screw, wishing the floor would swallow me. I seriously don't know what's wrong with me.

Leave her alone, Bent.

My stomach drops as I watch something flash across her face. For the life of me, I can't tell what it is. It could be excitement, uncertianty, shock, anticipation, want... God, I just don't know, but I wish I did.

It takes her only a second to make a face that I recognize, but it drags out like an eternity.

"Mmm." Her lips twitch out to the side, and those round eyes scrunch up. "You?" She shakes her head. "I think I'd slam the door in your face, seeing how you're so much trouble." We exchange soft lingering smiles, and I swear to God she glows while pushing a lock of hair behind her ear. "But honestly, how could I be nervous around a friend?"

Friend.

The sweet euphoria crashes. The word might as well be a cannonball plastering right into me. My vision drops to the table, and I force a chuckle. "Yeah, that's true." When I dare to look up again, I'm hoping my gaze gives nothing away. "We've known each other too long for that, huh?"

She nods and reaches for a piece of sushi. "Too long, indeed."

Quiet hits the table when she puts the food in her mouth and chews away. I reach for a piece too. Not because I'm hungry, but out of a need to appear unaffected.

Too long.

The phrase is another shot fired. Now my chest aches. We have known each other too long. At the moment, our familiarity has me longing for so much more than just friendship because what I slip into with Nora feels like home, and fuck, what I wouldn't give to have all of her—mind, body, and soul.

I only wish she felt the same way and that my heart wasn't so frayed.

Chapter 6

Nora

"So, Bentley asked you out, and you let it slide?" Tessa's hand slaps onto the crook of my elbow, forcing me to steady the steering wheel as we drive in my car.

"He *didn't* ask me out. He was— "

"*Pff.* Sure, Nor." I watch her wave her hand out of the corner of my eye. "Yeah, I don't know which pill you're taking, red or blue, but he asked you out."

My mouth hinges open to speak, but I'm cut off.

"*And* not only did you ignore it, you also didn't give him hell about all the other times he's left you cold in the past."

"You're a pain sometimes." Stopping at a long light, I grip the wheel far too tight. "Why do I bother telling you anything?"

"Because you trust me. Plus, I'm a life guru."

My eyes go skyward, and I look across to catch her shooting me a rare toothy grim. *Only Tess.* Her usual pearly whites are smeared with deep mauve.

I bite back a smile. "Hate to break it to you guru, but you have enough lipstick on your teeth to resurrect Picasso."

Her mouth snaps shut. "Shit," she scowls and flips down the visor to check in the mirror. A long index finger works away at the smudges while I tug off again. "So are you going to say anything to him tonight, or are you going to let him flirt with you, then leave with some bimbo?"

"Seriously." An unsolicited growl leaves my throat, and heat seeps from behind my eye's. "I don't know what sort of piss and vinegar you drank tonight, Tess, but I swear, if you don't stop with the snark, I'll leave your grouchy ass all alone at the party."

Her sharp inhale hits my ears. "You wouldn't dare."

I dare a quick squint in her direction. "Watch me, missy. I'll do it."

"Hmp." She slouches hard into the passenger seat. "Abandoning me, that has to be a new low."

Part of my heart sinks at the lackluster and deadened reply. One of Tessa's biggest fears is being left behind. Be it a party, life, friendship, she always fears the people around her won't stick around. That's what really keeps her from reaching out and connecting with others, and she has her parents to thank for that. I just partook in reaffirming those fears, and guilt twists my stomach into a tight knot.

"Sorry," I croak out.

"Nah, forget it." She fluffs the roots of her hair. "I was being bitchy. I just don't like seeing you yanked around, Nor. That's all."

"I know." My fingers tap the steering wheel at a nervous rhythm. "But like you said, the only heart on the line is mine."

"I understand. I don't like it, but I understand."

There's a pause as I come up to the block where Bentley's friend Rich's house is, and I find a place to park. From the looks of it, it's going to be a packed house tonight. While I don't know Rich all that well, me and Tess are usually always invited to his parties—much like everyone else in this town.

With all this hullabaloo, I won't even see Bentley. I'm undoing my seat belt, using that reasoning to lessen my rapid heartbeat when I'm stopped.

"Just, uhh," Tess grabs my arm, "Don't be a martyr, okay?"

My eyes flutter at the statement. "Martyr like how?"

"Cut the shit, Nor." Silver eyes pierce right through my crappy attempt of false innocence. "Don't let that guy yank your chain and lead you around."

"I-I… won't."

"Liar." She arches a brow and gets out of the car.

I duck my head to shoot her a nasty scowl out the passenger door. "You're insufferable."

"You love me." She slams the door, hunkers down low to peer through the window, and jerks her thumb toward the house. "Let's go."

"Good grief," I mutter, tagging behind, locking the car with my key fob.

We get inside, and my initial suspicion is proven right. There's a throng of people in this mini house. The AC is probably cranking, but it'd be impossible to tell because its make-up-melting hot in here. The door ticks closed, and Tess is pulling me in tight.

"Great." Her tone is snide. "Looks like some douche invited every sorority girl in town."

My eyes go wide when I take a better examination. She's right. The place is packed with skinny, giggly girls stuffed into body con dresses, tight pants, and snug shirts. Clearly they aren't looking to talk to me and Tessa.

Wonderful. I wouldn't have come if I'd known it would be like this. As it is, I push through the chaos, with Tessa sticking to my side. I'm trying to make the most of it, searching out the familiar faces I know.

When I see Bentley, part of my heart bottoms out.

Somehow he's camped out in the cramped living room, seeming extra comfortable on the sofa. He tosses his head back and laughs while making merry with a blonde chick who, judging by her legs, seems to be taller than him. She's boldly making physical contact, her boobs against his arm, sometimes brushing his sleeve or the collar of his shirt—a navy collared dress shirt that's hugging his pecs and giving a better show than a stripper at a bachelorette.

He looks delicious.

A tinge of jealousy strikes my heart while I envision myself in her place.

I clamp down on my lip. *It should be me.* However, it's not, and from the way he's staring at her, he doesn't even know I'm here.

Once again, he's absorbed, lost in someone else who probably doesn't know the first thing about him. I picture him taking her to bed and debate walking over there to yank the hair out of her scalp. *Let it go...* I came here to have fun. I bite back the disappointment, slide through the gathering and continue to mingle.

Time passes, and I try to forget about Bentley and the loud girls hovering around, battling for male attention. I'm passing the time by chatting, escaping to the kitchen for snacks, and checking on Tessa, who's sticking to the wall, clutching her solo cup like it's a stress ball. Every time I check on her, she assures me she's fine and tells me to have fun. I make a note to buy her a tub of the ice cream she loves most because she's a trooper for putting up with all this.

After my millionth time to the kitchen, I'm stalking down the hallway trying to locate Tessa, who's done her famous vanishing act. I'm halfway there when a hand clasps my upper arm.

"And where are you off to, sunshine?"

Heat floods my body at the sound of Bentley's voice. When I turn around...

Jesus, take me now.

He looks even better up close. The dark navy of his shirt is in contrast to his light eye color and sun tan. It's hard not to lose my breath when I stare into that beautiful, unreal gaze of Grecian blue marbles that almost have streaks of white peaking through. There's no other eye color like it in the world. Now I really hate that girl from earlier.

My lips curl up in a tight, forced smile. "I'm searching for Tessa."

"Ahhh. I think she stepped outside."

"Oh." *Poor thing.* The party was too much for Tessa, after all. I don't blame her. I'm struggling myself thanks to Bentley. I'm in no state of mind to deal with him right now. He does funny things to my head. My knees are shaking all the way down to my shins from being this close to him. I need to leave. "I'll go to her, thanks."

My heart stutters when he stops me by latching a hand around my waist. He pulls me in closer than what's appropriate, then backs me into the wall.

The rapid beats of my pulse drum up into my ears, canceling out the low thrum of the music. His masculine scent has me wanting to slide down the wall and collapse.

Ungodly heat hasn't affected how damn good he smells. He's fresh, like he's just stepped out of the shower. I stop my fingers from touching his chest, even though I feel they belong there.

He throws me a megawatt smile that threatens to melt my panties off and ducks his head low. "You wouldn't be the one eating all the spinach dip, would you?"

My eyes widen, my mouth drying up at his smirk. I take a hard swallow. "Who's asking?"

"No one, but I know you." Desire strikes like a match in my belly when he leans in even closer, his gaze dancing with good humor. "There was loads of it till you got here. Now it's half gone, and you're the only spinach dip fiend that I'm aware of."

My pulse fails. "You-you noticed I was here?"

"Of course." He cocks his head. "Thank this." He reaches behind and fiddles with that one lock of hair that's always straighter than the others, and heat pools between my legs. "I told you it helps, but honestly, I always notice you," his eyes scan over me quickly, "Which, by the way, you look lovely tonight."

I have to stop myself from kissing him. "Thank you…" This is exactly what Tessa was talking about. He always makes me feel so important when he talks to me like this, and while I want to test the limits, fear rubs out the ability. What if it destroys our friendship?

No. Living off the fragments is much better.

Willing a resolve of steel in my veins, I counter the all-consuming thought of being truly important to Bentley with some banter. "I'm glad you think I look nice. I wish I could say the same for you."

He throws his head back and laughs, replicating the moment from earlier when talking with the blonde.

I grit my teeth for strength because I'm about to push him

into the nearest bathroom and beg him to have me.

"Sharp-tongued." He taps the tip of my nose, "That's what you are, and I like 'em feisty."

That talk makes me want to fold into his arms. I wish to God that Bentley knew how much his words affected me. For him, this is nothing but good fun. It takes every ounce of strength I have, but I manage to toss my head back and smirk, concealing the compounded desire trailing through my body.

"Then allow me to exercise my wit." I fold my arms and squint. "I bet instead of eating party food like a normal person, you brought gross, meal-prepped chicken."

"Watch your language." His brows hit his hairline. "It's not gross. I have goals."

"Whatever." I skirt past him. "I'm going to find Tessa."

My departure is stopped with Bentley's hand clasping my wrist.

"I'll come with you." He takes the lead, airing out his shirt and shooting me a grin. "It's too cozy in here."

Words fail me for a second while straggling along behind him. The connection of his fingers around my wrist sends a wave of heat between my thighs, and my core tightens. I'm glad the noise around us is covering up my loose, uncomposed breaths. I need a distraction. Because if I keep focusing on the hormonal overload he's releasing inside me, I'll go insane. Normal conversation is a must for me right now.

As he leads us through the crowd, I tap his shoulder. "How is your sister, Lena?"

He snaps his head around, eyes wide while quickly scanning the crowd. I watch him make eye contact with something or someone. When he returns his gaze to mine, his eyes are tight. "I'll tell you outside."

"Okay." My head tilts in curiosity. He's never hesitated to talk about her before. I decide to hold off on further questions, and we slip outside together.

The air is crisp with the sun setting, yet not so cold where I can't enjoy being outside. Tessa isn't around, but there are a few stragglers out here. I suspect that, like me, they are probably tired of the noise and heat inside. The small crowd is quietly conversing, casually sipping on drinks. Someone's even busted out a speaker, and eighty's tunes are crooning off in the background. It's a much-needed change.

I send Tessa a quick message.

Everything alright? I can't find you.

She responds instantly.

I'm good. Just slipped off. I'll see you soon. Let me know when you're ready to leave.

I'm returning my phone to my pocket when Bentley catches my attention.

"Hey, our spot is open." His mouth perks upward. "Up for a chat?" He jerks his head, giving me the silent order to move.

A mad flutter kicks up in my stomach, and I can't refuse. I nod and slink past him, heading straight for the built-in garden box on the offside of the house.

Anyone can see that Rich isn't a gardener from all the dirt and weeds living inside, but that doesn't matter. Bentley and I make use of it at parties by sitting on the brick ledge and chatting it up.

While my butt is adjusting to the cool sensation beneath me, my limbs flood with fire due to Bentley sitting beside me. It's a repeat occurrence that never dies. *Damn what this guy does to me…*

"To answer your question, Lena is doing great."

"Oh." I try not to squirm on the bench. "I'm glad to hear that. Sorry if I pried back there. I—"

"You're good." His sleeve brushes against mine when he spreads his arms. "Sorry if I was weird about it." He briefly glances back to the house. "There's a mega douche in there who'd do anything to get to her. It's best if he doesn't know she exists."

My lips purse together. "Protective? That's a new one."

"Hey." he shrugs. "What can I say? I love my family."

"Now, that's *not* new." Bentley does love his family, and if my heart were capable of melting into a pool of nothing, it would, because this side of him, the warm and affectionate one that has him doting on his family, is hotter than any of the winks he throws my way.

I rest my elbows on my thighs, propping my chin on my knuckles. "Is Lena still dating that attorney?"

"Yeah." He spreads his legs and leans forward to dangle his hands between them. "Betcha they get engaged before the end of next year. Which is good." One side of his mouth hitches skyward. "They fit, ya know?"

"You mean unlike you and that blonde last summer?" I smile, recalling the slim, shrilly girl that he briefly dated. Briefly meaning three weeks, but it was long enough to make me rage with jealousy.

"Oh, ouch." He rubs the nape of his neck, ignoring my giggle. "What's bringing that around? Also, that's not nice."

I shrug. "That blondie that was talking to you earlier reminded me of her."

His brows lower for a flash. "Well, if you're going to bring up exes, what about that dick you dated last year?"

"What dick?" My head cocks.

"The one that ditched you at the restaurant. Remember? You called me, and I had to pick you up."

"Martin." I smack my forehead. "Touche'." Giving him a side-eye glance, I scowl. "Don't smirk like that."

"Fair enough." That half-smirk explodes into a full-blown smile, and he leans into me. "How is your family doing? Your Dad recovered from knee surgery yet?"

I nod. "He recovered so fast, it's crazy." A giggle slips out. "Dad swears it's the salty air around him. He claims it's good for the mind, soul, and body."

"Ha! I think that's the beach in general. It makes everyone feel better." My vision dips down as I watch him absentmindedly pluck at a button on his shirt. "And your sister, Carly? How is she?"

I let my head fall back in frustration. "Decidedly, Carly.

She's begging for me to move and join them in Florida to be a bartender on the beach."

He lets out a snort. "That's not you at all." His shoulder presses into mine. "But I bet you'd look hot in a bathing suit, serving up drinks."

I full out laugh, a flush hitting my cheeks. "Well thanks. I'm not sure how Dad would feel if I decided to go that route. He wants me to move too. So does Mom."

"You're not, are you?" He jerks upright, and it could just be me, but I swear there's an alarm tightening up his features. "Moving, that is?"

Or am I seeing things? I decide on the latter because I can't imagine my presence here means *that* much to him. "I mean, I wasn't planning on it, but—"

"I'd miss you if you left." His voice is soft, and I know I'm not imagining that.

"Bentley—"

"I mean it, Nora." My pulse rattles hard when his gaze lowers to my mouth. "Colorado wouldn't be the same without you."

He reaches out, placing his hand on my knee, and I feel the electricity in his touch—like he's the current and I'm the conductor. A surge shoots through me, making my heart beat in hard unsteady thumps, and I huff out a breath.

"Bentley—" Whatever else I want to say vanishes—all thoughts jumble around in my head.

"Fuck, you're pretty when you look at me like that."

"Like what?" My voice is barely a whisper.

"Like I mean something to you." He tightens his grip around my knee, and the air grows thick and heady, making the world around me drown out.

I swear he's going to kiss me. He's leaning forward. I can smell him, and my nose picks up on the mixture of spearmint and whiskey leaving his mouth. My eyes are drooping closed, but my blood freezes when he stills.

"Nora…" His voice is sex, and my limbs wilt, "How would you like to share a few drinks with me, sweetheart? Loosen us up a bit so we can have a *real* discussion?"

Each breath I take is audible. I want to tear my eyes away, but my line of sight stays on his mouth. I nod.

"Perfect," he purrs, and squeezes my knee one more time. "I'll go get them. Don't you go anywhere."

He gets up, shoots me a wink over his shoulder, and saunters off.

I expel a huge blow of air before gasping it back in again. *I'll need that drink.* The weight of his words make me think of just one thing—he wants to talk about *us*. This is it—at least that's what my racing heart is screaming. I just hope I'm ready for it.

My hands are shaking from pure anticipation as I prep my heart and mind for an amazing night. Hunching over, I seal my eyes shut to clear my headspace. If this is going to happen, I want to at least appear composed when Bentley comes back. I'll be damned if he returns to find me giddy.

I wait. The temperature drops with more of the sun disappearing, but all I'm doing is repeating the words. *Confident. Composed. Confident. Composed.*

It's not till I've looped it in my brain for what I think is the millionth time that a sudden twist in my gut alarms me something's gone wrong.

"Where is he?" The moon is taking over its night shift, and I know Bentley's been gone a lot longer than he should be. He told me not to 'go anywhere,' but this is stupid. I opt to abandon the dead garden and search for him.

Maybe he got tied up talking to someone. That's my hope and prayer while I meander through the front yard, keeping my eyes peeled. When I don't spot him there, I go into the house.

A heatwave engulfs me as I enter the clamorous crowd once more. Even through the mess of action, I can see he's not here. Peering down the hall, it's the same.

Lots of folks, but no Bentley. The kitchen is next.

I'm rounding the corner, and a soft moan hits my ears.

Then, all I recognize is my existence crumbling apart from under me and a massive ache combusting in my chest. *Holy shit.*

I bow over at the sight of Bentley with the leggy blonde from earlier. He has her pressed into the wall, one hand groping her boob, with his tongue jammed down her throat.

Her hands are roving his body, tugging at his shirt, threatening to rip it to shreds. My eyes trail down—the hurt fractures deep into my core. This chick has actually kicked off her heels to make herself more accessible, allowing Bentley's knee to wedge between her legs.

I wouldn't have to do that for him. I'm the perfect height for him… *perfect.*

Perfect. That's what my heart whispers every time I'm with him, but when I see him like this, giving himself away to someone else, the words scream and boom into my soul. I'm perfect for him, so why can't he *see* me?

The ache that exploded in me seconds ago transforms into a shatter, ripping through my body when I catch sight of two glasses filled with whiskey sitting on the counter. *Our drinks.* He started what he set out for but never finished it.

I was forgotten… for this. For her.

The view of Bentley blurs with the tears seeping out my eyes. My lips quiver and I bite back a bitter sob. I make a haste decision of not bawling in public. I turn on my heel and rush out the door, slamming it shut, not daring to look back.

I jog to my car, the tears on my cheeks slicing into my skin against the cool breeze. The breath in my lungs is sharp and piercing while I gasp on my own sobs. I've dealt with Bentley forgetting about me before, but this? Seeing him make out with another woman after he'd brought my hopes up so high is a death blow to my heart.

Reaching the car, I unlock it and plop hard into the seat, trying to sniffle the hurt away. I'm also quick to note I'm not alone. Tessa is here, examining me with a wide and seemingly baffled expression on her face.

"What happened in there?"

A sickness sweeps through my stomach, and I hang my head. "I don't want to talk about it."

"No need." Her tone is curt. "Judging by your tears, I can guess. Bent—"

"Tess!" I bang the steering wheel. "Please. I don't want to discuss it." My voice releases its own whimper at the end, betraying the strength of my outburst.

"Nor." Gently, she pats my arm. "I'm really sorry. Really, I am."

"I know." Brushing a few tears away, I force myself to sit up straight. "You were right. Like always." Letting my head fall back, we sit there quietly—my heart plummeting in a never-ending free fall.

All I can see is Bentley, but I'm doing everything I can to wash the image away. Wash him away.

After several moments, when I'm better composed, I throw Tessa a side-eyed glance and cock a brow. "How'd you get in here anyway?"

"Whenever we go to parties, I always take the spare car key you gave me," she smirks. "I can sit in here if I get sick of people and not look like a freak."

Silence hits again. After a long while, I take a huge inhale of air, then breathe it out. My shoulders fall with the action, and I completely deflate into the seat. I shake my head, painfully accepting the truth. Enough is enough. *I have to let him go.* The thought is wrenching my heart into a painful knot, but I can't continue to do this. *I'll go mad.*

Whatever it takes, I *have* to move on from Bentley—and I think I know where to start.

"Nora—"

"When does Trevor get here?" Sniffling, I stop my tears and glance at Tessa.

Her mouth hinges open, and her eyes do a double blink before she gives me an answer. "Next week. Why?"

"Good." I nod and start up the engine. "I'm hoping he'll ask me out."

"He will." She sounds like a yes and amen while sitting taller in her seat. "I'll be sure he does."

"Great."

Pulling out of the parking space, I slowly roll down the street. Passing by Rich's house, I dare to look at it once more. *Never again.* That's all I repeat as the building gets smaller in my rear-view mirror. Even though my chest wants to collapse, and I'm on the verge of tears, I decide that as I drive away tonight, I'll leave Bentley behind... forever.

Because he's never been mine, and now I see he never will be.

Chapter 7

Bentley

The girl from the party is in my bed.

I'm balls-deep in her.

I've been pumping in and out of her for far too long. She's taking it all. Screaming my name. Writhing under me. Bucking against me. Touching me in all the right spots—building up my ego like I'm a damn sex god.

It should feel right, good, and be what I need, but it all seems so fucked up.

This should be Nora.

It almost was.

Instead of a splay of blonde hair flaying around the sheets, it should be brown. My fingers should be tangling in it, and I should be drowning in her. But I'm not.

I'm not sure what to make of it. Did I fuck up or save us both? I can't tell.

All I know is when I left to fetch those drinks, I had a huge 'what the fuck are you doing?' moment.

When the blonde from earlier came up and flashed me her tits in the empty kitchen, I took it as a sign of providence. A reminder that Nora is sacred, and I shouldn't mess with her.

So I didn't.

I abandoned the idea of telling Nora how I feel about her. Plus, she wasn't even there when I left the party. Now, I'm here, banging someone who means nothing, and for the first time in forever, I feel dirty—like a layer of grime exists on my heart and will never leave. Each shove of my dick into the woman underneath me hollows out my chest a bit more.

Numbs me harder.

Reminds me of the bastard I am and why I don't deserve Nora to begin with.

I can't drive the sensations away, and I can't get off. Not with the wrong person in my bed. Everything that's not right about her is chasing pleasure away. I leave my eyes open, staring down at my sin of betrayal.

I couldn't care less about this person, and I'm using her.

So I fixate on the person I *do* care about.

Nora. Nora. Her name won't stop playing in my head, and I don't want it to. I welcome her, imagine her… picture my wildest dreams of happiness coming true. It becomes all too real.

My eyes close. "Fuck."

A cascade of rich hair.

Sugary candy eyes.

Milky skin.

Suckable pink lips. The bottom one, fuller than the top.

An assault of light perfume that always leaves my cock hard.

Perky tits. A round ass. Hourglass shape.

"Holy shit." My teeth grind, and I pump harder. "Yes."

"Oh, God yes. Yes!" It's Nora's voice.

Gripping around her waist, I feel *her.*

Perfect. She's just so fucking perfect in my hold. Praise for this woman spills out of me. "Holy fuck, baby. You're amazing. Just so—ahhh—incredible. Beautiful. I-I can't…." My entire body coils and flexes. Every inch of me quakes. My fingers grip into the sheets—I fist them tight. Nora lets out a squeal. My body and cock jerk. The release is incredible. Blackout, neck-snapping, out-of-this-world amazing. I moan with each pulse of the sweet undoing. "Fuck yes." Throwing my head back, the last of me expels into her. "Yes, Nora, yes."

"What? What the hell did you just say?"

I freeze. The voice isn't Nora's. Not even close. Same for when I open my eyes. It's all blonde, blue, and fake tan, and I pull out fast.

Those blue eyes are scowling at me, no doubt damning me to hell. She pushes at my torso, forcing me away. "What did you say?"

"Nothing." Raking through my hair, I sigh, frustration and sickness kneading themselves in my stomach. "I didn't say anything, and you should go."

"Wow." She lurches upright, flipping me off in the process. "You're a real dick. You fuck me, then call me by some other whore's name—"

"Out. Now." Fury pops in my veins at the abuse of Nora. "The only whores here are me and you," I sneer, loathing everything about her figure. She's too tall and flat-chested, and while I hate this girl for bashing Nora, I hate myself even more. *What was I thinking?* "Party's over. Now get the fuck out of my bed and go home."

"Gladly. Dick." Her long legs swing off the side, and she's snatching up clothes faster than a laundry maid. "You should consider getting some therapy. You're seriously fucked in the brain."

Hot shame sears through my heart like burning coals. "No doubt about it." I peel off the used condom, desperate for a shower. "Make sure you lock the door on your way out."

"Fuck you."

"You did. Can't say I want a repeat."

She cries out another obscenity, but I'm gone, already in the bathroom clutching for the shower handle. Only when a shit ton of steam billows do I get in.

It's useless.

Contamination and filth rest all over me. I can't get the water hot enough. Can't scrub hard or long enough to get rid of the impurity.

It grows ten times when Nora's face flashes before me.

The hope in her eyes when I said I wanted to talk was real. The expectation emitting from her was genuine. The way my heart soared when she stared at me like I had worth was indisputable. The same goes for the lightning bolt that blasted through my soul when I almost kissed her.

The feel of her on my lips pulsed thick in the air before I tasted her. And how I wanted to hold her in my arms was coursing through my veins before I even laid a finger on her.

Tonight at the party, I felt alive.

No.

I *was* alive and shot it all to hell.

Or did I?

She was long gone when I left. Does that mean I don't matter? Maybe I'm imagining everything, and Nora doesn't care about me at all.

The thought of her not caring sends a raw ache through my body.

Fuck my life.

Because while I *shouldn't* want her to care, I do... to the point that it scares the shit out of me.

The last time I cared, it ripped me to shreds.

I know Nora is different from Ivy, but now, I'm broken too.

The Bentley that believed in lasting love is dead. Or at least he should be. But each smile or kind word from Nora revives bits of the person I laid to rest years ago. The harder I fight, the further I slip into her, and it shouldn't be like this. Not after I vowed never to cherish again.

But this is who I am now—my source of driving demons away proves uncomfortable. The mindless fucks I partake in are supposed to leave me feeling better, not like a cheating sack of shit.

Because that's what's happening.

Every time I'm with anyone other than Nora, my heart twists with betrayal, and each meaningless encounter reminds me that I'm a fraud. Nora's name should be the only one on my lips, and my soul tells me she should be the person in my bed. Every. Fucking. Night.

"Damn it." I rest my head on the cold tiles and ball my hands, my stomach lurching into my throat.

Why did I ever have to meet or want her?

All I'm good for these days is a fast fuck. Nora deserves better. With how my life has gone the past few years, I know I'll hurt her.

And that can't happen. It just can't.

Sinking down to the floor, I cover my face with my hands. I stay there till the water is freezing cold. Even the pounding ice on my back fails to shock any remarkable feeling in me other than hollowness. Hollowness so deep, it pulses through my bones. The truth is I'm not worth anything to anyone, and now I seem cursed to fixate on the one woman I should never have.

It's two weeks later, and I'm at a barbecue, but I'm not focusing on the party—something Rich has noticed.

"Hey, man." Rich nudges my arm, almost knocking my phone loose. "You going to look at your damn phone all night or what?" he asks, bumping into me again.

"Really, dude." Annoyance sizzles in my veins. "Do you have to ride my ass for everything?" I grunt and pocket my phone. "If it makes you feel better, I'm texting work."

He stops and pockets one hand, giving me a once-over. "You damn liar." He walks away, returning to the BBQ grill in the backyard of Al's house. He's a friend of Rich.

Scrubbing over my face, I take a moment to hide away from the party. *I am a liar.* My phone obsession isn't work-related. I've been checking to see if Nora's returned my text from yesterday. She hasn't. I open our thread one more time.

You coming to Al's tomorrow night?

Nothing—shit.

Al is selective about his invites, but he knows Tessa and Nora, so I was sure they'd come, but they are proving me wrong. A bitter taste hits my mouth while reading each message since Rich's party two weeks ago. She's been busy, unavailable, and slow to respond.

Even my invite to sushi was shot down, and that gutted me.

There's a dreaded thought that crosses my mind—what if she spotted me and that dumb blonde in the kitchen that night?

I didn't want her to see that. I should have taken the girl to another part of the house, and if I'd been really smart, I wouldn't have done that at all. Fuck, I'm stupid sometimes. Guilt tidal waves through me at the blunders I've made so often.

I grit my teeth. Gawking at the ignored message once more, my finger swipes across airplane mode because I'll go crazy if I don't.

Don't cherish, don't care, and don't get Nora entangled with your broken-hearted shit.

Forcing myself to buck up for the time being, I linger around and shoot the shit with a few guys Rich works with.

An hour or two later, I decide to split, since I don't feel any better in the end.

With my pent-up mood, I might hit up a few girls to see if any of them have some free time. I could stand to let off some steam. I'll deal with the guilt later.

I'm stalking through the house, phone in hand, scrolling through the names of a few available girls when my pulse accelerates. It's the effect of a sound I know all too well.

Nora's voice.

I'd know its calming tone anywhere—be able to track it down through any crowd—find it in a sea of screaming people—because that's how hard I'm wired for her. I can always find her, even without trying.

It's coming from the kitchen. Lies of me not caring wash away. Her not getting back to me is trivial when I hear her sweet laugh and know she's mere steps away. My footsteps quicken, and I'm reaching the end of the hall.

I stop.

Fuck.

We're head to head, meeting up at the same time, and she looks incredible. Her eyes are wide while gazing into mine. Also, something has her cheeks bright pink tonight.

That flush color is dumping every ounce of blood straight into my heart—God, how I want her.

How I want her to *want* me.

I swallow hard and try to smile. "Hey." The salutation is weak, the same as I am for her.

Heat throttles through my body when she gives me a shy return. "Hi."

"Long time no talk." I fold my arms and lean a shoulder into the wall.

"Uh-yeah." She tucks back a piece of hair and drops her gaze. "Yeah. Sorry. I've uh-just been a little busy."

"Doing what?" I force a chuckle. "Ignoring me?"

"No." Her eyes deaden. "I've just been busy."

Hello, tension. It's here… and so thick, I'm sure only a chainsaw could cut it. My shoulders tighten as I try to remind myself to stay calm. All I have to do is determine what the cause is. *I'm sure I can soothe it over. She's my Nora.*

"Hey, no big deal." I pat her shoulder lightly to see how she'll respond. Hope flickers in my chest when she doesn't back away. "Sushi is always there for us. Next time you're down, let me know. I'm just glad you're okay."

She glances up and nods. "Thanks." I garner a smile out of her.

My smile widens, and I lean harder into the wall. "I was getting ready to leave, but since you're here, would you like to go out back and grab some food?"

"Oh, uh…" She takes a step back, which I find weird. Nora usually doesn't put any distance between us.

Panic surges up my spine, but I refuse to give up. I hang my head to meet her eyes. "I'll even forget about my ripped bod and meal-prepped food to share a slice of cheesecake with you." I wink. "Your favorite."

She huffs out a breath, her eyes darting around the room. "Bentley—"

Don't lose her. Because I feel like I am. Her silence is slamming down a wall between us, and despair is nestling deep into my chest as I watch her fade away. "I think it's from Costco, but I bet it will cut it for one night."

She shakes her head, and panic rolls through my limbs.

"Nora?" I reach out, a sharp pain riveting through my fingers into my chest when she steps back again, taking herself out of my reach. "What's wrong?"

"Nora?" A deep voice comes from around the corner. "You good?"

I go stark blank when a tall guy rounds the corner.

He's looks like a pathetic excuse for a biker with his leather gear, black hair, and chains. My vision goes green when he places his arm on Nora's shoulder like he's claiming her. Bile hits my throat.

He bounces a glance between us before settling on her. "Who is this?" I observe his fingers tightening around her shoulder—then, he tugs her in tighter.

I glue myself in place. All I want is to snatch her out of his arms when Nora's fingers lightly graze his torso. A plea rests on my lips—*Touch me. Touch me everywhere.* The desperation to place her hands on my body courses hard through my chest. Fuck this douche she's brought tonight. She should be with me. My fists ball so tight with the idea they go white-knuckled.

"Trevor, this is one of my friends, Bentley Harris."

Kindness shines in her eyes while she stares up at him. The look has a huge pit shredding through my stomach. She's never looked at me that way. Not ever. It reminds me of the truth...

That I'm nothing special to her.

"Bentley," she gestures at me. "This is Trevor Stevenson. Tessa's brother."

Fuck. I want to fall to the floor. This is her best friend's brother, and frankly, how am I supposed to compete with that?

All I do is nod. He barely returns it. A few seconds of less than warm eye contact, and I flick my gaze to Nora and try to smile. She's off the market—maybe for good this time. I've never seen Nora in someone else's arms after only a few weeks of dating. *Fuck my life.* "Hey, good to see ya."

"Yeah. Same here. Have a good night, Bentley."

"You too." That's all I can mumble, pushing past them.

I can't even glance back. The pain plowing through me is too great. My heart beats as if glass is embedded in it. Seeing her in someone else's arms is agonizing—this time, the pain cuts deeper than any other.

It's always uncomfortable watching her with other guys, but this one? My gut might as well be a punching bag because it literally makes me sick and bruised inside. Walking out without a second glance is the better option.

At least I won't look like a pussy. I can save my dignity in front of douchebag Trevor.

Better still, Nora will never catch on to my true feelings, and that's for the best. The last girl who knew my heart made sure I'd feel unlovable forever—she accused me of being boring, a dull pain in the ass—her words replay.

"I had to fuck all those other guys to remember what a good fuck actually felt like."

I've lived several years proving her otherwise—cursing that woman every time I banged a new girl and got her to scream my name. It's exciting, but it's poured me into a mold of nothingness that I can't break free from.

And Nora?

Well, let's just say that beautiful unsullied princesses like her don't belong with guys like me. They belong on a pedestal, which is where I'm keeping her. Nora deserves the world, and after all the revenge I've feasted on, what I have left to offer isn't worth shit. All that remains of me are broken, worthless pieces.

Nobody wants that, especially not her.

Chapter 8

Nora

"Pretty sure I found a new job."

My head bounds up at the voice of my co-worker, Wes, who's entering the compounding area. It's a small room at the back of the pharmacy with overpowering fluorescent lighting, but the other two pharmacists and I occasionally use it to hide away from our boss, Laura, since she despises all of us.

"Really?" I set down the prescription I'm mixing up and lean against the lip of the counter. "Where are you going?"

"There's a local pharmacy downtown. Someone retired, and I nailed the interview." He straightens out his lab coat and shoots me a glossy smile. "With all the hell happening here, I figured screw the bonus. I'll find some way to pay it back."

A bitter taste hits my mouth. It's so wrong, but my instinct is to loathe his good fortune. Out of all three black sheep, Wes is the most accepted by Laura. Probably because he's kind of cute. I need it more than him.

Worse, one less person will mean more of Laura's direct attention. A queasy sensation burrows deep in my gut at the idea.

Congratulating him isn't even an option because I know it will sound forced and insincere. Needing a distraction, I pick up the cylinder tube for my compound and fiddle with it in my hands.

"When will you start?" The question comes out flat, and guilt pricks at me.

"If it all goes to plan, next Thursday." Either Wes is socially clueless, or he's ignoring my lack of enthusiasm because his shifted smile remains fixed.

"Cool." An awkward grin plays on my lips, and I pop off the lid, ready to put in the cream. I have a dollop of mixture resting on my spatula when the second black sheep barges in. Susie.

"Nora." Her shrill voice bounces off the walls, and her body is tight while glancing over her shoulder. "There's someone here to see you."

My brows shoot up. "Me?"

"Yep." Tight pin curls bounce with her nod. "Tall, smoldering hot. A model maybe."

Trevor. A warm flush flickers inside, swirling upwards until my earlobes burn.

He playfully warned me about stopping by for a visit. I told him not to bother, but like his sister, he's not one to listen well. "Thanks." I cover up my compound and slide past Wes and Susie with a smile.

I'm pretty sure their eyes are still on me when I go out into the store. At least I have Trevor to counterbalance the rough news.

Rounding the corner, I catch a glimpse of glossy raven hair that peeks above our tallest shelves. The slicked back and parted styling tells me it's Trevor for sure. My heart kicks up—anticipation sitting heavy in my core. His leather jackets, spiced cologne, and killer quads do funny things to my reasoning. I always go dizzy.

Smoothing down my hair, I hide that one strand Bentley always points out. *Crap.* I don't want to think about him. Lord knows the guy probably never thinks about me. I push the blue-eyed fiend far from my mind and focus on Trevor.

My mouth practically waters coming from behind. Trevor's not in leather today. He's donning a black button-up dress shirt, and the sleeves are rolled. It shows off sinfully roped fore-arms and rippling tats. "Hey, stranger." The greeting is a strug-gle, almost getting stuck in my throat.

He glances over his shoulder. Silver orbs and high cheek-bones make his simple smirk more indecent than it should be. "Hey, dream girl."

A heaviness rushes between my legs at the deep tone of his voice. "I told you not to come."

"And keep me away?" He turns to face me head-on. I'm greeted with a view of muscle upon muscle. As his eyes rake over my body, I duck my head to hide flaming cheeks, which I'm sure are red.

"I thought I made it clear I wanted to see you in your uh—" he points to the white coat hiding the top half of my body, "— whatever that thing is."

My shoulders shake hard with a laugh. "It's a lab coat."

His sculpted brows scrunch together. "Sexy." He takes one step forward, stares down at me, and lowers the volume of his voice. "But I think it would look better off you."

I nod. "I'm sure it does. These aren't the most attracti—"

"Most likely, it'll look best on the floor." He folds his arms across his chest, and his pecs bulge. "Bonus points for you if *I* get to be the one that peels it off you."

Heat swells in my stomach. I stand still, my mouth agape. A reaction doesn't hit me until he laughs. "Well," I let out a breath, and my spine rounds, "You don't beat around the bush, do you?"

"Bulletin." He pockets his hands, hunching his shoulders. "Tess and me both say what's on our minds. Remember that, and nothing should catch you off guard." Taking one more swaggering step forward, he frees one hand and extends it to me. "I didn't know this place is connected to a coffee shop. Let me buy you one."

My eyes dart to the clock. I have exactly twenty minutes before Laura returns. "Okay, but we'll have to be quick." Grab-bing his hand, I spur us into action, pulling him behind me.

"Wow. Don't be so eager," he says, catching a long stride. "You'll give me the wrong impression."

My brows quirk together as I tilt my head back. "What impression would that be?"

His mouth curls. "That you're dragging me to a bathroom because you want *more* than just coffee."

I slow our pace and brush my hip against his thigh. "Maybe I do, but it's just not the right time." When I look up again, I clamp down on my lower lip then pull it out slowly between my teeth. I don't miss the hard-set flicker lighting up his gaze while he watches me.

A low grumble leaves his throat. His hand grips around my waist, and he pulls me tight into his frame. "Keep that up, and I'll make sure the time is right. We won't make that movie tonight." He threads long fingers through his hair. "If we don't make the movie, we'll piss off Tess, and nobody wants that."

I snort through my nose. "You're scared of your sister?"

He tilts his head back, laughing. "Always. You ever seen her pissed?"

Solemnly, I nod. "She took a bat to an ex's car after he stole money from her."

"Then you understand it's nothing to screw around with." He shoots me a grin. "Besides, I want to stay on her good side this time. No arguments this visit."

"You two have your spats, don't you?" My eye trails over the tatted phoenix spanning across his forearm. I obsess over its spanned-out wings and make a bold move to trace it with my index finger. Satisfaction hammers in my body when he goes rigid at my touch and tightens his grip.

"We have." He shuffles me closer. "But it won't be like that this time. I also won't stay away as long. It's all going to be different."

"And what will make it different?" I clasp my fingers around his arm.

Looking down, he gives me a smile that could put cupid to shame. "You."

Chills race down my spine, my pulse beating out of synchronization. I relish in his chuckle and the gentle way he brushes my hair while uttering my pet name, 'dream girl.'

With our hands entwined, I lean my head on his shoulder

and close my eyes. Pieces of my heart surrender to Trevor's. With each passing day, I feel him slowly steal more of me. Part of my brain tells me it's too fast too soon, but the other side says this is just right.

For the first time in so long, I feel like someone *sees* me, and that can't be wrong.

It just can't be.

Every item in my closet was lying on my bed before I stepped out the door this evening. I changed a million times but finally decided on a neutral color palette of white and beige clothing, and nude Jimmy Choo heels that my parents gifted me last year. The shoes alone have me feeling more than ready to stand next to Trevor and Tess while hitting up the town tonight. The goal is dinner, movie, bar, piano bar, then sleep.

My ass probably won't even make it to the bar since I'll be ready for bed, but Trevor doesn't need to know that yet. He'll find out the truth like Tess did years ago. I have the nightlife endurance of an old woman.

I'm already yawning here in the theater. Pasta for supper was way too heavy.

Waiting in line for our tickets, I lean harder into Trevor, whose arm and spiced fragrance are comfortably wrapping around me.

"What's your favorite movie snack, dream girl?"

"I like sour punch straws," I say, brushing a random strand of hair out of my eyes.

"Really?" His voice perks up. "I would have taken you for a Reese's kind of girl."

"Peanut butter?" I stick out my tongue. "Now that's gross."

"Hmm." His lips mull down. "Tess told me you liked chocolate and sweets. Not sour."

"I like all of them, but not peanut butter." I send a squint in

Tessa's direction, who's standing on the other side of her brother. "Spilling my secrets?"

She tilts her head and shrugs. "Just trying to help him out. You'll thank me later. Nobody can mess things up better than him."

My eyes go skyward. "Thank God you don't know my bedroom preferences."

Tessa gives me a bored stare while Trevor tips his head back and laughs.

"I'm kind of sad she doesn't," Trevor says. His index finger tucks under my sweater to make small circles on my bare shoulder for a brief moment. My blood simmers.

The strength in my knees wanes from his touch as I flick my vision up to him. "Something tells me you're about to find out what they are for yourself."

Silvery eyes twinkle, and he ducks to better meet my gaze. "Good." He rumbles out the word, and lust clenches in my core.

"Gross." Tessa's off-put voice cuts through our magic. "Here." She fishes out some cash from her pocket and shoves it Trevor's way. "Pay for the tickets. I'm going to the bathroom to puke."

Trevor finger flicks the back of her skull. "It's your fault for telling me she was single."

She gives him a nasty scowl then disappears.

We look at each other after she's gone and smile.

"Thanks for sticking around with her." He pats my arm. "She'd be pretty lonely without you."

"I'd be lonesome without her too." I fluff out the ends of my hair. Looking at the restrooms, I determine it seems kind of empty and decide I'd better pee now. I plan to drown myself in snacks tonight, and soon my arms will be full. I rub his flat torso and slink past him. "I'm going to join Tess. I'll be right back."

"Don't talk about me too much."

He hollers it loud enough, so I snap over my shoulder to look at him. One glimpse has my heart in my stomach. He's smiling at me—ripped upper torso deliciously filling out his shirt, muscular legs spread wide in a dominant stance, his tall frame hovering above the crowd—real perfection.

Yeah. He's hot. I give him a wave and break my stare to look dead ahead. God bless Tessa for giving me a live one. She's a real pal.

I jump. Gasp. Freeze.

It's Bentley.

He's in front of me, a few feet away. Neither of us moves. We stay put, opting for the crowd to swim around us. His eyes are deadlock set on me. The burning unblinking look sends a prickle through me—head to toe.

Is he mad at me?

For once, I can't tell, probably because I've never seen him pissed. I've witnessed irritated, hungry, tired, grumpy, stressed, but not anger. A lump lodges in my throat, one I can't even swallow through.

A curvy brunette with finger waved hair comes up beside him and shoves her purse his way. He accepts the tiny clutch but never acknowledges her, not even for a beat.

Nothing familiar registers on my end. My heart should be dropping to the floor. I should feel sick and abandoned like all the other times, but there's none of that. Not when his eyes belong to me.

His date doesn't even take note I'm here, per usual. Another blind girl. She flicks his collar with a red-painted fingernail and flits off to the bathroom.

It's only after she's gone that I dare to approach, and for the first time, it's hard. The manic thump racing through my ribs reverberates throughout. It strengthens with each timid step, and when we're closer, it takes everything in me to manage a stilted smile.

"Hey." My voice squeaks.

"Hi." His reply is dead—the same goes for his pale complexion and glassy stare. Everything about him seems dull and lifeless tonight.

"How's it going?"

No answer. Only a stare.

The silence makes me feel knee-deep in shit, but running from an old friend seems stupid. It's probably all in my head, and maybe he just didn't hear me. I scoop hair off my neck and force a bigger, more sincere smile. "You brought a date tonight?" It is odd for him to bring girls out in public. From my experience, they occupy his bed longer than his real free time.

"Mmm-hmm," he nods, then stares downward.

"She's pretty."

Nothing.

My skin crawls, and I can't understand why this exchange is so awkward. We've talked about our dates before, even joked about the bad ones, so why is this different? "Is...uh... is she nice?"

His head jerks up, his ocean ice laced with icebergs. "Not really, no." There's no eternal smile plastering on his face. Tonight he's straightlaced, stoic, and arctic. "If I were to be honest, she's really unpleasant and annoying."

I can't form a response, thanks to all the words sticking in my throat.

"Ya know, I wanted to see this movie with you." He dares a step closer, and my toes turn inward. "I sent you a text. I even called."

"Oh." It's not in my head. Guilt weaves tight in my heart about flat-out ignoring him. "I'm sorry, Bentley. I've been so busy. I—"

"Yeah. I can see that." That cold gaze of his darts past my shoulder right in Trevor's direction.

I sigh hard, my shoulders deflating, a lump forming in my stomach. "Bentley, please don't be mad. I—"

"Shit. Don't look at me like that." He squeezes his eyes closed. "I'm not mad, Nora. It's been a bad couple of weeks, and I just—" Refocusing on me, he takes a step closer.

A frown paints over his features, the sadness in it spearing right into my gut.

"I wish it was you I was seeing this movie with." His voice falls to a mumble, and he stares at the floor. "This sounds stupid, but... I wish this popcorn was over buttered because of you and that I was bitching about it."

"Bentley—" His words hollow out my chest then fill the void with shock. *It sounds like he cares*—It sounds like too much for me to handle. I shake my head and stumble back a step.

Bentley is tempting, beautiful, my Achilles, what my heart beats for, and everything I've obsessed over for the last two years, but I won't be disloyal to Trevor.

I've never been a cheat, and I never will. It doesn't matter who it is. If any part of this is him sulking due to my distance, then that's too bad.

It's hard, almost impossible, but I stop the churning of guilt. This has nothing to do with me. I won't take the blame for his foul mood. If we want to talk about ruined plans, I could throw plenty of shade his way. *I'm only here because Bentley hung my heart out to dry.* I'm sure Bentley doesn't know it, but he did that, and now I'm moving on. I won't let this display trick me. *He doesn't care about me.* He doesn't *see* me. He's just off tonight, and mad I ignored him.

I sigh and shrug. "Bentley, I'm sorry if you've felt ignored. You're my best friend and always will be."

He lifts his head. No smile. "Nor—"

"Next time there's a movie out, all of us will go together."

"All of us?" His brows snap together.

"Yes," I nod. "You, me, Tessa, Trevor. I'll make sure you're included."

His eyes narrow, but it looks more like hurt than anger. "I don't want—"

"Nora." Trevor's voice comes up from behind. He stops beside me, places his hand on the small of my back, and stares at Bentley. "You? Again?" He doesn't sound pleased, but he also doesn't sound pissed. *Surprised* would be more like it.

"Yeah." Bentley's jaw clenches. "Me again." His gaze slides over to me, and he nods once. "Thanks for that, Nora. That would be great. I'll see you later." Turning on his heel, he strolls away, his posture slouching.

I chew the inside of my cheek, guilt roiling in my blood. I hate seeing him like this. Whatever has him off-kilter tonight is terrible.

"Can't say I like the way he looks at you." Trevor's eyes are pinpointed on Bentley, following him through the flowing crowd. "Seems to me he thinks you're his dream girl too."

"I'm not." I grab onto his built bicep, shoving the feelings for Bentley away. "He's just a friend."

"Ahh." He pats my hand then urges me to move to the concession stand.

We've only taken a few steps when he stops us and twirls me into his arms.

"Nora, I *know* who that is." His eyes burn into mine, brows halfway scowling. "I know who Bentley is to you."

"But how?" My mouth falls open.

"Tessa told me about him."

"Of course." My shoulders deflate. *She's a blessing and a curse.* "What did she tell you?" I can't hide the lackluster tone seeping through my voice.

"That you had a serious crush on him," he says it low, almost grumbling, and I know he isn't pleased.

"Exactly." I straighten my spine. "*Had.*"

"So?" His arm snakes around my waist, and he tugs me into a hold that feels possessive. "You think you can turn that on and off like a light switch?" A huff blows out of him. "That's not how attraction works, hun. It's either there or not."

"Well, it *was* there for me." We move in unison and join the back of the line. I avert my gaze forward and hold my head high as I glue my composure together. "It's not anymore, and it *never* was for him."

He sucks in air through his teeth. "Yeah… I wouldn't be so certain of that. Those looks he gave you—" he pauses. "I didn't like them, Nora."

Nervous adrenaline spikes in my body—and I almost sense that I'm spiraling, but I won't let that happen.

I won't lose this man because Bentley was off tonight. I turn into Trevor, placing my hands on either side of his waist, and remove the space between us. "But were you uncomfortable with me? Did I do anything?"

"No." The corner of his mouth pulls up, and the tightness dissolves in his gaze. "Whatever I saw, you seemed to handle it like an unavailable woman."

The corners of my eyes crinkle, and I use that acknowledgment as the eraser to our problems. "Then I hope that's what's important to you."

"It is." He strokes the back of my hair.

"Good." Tightness flushes out of me from limb to limb.

Taking a second to observe where Bentley last stood, I shake my head and gaze up at Trevor. "As for Bentley, I don't know what his deal was tonight, but I assure you, it's not like that for him. Whatever interest you *think* you saw doesn't exist."

One brow arches up. "Uh-huh." He winces and looks away. "Keep telling yourself that. I know what I witnessed."

I hate the refusal. For whatever reason, it sits bitter and sour in my stomach, but I'm not going to ruin our evening with a fight. I face the concession area again and grab Trevor's hand. After giving it a firm squeeze, I get one in return. My mouth curls up.

It will all work out. I have Trevor now, and even though he has his doubts, I know it won't be long before he sees what I really am to Bentley.

A convenience.

Nothing but a simple, easy convenience.

Fragments of You

Chapter 9

Bentley

"Damn. You're ugly when you scowl." Rich's voice rings louder than the bar crowd around us. He taps the neck of his beer bottle on my glass—his way of fully getting my attention.

I rip my eyes from the TV and slip my mask back on. It's fallen off during a moment of brooding.

He scoops long black hair out of his face. "Last time you looked like that was when a girl fucked me instead of you."

"I didn't care about that." My eyes droop. "I was sick that night. Besides, she was too tall." I hunch over the table.

Son of a bitch is telling the truth.

I was sour about being overlooked that night. *Guess not much has changed.*

The past three weeks have been hell.

Actually, ever since I heard Ivy's name last month, I've been different. That name was a wrecking ball to my so-called healed heart. I realize now restoration was a lie—I've always been broken. I still can't figure out where to place the pain. I've been overworking myself in the gym, at times, punching the sandbag till my knuckles bleed—fuck gloves.

But the last three weeks have been an intensified type of

hell.

It's all because of Nora.

Trevor commands her attention like no one else. Past guys never interfered with our contact before. Dinners and movies became non-existent, but I've never been flat out ignored… until now.

Last week everything climaxed. Seeing her at the theater with Trevor gashed a hole in my chest. When I caught her smiling and laughing after days of not responding to texts and calls, my self-worth bled all over the fucking floor. It pooled around my feet and seeped away to misery.

I'm sitting here tonight having a few drinks with Rich and his coworker, hoping to lessen the sting festering in my chest.

So far, it's not helping one fucking iota.

"Women." Brock, the guy with us tonight, shakes his head. "I can't think about women." His voice is barely loud enough to hear, same for his sigh. "Thinking about anyone is hard after my, uh…"

"Divorce." I stifle an exasperated stare. "Yeah. You've said that."

A million times.

Seriously, all this guy has done since we met up tonight is moan about his cheating wife. I know it sucks. My breakup with Ivy made me pray for death. But the difference?

I don't cry about it to people like a little bitch. Unlike this dude, I keep it all to myself. Rich doesn't know about Ivy.

No one here does.

I take a sip of my ale, thanking God my dignity remains intact.

"Yeah, man," Rich says, his attention diverts to the game, "Sorry to hear about that and all, but you know my saying."

Brock gives a pathetic shrug. "I think I forgot it."

Rich takes a long guzzle and places the drink down. "If you want to be disappointed, fall in love." He places both elbows on the table and stares at Brock, deadpanned face. "If you want to be totally destroyed, get married."

The words crash down harder than a boulder plunging through a glass roof, and I swear Brock tears up.

"Wow, Rich." My shoulders fall as flat as my voice. "Remind me to hire you next time I need a pep talk."

"Hey," Rich frowns. "Just keeping it real and speaking from what I know." He coolly looks at the screen. "Every man in my family has gone through hell. Dad, Uncles, Brothers, Cousins? None of their marriages lasted. I'm not even gonna try."

My brows furrow, his words bristling my nerves the wrong way. "My parents are happily married and dated all through high school. Not everyone has a bitter experience."

"Ahh, yours are the rare ones, then." His dark eyes are stoic. "A flower surrounded by shit."

"Great analogy," I bite out. "I'll tell my parents you said that—they'd be thrilled."

He throws a sly smirk and grunts.

"I can't blame you, Rich," Brock says. "If I had known divorce was this bad…" He palms his drink between both hands. "Have you ever had relationship problems, Bentley?"

A sharp twinge snakes through my heart. Thoughts of my fucked up affair with Ivy and even Nora's distance lash across my mind. I numb it all, sending rejection back to whatever rotten hole it came from.

"Sorry." I settle into the chair. "Never met anyone I cared that much about."

"Which is why we're friends." Rich toasts to me, a massive grin on his stupid face. "However, if some chick ever captures me by the dick, shoot me in the fucking head." He ignores a shocked sound from Brock. "Death would be better than losing my balls."

"Jesus, Rich." Brock's eyes are wide. He looks at me. "Do you share the same views on commitment?"

"Depends," I say, bringing the cool rim of the glass to my mouth. "You shouldn't be surprised. Lots of guys have the same sentiment as Rich—" I shrug, "—as us."

"To each his own then." Brock shakes his head. "I don't think I'll ever be as bitter as you, Rich." He polishes off his beer and squints. "And never say never." He stays fixated on the TV playing a college game. "Females are tricky. If you're not careful, one of them will have you by the balls before you know it."

"Hell no." Rich waves his hand in the air. "Not me. Not unless someone girl can prove to me they can have a heart—which won't happen. If anyone is going to get castrated, it's Bent." He waggles a finger at me. "You're too fucking soft, not wanting to make women cry. It's going to get you in trouble."

"What?" I turn my palms up. Irritation flickers in my veins. "And you enjoy making them cry? What's the pleasure in it? I think it's stressful."

"No pleasure." Rich motions at the server. He wants another drink. "I just don't see the point in sparing girls their feelings. They don't spare ours. If I'm going to send them out the door crying after a satisfying fuck, they might as well know there's zero hope of a repeat." He raises a brow. "There's nothing more annoying than a girl who won't leave you the fuck alone."

"Shit, Richard." Bile hits the back of my throat. "You're a real dick."

He always has been, but damn. What I'm hearing from him tonight would disgust even the most devout libertine.

"No," Rich says. "I'm honest."

Which is why you don't know about Lena.

I remind myself of this frequently. Anytime I slip up and think he's a halfway decent person, he fucks it up with talk like this. The thought of him laying his hands on anyone I hold the slightest regard for curdles my stomach.

"So, the party I'm having Friday…," Rich props his calf on his opposite knee and nods at me. "I think—"

"I'm not coming."

"Not coming?" Rich's mouth falls open. "You're shitting me."

"I'm not." I shake my head. "I'm tired."

Attending a party sounds like hell. The idea of cruising around his house, prowling for some random girl to dick in my bed is nausea-inducing.

I don't need a fuck. What I need is to sit my ass down and figure out what the hell is wrong with me—sort through why I've been so damn moody.

Besides, Nora won't even be there.

There won't be any moments where I break away and tease

her. Fixating on her scent and hair while my heart palpitates in my throat won't happen.

She'll be with Trevor. A bitter taste coats my taste buds at the idea.

Rich doesn't even notice. He leans back, casually wrapping his hand around the fresh beer the server just brought. "Well, screw you too, dude." He nods at Brock. "How bout you?" A chime rings out as he taps the top of the bottle. "Bet I can find you someone who will fuck away your pain."

"Nah, man." Brock rolls his drinks between his hands, a drink he hasn't really touched. "I think I'm good. I've had a long week, and then I'm supposed to see my kids."

"Hmm." He cocks his head. "Okay, you bunch of pussies." Picking up his drink, he prepares for a swig. "More for me. The more, the better, ya know. Can't have your dick in one place too long."

I fall silent. A sadness tides through me—one so heavy it pulls my heart through the damn floor, weighting me into the chair.

He's such a fool.

There was a time when one person would have been good enough for me. Moments linger where I remember how much pride I took holding her in my arms.

Just like Dad.

Every time I made Ivy smile, I felt myself foraging in Dad's footsteps. I had no doubt that I could make her happy the way Dad makes Mom happy.

A weight hits my chest. I was supposed to be like him. Provide for, care, and love the way he does.

The past slurries in my brain as I drown out Rich and Brock. I know it's the beer since I haven't drunk in a while, but right now, all of Dad's soapbox moments on morality are weaseling their way into my head, prickling at my heart.

"Your Mom and I never had a breakup."

"All that bullshit about young love not lasting is just that. Bullshit."

"The only way to be truly happy is by staying with one woman."

"A Harris man is a faithful man."

"Treat a woman right, and she'll stay with you forever."

The last one always fucks up my insides—knotting my innards into a cluster of pain and guilt. It's the one Dad said the most when I lived at home. It's the saying he pounded into me, over and over.

And I believed it, until it crashed down on my head. The crash being Ivy. I let the most painful part of her words replay.

"Ask your friends how loud I screamed when they fucked me... sometimes two at a time."

Seven years later and a wicked crack breaks across my heart with the recall. I ball my fists.

Friends.

The word haunts me to this day.

All my friends, except one, fucked her, and I didn't even know it. Not until my nineteenth birthday, the night I was going to propose.

I thought all my dreams were going to come true. Instead, I caught her in *my* bed fucking a long-time 'friend' Liam. When I walked in, I remember seeing the horror on her face. Then it switched to laughter.

"It took you this long to catch me. God, you're dumb. We've been placing bets on when you'd figure everything out."

After a fistfight with Liam, all I recall is going to a club and fucking the life out of the first girl who'd have me.

I've been rotten ever since—never stopping long enough to let old gashes heal. By now, I'm sure that inside, all I am is gangrene and filth. Part of me blames my Dad. His fairytale horseshit pumped me full of lies, driving me to all the easy sex I opposed for years. I had offers all the time but wanted to be 'more than a fling.' It wasn't until Ivy crumpled and tossed me aside that I actually called those offers in.

And it's his fault. If Dad hadn't made me his guinea pig for his beliefs, I wouldn't have been catapulted over the edge when I discovered the truth about Ivy.

Fuck, life sucks. I rub at my chest, hoping the gape gnawing at me will leave. Maybe more beer will help.

I take another sip. It suddenly tastes like piss. When I look around, my head throbs. There are too many people and too much noise.

I spot a girl sitting at the bar with her friend. She makes eye contact with me, pokes out her tongue, and winks. Repulsion slithers down my spine and wraps around my stomach.

I'm done.

Tonight, I don't need something easy. I need something real. I'm sure as fuck not going to find it here.

Sliding out of the chair, I push the beer away. "I'm going to call it." Being home with no background noise sounds perfect.

"Wimping out then, hey?" Rich places his second empty beer bottle down.

"Yeah." I nod. "I'll hit you up later."

After a brief goodbye to Brock, I unpocket my keys and go to my car.

At first, home is the only place I'm thinking of.

My bed. A protein shake. Maybe a few chapters in a book. A shower. It all sounds great.

Until I realize I'm not driving home. My car is on the road leading west of town. I'm going to the field. The one that's away from the city lights so I can see the stars.

I guess the heart knows what it needs.

My foot bears down on the pedal as I abandon the nightlife.

Twenty minutes later, I'm whipping up to the electric fence, pushing my trespassing luck for whoever owns this land. I want to be as close to the field as possible.

I climb out and, despite the cold air, tug off my jacket and lay it on the hood. Careful not to scratch the paint, I sit my ass down. First, I take a few stilted breaths, tugging my knees in tight. But the longer I sit, the more I relax, and the more my blood pressure drops.

The night wind hugs me as I become in tune with the nature around me. Crickets. The occasional hooting of an owl. Rustling leaves. Blades of grass rippling at the touch of the breeze.

I absorb it all.

Then when my eyes pull up, I see the blanket of stars. Bright and bold. I smile and lie back—my head on the windshield—hands propping behind my head.

"Nature heals. The stars are the best at it. Look at them, and you'll feel better."

It's Mom's saying.

Over the past few years, I haven't stargazed long or hard enough. It's to my downfall. Right now, there's no weight in my heart. A bit of sadness swirls in it due to my shitty lot in love, but that lead weight that pinned me to my chair at the bar has vanished.

A chuckle slips out. Maybe I'm a fool for sitting out here, believing my Mom's story about nature being able to heal me, but at the moment, all I know is she's closer to the truth than Dad ever was.

The stars do help, especially when my eyes lock on the brightest one.

Dad's beliefs, on the other hand...

Rich is partially right.

Love does lead to destruction. At least in my case. If it didn't, I wouldn't be out here, looking at the stars hoping they'll suture the split residing in my heart. I sigh. Dad's the one who's wrong.

Love isn't anything great.

Love isn't anything except a big lying bitch.

Chapter 10

Nora

"Davis." Laura's voice grates on the other side of the bathroom door. "You good? You've been in there for an awfully long time."

Crap. I lower my phone, covering part of the screen. "Yeah, I'm good." Not to mention it's only been five minutes.

"Ok. Well, hurry the hell up. Scripts aren't going to check themselves."

Once she shuffles away, I glance skyward and bring the phone to my ear. "I have to go back to work, Carly."

"Why?" Her voice bristles. "I thought you were on lunch."

I'm not. "I know, but-uh —" I can't tell her Laura's going to chew my booty out for stealing time in the work bathroom. Any slip up on that will blow all the big talk I've made over the past several months about my 'sweet life'. "There's a customer who wants to see me." I'm glad Carly can't see the grimace on my face as I lie through my teeth.

"They can wait."

"No. Not really, Carly." Annoyance simmers in my gut. "They —"

Uhhh." Air huffs into the phone. "You haven't even said hi to Dad yet. That's literally the only reason why I called since his phone broke."

"Tell Dad—"

Bang. Bang. Bang.

"Davis." Laura's voice sends me leaping. She's back with hell marching behind her.

Instinctively, I hide my phone, even though she can't see it.

"We need you out here," she growls. "Now."

Judging by the tone, she's going to claw at me quicker than a hellcat when I step out of the bathroom. I quickly bring the phone to my ear and barely whisper. "I have to go."

"No—"

My thumb hits the end call, and I turn off my phone. If I don't, Carly will call back right away, and Laura is bound to hear it. She's waiting for me out there. I can sense her ugly soul on the other side of the door.

Trying to make good of a lie, I flush the toilet and run the sink water. I even dispose of a paper towel, so she can hear it pulling through the dispenser.

Stepping out, I flick off the light and become rigid. Thar she blows.

The old battle-ax is standing a foot from the bathroom door, knuckles on her hips, her shoulders slouching so low I think they're competing with her saggy old boobs. I don't know if it's from hard living or maybe just too many days out in the sun, but Laura has seen better days. I'll never be the one to tell her, but that cropped perm and brassy hair do nothing to counterbalance all the lines and wrinkles coursing her face.

My hands go clammy, and I soothe them over my pants. She's going to say something, she always does. *Three...two... one...*

"What were you doing in there?"

I force my best poker face. "Going to the bathroom."

"For seven minutes and twenty-two seconds?"

Wow. I keep my jaw sealed because if I don't, it will fall wide open. *She actually counted.* Part of me finds it impressive how stupidly obsessed she is.

Her top lip snarls up. "No bathroom break, not even an elephant-sized shit takes that long."

Classy. "Sorry," I counter, folding my arms across my chest. "Blame aunt Flo. Her arrival isn't always timely, or um—" The pause drags out exactly the way I hoped. "—neat."

Her overly plucked brow arches. "I don't believe you."

"Then ask Susie." A curt smile perks up my mouth. "We're synced."

"So you keep saying." Her eyes narrow. "I might ask. For now, go back to the counter and check prescriptions. The flu is running amok. There are enough Tami-flu scripts being called in to supply a warehouse."

I nod, slide past, and return to my spot.

Soon, I'm knee-deep in comparing the illegible handwriting of doctors to the bottles of medicine in front of me. I've just checked off on a massive order for a family with strep throat when one of our clerks from the main floor comes to get me.

"Sorry to bother you, Nora, but there's a guy here who has questions about allergy pills."

My brows come together. "Allergies? In this weather?"

She nods. "That's what he said."

I'm considering passing it to Laura or Susie since I'm too busy. I have a stockpile of prescriptions to check before they can go out the door, and a doctor's been on hold waiting to call in a script for way too long now. He's bossy, rude, and hard to understand, so no one ever wants to talk to him, but we can't ignore him forever. "I don't think I have time."

"He asked for you."

"Oh, very well," I sigh, glancing at the phone with its red beeping light. "Remind one of the other pharmacists that Dr. Langer is on line two. New script."

Grumbling, I go out the security door and onto the store floor. Most days, I love interacting with patients, but today isn't one of them.

Carly called me, chewing my butt out that I haven't called in a few days. *If she wasn't such a brat.* I love my sister, but holy shit.

She blows money, shirks responsibilities, criticizes me for my dreams, then wonders why I rarely phone home. Combined that her call got me in trouble with Laura has exasperation resting in my veins.

And work? Well, that's always a bitch, and I have nowhere to go with it.

My heart wants to tell my folks about my situation, but I can't. Dad doesn't understand toughing things out, all he does is rescue people, and I don't want that.

I'm rounding the corner, heading to the antihistamine aisle—frustration still brewing and cooking like a stew.

A hand wraps around my wrist. I squeak while being yanked past my destination.

"What the—" My hands flap to pull away—instead, I'm pushed to a darkened nook that holds a door leading to the stockroom. I blink, adjusting to the dim surroundings, but reality blanks out when a flat stomach, ripped thighs, and a leather jacket grinds against my body.

Triple that when hot lips overtake mine and spiced cologne engulfs me.

Trevor. Holy mother of mercy.

His hotter-than-sin mouth dominates me. His hands cup my face while his tongue lightly brushes my lips. He's been doing this to me all week—kissing me till I'm dizzy, clutching his arms, so I don't fall to the ground. This time is no different. The wreckage is the same. My clit throbs, my knees shake, and my panties become slick right on cue.

He pulls away, and I'm panting. When he looks into my eyes and smiles, I'm positively devoid of air. "Hey, dream girl." He waggles his brows. "Surprised?"

"Trevor." I rest the back of my head against the wall. "Do you have any idea how much you scared me?" I'd like to look around, but it's hard with my face between his hands. "I could get in huge trouble."

"For what?" One of his brows quirks up. "Kissing your boyfriend?"

"No, for making out—" I stare into his ever handsome face and blink. My mouth dangles open. "Boyfriend?" The word is barely audible.

"Yeah. That's right." He sweeps his tongue across his

mouth, darkness flickering in his eyes. "Come here, girlfriend. Let me taste you again." He lowers his head, heading straight for my lips.

"Just a moment." Pressing my hands against his face, I intercept the kiss, blood whooshing through my head so I can hear the humming in my ears. "Shouldn't we talk about this first?" I drop my hands and fold my arms across my chest.

He shrugs. "What's there to talk about?"

"I-I-mean…" I turn up my palms and wave them in the air.

"You like me, Nora." He lowers his frame. "And I clearly like you. We click, so I don't see the need to complicate things. Do you want this or not? No pressure if you don't, but I do. I *really* do."

My stomach whirls with uncertainty, but my heart responds differently. It drums hard against my ribs, the rhythm echoing in my neck as I look into his gray eyes rimmed with black. My hand finds itself on his stomach, fisting at the black tee under his jacket.

His body coils. "Is that a yes?" He scoops back the fringes of my hair with his large hand. "Because the way you're touching me makes it feel like a big-time 'fucking yes'."

My chest lurches with a hard breath. I stare at his mouth and become parched. "It's not a 'no'."

A smile spreads over his mouth. "Fuck yeah."

Before I can think, his mouth is on mine, and whatever we've just acknowledged detonates in me. Heat blossoms through my whole body, my core clenches hard with need, and I flood, desperate to strip him of his clothing right here in the damn store and taste him with my tongue.

He groans, threading his fingers in my hair.

I push the jacket off his shoulders and—

"*Ahem.*"

"Shit." While leaping in the air, my head snaps toward the voice.

It's Laura, and boy, if looks could kill, Trevor and I would be drowning in our own blood.

There's nothing to say. All that rises is a gurgle from the back of my throat.

With a hard scowl on her face, she steps up close, so close her coffee-tainted breath sweeps across my face. "You're fired. Go. Home. Now."

My shoulders collapse onto the wall, and my lip trembles—my gut binding around itself into a wadded ball of sickness.

She turns on her heel, returning behind the counters without another word.

Great. I've just lost my damn job, and it's by my own hand. I try to breathe. All I get is a whoosh of stale air that does nothing to help me. Tears swell up in my eyes, and the floor blurs.

"Shit, Nora." Trevor rubs his hand up and down my spine. "I'm so sorry. I shouldn't have done this."

"No." I shake my head. "She's had it out for me for a long, long time. It was bound to happen." It's the truth, but it doesn't lessen the sense of gloom rolling through my body. I close my eyes and rub over my face. *I have no idea what I'm going to do.*

But I do know I won't be telling my family about this. Carly's snark is enough to keep me away—forget about the humiliation of losing my job.

A failure. That's what I am right now. The word is a knife to my composure, and a sob slips out.

"Come on, let's get out of here and go to Tessa's." Trevor grabs my hand, intertwines our fingers, and guides me down an aisle. "I'm going to give you some hot tub time, and then we'll figure this out." He walks, pulling me with him.

"How can you help?" I tag along behind, struggling to keep up with his long strides. "You don't know anyone here?"

"Trust me, dream girl." He looks at me past his shoulder. "I'll take care of you."

The way he says it—strong and upbeat—it's therapy to my soul. I finally manage a composed breath.

"Now," he says. "Let's go to Tessa's and figure this shit out."

"Oh, way to go, you idiot." Tessa flicks Trevor upside the

head, bullets spitting out of her fiery gaze. "You got her fucking fired because you couldn't keep it in your pants?"

"Will you shut up?" Trevor rubs at his skull. He takes a wide stance, anchoring his position, standing tall over his sister. "I wasn't having sex with Nora against a wall, Tess." He ignores her hard snort. "We were kissing."

"Uh-huh," she nods, one brow cocked up. "At her workplace, shoved into a corner like a stupid teenager." Rolling her eyes, she walks over to a dining chair and plops down into it. "Honestly, how dumb are you? You knew she had problems with her boss."

Trevor scowls. "I was trying to make her feel better."

A place behind my eye pounds, and my shoulders tighten. "I can't believe this." Some of the frustration is from my situation, the rest of it from watching Tessa and Trevor fight these last few moments. I look at Tessa. "What in God's name am I going to do?"

"You'll move in with me if you have to, and you'll look for another job."

"No, Tess." My stomach falls to the floor. "You already do too much. I don't want to put you out."

"You won't," she smirks, "Because you won't get dinner unless the floors are scrubbed every day."

That makes me snort. Only Tess could make me laugh about something like this. However, it doesn't last long. "Oh, no." My heart plummets into my shoes when my biggest problem smacks me in the head. "How am I going to pay back the bonus?" Life leeches out of my face, and I stare blankly at the floor.

"We'll figure something out," Tessa says.

A groan releases from me. "Tess, no. You don't understand."

"Hey." She sits upright. "Shut up with the negativity, Nor." Her head tilts. "We got this. Now breathe and stop freaking out."

Taking a few inhales and exhales, repeating Tessa's words over and over, I try to calm my racing heart by taking a cool sip of water.

"So," Trevor says, leaning his butt against the counter, "I

don't know if this is a good time to bring this up, but I have a surprise for, uh, Nora."

"Me?" My head bounds up.

"*Pff.*" Tessa's blow of disbelief hits the room. "I think you've given her enough surprises today, but go ahead and spill."

"I've rented a cabin for next weekend."

"Oh." Some of the hell imploding around me disintegrates, and a corner of my mouth tugs up. "That sounds really nice."

"Yeah," Tessa chimes in. "It does. Where is it, and what day do we leave?"

Trevor rubs at his chest. "So it's in Evergreen and uh…" He pauses, licks his mouth, and smirks. The look is sin in itself. "And uh, Nora and I leave Friday night."

"What?" Tessa and I say it in unison.

"That's correct." He nods and looks at me, that direct stare that's mine and mine alone. "If you'd like Nora, I want to treat you and have you *all* to myself next weekend?"

My pulse accelerates like it's been injected with octane. I nod and smile, anticipation coursing thick through my veins.

"I can't think of anything better."

Chapter 11

Nora

"Wow, this view is amazing." I look out the steepled cabin window and press my hands to the chilly glass, admiring the view all over again.

Pure snow overlays the ground in thick sheets. The blinding white contrasts with the dense enclosure of pine trees that look like they've been dusted with sugar. Only those two things exist for miles. I think Trevor picked the most secluded cabin he could find. However, I wouldn't call this a cabin. *Mansion* would be a better fit. Eight bedrooms, five baths, an enclosed pool, movie theater, and a bowling alley—yeah, 'cabin' is a stretch to me. But, the last day and a half have been perfect, washing away my troubles of being jobless for the time being.

A thrill races up my spine when the bathroom door opens from the adjacent master suite.

"I heard you say something about the view?"

I look over my shoulder to see him stark naked from his shower, raking through wet locks of hair. *Damn.* The water droplets still clinging to his body slide down his abs, forcing my attention to his tapered V and semi-hard cock bobbing between his corded legs.

My clit slickens. I secure the blanket around my body, a flush hitting my cheeks as I remember I'm naked under it. "I did. I was saying how nice the view is."

"So I heard. Only..." He strides towards me, running his tongue over his lower lip. "I wasn't out here when you said it, so I think you're mistaken."

My heart drums in my throat when he collides into my body and forces me backward. He pushes against me till my ass is pressing against the glass—a thin blanket being the only shelter from the chill it omits.

His throat racks with a hard swallow. "Lose the blanket dream girl."

I shimmy my shoulders under the covering, straining to look up. "But the glass is cold."

"Good." He says it parched, with a spark catching in his gaze. "It will heighten the sensation of what I'm about to do to you." His long fingers gently force the blanket open. He tugs it out of my grip and lets it float to the floor. Silver eyes comb over me once, and he sucks in air through his teeth. "God, you're so fucking sexy."

His hands grip into my butt cheeks and boost me up, taking me off my feet.

A shriek escapes when he secures me against the cold window.

"Mmm," he moans, taking his mouth to my throat. "I like that sound. It's even better when I'm inside you."

"Oh my God, Trevor." I wrap my legs around him, straining to fully surround his broad build. I accept the chill to my back, his ungodly heat to my front, and let the room black out.

He works me in expert fashion. Palming my breasts the way I like, kissing my neck in the manner that causes my clit to wet in heavy anticipation—he does it all and so perfectly.

He's been like this the whole time we've been here. Without the constant company of Tessa, we've been ravaging each other any chance we get.

We still have a day and a half left here, and parts of me are already sore, but I have zero intention of stopping this. I've needed this for far too long. I prepare to do the side-to-side walk after it's all said and done, choosing to enjoy the thrill for now.

After one mind-melding release that leaves me echoing his name, we move to the bed.

I urge him to lay down, then I drive him nuts, kissing up and down his body—paying extra special attention to that phoenix tattoo, and his cock. I tease him till he begs me to ride him however I want, which I gladly do.

I ride him till he builds up to a release that has him flipping me over, slamming into me so hard I can feel my brain knocking against my skull.

When he's done, he collapses onto me, and we stay motionless for heaven knows how long.

"Damn," he finally says, rolling off of me. "That was better than the last time."

I snort. "You said that the last three times."

"And I'll keep saying it." He coaxes me into his arms. After throwing the blanket over us, he holds me close. "I'm glad we broke away and came here. It was getting hard finding time with Tessa always up in our asses."

"I know." I trace my finger along his chest and giggle. "I love her, but if she wants us to be a couple, she's going to have to give us more privacy."

He chuckles, soothing over my hair. "I know. It's too bad she's so lonely."

I frown. "Yes, she is, but you're different. You have friends back home, don't you?" I tilt my head up and peck along his jawline.

"Too damn many," he sighs. "Tessa and I are opposite in that area. I like having people around."

"She does too." I lie on my back and look up at the ceiling. "She's just scared because of your parents. They didn't invest a lot of time into either of you. I think she sees it as a reflection of herself, that something's wrong with her."

He shakes his head. "Those two..." He reaches over and softly strokes my belly. "Do they ever call her? I mean, have they called recently to talk to her or anything?"

"Not that I know of." I tuck part of the sheet underneath my armpits. "I think they sent her some money a while back, but that's all I know."

"Did they now." His voice flat-lines.

"What do you mean by that?" It's a tone I haven't heard before, and it has my brows melding together.

His eyes widen, looking my way. "Oh-uh-nothing. I just mean that's how they do things, you know? It's-uh… all money-related."

"Oh." My brows lift when catching the full meaning. "Yeah, it's safe to say that. She's complained about receiving money multiple times."

A huff leaves him. "Not that she needs it. I bet she makes a pretty penny where she works. She's always been smart." One side of his mouth curls up, and he turns on his side to face me. "Has she ever helped you out before? I mean, you're all she has, so I bet you've been on the receiving end more than once."

"Once or twice, yes." A yawn trails out as I sink deeper into the covers. "I always try to keep it even, but she has helped me a lot. That's why I don't want to move in with her. I know she'll end up paying for everything."

"Ha!" He tilts his head back. "Like that's a bad thing."

The reaction strikes an odd chord in my chest, and I frown. "It can be if it becomes too regular. I don't want her to think I'm using her."

"No way." He shakes his head. "That will never happen."

"It could, though—"

"Not a chance." He pushes a lock of hair behind my ear, smiling while gazing deeply into my eyes. "Matter of fact, I bet she'd do anything you asked."

I shrug, unsure how to respond to that. I'm sure Tessa would, but I've never wanted to be *that* friend… I've always just wanted to be *her* friend.

"I gotta pee." He leans over, giving my mouth a gentle kiss. "You ready for another round, dream girl?"

"Ooh." I cup his face in my hands, my pulse racing in anticipation. "If you can work me right, I will be."

"Well…" He cocks a brow. "We already know I can, so I'll take that as a yes."

He slides out of bed and saunters into the bathroom.

I sink into the mattress and close my eyes. My body is already humming at the anticipation of experiencing Trevor again. *This trip is just what we needed.* We're screwing the life out of each other and then bonding by talking after each occurrence. My head tilts back, and I wonder if this is the one. *Our kids would be beautiful.* They'd have to be with Trevor's genetics.

The thought shatters, my eyes flying open when Trevor's phone vibrates with a phone call. I figure it's Tessa bothering him since I ignored her call a couple of hours ago, so I peek over.

No.

A gasp knots up in my throat and stays there.

The picture popping up is *not* Tessa. It's a chick with auburn hair. Trevor is standing behind her in a shot that they snapped in a bathroom mirror. They're naked. Trevor's cupping her breasts with his large hands, his chin resting on her shoulder.

Nausea waves in my gut, and with a shaking hand, I pick up the phone and accept the call. "Hello?"

"Hello?" She snaps, a harsh, nasal accent blaring in my ears. "Who the fuck is this? What the fuck are you doing answering Trevor's fucking phone?"

"I…" My breath shakes, shuddering out my mouth, and my voice loses its strength. "Uhm…who are you?"

"Uh, first off, *bitch*," she bites back. "I'm the fiancee, so you answer the fucking questions."

I slap my hand over my mouth, bile rising in my throat while my heart bleeds out from a vicious crack splitting across it.

"I'm only going to ask one more time bitch. Who. The. Fuck. Are. You?"

In a panic, I end the call—a hot spew of tears bursts out my eyes as I bow over, clutching at the raw piercing pain through my chest. My self-worth shreds apart into nothing, and all I sense coursing through me is filth.

The cell phone buzzes again, and Trevor steps out. I look up.

The sight of him…

This disgusting, vulgar, putrid thing that just put his dick inside me has a smile on his face. The disgust running in my veins catches fire and explodes. I clutch the phone tight. *Mother fucker.*

Trevor tilts his head and furrows his brow. "Hey dream—"

"FUCK YOU!" I hurl the phone. It shatters on the wall, barely missing his head.

He ducks and dodges flying pieces, covering his face with his forearms. I'm flying out of the bed when he lifts his head and drops his hand, looking at me wide-eyed.

"What the fuck, Nora?"

"WHAT THE FUCK?" I charge his way, shoving against his chest, moving him an inch back. "Did you really just ask me that? What the fuck is wrong with you, Trevor?" My lip trembles while holding eye contact. "Fiancee? Are you fucking kidding me?"

The shocked expression on his face turns to a scowl. "You answered my phone?"

I scoff. "I only looked because I thought it was Tessa." A once-over of him has repulsion swirling deep in my core. My fists clench. "Imagine my horror when I saw your hands all over some other woman's bare tits."

"Shit." He swaggers a step back and covers his eyes with his hand.

"Yeah, shit. Which is what you are." My jaw clenches at the sight of him. "Nothing but a fucking disgusting piece of shit."

I'm not able to look at him anymore. All the hurt, pain, and betrayal implodes. Air sticks in my lungs, making me think the life is being squeezed from me, and I can't stay here. The only thing I can think of is collecting my clothes scattered all over the room.

My bra is the first thing I see. It's draped over an armchair, and I lunge for it, slipping it on.

"Nora..." Trevor crosses the room—his voice is high and tight. "Nora, wait. I-I can explain—"

"Explain?" The word shrieks out of me. I reach for my shirt near the fireplace and toss it over my head. "There's nothing to explain, Trevor. You fucked me, and you're engaged."

He extends a hand my way. "It's not like that, Nora. Really."

"Really?" Fully aware I'm still nude from the waist down,

I place my hands on my hips. My panties and pants are on the stairwell. There's this immense need to have them on and be clothed, but I steady myself long enough to look him in the eye and control my voice. "Are you engaged to her or not?"

His shoulders rise with a deep breath. "I am."

Bastard. I squint and tilt my head, revulsion hitting my veins. "Then there's nothing to explain." He moves for me, but I dodge out of his way. "Tessa is going to kill you."

His eyes go saucer wide, and his mouth falls open. "N-no, don't tell her. Whatever you do, please—"

"Should have thought of that before you fucked two different women."

Dashing for the bedroom door, I snag my undies and jeans off the railing while flying down the staircase. I'm not staying here a moment longer. I'd rather be outside dying of frostbite than looking at this cheating, lying snake.

"Nora?" I'm halfway down when Trevor emerges out the door frame. "Where are you going? There's no place—"

"I don't know." I spit. "But I'm *not* staying with you."

"Nora, wait."

I don't—can't.

Running into the kitchen, I retrieve my phone and purse while sliding into the rest of my clothes in a hurry. Clutching my ski jacket, I scramble for my gloves. When I find my snow boots, I jam my feet inside, not even bothering to tie the shoes as I hear Trevor approaching.

He's still naked, wearing only horror and shame on his face.

"Nora, please." He pleads. "Don't go. If something happens to you… Damn. Just please stay or let me drive you back."

I open the front door and dare one cold look back, heat hitting the back of my eyeballs. "Fuck off, and don't follow me."

"Nor—"

The door bangs shut behind me as I step outside. Tears dribble down my cheeks, and I suck in an icy breath when a gust of wind kicks up. The wetness cuts at my face like knives on my flesh, and I have no choice but to stop crying and start walking.

My destination is the twenty-four-hour diner a few miles down the road, and my hope is to make it there before dark. The sun is already setting, and any bit of warmth it gives will soon disappear. I quicken my pace.

Crunching through the snow, I'm cursing the whole time, trying not to bawl, hating myself, wanting to fall apart, wondering if I already have, and questioning why this had to happen to me.

I'm swirling and drowning so bad that I barely notice the diner when I finally reach it. Looking at the neon sign, sniffling with a frozen nose, the remaining pieces of my heart deflate. I frown, staring at the lights shining through the windows, and sigh. *"How am I going to get home?"*

I'm over two hours away from home, stuck up here in the mountains. My only option is to call Tessa. She's going to freak, but I know she'll be on my side and that she'll come to get me.

Unfortunately, she doesn't answer.

After the tenth time, I give up hope, and a tear slides down my cheek. I'll need to find someone else.

I'm scrolling through my contacts, hoping to see a name I can count on—someone who won't judge. I have a few good acquaintances, but the circumstances make it too humiliating to call.

"Damn it." I sniffle, failing at controlling the tears that fall down my face in droves, hopelessness starting to take deep hold in my chest.

I have no one.

Scrolling once more, I freeze when I spot a name that meets all the rescue criteria.

Bentley.

He'd help me. He's rescued me from bad dates before, but there's only one problem. I don't know if he'll answer. Most times, my phone calls go to voicemail, and with our distance lately, he has zero reason to answer. I pause, holding my thumb over the name, struggling to breathe. After deliberation, I decide it's worth a shot. If not, I'll have to wait for Tessa.

I hit the call button.

It rings once.

He's not going to answer. He never does.

It rings twi—

"Nora?"

The sound of his voice has my heart catching in my throat. I grip the phone tight. "Bentley?"

"Hey." His voice sounds tight. I wonder if he knows something's wrong. "What do you need?"

"A ride." Bundling my jacket tight around me, I shiver with the cold, and looking at the diner turns out to be a massive mistake. Wetness hits my eyes. The entire building blurs, transforming into a myriad of neon smears. "I'm in Evergreen, and..." My lip trembles, and a throb of hurt pounds deep in my ribs. "I'm stranded."

"Shit." He pauses. "Don't panic. Just... shit! One second."

There's background noise, and I swear I hear the muffled voice of Bentley saying, "You're going to have to leave. Now."

My stomach plunges to my toes. *Is he with someone?* I take a hard gulp. *I shouldn't have called.* "Bentley—"

"Send me your location." He huffs into the phone. The rustles and sounds coming through the speaker match the panicked tone of his voice. "I'm coming to you, Nora. I promise I'll be there. I'll be there soon as I can."

A sob bites out, and a hot well of tears gush down my face as a fresh ache splits down my sternum. I nod, choking over my own words. "O-okay."

Dropping the pin, I send it to Bentley. When the call ends, I fall to my knees and bawl, not caring who sees me fall apart.

Chapter 12

Bentley

I've known Nora a long time, and I've seen her go through some shit, but the sight of her when I got to the diner ten minutes ago—red-eyed and puffy-nosed, as if she'd been crying for hours—nothing could have prepared me for that. Nor for the way my heart fell and smashed to the floor.

Thank fuck she called when she did.

The thought of Nora being stranded here… I don't even want to finish the idea. Sickness spirals in my stomach when I consider she was almost too late. A few moments later, my phone would have been off. I would've been trying hard to screw away the mysterious ache that's been with me for far too long. Weeks later, and I still don't know what the hell is wrong with me. Nothing is helping.

Not that it's important.

I'm here for Nora, and I need to put on a strong front. Hiding away the misery fermenting deep inside, I approach the table with her favorite cola in hand and frown.

Fuck.

The slumped sight of her isn't any less distressing than it moments ago. She looks like hell.

"Here, sweetheart." I take the seat across from her and push the beverage her way. "Have a drink." Seeing her a after two weeks of separation sends my pulse into a frenzy. The cola's a measly offering of comfort, especially when it's stacked against the desires heating my blood.

I want her in my arms.

I want to watch her tears stop *because* she's in my arms. And this impulse to sweep away her pain with my mouth won't stop bubbling under my skin. I want to kiss that fucker out of her mind—out of existence. Then I want to make her smile at me the same way she did for him.

I want to make all that happen as soon as I get done feeding Trevor his own dick. He screwed with my Nora, and nobody does that.

Mother fucker.

My heart sinks when her soda goes untouched. She sits, her eyes glazed over, unblinking.

"Nora. Say something." Reaching across the table, my fingers brush her knuckles. Thunderous flutters swell in my stomach, and I can't push them down. "Sweetheart?"

Her gaze meets mine, and fuck, she looks shattered. Fragments of pain and betrayal swirl in a pair of eyes that until tonight always seemed to dance with excitement and joy. My sunken heart bottoms out.

He's wrecked her. Torn her apart.

I only recognize it because I've lived through it—I've yet to recover—bits of me are still missing.

Gently tapping my forefinger on her hand, I hope the rhythmic touch will somehow revive her. "He's not worth it, you know? They never are."

I would know.

I cried over Ivy for months. She never gave a shit.

She sniffles. "I feel like he *is* worth the tears." A deafening pause rolls in. After a second, she winces and looks away. "I shouldn't have called you."

"I'm glad you did." My voice softens as I place my hand over hers. "Really, Nora. I'm happy you trust me enough to call."

"Trust?" She scoffs, staring ahead. "What is trust?"

A sharpness pricks away in my chest. It pokes at the memories of what I've been through. Agony and unfaithfulness have hit us both. Right now, it's tethering me to Nora more than ever before, and I can't let her go. I rub my thumb over her soft skin, not ignorant to the way my pulse ticks harder in my throat.

I try to smile. "Trust is what we have, Nora."

"Is it?" Her voice goes hard.

"It is."

She looks at me with a narrow gaze.

"I trust you, Nora." The corner of my mouth lifts. "I trust you more than anyone." The one I don't trust is myself, especially around this fragile version of her.

I don't recognize the tearful, decimated creature sitting across, calling out to me—coaxing me to be the protector I once was. And right now, I believe that defender is still there. She makes me hear him, even if I don't want to. I swallow hard while staring at her, my mouth dry, and each thrust of blood pushes an ache through my arms.

God, how I want to hold and touch her.

Instead, I take my hand away.

This isn't the time to want her affection—not when her world has just crashed down.

Selfish bastard.

She called me here to help her, and I'm determined to do just that.

"Come on." I pull to my feet. "Grab your drink, let's go out- side. I want to show you something."

"What is it?" Her brows furrow. "There isn't anything out here."

"There is." After tightening my scarf, I jerk my head for the door. "Just come on."

She replaces her gloves and leaves the table.

I hold the door open for her and step outside. There's a snow-dusted bench a few feet away. It caught my eye while I was walking in, and I'm going to make use of it.

"Wait here." I tap her on the nose and stroll over to it. With my hand protected by the leather, I make quick work of the snow covering the top. When it's clear, I sink down on the left side and smile at her, patting my hand on the free end—a silent request to join me.

Her head tilts. A second or two later of examination, she pockets her hands and complies.

She sits further away than usual. Most nights, I can brush my sleeve against hers. I don't know if she's ever noticed it, but I do. Anytime I feel her, my heart quickens. Often, I make 'accidental' touches happen more often than they should… but it won't be occurring tonight.

Probably for the best.

A sniffle from her makes me glance over.

She's frowning, her eyes and brows in a near scowl. "It's cold." She bundles her arms around her chest.

"It is." A smirk works across my mouth. "But it's also beautiful. Look." I point to the stars. "Look above us."

Across a dark ribbon of navy, silver dots twinkle. The dim lighting around is enough for us to have a great display of their magic. Being high in the mountains, I think I'm almost close enough to clutch them in my hand. Almost.

"It is beautiful." There's a lightness in her voice, and I glance over. For the first time tonight, those pretty sugar lips are curving up a bit.

"That one? See it?" I point to the brightest one. "I like the ones that stand out."

"I always look for the little dipper." She ducks her head, examining the sky, and then finds it, her dainty hand lifting to point it out. "That was the first constellation Dad told me about." She releases a sigh. From the gentleness, I assume it's a relaxed one.

Silence falls. I don't push for conversation. What I'm doing seems to be working, so I will let her sit here until she's ready to leave or talk. A breeze brushes around me. I slouch, dangling my hands between my thighs, trying to downplay how fucking cold it is out here. I still can't believe she walked here in these conditions.

"Why the stars?"

I avert my attention over. She's staring at me with a soft gaze, rubbing her long index finger down her neck.

Fuck, she's gorgeous.

Even with wisps of uncombed hair poking out and red-rimmed eyes, she's knock-out beautiful.

A weight anchors heavy in my chest. It's begging me to buoy on to her lifeline… to be with her and make her *feel* me. But it'd be too much, and I'm not the person for her. I push the urge away and shrug. "Mom always took me outside to stargaze whenever I was upset. She says nature has a way of healing. It stuck. Whenever I'm hurt or upset, I look at the stars. Even if it doesn't fix anything, it's calming."

She huffs out a breath. "I can't imagine you ever getting hurt. You're too busy being happy. Doing whatever you want."

Happy.

I don't even know what that word means anymore. My eyes hit the ground. I flick my vision up when a sad laugh escapes her.

"I bet you never look at the stars. At least not anymore."

A knife twists then shreds, right through my heart, and fuck, I think I'm going to cry. "Then you think wrong." I can't face her, so I stare at the bench, clearing my throat. "The last few weeks, I've been looking at them a lot. Probably more than anyone on the planet."

She shifts her weight side to side. "I'm sorry. I didn't know." Her voice weakens. When she starts again, it's half the volume it was. "You usually seem so upbeat. I'm sorry."

"Don't be." I croak out the words—her sympathy knocking hard on the door of my composure. I'm thankful she's not asking questions as I rake my fingers through my hair. "Life is a bitch sometimes. It doesn't matter who you are."

"Yeah. You got that right."

Sucking in a huge breath, I glance her way and try to smile. "Enough with the heavy, huh?" Too much of this, and I'll be crying with her. I stand, extending my hand. "Let me take you home."

Pulling to her feet, she slips her hand into mine. Somehow even with our gloves on, breath snags in my lungs.

Fuck. My fingers tighten around hers. I'm holding her hand.

It's secure in mine while escorting her to the car. Blood drums hard in my ears, coursing stronger the longer our connection lingers.

We're silent while heading to the car. All I hear are the things that shouldn't be there—our steps, far too loud for how light we're walking, and my swallows, obnoxious and ear-catching—the pounding of my pulse booming under my skin.

She's unraveling me.

My heart is unwalling itself and dying to tell its secrets, pushing me to the point where I'm contemplating sharing my past about Ivy.

Nora would understand.

Even sympathize. A confession rests on my tongue, but a vice of terror chokes all the words away. I stay mute, balling my free hand rhythmically, hoping she can't sense the pain and yearning radiating off me.

Control. Control.

I snatch my hand away when we get to the car and make quick work of escorting her in. Walking over to my side, I'm scrambling to abate the tide of craving sweeping me under. It's matching my heartbeat, shooting up my throat, then falling to my stomach with a twist. When I get to my door, I'm raking through my hair, and my breathing is fucking shot.

Not good—we still have a two-hour drive.

Fuck.

I close my eyes, squeezing them tight.

She needs my help... not me.

She'll never need me. The truth of those words causes a sting of rejection to wrap around my body, but I'm able to compose myself again. Breathing easier, I climb in.

I close the door, ignoring her scent that's permeating my car. A scowl breaks out when it's not just hers. It's mingling with *his,* and I fucking hate it. Hot blood scorches my nerves, and I push back a snarl.

"Thanks for picking me up."

My head jerks up at her weak voice, but my breath sucks in hard. Her eyes are right in front of mine, large, round, and brown.

Mixed fragrance or not, the desire to have her pricks away at my skin.

I lower my head, hands shaking while I buckle the seat belt, and I hope she doesn't notice. "No worries." I focus on the wheel, unable to lock eyes with her again. "You know I'd do anything to help you."

She doesn't respond, and I'm dying to know what's racing through that head of hers, but I don't dare ask. I'm a fucking mess already. Starting the car, I begin the long drive home, clenching the wheel the whole time.

Later, out of the corner of my eye, I watch her tilt the seat back and relax into it. She sighs but says nothing. Very little enters my mind of what I should be saying. All that runs through me is what I *want* to say.

"Have you ever considered us? Have you ever wondered what we'd be like together?"

Tonight, it's too improper to voice, and I can't for the life of me figure out why the hell I'd even want to ask her that. Sure, I've wanted to take her home with me. Numerous times. But a real relationship? That's something I kicked to the wayside long ago. I shake my head, trying to rattle the thought away.

"This might be really inappropriate," she says softly.

My spine straightens. Anticipation has me grasping for a hard swallow, and while I shouldn't prod, I have to know. "What is it?" I sound parched asking it.

"I just…" She sighs again. "I think what makes it hurt the most was all the snuggling afterward."

My brows lift at the subject. I can't believe she wants to talk about this. The idea of her with Trevor makes my jaw clench so hard it sends an ache to the bones. This is the last thing I want details about, but I can't cut her off. I just can't.

"Sorry," she says. I look over, and she's chewing on the inside of her mouth. "We shouldn't be talking about this, but I have to get this off my chest." A pause dangles in the air. "You know what, never mind."

"No." I force a deep breath. "It's okay." It's not. Not really, but, yeah. "What is it?"

"This might sound dumb," her brows pinch into a pensive look as a pink tint climbs in her cheeks, "But snuggling has always been a big deal to me. For me, it's more than just… than just…" She waves her hands in the air.

"Sex?" My direct word choice cuts through the air.

She nods, averting my eyes.

"That's because…" A clamp wrenches around my chest—memories of Ivy gouge at the scales covering my wounds. My shoulders tighten, but I continue, "That's because it includes vulnerability." The words croak out of me. I shrug, patting down the tension trying to climb in my body. "Anyone can fuck, but holding that person in your arms afterward makes it real—gives it meaning."

The confession has me reliving the past. I feel Ivy and how I used to stroke her hair when we finished. The way her curls tangled in my fingers lays fresh in my mind, and I remember everything we did. I used to love how her legs would remain draped around me, even though they were shot and shaking. And I'd always fall asleep on top of her because she liked it. Or at least she claimed to, but that obviously wasn't true.

I haven't held anyone after sleeping with them since. It's too damn painful. A sense of loss clenches around my midsection, and I grip the wheel tighter, bile hitting my throat.

"Yeah." I'm drowning in what died years ago. There is no road in my line of sight—all that registers is black. "It's vulnerable. Which is why I don't do it."

"What?" Nora's shocked voice cuts into my thoughts.

I jerk my head over.

Did I say that out loud?

Her wide eyes and dangling jaw tells me I did.

"*Shit.*" Heat billows under my clothes. I rip my eyes away and stare again at the road. "You probably didn't want to hear that. Sorry for making it weird."

Why can't I control myself with her?

I'm always saying stupid shit and giving myself away. Thank God she's gracious about the whole thing. Her easy and calm tone has my shoulders loosening.

"It's fine. Really. I'm the one who brought it up." Her mouth barely lifts with what looks like a sad smile. She relaxes into the seat again, and shortly after that, she falls asleep.

Thank God.

The silence is just what I need. Much more of this, and I'll be begging Nora to give me a chance. At what? I don't fucking know, but the way my heart hums around her tonight has me realizing this woman is becoming more than the sunshine I flirt with and fantasize about.

While stopped at a light in town, I take a long glance over.

Her peaceful, sweet face peeks through dark strands of chestnut hair—her milky skin contrasting too perfectly even in the dark.

A compulsion to touch her winds down my hand. I reach out, gently brush hair out of her face and...

Fuck.

She sizzles like wildfire against my skin, but I don't want to pull away. I *want* her to burn me, and I want to sing her praises while she does it. My hands shake when I realize I want it to happen every single night.

"Damn it," I whisper it, unable to tear my gaze from her. "Damn you, Nora." I grit my teeth, tapping my fist on the wheel.

For the first time in forever, I want to surrender again, and it's to this woman. Part of me wants to give Nora Davis all the fragments that remain of me. And holy fuck, that's terrifying.

Fragments of You

Chapter 13

Nora

"That was my Mom." Tessa rejoins me in her living room and settles down on the navy sectional.

"No way?" I cough, mouth half-filled with ice cream. "You mean she actually called?"

"After I bitched about her silence, she did." One side of her nose pulls up. "It took her a while, but she called. I guess she finally, quote-unquote, 'found the time to fill me in about Trevor.'"

My brows knit together. "Seems a little late after you told her you were going to chop off Trevor's dick and run it over with your car." That was over a week ago.

"Trust me," she holds one hand up and shakes her head, "Calling is her way of showing concern. It's pathetic as hell, but that's as good as it gets."

"Why am I not surprised?" They've always been crappy. "So?" I pick up some of the dessert on the tip of my spoon. "What did she say?"

"That Trevor was probably only here for one reason, Money." She folds her legs under her and sighs. "Mom and Dad cut him off last month."

I become motionless, my pulse beating out of sync. "What do you mean they cut him off?"

"Like—" she jerks her fingers across her neck, "No more money. Nada. They even cut him from the will. They're giving everything to me, and I didn't even know about it."

"What?" The spoon clatters into the bowl as it slips from my grasp. "But why?"

"Drugs." Her eyes dull, and she readjusts the gray sweater slipping down her shoulder. "He began dealing drugs, and he started the new venture with Dad's money."

My hand claps over my mouth. "Oh, damn."

"Yeah, not a good thing for a board member of the DEA to be funding. If that shit got out, it would cost him everything."

I look at Tess and shake my head. "So he came for your money?"

"Apparently." She shrugs, jerking her line of vision away. "Glad my parents decided to keep me informed."

I know that shrug and the wince on her face. It's one I've seen far too many times over the years. She's hurt. "I'm sorry, Tess."

"Eh." She waves her hand like she's brushing my words aside, but I know she doesn't mean it. An ache crashes into my chest for her. "He was always a little shit. What pisses me off is what he did to you."

My frame sinks against the pile of pillows behind me, and a dull thunk replaces the rawness that first ate at my heart after Trevor. "Honestly, I'm good."

Her brows scrunch in disbelief, but I shake my head.

"Really, I am."

Over the past week, the wound that ripped through me at the cabin has slowly begun to close. If I'm being realistic, Trevor was hot and pushed all the right buttons, but we weren't together long enough to get too entangled. It sucks that I was the *other* woman, but thankfully it ended before I fell in love with him.

I'm fortunate.

However, Tessa is not. The misuse of her has my afternoon sweet-tooth going sour. He could have hurt me all day. But not

Tess. She doesn't deserve it—not to mention it's his damn sister. Family is supposed to be everything, but for her, it's nothing. I place my bowl on the floor, no longer hungry. "I'm sorry I got so hung up on how much he liked me. I wish he would have just left us alone."

"You're not getting it, Nora."

My mouth snaps shut.

"I'm not sure he even liked you. I think he was using you the whole time. He probably saw you as a way to get access to my money."

I gasp. Something in my ego shatters, and a new hurt cracks my heart open, burrowing itself deep in my sternum. I don't know why I haven't thought of that until now, but Tess is probably right. To sit here and think a guy *that* sexy saw anything in me is stupid flattery. My plane of vision drops to the couch, and I pick at a fraying thread, shame and betrayal stinging my cheeks.

"I'm sorry to say that, Nor." Her tone is flat, just like my feelings.

"No. It's okay." I shove the abrasion of Trevor's insult away. I'll lick my wounds later when I'm not with Tessa. This needs to be about her. "You're right." A frown twists across my face when I recall how he asked about money and their parents during our brief talk. "He did mention something about your funds. He even asked if you helped me out in the past and said you'd probably do anything for me. It seemed weird—I just didn't question it."

She squints. "I knew it. Dirty bastard." With a sigh, she plays with the ends of her hair. She's opted to leave it out of a bun today, and I've forgotten how long it's gotten. Her pale fingers comb through the midnight waves. "Well, he was right about one thing."

My brow pulls up. "What's that?"

"About me doing dumb things for you," she smirks. "While you were gone, I went to your pharmacy and paid back your bonus."

"Tessa, no." My palm smacks against my forehead. "The amount of that bonus, was…"

"A lot. A whole damn lot." The smirk she's wearing travels up, hitting the corners of her eyes. "So whenever I call asking you to bring me a soda, you better not give me some bull crap about being busy. That shit's not going to fly anymore."

I can't even laugh. The astonishment of what she's done overrides everything else. I'll never be able to pay her back.

"It was the least I could do after Trevor fucked you over and made you lose your job." She jerks upright and points her finger to the door. "Now go out there and find a halfway decent pharmacy. I can't have you running off to Florida. I need you here."

A huff leaves my lungs, the humor catching up with me. "I didn't know you cared so much."

She grimaces. "Nothing to do with that. You're the only one who really uses the hot tub, that's all."

"Ooh," I lift my chin. "Okay. Sure."

"I mean it, damn it." She scowls, but it falls right in with her using a crappy excuse after she's done something kind. Deflection is her usual go-to for anything that makes her uncomfortable. Still, I won't let her get off without some appreciation.

I squirm in my seat, trying to swallow past the lump of gratitude knotting up my throat. "Thanks, Tess, really. I won't let the opportunity go to waste. I'll make you proud."

"Uh-huh." Her head tilts back, and a brow cocks up. "Speaking of making me proud, one thing I'm *not* proud of... you calling Bentley to come pick you up."

"Stop." I take a pillow, throw it over my face and fall back onto the sofa. "Come on, Tessa."

"What? You think I was going to let that slide? I did for a while, but now things have settled down." I hear her scoff. "Really, Nor, out of all people, that's the one you call?"

"It's not like I had a lot of options." The pillow falls off my face onto the floor. When I catch a glimpse of Tess, her lips are puckered, and she's shaking her head. I sit up, annoyance bristling up my spine. "You and Bentley are about the only people I'd trust in a situation like that. You didn't answer."

"So you should have waited for me."

"And what?" My eyelids droop. "Slept on one of the booths

at the diner?"

"Maybe."

My expression sours. "Talk about stripping me away of all dignity. That would have done it."

"Better than placing yourself back in his grasp again, I'm sure. I bet he's flirting with you more than ever after 'rescuing' you. All you did was puff up his ego."

I shake my head, lips pulling down. "Not really." She tries to cut me off, but I talk over her. "Yeah, we've gone for sushi a few times, but it's different."

"What do you mean different?" She props an elbow on her thigh and rests her chin in her palm. "Are you referring to you or him?"

"Both of us. He's," I gaze at the ceiling trying to find the right word, "Nicer?" I frown in contemplation. *He's always nice to me.* "Maybe more genuine? I think that's it, and I'm not interested in him anymore. That ship has sailed."

"Sure." She drags out the word long and loud.

Ripping the pillow from behind me, I chuck it at her. "Say what you want, doubting Thomas, but it's true. He's just a friend."

"Bet that resolve's gonna get tossed out the window faster than it started."

"No way. You just watch. Tonight at that going away party."

"I won't be watching because I'm not going."

My mouth falls open. "But this guy is *your* coworker. He invited me and told me Bentley's going too."

"Yeah, about that. *You* dated Quinn and ended it on friendly terms. That's why he invited you. Bentley helped our company and Quinn with investments one time, so of course he's going to invite him. Me?" She shrugs. "Eh… he's already not my favorite. Plus, he looks like a famished version of Mr. Bean."

"Does he?" My head tilts. I stare at the floor, trying hard to remember exactly what Quinn looks like. We only dated a few months, and I haven't seen him in a while, but he's a nice guy. We met at a Christmas party through Tessa's work a few years back. He was polite, but we just never sparked, so things ended rather quickly. I frown when remembering his eyes. "I don't think he looks like Mr. Bean."

"He does. I don't know why you can't see that, but he does, and I think he's annoying, so I'm not going. Have fun for me." She pauses and gives me a downward stare. "Only, not too much fun. Watch out for Bentley. I won't be there to check on you, so don't lose your head. I don't know what it is about him and social gatherings, but they bring out the worst in him, so be careful."

"I'll be fine." I stand from the couch, needing to leave to get ready for the party. She rolls her eyes, and my hands fly to my hips. "Trust me—I'm telling you everything is different."

"I'm hoping so. Just be smart."

"Always am."

She responds by slinking back into the sofa and crossing her arms. "Sure, Nor. Sure."

Chapter 14

Bentley

"Quinn. Hey man." We exchange a firm shake and a pat on the arm. "So you're finally getting out of here, huh?"

"Sure am." He pockets one hand. "Met a girl online, and I'm going to move and marry her."

I stop a wince.

Worst. Fucking. Idea. Ever.

But it seems late to tell him that. His house is packed up and ready to go. Minus a box or two, all that's here are some lawn chairs and a collapsible table with food on it.

I nod instead, "Awesome, man. I wish you luck."

"Thanks."

We chat a little longer before I head into the kitchen, deciding to scrounge up something decent to eat. Work was a clusterfuck of problems, and I skipped lunch, so I'm famished.

I'm hogging all the raw broccoli from the veggie tray that no one's giving a shit about when I hear *that* laugh. A giggle that makes my head swim. It releases a shiver up my spine. Nora's here. Looking up from the food table, I'm stock-still, instantly bewitched.

Of course she's here.

I'm pretty sure she dated Quinn a while back, but I can't figure out why. I've seen better.

She's talking to him, looking more refreshed than when I picked her up from the diner, or even when meeting for sushi the other night. There's color in her cheeks and a spark in her eyes—she's smiling wide and listening intently to whatever he has to say.

A corner of my mouth tugs up.

Steady.

It's my go-to word from her. Right now, I can't see the heartbreak that smashed her apart. All I detect is her sweet, easygoing spirit—a brightness that's making her stand out like a fucking angel.

I swear she's glowing.

My heart slams against my ribs so hard it thunders in my damn stomach. She tosses hair off her shoulder, and my hand goes limp. The plate wobbles and I drop it. Broccoli scatters— green tops dancing across the white tiles a few times before tumbling to a stop.

"Shit," I stoop down to my hands and knees, scrambling to pick up the food, wondering if I should eat it or throw it away because I'm still hungry. My pace slows when a pair of red ruby heels halt right in front of me.

"I didn't know caterers came so hot." The voice is smokey and way too confident. It's definitely not Nora.

My eyes trail up. Whoever this is, she's leggy and tanned. Finished scooping up the food, I stand and get a better look. She's attractive. Not a punishment, that's for sure. Her hair is a short glossy blonde—a compliment to vibrant blue eyes. She's also stacked, and despite being leggy, we're nose-to-nose.

And I do mean nose-to-nose.

This girl is practically breathing down my neck. I try to smile and take a step back. "I'm not a caterer. I'm just hungry and uncoordinated."

Or stupid.

I only dropped my plate because of Nora.

"I know," she purrs out the acknowledgment. "But my real

question is *how* uncoordinated?" She closes the gap, and long red painted fingers clench around my bicep. "Like, you can still get me off, right?"

My eyes widen, heart stopping from shock.

I've heard of cheap and fast, but this is free and instant. Aversion flares in the base of my stomach. "I'm sorry?" My fingers clutch around hers, and I break her grip, forcing her hand off my arm. "Who are you?"

Her tongue trails across her mouth while she looks at mine. Her dark blue eyes track slowly up my face until she meets my gaze. After a sly smile, she tilts her head forward. "I'm Tonya." She makes a quick glance over her shoulder. When she makes eye contact again, her volume has dropped, "Jessie's friend."

My head jerks back. "Jessie?" She nods. My brow furrows. "Who the hell is that?"

It's a lie. I know exactly who Jessie is because it's an annoyance. She hung around for weeks last year and pestered me until I fucked her. A mistake, since she sucked in bed.

"Uhh." Her eyes dart around for a moment. "I'm surprised you don't recall her. You were with her a lot last summer."

I shrug. "Sorry. I don't keep names."

"Not a big deal." Her gaze rests on my pecs, and the corner of her mouth glistens like she's drooling. "Even if you don't remember her, *I* remember you. I also remember her saying you were the best lay she's ever had."

"She said that, did she?" I fold my arms and take a step back. "And what? You saw me and thought you'd get the same experience?"

"Maybe."

She takes a slithering step toward me. The tight dress displays every dip of her figure. She presses her thigh against my leg, and her body heat collides with mine. A light floral fragrance flies up my nose as she lightly taps her knee against my balls, and it almost feels good.

Almost.

Her lips threaten to brush my lobe, and her breath fills the shell of my ear. "She also said you had the stamina of a stallion. Why don't you show this naughty girl if it's true or not?"

She talks dirty.

Her attitude and words are an apple of sin, dangling right in front of me. Some of the aversion drains away. Locked eye-to-eye with her, a smile curls on my mouth.

I'm sure she'd be a great ride.

Better than great, actually.

Her finger traces the outline of my jaw and goosebumps form on my skin to chase after her touch. "What do you say, champ? Up for making me scream all night?"

A movement in the background drags my vision away from the temptation. My senses drop into a black hole, and the room drops away. I know this chick is still in front of me, but she's not registering. I can't hear her. I can't see her. All that exists is one person.

Nora.

She's still talking to Quinn and some other guy who's now standing beside him.

My throat tightens, eyes going rogue. I'm helpless to stop them from combing over every inch of her snug body. This week, she's been a damn force field, pulling my attention to watch her wherever she goes. She moves across the room and air snags in my chest.

Fuck.

I double blink.

Have her hips always swayed like that?

With each step, her hips swing, indecently circling one way before catching and rocking in the other direction. It's a titillating dance that has my heart beating in sync with her chosen rhythm. My fists clench. I want to palm her hips between my hold to experience what that movement feels like. Then I want to coast my fingers up to her breasts and—

"Hey!"

My crash back to reality is met with the red-heeled lush flicking my ear lobe. Blue eyes flood my vision, and dislike pulses in my blood. *I don't want blue.*

It's brown that I want to get lost in—deep sugary brown.

"Welcome back." That smirk from moments ago is fixed to her face. She traces a finger on the outline of my shirt collar and breathes against my neck, "Now what do you say? You ready for a wild night?"

"I—" My ear catches the ring of Nora's laugh, and I can't help but look at her. The sound is sweet fucking nectar to my ears—my personal kind of bait. I bite down and sink, "Sorry." I slide my vision briefly to the other girl. "Find someone else to fuck you."

"Hey, you douche—"

The rest of Tonya's insult cuts off as I slide past and stride towards Nora.

Halfway across the room, Nora makes eye contact and smiles. The plate in my hand wobbles, and I clasp my fingers around it, hoping not to drop it again.

Coming to a head with her, a lump forms in my throat. I struggle to swallow through it while giving her a wink, "Hey, sunshine."

"Hi." Her casual tone has my blood pumping a mile a minute. She looks too damn delectable up close.

I gesture at her clothes. "You dressed up." She's in a cream blouse and a tight black skirt. It's hugging her in all the right places, and it's making me hot. So heated, I regret wearing this sweater.

She shrugs, resting her shoulder blades on the wall. "I figured it would feel nice to look nice." Her teeth tug at her lower lip. "After all that crap last week…" Her eyes dance around the room as she refers to Trevor. "Well, yeah. I just thought it would be nice."

My heart thumps harder the longer I stand here—its beats competing with the noise in the room. And I'm convinced there's no way she's always been this sexy. Cute, yes. Gorgeous, absolutely. But not sexy. I would have noticed by now. Something's changed, and tonight, her giddy jabbering, tight clothes, and flushed cheeks have a carnal urge devouring all my common sense.

Our car ride home flashes in my mind. Remembering how she burned me—that feeling of wildfire against my fingertips sucks me under. I step closer to her, propping my hand on the wall next to her head, and breathe in deep. *It's all her.* There's no one else's scent on her tonight, but I *do* want it mingled.

I would smell good on her. Really damn good on her.

Her hips wiggle against the wall with a shift, and I can hardly breathe.

"Are you offering me some food?" Her voice is soft.

My eyes snap to the paper plate that's creating a barrier.

Shit. What the fuck am I doing?

Embarrassment implodes in my stomach. What happened just now? My behavior has to look off. I've said nothing this whole time, and my hand is still near her head. I probably look like a creep.

"Possibly." My eyebrows raise.

"Hmm." One corner of her mouth pinches. "If it were spinach dip, I'd say this is a worthy offering, but it's not."

I laugh, lowering the plate and my arm to give her some space. "Just as well. I dropped it on the floor."

"I saw that." She gazes past my shoulder. "Did it have anything to do with her?"

I don't look back because I don't want to. My eyes only want to drink in Nora. My throat goes dry, and I shake my head. "No." The parched word is all I can manage.

"No? You're quiet tonight." She tilts her head. "Nothing else?"

"Finally got us those drinks." The guy who was standing next to Quinn earlier emerges with two drinks in hand. He gives Nora a sheepish-looking grin and passes one off. "Sorry it took so long."

"Oh." Her candy eyes light up, and she accepts. "No worries. A good water is always worth the wait."

Water?

My brow furrows. Irritation rolling down my spine. Who the fuck gives a girl water at a party? But Nora doesn't seem opposed. In fact, she's not even looking at me anymore. Her eyes are stuck to this dude, and it seems like anticipation is on her face.

What can he have for her?

His appearance is duller than vanilla ice cream as he unpockets his phone. He clicks it on, scrolls for a moment, then passes it off. "Here's a picture of the blueprint I've drawn up."

"Oh wow," she says. " That's really cool."

Whatever. She doesn't mean it. She can't. I know Nora, and this voice is pure pleasantry… at least I think it is. But a sting festers in my chest at how brushed aside I feel. When she doesn't look at me again, a slight panic floods in my chest, and I try to reassure myself. *There's no way she's into him.*

But then he escorts her to another part of the house, and my hopes bottom out.

You've got to be kidding me?

She doesn't even say goodbye as she follows him down the hall to look at a moving box that's still open. There's something in there that he's showing her, and whatever it is, Nora is giving it her full attention.

I blow out a huge sigh and find the nearest corner. Disappointment looms over my head the longer I stand here. I try to forget about her and look for someone else to talk to.

Pointless.

Everywhere she walks, my eyes follow. Every time I catch sight of her smile, my heart thuds against my ribs. Whenever I hear her laugh, desire prickles in my veins. When she randomly twirls hair around her finger and clamps down on her lower lip, my pants get tighter.

She's not even doing anything extraordinary. Everything I'm witnessing is so simple. So her. Yet desire is dousing me, catching in my blood and taunting me to press her ass into the wall and kiss her like she's never been kissed before—to taste her the way I've done in my dreams this past week. People around us be damned.

She makes eye contact with me, and I lose my breath. I can't inhale, can't exhale. It all gets stuck inside. Even my hands shake.

What the hell is going on with me?

I scrub over my face. This isn't normal—even Ivy didn't make me feel like this. I need to get out of here. Leaving this early would look bad, so I opt for the next best thing—to step outside and take a breather.

It has to be the heat.

It's the only explanation for how stupid I'm acting tonight. After some fresh air, I'll be back to normal. I slink out the back way, undetected, but even then, I steal one more glance to look back and see her.

I just have to.

My heart leaps into my throat, and butterflies pound at the sight of her tipping her head back and laughing.

"Yeah," I murmur, tearing my eyes away. Stepping outside, I let the door close and force a deep breath. "It's just the heat."

Chapter 15

Nora

I'm about to go out of my head. Scott, Quinn's cousin, has done nothing but pester me this last hour. It's obvious he's trying to hit on me, but his personality is that of a stick—a dead one.

He's super nice, so I don't have the heart to tell him that explaining the science used to construct buildings isn't the way to my heart.

I've gone around the house hoping I'll shake him off. I'm also scoping around to see if there's anyone else who's free to talk and break up our party of two. I would chat it up with Bentley, but he doesn't seem like himself tonight. Rather than being the life of the party, he's kept to himself, which I find strange.

But even without Bentley, I finally catch a break.

"Could you excuse me?" Scott says in his gravelly voice, "I need the men's room."

Thank god. The relief shooting down my knees makes them sway. This last speech about the role specific gravity plays in the stability of buildings almost killed me. "Sure, no problem." My chance to escape has just presented itself.

"Cool." He gently shakes his finger at me and chuckles. "Don't you go anywhere."

My heart skips a beat… not in a good way. "Oh…uh-I-uh—"

"I'll look for you if you slip out on me." He walks away before I can refuse him.

Well, great. Leaving now would make me feel like the worst person ever. I blast air out of my mouth and decide to suck it up. It's only for one night. I won't die. I've never been that girl to take a low jab at a guy who isn't for me. I refuse to crush his ego by bolting on him.

Looking around the room, I notice that Bentley isn't here. Neither is that woman from earlier. They probably left together, but for the first time since I've known him, I don't care. There's no ache gnawing at my chest tonight.

Whatever was there for Bentley, I've laid to rest, and I hope they're enjoying themselves. A smirk pulls across my mouth. Tessa is so wrong. About everything this time.

I'm making a mental note to tell her that when Scott re-emerges. Dread crashes over me, and I groan. He's looking down at his phone, and I'm foreseeing another scientific special on construction. My gut tells me I should have stepped out when I had the moment. Thankfully another opportunity opens up when Quinn motions for him to come over. It's the perfect second chance for an escape… only they are right by the front door.

Frantically I sweep the room for option B. When I notice the hallway leading to the backdoor is free and unmanned, my legs are carrying me away from the party before I can blink.

Freedom swirls around me as my fingertips brush the handle to the back door. Successfully stepping outside, my limbs go lax, and I absorb the atmosphere around me.

It's colder than blue blazes out here, but at least I'm unbothered and don't have to endure an earful about construction.

"Got stuffy in there?"

I jump at the voice of Bentley.

"Sorry," he says softly.

With my eyes adjusting to the dark, I spot him across the yard, propped against a brick shed, chilling out in the cold air. After staring at Scott all night, Bentley looks like a snack, and my pulse elevates. Even the dull smirk he gives me looks amazing.

"Didn't mean to scare ya, sunshine."

"No, you're okay." I bundle my arms across my chest for warmth, tamping down the heart flutters I just felt. "I just thought you'd gone."

He rakes over the top of his hair. "I needed a breather. Looks like I'm not the only one."

Strolling slowly through the grass to join him, I sigh. "I'm trying to get rid of a shadow."

"Ah yes." He nods once, sounding droll. "The blueprint guy. He seemed like a good time. You two gonna have kids soon?"

"Shut up." I bite back a snort. "Seriously. You don't even want to know how much fun he is." I ignore the chill from the air slithering down my back, tucking myself in tighter to the corner of the building. "He's been following me all night—you'd think he'd give someone else a chance."

"Ha." Bentley laughs and leans fully against the brick building. "He won't if he's smart."

The sleeve to his leather jacket brushes my blouse, and the chill disappears—a warm flush radiating in its place. It's not in my head. Bentley has moved closer to me, and as my words fall away, so does all my big talk to Tessa. I take a stiffened swallow, praying he can't hear it.

"Hey." He nudges my shoulder, and I can sense the smirk even though I'm staring dead ahead. "Who's the quiet one now?"

I try to force a giggle. "Me, I guess." That same fake laugh catches in my throat when I look at him and see *those* eyes peering into me. Their true color is dimmed at the moment, but the intensity is apparent. They contrast against the soft streaks of moonlight. My heart is thumping against my ribs, and my throat is closing. "Sorry, I'm just annoyed, is all."

The corners of his eyes soften. "Hey, no worries."

The back door across the lawn flies open, and I spot the lanky silhouette that's hounded me all night.

I sigh, my limbs wilting. "Dammit."

"Looks like someone's missing you." Bentley retorts with a dry sarcasm in his voice.

I groan. "He's so nice, but I really want to be left alone."

"I could always—"

"Nora?" Both of our heads snap in Scott's direction when we hear Scott's gruff voice hit the air.

My heart plummets right into my stomach. "Great," I mutter the complaint softly, but the next breath I take is loud when Bentley slides closer to me and lowers his head, closing the gap between us.

"Are you in need of another rescue?"

"Another?" The word chokes up in my throat. I can barely stand to give him a side-eye glance while my pulse drums in my head.

"Yeah." His tone is gentle and scorching hot... like sex. Just like the night he ditched me at that party—and while I should, I can't stop listening to him. "Let me help you get rid of him."

A frost trails in the cold night with each word he utters. He ducks for my ear, and I push away the tremble coiling in my stomach.

"How?" I calm my voice and look at him, our height almost identical tonight thanks to my heels.

His vision dips to my lips, then slowly floats back up to my gaze. "Pretend you're making out with me."

The earth drops from under me, and the shock palpitating in my chest vibrates down to my knees. I couldn't have heard that right.

Bentley's sun-kissed skin glows as the moon briefly peaks from the clouded sky. It grants me a full view of that sly smirk he wears, the one that always leaves my heart twisted in knots. Tonight it hits a new high, injecting a pool of heat between my thighs. "If he catches us, he'll take the hint."

"And if he doesn't see us?" My voice is cynical, but each fiber in my body is burning to fall into his arms.

"Then, hey," he shrugs, "I've finally gotten to kiss you."

I freeze. *He can't mean that.* But there's no other way to interpret what he's said. I struggle for a swallow.

"Nora," Bentley cocks his head. "Whattya say, sunshine? Want me to get you out of a spot of trouble for the night?" He turns into me, plants one hand over my head, and leans in. "No strings attached, and we won't make it awkward. This is just between friends. I promise." He takes a hard breath and repeats it, stuttering. "I-I promise. Friends only."

Don't do it. The voice ringing in my head isn't mine, and it's the most logical sound I've heard all night. "Bentley—"

A shuffle of footsteps crunches in the grass, heading in our direction.

"No time," Bentley whispers the words then his lips, warm and gentle, meet mine.

He's perfect with his kiss. The sweet enveloping pressure of our connection shoots straight through me, rendering my knees nearly useless. I'm about to wobble when he grasps me by the shoulders, and my fingers automatically rest on his chest, like I was supposed to touch him there all along. Starved to feel more, my fingers work under his jacket to rest on the front of his sweater.

There's a resonant thunk occurring under my right hand. Maybe it's my imagination or futile hope, but I swear it's picking up in pace, just like mine is.

Somewhere out in the distance, footsteps draw near, then stop. Bentley's kiss deepens, then his tongue lightly traces over my lips, and my nails claw into the front of his top. A beat later, and I hear what sounds like a retreat from the oncoming approach.

Scott left, still, Bentley isn't relenting. His head tilts, deepening our lock until I wonder if he's ever going to stop.

And if he won't, then I must. This can't carry on. It isn't wise or safe, not in the state my heart is in, bruised and battered.

I pull away, and we're both huffing—our breaths colliding in the air. I manage a sheepish smile. After all these years, I finally experienced Bentley in a way I never thought possible. I ignore the buzzing in my ears and the way my head floats as I pat him on the chest. *It was amazing. Now it stops.*

Glancing to the back door, I take note that for sure, we're alone. Bentley's plan worked. Flicking my eyes to Bentley's, my heart shakes behind my ribs—his gaze piercing straight through me, his head far too close. My throat closes up, nearly strangling out my words. "*I think he's gone.*"

"Yeah." The response heaves out low and soft as his gaze stays transfixed to mine. I assume he's about to walk away, when—

He crushes me against his body, yanking me into his arms. Bentley's lips don't merely meet mine. They crash down, and he moans. The sound shatters through my control, and I fling my arms around his neck while arching and grinding against him.

Brick scratches against my back, and I realize he's moved us. His delectable planes, lean and athletic, press into me, causing my nipples to pebble. Bentley finally elicits a mewl from me when he sucks my lower lip, then rubs it between his pearly teeth. The action is a mix of pain and comfort, and I combust. My sex throbbing with each minute shift of his mouth. He sucks in a cool breath until my lips feel like frost and my head goes hazy.

His fingers gently wrap around my throat but refuse to apply pressure. The gesture feels like a request—like a desire he has, but one he won't engage in.

Bentley is everything I ever wanted, and more.

I go limp, sagging against the rough red stone, ignorant to the discomfort it should cause. I can't stop it. My hand crawls, inching towards the grasp resting on my neck. The ways I *want* him to take me are shameful and unspeakable. I finally place my hand over his and squeeze ever so slightly, hoping he'll catch the hint.

He goes motionless, and at first, I wondered if I've pushed him too far. Then he breaks our kiss.

His breathing is heavy and uncontrolled—the faint smell of whiskey and spearmint sweeps over me as he stares deep into my eyes.

"Fuck," he whispers, scanning every inch of my face. He strains for another inhale, and his eyes droop. "I'm so screwed with you."

His mouth collides with mine again, and his fingers jut into the back of my hair in a possessive clutch. He commands my head back and tucks me into his body all the way, making our kiss and connection like a vacuum.

This time when our kiss ends, he growls—the sound bolts through my stomach, and I know I'm done for. He could take me on this lawn, and I'd do nothing to stop it. The zest of his cologne flies up my nostrils, and I nuzzle his neck, praying he'll never vanish.

"Nora…" His fingers stroke through the back of my hair.

"Hmm?"

"Let's get out of here and go to my place."

My neck and shoulders tighten. My resolve is leaping out the window, descending to its destruction. "Is-is that wise?"

"The fuck if I know, but all I know is that I want it. I *want* you." He pulls back and cups my face. "And right now, I can't stop myself." I notice the hard swallow he takes. "I'm tired of fighting the one thing I can't stop thinking about."

His thumbs soothe over my cheeks, and I go breathless, stolen off the confession I want to make in return.

"Come back to my place, baby." The words are gentle, melting the rest of my resistance. "Let me know that I'm not going crazy… that what I feel for you is real. That you want me too."

I manage a small nod, a shallow breath, and a weak reply, that's tumbling out on its own—because of course I want him. I've always, only, wanted *him*. "Okay."

Bentley grabs my hand and hurries me out the side gate.

Following behind, all I can think about is how I should be stopping this, but all my heart tells me is that it's way overdue— that at last, it's finally going to get what it's always longed for— the man who makes me feel like my soul is complete—Bentley Harris.

He's finally mine.

Fragments of You

Chapter 16

Bentley

One of my hands is on the wheel—the other resting on Nora's leg. Anticipation of having her winds itself through each fiber in my body, shooting out through my fingertips, but I know this shouldn't be happening.

Stop. Bentley. Stop.

The voice does nothing to stop me. If anything, my heart beats quicker, and my thumb brushes over the silky smooth skin of her thigh. I want to groan as her hips shift side to side.

Shit.

Her reaction—a silent admittance of her arousal—sends my foot throttling down on the pedal. I take a corner harder than I should and, recalling how we left the party, a lump forms in my throat. *I knew tonight was different.*

Pinpointing it was hard, but watching her enter the party had a whole different feel, and when she joined me outside, I knew right then and there I was screwed. The way my body gravitated towards her confirmed it. And my rescue? That was nothing but a ploy—a desperate lie of my existence from being parched to drink her. One taste left me a prisoner for more as m still suffering from dehydration. I need her—badly.

The craving for her continues coursing through me when I whip into my driveway a few minutes later. As I climb out of the car, reality is distant and clouded—the ground beneath me isn't real anymore.

My skin tingles and my hands shake while I undo the lock to my house. Nora's presence floods from behind like a damn tsunami that's about to crash over me.

She's waiting, not saying a word, but I *feel* her and those velvet eyes branding into my back. Finally, after twisting the knob and pushing the front door open, I spin and face her.

My heartbeats are paralyzed. I'm lost while staring at the most beautiful sight in the world.

Nora—her cheeks flush, eyes bright while averting my full attention. Her mouth is plump, begging me to taste her. One of her shallow breaths makes mine pause, and my pants tighten as I notice the mounds of her tits cause a rising under her blouse. A growl from me gets lost in a frantic swallow.

Daring a step forward, I use the sounds of my shoes shuffling against the pavement to remind me I'm not dreaming. Reality is confirmed when my fingers wrap around her wrist and fire laces in my veins. She burns so sweetly I want to fucking die, and she's mine. All mine.

I pace backward, facing her because I can't look away, and once we're inside and the door clicks closed, the still between us is deafening.

She slouches to rest her back against the door, and I don't know why but my heart races wild at the sight.

I cage her head with my hands and dare to move closer. Close enough that our united inhales make our chests connect.

My next breath is unsteady when her hand skims up my torso. Her touch is so light and gentle, but holy fuck, how it makes my blood explode—makes my mind levitate with euphoria. A sigh leaves me.

The urge to touch her drives down my arm, and I cup her face, grazing her mouth with my thumb. "What are you thinking about, sweetheart?"

Usually, she's so easy to read, but tonight, she's a mystery. The eighth wonder with her soft silence and rounded gaze. I lightly press my lips to her neck. My chest jolts when she shudders, and her touch becomes more aggressive. "Talk to me, baby." My voice is dry. "Tell me what you're feeling. Give me some direction."

Her head falls back with another pass of my mouth on her milky skin. "I'm thinking that I like the feel of you against me."

My cock hardens. "Oh, baby." I toy with the first button of her blouse, my skin burning a million degrees. "I like the feel of you too."

She pauses for another rattled breath followed by a light moan. "I'm also thinking that I'm dying to have you inside me."

"Fuck Nora." My fists clench, knuckles grinding into the door with those words twisting their way into my soul. "God. You know how to make me feel good. I'm dying to be in you too."

Through a blanket of long lashes, she looks up at me and swallows. "Kiss me."

The command shreds my composure. I grunt, and our lips collide. The explosion of what we are together is pure carnage. It's ripping me apart, and I'm not sure I can breathe without the taste of her on my tongue.

She's life. She's everything, and the only way I can stay alive is to drown in her.

My frame is flush against hers. A light moan from her gets lost in my mouth as dainty fingers clutch around my neck. Our tongues find each other, and we feast, tasting and relishing as I push harder onto her, expelling all her breath, taking it as my own. I strain painfully against my pants and shudder when she opens her legs to rub against my dick.

My mind shatters. Quakes jolt down me from limb to limb, sending my eyes rolling to the back of my head. I break the kiss—teeth gritted in pleasure. "Fuck, Nora. Holy shit… you're just so—"

I can't finish.

Damn.

I want to tell her how beautiful I find her, how her perfect lips sear past my mouth and brand into my heart. I want to confess how she's haunted me in my dreams this last week. Tell her that tonight, while standing out in the cold, I felt her in my future. I want to confess how crazy she drove me when I knew she was with Trevor and tell her never to do that again.

It all gets lost on the way out.

Years have passed since I've bled my feelings out to anyone—peeled back my lies and bared my true self—or showered someone with abundant praise.

Nora's worthy of it all, but I'm not there yet.

Yet.

I kiss her again, hoping she *feels* what I want to say.

A desperate frenzy claws at my composure the longer I'm exposed to her. Each inhale of her scent increases the thunderous plunks ravaging through me. Passing seconds unravel another thread to the fabric of my barely-there composure. When control eventually combusts, I'm left panting, starving for more.

My fingers move, deftly trying to make quick work on the buttons of her blouse. I fail as the buttons fight me, refusing to slide through.

I grumble in embarrassed frustration.

Women's clothing is something I learned the tricks of long ago, but tonight, I can't undo a single one. Frantically, I tug at her skirt.

Fuck.

I can't find the zipper. Our kiss breaks. With shaking hands, I rove around her hips, searching for the cool feel of metal. Nothing.

She's unmanning me—reducing me to a schoolboy in my own damn house.

"Shit. Shit. Shit." I clap my palms against the door, hands shaking harder.

"Allow me," her voice is breathless yet sweet. She's calm, holding deep eye contact. The undivided look has oxygen snagging in my lungs.

Reaching behind her, the sound of her zipper drags out. I clench my fists to keep from ripping her outfit apart. Teasing me hard and painfully, Nora works each button, making small circles around the shiny black fixings before undoing it and moving to the next one.

The unsteady tightening of my cock is going to be the destruction of me. The bundling of my nerves is going to make me shred apart before she's even halfway done.

My chest heaves harder each time more skin peeks out, and she's only on button number three. "Oh, Nora," I breathe her name, lace from her bra showing itself, granting me a view I only dared to dream of. It's creamy and tantalizing—like her. "Baby, you're going to drive me insane." Reverently, I soothe over the exposing flesh and unmentionable with my knuckle.

Grazing over her bra strap, she burns like sweet fire on my fingers. I could live being engulfed by her for eternity. When the last button pops undone, she raises one brow, and at a pace meant for torture, barely flays open her blouse.

"All yours." She whispers it in that honey voice—the one that sends my pulse into a rage.

I fall against her, throwing the garment open fully, caressing her breast, kneading it with my left hand.

Her head tilts back—her body slides partially down the door. "Oh my God."

That moan, the feel of her body fitting perfectly into mine, is too much. The room blacks out. I kiss up and down her exposed neck before capturing her dainty ear lobe between my teeth. When she groans again, I thrust against her, jeans and all. "Nora. You're going to be the undoing of me." I lick sweet supple skin right behind her ear, and she arches against my abs.

"And you, me." One firm tug at my pants, and she unlatches my belt and unhooks the button, loosening them at my waist. I'm tempted to ask how she's learned that, but I know I'll hate the answer because she didn't learn it with me.

I work on her, ripping her skirt down, not caring it isn't fully unzipped with it straining over her hips.

Delicate fingertips catch at the hem of my sweater right before she peels it off. My skin fires up along with my heart each time her fingers graze my skin. Bare-chested, she stops and takes a moment.

I smirk as her eyes rove me, a look of lust laying heavy in them. "Like what you see, sweetheart?"

Those lips of hers part when she nods. "It'll do." The

words barely breathe out as she traces along the V of my hips.

My vision falls to the brown strands of hair curling around her collar bone, and my mouth dries up. "You'll more than do." I grasp around her hips and yank her into me with a growl.

Lace from her bra chaffs my skin. The subtle pain and pleasure combine into a beautiful duo that has my pulse humming with contentment. I bare my fingers into her ass, muttering a curse when I discover she's wearing a damn thong. She's perfect. Hoisting Nora up, I position her legs around my hips and secure her back to the door.

The fabric on that barely-there V thong is drenched, and her heels are pressing into my spine, threatening to poke me. It's the hottest thing I've ever had the pleasure of experiencing, and the sight is pure heaven when I look up into her eyes.

Everything except my thumping heart goes still. A piece of my wall cracks away. Praise flows off my tongue without thought. "You're my happiness. Do you know that?"

Her gaze is round and wide while shaking her head. In the moment, it makes me feel like I'm made of glass. Like she sees through every fucking inch of me.

I love it.

"You are, baby," I whisper, brushing my thumb over her cheek. "You're the only perfect thing in life."

My lips find hers. At first, I want to be gentle—to reverently worship what's been out of reach for so long. She whimpers out my name while I whisper kisses along every inch of her upper body. Shoulders, neck, sternum, the swells of her breasts, the peeks of her collar bone—my lips make love to this delectable body of hers. The taste of her heated skin and perfume mingles in my mouth. The sweetness is tailored to my preferences. The flavor elicits a rasp out of me as I drag my lower lip along her flesh.

"God Bentley. That feels incredible."

My cock throbs in rhythm to her cries, and my blood rushes fast each time she pants. I sing out her name when her fingers run through my hair. "Nora. Nora."

"Mmm," she moans, her spine lurching off the door. "Bentley. Yes. God, yes. Kiss me just like that. Kiss me like that everywhere. Please. Oh, please."

Fuck. She fragments me and my softness. I grunt. My teeth nip at her tit, biting through the forbidden lace. My cock stiffens harder at her squeak. The raw energy pumping harshly through my veins pushes me near a cliff's edge.

I can't do this much longer.

But I won't screw her against the door. She means so much more to me than that, and for this, I want her properly beneath me so I can stare into those eyes while I rock her world—my ultimate dream.

I have to move. Now.

Securing her into me, I move away from the door. My mouth tangles on hers. We pant against each other as I carry her through the house. Her legs grip around my waist, cinching the air out of me. My only regret is that she's not squeezing tighter. I want to lose every fucking breath to her and her alone… forever.

I stumble into the room and lay her on the bed. My hands explore her pert body. Taking dangerous liberties, I undress her, taking extra time to coast my fingers along her hips, pluck the lace of her thong, and trace around her nipple until it pebbles with need. I drag out the process until she begs me to hurry. When she's fully naked and desperate, I stand up, taking her in.

"Fuck, babe." My heart slams against my ribs. "You're gorgeous."

"Thank you." She stretches her arms over her head and smiles.

Seeing her spread out under me, a ravenous demand for more lashes hot in my stomach. I bend down and run my tongue over the course of her torso.

Her spine jolts with a wicked bow, and her legs clench around me. When I give her another pass, she whimpers, and her knees quake.

I groan at the response, palming one of her breasts. "You like that baby?" I work my body up against hers, brushing against every inch of her skin until we're face to face. Satisfaction swallows me up at her wiggling reaction. Clasping my hand behind her head, I force her eyes on mine. "You like the feel of my tongue on you?"

Her face pinches together with pleasure as she nods, and she can barely speak. "Yes-yes-I—"

"You what?" I grind my clothed cock into her naked thigh, and we both curse. My heart wants to burst when she hisses my name, her eyes sealing closed.

I can pleasure her.

And I'm determined to grant her whatever she desires. I lower my head to her ear. "Tell me what you want, Nora. I'll give it to you. You want my tongue on your clit? I'll do it, baby. I'll feast on you like you're my personal fucking buffet."

Air pauses in my throat when she becomes motionless.

Was it too much? I know nothing of bedroom Nora. Perhaps my offer was an overload.

But my pulse jump starts when she opens her eyes and looks at me in the bright moonlight.

It wasn't too much, because what I see has my fingers clutching into her thigh and my blood running with fire.

I see heat, uninhibited cravings, and desire, all swirling in a droopy-eyed half-smirk. She wets her mouth. When she speaks, it doesn't sound like her at all. She's calm, powerful, collected, and hotter than sin.

"I want you to take your pants off and fuck me. Hard."

I'm moving faster than I can think. My jeans and briefs are ripped off—my nightstand is open, a condom wrapper is on the floor, it's already on. But in the craze… in this crazy stage of wanting her, I stop long enough before entering. With me lined up and ready, I pause, taking a moment to stare deep into her eyes.

My swallow is strained. "Nora." Her name leaves me in a croak. "Are you sure this is what you want? You're positive—"

She cups my face with one hand. There is nothing else. Just her. "Positive."

My blood thrusts, taking my body with it as I enter her in one fell swoop.

She shouts.

I clench the sheets thinking my heart will fail. It's missing several beats that should be there, and I have to close my eyes for a moment. She's tight and sweet. "Fuuuck!" My arms quiver, threatening to collapse from pleasure. I only shift a little, but it has my head snapping back and a primal growl tearing from me.

She feels too damn good to be real.

"Bentley." Her fingers rest on my abs as her voice twinges with concern.

I clasp my fingers around hers and force a breath. "I'm alright, baby. I just…" Sweat beads on my neck. "You just feel so incredible." Taking controlled breaths isn't possible. I pant, heave, and chuff for even the slightest breath. I finally manage a full-blown thrust in and out, and I know this is paradise. More so when she writhes underneath me and calls out my name.

"Oh, holy shit Bentley." Her fingers clench into my triceps. She sounds like she's on the verge of tears. I fucking love it. "Do that again."

"Anything you want."

I do it again. And again. And again. Each time groaning in a voice I don't recognize, thinking I'll blackout from the ecstasy of it all. It's not until several thrusts later my adrenaline kicks in. I'm pumping in a steady rhythm when my eyes flutter open.

I'm staring down at a vision.

Brown tousled locks.

Perfect breasts.

Beautiful skin.

Curved hips.

Her creamy slim silhouette contrasting on the dark sheets.

She's an angel.

Her voice and scent fill the room, engulfing my head.

I listen intently. Each gasp and moan etches itself into me… and I know it's all there to stay.

She's a part of me. Always has been, always will be.

"Faster, Bentley." She bucks her legs. "Please go faster. Harder."

I slam into her. Hard. Fast. Like she ordered. And why wouldn't I? She's the master. I'm her slave. Her requests are the whip.

When she spills over the edge, I prevent myself from doing the same. I want to indulge her, force her beyond herself. That becomes my focus, and I do everything to hear the screams of my name mixing with her cries of pleasure. Each time I succeed, satisfaction zings across my chest, and I'm hell-bent on chasing the feeling again.

I make it happen.

Over.

Over.

And over.

Until I'm drenched in sweat—my hair is damp, with beads of salt rolling down my body, fatigue pinging in all parts of me.

She finally goes limp, and I think she's done. I lessen the pace, readying myself for the release I've delayed for too long.

"Please, Bentley." She's panting, long hair sticking to her face, rolling and arching her spine. "More. Do it again. Please."

A primal urge rips through me. I pull out, grab her ankles and yank her down the mattress. "You're pushing me, Nora." Peeling her ass off the bed, I hook my elbows behind her knees and force them up to her ears.

She's exposed, mine to do what I like with, with nowhere to hide. *Mine. All mine.*

Laying over her, my fingers grip tight in her hair, and I force her attention. "Look at me, Nora. Look at me when I fill you."

Hazy brown eyes meet mine. I thrust in, and they go wide. She screams when I hit the hilt of her, and my frame stiffens.

"Too much?"

She shakes her head.

My breath staggers. A wicked shake seizes my limbs. "Feel that? Feel me all the way inside you, sweetheart?"

Her lip trembles. She nods, tears filling her gaze.

"So do I. You feel fucking amazing. *You* are amazing," I say, panting.

I jackhammer myself in and out. My fingers tighten in her scalp with each movement. We're both shouting with each stroke. Each of my muscles clench and release in a wild build-up.

She throws her arms around my neck and kisses me, moans and groans escaping her as she squeezes my throat.

Fuck.

I huff, crumbling apart with each thrust.

She locks eyes with me again. A quiver of arrows hit my heart. Besides a paradise of caramel brown, the only color around me is white. Beautiful pure white, and it's coming from Nora.

My Nora.

This time while saying her name, this beautiful creature is finally here with me—just how I've always wished for. "Nora." It resonates like a gong, echoing in my very being. I say it again. "Nora." My heart sings and hums. The word is music. When I repeat it a third time, my soul floods and spills over.

Impossible.

I'm the one inside this woman, yet she's filling me, consuming whatever's left from the wreckage and pain of the last several years. A massive ache seals up, and I'm home. Safe, protected, loved. My brokenness is complete once more. I've found the lost parts of me.

Holy fuck.

This woman means more to me than my own life.

My head rests in her neck, and I shout out her name as I thrust harder and deeper. My voice muffles against her skin as her smell and taste dominate my senses, as I unravel—giving myself to her. It's not just my pent-up tension that's being released—I'm pouring my heart and soul into her with every pulse I make.

Everything I am or ever will be is hers.

All the things I've hoped to become.

She takes it all.

She doesn't even know it.

When I'm finished, I unhook her legs, and my body slumps onto hers.

All I hear are battered breaths for a while, and truthfully I don't know where I am for the moment, not after something like that.

"Wow." Nora's arms fall lax to her side, her legs shaking. "Just wow. That was... that was incredible. Bentley, you're amazing."

"No. You're the incredible one." I lay beside her, practically crumbling into the bed—my heart so full, it's about to burst out of my damn chest. I fucking love this woman, and my blood pumps with life because of her.

Hers. I'm all hers, and already aching for the next moment to be inside her again.

I reach for her hand, threading our fingers together as we pant in unison, gazing up at the ceiling. This silence, this *oneness* concretes the knowledge that my soul no longer belongs to me— now I need to tell her I love her. But how and when? Tonight? Now? Over breakfast?

"Bentley?" Nora's soft and spent voice cuts through my thoughts. "Can we do that again tomorrow?"

That's the sweetest request I've ever heard—the petition that lets me know she wants me.

I squeeze her hand, a smile tilting my mouth, deciding I'll tell her about my feelings in the morning after we wake up. "Absolutely, sweetheart. We'll do it as many times as you'd like."

She giggles—a sweet reply that makes my pulse slow with euphoria. "Then I'll count on you waking me up with kisses."

"Depend on it." Re-positioning, I bare my weight on my elbows and lightly kiss her forehead. "For now, let's get some sleep, huh?"

"Please. After that amazing session, I need to recharge." She rolls away, tucking herself under the sheets.

I remain sitting up, my back resting against the headboard, admiring the look of her filling my bed and of how the moonlight pours over her perfectly. Nora Davis was made to be here, and as the minutes tick past and her breathing slowly becomes steady with deep sleep, I know she was made for me.

Me.

Me?

Fuck. My heart sinks as a wave of shame floods over me. If I was standing in front of a mirror, I doubt I'd be able to look myself in the eye, because have I taken a good look at myself lately?

Lying to my right is a soul so sweet and pure it glowed in my bed only moments ago. The man watching her right now doesn't even deserve to touch Nora, much less fall in love with her.

I'm rotten and worthless.

I've banged meaningless women for the hell of it. Forgotten names, twisted hearts, plucked apart egos, lied, and have backed out on Nora too many times to count. And now I think I deserve her?

What a presumptuous fucking thing to do. And damn me since I've tampered with the untouchable. Nora deserves more than my pathetic weak ass.

Guilt slices down my sternum when Ivy's face flashes before me. What Ivy did was wrong, but what if it only happened because I was a failure? A fresh burn forms behind my ribs, putting me in my place.

I'm only good for the temporary, never the permanent. Fast and short lived, remember Bentley?

Sitting here for beats too long, panic floods through me as a massive 'what if' plants itself in my soul.

What if I can't keep Nora happy? So far, there's been every bit of proof in life that I can't sustain anyone's well-being. So when Nora gets bored with me, how quickly will she decide to move on? Worse. How will I deal with the pain of losing her?

I don't think I can. Just the idea is making my molars grind, and a headache of agony forms behind my eyes.

More importantly, I don't want to see the look on her face when I disappoint her—when she reaches the day that I disgust her so much, she decides to move on. I don't want to see the ways I'm going to let her down.

Because I will. It's proven that's all I *can* do.

She's better off without me, and it'd be in her best interest to never let Nora get entangled with my heart, or to hear the burden of my feelings.

As the deadly silence of the night wraps around me, sending a chill down my spine, a realization dawns on me—I can't tell her I love her. I don't deserve to tell her.

Fuck.

I can't even stay here. I can't stay here and hold her. It will only make my shortcomings harder for her in the end. Leaving is the only option I should be considering.

With shame pulverizing my guts, I slink into the bathroom, trying not to cry. Closing the door, phone in hand, my shoulders are heavy. All the rightness I felt while inside Nora is gone. Now all I can feel is how wrong it was—how I touched something I should never have even looked at.

The only way for her to escape me now is through distance. The thought makes my heart feel like it's being ripped out and squeezed to death.

Let her go. I have to let her go.

I open my phone and look up the soonest flights from Colorado to Washington State. I'm going home.

For a long time.

My insides lurch at the first option. There's one leaving in three hours. A red eye flight. I love it. I also hate it.

Daring to look out of the bedroom, my heart sinks. I'm leaving her—leaving her while she sleeps with my heart in her hands.

I dress, pack a duffel bag, and grab my wallet and keys. It takes less than fifteen minutes.

Walking out on the one thing that brought me back to life and reminded me I could *feel* again takes less than a moment.

My steps slow as I tentatively walk to her side of the bed. Even her silhouette that's half-masked in darkness looks angelic. Stooping down, I wisp a tendril of loose hair away from her face and bite back a sob.

"I love you." The words are thick in my throat, nearly choking me. "Always."

That last word booms in my ears as I quicken my steps, escaping outside.

Tears pour out my eyes the moment the front door clicks behind me, making it hard to see. Each step away from Nora fractures my soul, causing a growing ache that's more agonizing than the last. It whirlpools through my chest and lands in my stomach.

When it crescendos, I'm only halfway to my car.

I have to stop and fall to my knees. Bending over the bushes, I hurl out the contents of my dinner. Through dry heaves, I crunch my knuckles into the concrete and sob.

Fuck, what I wouldn't give to go back into that house and hold her until I'm gone from this life, but I won't make Nora choose that. Nora Davis won't waste herself on me.

She deserves so much more than this busted-up man who is nothing but a disappointment.

Fragments of You

Chapter 17

Nora

I stir in bed. Warm euphoria and Bentley's scent encase me while the sheets tangle around my ankles.

I'm deliciously sore in all the right places, and I'm dying for the tenderness to grow after another repeat. Last night was mind-melting incredible after waiting for so long, and Bentley was more than I could have ever imagined. He was so attentive in ensuring I was satisfied, so generous with meeting my requests, fixated on ensuring my pleasure before reaching his own. He was so, so perfect—in every way. *Good things do take time.*

My head and heart are still on cloud nine at the moment, and I feel weightless in the mattress... *his* mattress.

His.

A tired smile creeps over my face. I bury my nose in the pillow and sigh. When I think of having Bentley inside me again, my clit throbs. *I need him now.* I turn over, desperate to see him shirtless in bed while sun rays peek through the curtains.

Nothing.

He's not here, and I can't help but notice that his side of the bed looks undisturbed. It strikes my heart like a bad omen. *"Bentley?"* His name is a whisper. I scan the room and climb out of bed.

My feet hit the wooden floor, and I tiptoe over to the bathroom and knock twice. "Bentley?" There's nothing but darkness spilling out from the crack under the door, but I still obey the compulsion to push it open.

It's empty.

I rest my fingers around the handle and gaze around the room. My head tilts when my line of sight falls on the bedroom door. *He must be making breakfast.* He's wronged me so many times, but he wouldn't do this. I know he's still here. He promised me a repeat of last night, so yeah, he's here.

Traveling across the room, I smirk while opening the door, naked—his words after stripping me of my clothes last night replay.

"Fuck babe. You're gorgeous."

I'm anticipating his mouth hanging open at the sight of me, right before he has his way with me all over again—maybe even on the countertop. I giggle. *I can't wait to see the look on his face—*

When I step out into the hall, my heart plummets to my feet. It feels like a wasteland, and there are no signs of food. No smells of coffee, eggs, or toast. It's all silence. *Oh no.*

My fingers clench into my palms. "Bentley?" I scan down the hall, eyes bouncing off the walls like I'm trying to conjure him out of thin air. The soles of my feet pad against the hardwood with my timid approach. I reach the end of the hall and poke my head into the living room. "Bentley?"

Nothing. Unease begins to simmer low in my gut. I force a deep breath. No. He's here. Probably in the kitchen, he just didn't hear me.

I tiptoe. "Bentl—"

The kitchen is dark, no lights, not even a smidgen of life, and now I sense it in the whole house. There's a deadness residing here—one so thick and heavy it's permeating the walls.

I venture towards the entry of the house, and peel back the curtain to look out the front window.

His car is gone. The curtians drop from my grasp. After resting my back against the wall, I pinch my eyes shut, tapping my finger against my forehead. *Did he go to get food?* Maybe he left a note? I scour through the house, checking the countertop and any tables in hopes of finding a quick note—anything to indicate that he'll be back soon.

I don't find anything.

No. No. No. This isn't happening. He wouldn't do this—but I can't help feeling that he has. My heart taps hard against my throat.

I decide to search the house again—each room. There's not many, his place isn't that big, but I go over every room. Tears well out of my eyes. Every time I come up empty-handed, I whimper a bit louder.

All I see is smears when I return to the living room—a pit shreds through my stomach, the silence chokes me.

I feel my fingers clutch around my throat while scanning the empty room, trembling. "B-Bentley?" I heave out his name, while a sob echoes off the walls. Rapid breaths resound in my ears. My lower lip quivers. *"Where are you?"* The first time I whisper it, then my eyes lock down the hall. "Where are you!"

My scream reverberates in the house, eyes sweeping around the room in a panic. Then I spot my purse on the floor.

God, I'm being stupid. Why not just call him? Plastic scrapes at my nails as I fish out my phone with shaking hands. There are a few missed calls from Tessa. I ignore them and go to my contacts. I'm trying hard to stop my sniffles while hitting the call button, but it doesn't matter—it goes straight to voicemail.

It's happened, and the slight sting radiating across my mouth as I slap my hand over my face is the chaser to my shock. The ache of him leaving me slices through every fiber of my being.

I look out the window again, staring at the empty driveway. *He's gone.* The truth of what he's done reaches out, stabbing into my heart. "Nooo!" I fall to the ground, ripping the window dressing and pole to the floor. It clatters around me while I sit on my knees and wail, my screams bouncing off the walls.

I'm rocking back and forth, clutching at my chest, sobbing. I swear my ribcage is busted from the inside out. Jagged bones stab at my heart and lungs with each beat and breath that occurs. It hurts. It hurts to breathe, hurts to move, hurts to think that fucker did this to me. All I can do is rock, the floor nothing but a blur under me.

I don't even know how long I've been crying. All I'm aware of is that I sob harder than ever, and that I'm broken. A broken fucking mess because I meant nothing to him.

My voice is hoarse when my phone goes off. Rubbing tears out of my eyes, I look for where it is. Spotting it face down a few feet away, I crawl to it. When I manage to pick up and flip it over, the screen is shattered... *like me.*

It's Tessa. I'm not even sure if the screen works, but I slide my fingers to accept the call. "H-hello?"

"Oh my God, Nor, where the hell are you?" Concern rings tight in her voice, and that's not something I usually hear. "I've been trying to call you all ni—" A heavy pause hangs over the line. "Are you crying?"

I sob. "Yes. Yes, I—"

"What happened? Where are you?"

I take a hard swallow, she's going to hate me for this, but right now, Tessa is the only one who can pick me up since my car is at Quinn's house. "I'm... I'm at Bentley's."

"Oh, Nora." She sighs. Judging by her soft tone, I take it to be one of sympathy. "You slept with him, didn't you?"

"Yes." Curling up into a ball, I hug one arm across my shins. "Tessa, he's gone."

"Oh shit." I barely hear it.

"I've tried to call him, and it went to voicemail," I whimper again. "He left me." The admittance gurgles out. I sob and hang my head. "Tessa...he...he..."

"I'm coming to get you."

My head snaps up. "Okay. Um-okay." It strikes me that I'm still naked. "I need to find my clothes."

"Find them because I'm going to be there soon." She hangs up.

Her words act like a spur. I scramble to my feet, pushing tears off my cheeks. After finding my blouse in the living room, I return to Bentley's room for the rest.

The bedroom is a cruel whip of pain, flaying apart my

composure until I'm a mess. I'm sputtering through my snot while climbing into my skirt. By the time I leave his room, I can't breathe, and my head throbs.

Tessa isn't here yet, so I slide my spine down the front door, allowing the sorrow of being tossed aside to shred through my very being until my soul is dismantled and worthless.

I cry until she arrives, wondering the whole time why I ever trusted myself with him to begin with. I've forgotten once again that he never *sees* me.

Fragments of You

Chapter 18

Bentley

I'm outside, my hands dangling over the railing of my parent's balcony. The air is probably cool, nipping at my exposed arms, but I can't feel it.

Numbness overpowers my outward senses, and I'm almost used to that by now.

I guess that's what happens when your whole existence is agony.

I've been home for two weeks and haven't been able to feel a damn thing besides the beating of my heart. Each pulse rattles through me like I'm stuffed with needles. It hurts. Anytime I think of Nora, the pain crescendos, and it's like a machete's hacking away at my being. I feel amputated from her, and empty.

Pulling out my phone for a second, I sigh. Yesterday afternoon, her sporadic calls stopped. It's not hard to guess why she's tried to call. She wants an explanation.

I don't have one.

How do you explain to someone that while you were having sex with them, you discovered they're everything, and you're nothing? I remain uncertain if running out on her was the right ay to do things, but I do know that leaving her alone is what

I'm supposed to be doing. I should never have messed with Nora.

Nora.

Just her name. The familiar anguish travels up my spine, piercing straight through my heart. I interlock my fingers and clench them hard. My head drops, and I squeeze my eyes shut.

Stop thinking about her.

A dragging of the patio door jolts me upright as it opens, then shuts. The light shuffle of shoes tells me it's Lena, and I muffle a groan. She wants to talk. I know because *that* look was passed my way all through dinner. The one where she squints her eyes and tilts her head. It's my sister's pre-game of 'I'm getting to the bottom of your problems.'

"Hey, butt face. Wanna talk about it?" She's already starting strong, coming up to my side, holding two beers. She juts one my way and props an elbow on the balcony railing.

I shake my head and look dead ahead, hoping she takes the hint for once. "No."

"Well, tough shit," she bites back. "Because you're going too."

A growl hits the back of my throat when she places her can down and cracks the drink open.

Damn it. Irritation ripples down my spine. I came out here to be alone, not hounded. "Lena stop."

"Ya know, if all you planned on doing was brooding around like a damn grizzly, why did you come?" She arches a brow. "Mom and Dad are scared to poke at you, but I'm not, so what's going on?"

"Damn it, Lena." Wood stings my palm as I smack it against the railing. "Can't you take a hint? I told you I don't want to talk about it."

"Sorry." She narrows her eyes, voice scolding. "You lost that privilege after you made Gracie cry yesterday."

I exhale hard, still kicking myself over my snappish behavior. Gracie wasn't doing anything wrong. She pestered me while I worked out in our home gym. It happens whenever I come home, but yesterday after the millionth question, I told her to shut up and called her annoying. The poor thing bawled. When she ran upstairs, it compounded the pain that's been fracturing me from the inside out. I apologized, and Gracie forgave me, but I still feel like a dick.

"So," Lena ribs her elbow into my arm, breaking up my thoughts. "Talk to me, Bent."

Pinching my lips closed, I refuse to make eye contact and stare at the twinkling sky.

"Oh. Playing that game, I see." She tsk's. "Then I'll start with the most obvious. It's a girl."

I huff.

"Called it."

"Damn it, Lena." I scowl while lightly kicking my toe against a beam of the deck in aggravation.

With a dull expression, she taps her finger along the metal beer can. "And what happened that made you run away, because it must have been bad?"

My heart squeezes painfully, forcing a confession out, "I-I slept with her." The words drop a sick knot into my stomach, and I hang my head.

"What's new about that?" Her question is flat. "She have a boyfriend or something?"

"No. She's single." A somberness ripples down my back, and I frown. "I'm not Ivy. I don't fuck the taken ones."

Her lips pull down after taking a swig of beer. "If she's single, I fail to see what's wrong."

"It's wrong because she's…" Breath catches in my chest.

"Clingy?"

"Perfect." When I say it, I know it's the right word—I can tell by the agony in my sternum lashing through me—reminding me how ugly I am after all this time. "And I can't give her what she needs.

"Perfect?" Her voice sounds riddled with doubt."Bentley, nobody is perfect."

I think of Nora, her eyes, laugh, smile, most importantly, her heart. Never in my life have I met someone so sweet or kind. My fingers clutch tight around the wood as a lump forms in my throat. "She is."

"Then you're delusional." She gently nudges the beer can my way. "If you're going around thinking you're the only one who's made mistakes, then you've been hanging around the wrong people."

I finally pick up the can and open it. "Well, you've never met Nora."

"I don't have to." Lowering her tone, she traces her finger around the rim of the beer can. "I don't have to because she's human, and we're all flawed."

"Then so be it. She's flawed." I hang my head while a wave of shame steals my breath. "But I'm worse."

"How?" Her voice rings out with shock. "How are you worse?"

"I just am." An invisible weight presses my shoulders down, and they slump. "I've used people, Lena."

"And she hasn't?"

"No. Not like me." The admittance makes me sick. I opt for a swig of beer before the feeling worsens.

"Bentley, you can't know that. Also," she sighs, "I think I know where this all stems from for you." She shrugs, tossing a long blond hair off her skinny shoulder. "And I can't say I blame you." Her back rounds while she rests her elbows on the railing. "We've skirted around it but have never really talked about how badly Ivy hurt you."

"Ivy didn't hurt me that bad." My denial is gruff as I block the words out.

"Bullshit." She snorts, the sound tearing like a knife at my composure. "I think she destroyed you, and that you blame yourself for everything that happened."

I've never told anyone that, and I hate how Lena sees through me. My hand tightens around the can until the outline of my fingers dents into the aluminum. "Why would you think that?" I fight the tremor in my voice.

"Because I know how Dad raised us. In particular, you. " She glances over her shoulder, briefly, shooting our house an un-amused scan. "Dad was always infusing you with this belief system about how taking care of a woman is everything. How the monogamous married life is the *only* life."

I opt to keep my head down, trailing my finger around the rim of the beer can, trying hard to hide the pain eating through my stomach.

"He always put so much pressure on you to be the best, then all that shit happened with Ivy. I know you put on a brave face, but I think Ivy cheating on you the way she did busted up all the faith and self-worth you had. And I think Dad's silence on the matter convinced you that you were a failure, that what happened was because of you."

Sorrow ripples down my body, taking my heart to the floor. My surroundings blur as tears well. "Lena—"

"Dad never told you it wasn't your fault because he's an idealist." Her voice softens, threading with an understanding I've never heard but have seriously needed. "Sometimes when shit hits the fan, he doesn't know the words to say, so he says nothing and just pushes through."

Raking through my hair, I close my eyes. Each possible emotion mixes up inside my chest and swirls until I'm unsure of what I'm feeling. It's as if all my thoughts and feelings have been nailed to a bulletin board and put on display the last few years because that's how damn accurate Lena is right now.

"Silence wasn't what you needed, Bent." Reaching out, she pats the top of my hand. "Dad should have told you that Ivy was just a rotten person—a bitch who slipped under our radar until it was too late. So please," her heavy pause makes my lungs tighten, "Allow me to say what he can't. It wasn't your fault, Bentley. It never was."

I blink, and with my hands shaking, my vision falls to the ground. "Then why wasn't Ivy happy? If I'm not a failure, what did I do to make her cheat on me?"

"Nothing. You didn't fail, and you did *nothing* wrong. You're a great person Bentley. You just had a bad experience." Resting her head on my shoulder, she gives me a quick side hug, patting my back. "Don't let one person convince you that you're a failure in keeping someone happy."

Keeping someone happy. Can I attempt to do that again for someone after all this time?

And also, what does Nora want? Hope sparks in my chest at this ludicrous thought that maybe she does want someone like me.

Nora and I have never had a heart to heart, where I've asked what she wants in a partner, so maybe there is a chance for someone like me. The thought of possibly being with her sends my heart soaring.

Until it crashes to the ground, erupting in flames when I recall what I did to her—how I left without telling her what happened. If there was a chance with Nora, I probably fucked it up, and now more than ever, I'm not worthy of her.

"I think you should talk to her when you get back, Bentley." She makes half circles with the beer can on the railing while looking down. "I bet if you talk to her everything will work out."

"I'm not sure I can," I speak so low, I can hardly hear my own words thanks to the nausea high-tiding in my stomach.

"What?" Lena's brows knit together. "Why not?"

"Lena, I..." The words get stuck in my throat, and I wave my hand once, almost wishing my sister away.

"Hey, it's okay. What is it? You know you can tell me."

The deep breath rattles as I blow it out, shame curdling my insides until the beer in my stomach is sour. "I've made a mistake."

"I'm sure it can be fixed." She's standing right next to me but sounds a mile away.

"Doubt it." My voice gives out, guilt taking away all my strength while it lashes in my sternum. "I left her."

"Left her?" Lena's head ducks low. "I don't follow."

My fists clench, trying to counteract the revulsion of my own actions as the emotion rolls through my body. "After I had sex with Nora, I left her. I left her sleeping in my apartment and came here without saying anything."

Her gasp is loud, cutting right into my chest. *"Oh, Bentley."*

"Yeah." My hand thumps against the banister. "I fucked up. After sleeping with her, I couldn't shake this feeling that I ruined her, so I bolted."

"Well, that was a big fucking mistake."

I grimace, tempted to slap myself for my own stupidity. "What do I do?"

"Are you kidding me?" Her brows lift, almost touching her hairline. "Talk to her. Tell her what happened."

"How?" I shrug, pocketing my hands, my ribs wanting to concave from the depressing question. "How do I make it right, Lena? After something like that, how do I try to smooth everything out?"

"I can't help you there." Her lips flip downward. "If you want Nora, you're going to have to figure out how to mend what you broke."

I suck in cold air while disbelief sucker-punches my core. I've been called sly and like-able. I've been told I could win over my worst enemy with charm and charisma—but burnt bridges? I don't know how to fix those.

Maybe I need to start learning.

"Hey." Lena breaks me of my thoughts. "You can do it. Talk to her, and be honest. We all make mistakes, so maybe she'll be able to heal if you give her time and rebuild her trust. Just try." She pats my arm and then turns for the house.

A small part of the sting festering inside soothes over. *Thank God for Lena.* "Hey, stupid," I call out to her, one side of my mouth curling up.

She halts and gazes past her shoulder. "What?"

"Thanks."

"You're welcome." She waggles her brows. "Now think of a way to close the divide you caused." The patio door opens, she steps inside, and then it closes.

Alone, I exhale a deep breath, letting my cheeks round out. *Close the divide.*

I have no fucking clue how to do that or if she's ever wanted me beyond friendship and fun. Fuck, how does she even feel about me? Was I a fling to her, or something more?

For all I know, she could be happy I'm gone and regretting what we did for a different reason altogether. But damn it, I have to try because Lena is right—none of us are perfect. Even if I'm the worst snake of the bunch, there must be something good in me, and I don't want to miss out. I don't want to lose the woman who brought me back to life. At least not without a fight.

Now the real question is, how do I do this?

It's been so long since I've tried to love someone that my heart is a dust jacket.

However, for Nora, I want to try to renew myself. For once, after all these years, I want to be better. I only hope I'm not too late.

Chapter 19

Nora

"Are you certain about going to this thing, Nor?" Tessa asks the question from her couch, sitting with both legs tucked beneath her. "You're going to see a lot of people that know Bentley, so he might be there."

I shrug, pushing out the light prick occurring in my sternum. "Honestly, Tess, maybe that's what I need."

It's been a couple of weeks since Bentley ran out on me. I called numerous times, and there was never an answer of any kind, so I gave up. The pain that ripped me apart is still here, but icing over, or so I keep telling myself. Especially tonight as I try to move on.

I'm dressed in jeans and a T-shirt, for pretty much the first time since the ordeal, preparing to go to someone's house for fight night. MMA isn't really my thing, but I need to do something. Wallowing around on the sofa isn't going to do me any favors.

Slinging my leather purse over my shoulder, I amble for the front door. "It will be fine." *I hope.* "And if Bentley *does* have the guts to turn up, I'm going to corner him and get some damn answers."

She frowns, snuggling deeper under her blanket. "I doubt that will happen. You know how slippery he can be. I bet he either avoids coming or runs some bullshit past you."

"I'm not going to let that happen," I sigh, hating how defeated it sounds. "Plus, I still don't even know if he'll be there."

All this time, and I don't even know where he is. I've driven by his house once or twice, and it looks abandoned. The front window is exposed from where I pulled down the curtain, and if he were there, I'm sure he would have fixed it.

"Anyway," I hike the shoulder strap higher, "Are you sure you don't want to come?" I put on my best sugary voice. "I'm sure we'll have fun."

"Forget it." She puts her hand up, rejecting my plea. Her nose scrunches up. "All that punching, screaming, and blood… no. Go and have fun, if that's what you're calling it."

I bite back a snort. "Okay fine. I'll bring you back some food if they have anything good."

"Cool." She readjusts her position and picks up her e-reader. That's how she's going to spend her night—reading till she falls asleep.

I say one last goodbye, then head out the door.

When I get to the intended house, there are way more people here than I expected.

And just my luck, it turns out, I don't know most of the people here. I've never watched a fight in my life, and I haven't a clue what I'm supposed to be keeping track of. I try to fit in quickly, screaming when everyone else screams and bobbing my head 'yes' to the numerous comments being made.

I'm floating along, which is about the best I can do, but eventually, I need a break.

The entry hall is where I seek some sanctuary. I'm checking my phone to see if Tessa's tried to contact me when a pair of heels tapping on the tile catches my ear.

It's a busty blonde named Helena, and because my luck sucks, I recognize her because she works with Bentley. A burn of hurt weaves through my ribs. The only good thing is that they haven't slept together. She's older and married, and I've never, not once, seen Bentley flirt with a married woman.

Her lips tweak up with a smile when she sees me. "Oh, hi." Her voice is bright, just like her red lipstick that sheens while catching the overhead light. "Nora?"

I nod. "Yes. Hello."

"It's been a while."

"It has." I tuck my phone away and try to smile. "How are things going for you?"

"Just fine." She tugs at the hem of her tight sweater and smooths it across her hips. "I didn't think a cute thing like you would be into martial arts."

I shrug. "I'm not really." For some reason, the flat way I say it makes her laugh, and I chuckle. Staring at her, all I think about is Bentley. Curiosity grabs me by the wrist and yanks hard, leading me to a subject I should avoid but can't. My shoulders tighten, yet my voice stays calm as I dive straight in, "I'm surprised Bentley isn't here. He likes MMA."

"Bentley?" Her brown eyes widen. "Kind of hard for him to be here when he's out of town."

"Out of town?" My heart begins a never-ending free fall. All the composure I had in my voice goes straight to Hades. "You-you mean he's gone?" When she nods, my chest shreds into two.

"He went home to be with his family." She casually looks down and uses one of her long acrylic nails to brush through a knotted strand of hair. "It was kind of sudden, but he's been working remotely while he's gone."

"Oh." I can't ignore how sick my response sounds, nor the way my stomach knots itself in my gut. He actually went home. Most likely the night he fucked me. Fucked me then chucked me out some side window of his memory, escaping to his family, leaving me with zero explanation and unanswered phone calls.

The last hopes of me thinking I meant anything to him explode—hitting my psyche right in the face all while mincing my dignity and scattering my soul along the way. I was nothing to him. Absolutely nothing.

I wrap my arms around my middle, hoping it will help dispel the hollowness engulfing me. Reality crashes back at the sound of Helena's voice.

"Oh, don't look so disheartened. I'm sure he'll be back." She winks. "You might have some competition, however. A lot of girls are upset about his departure."

A lot of girls. God, all I want is to crumple down to the floor and cry.

Instead, I try to distract her so she can't recognize the anguish stabbing at every part of me because I don't want anyone to know what's happened. That would be the end of my pride, and it's already been strung out to dry. I manage something that halfway sounds like a laugh and a smile, but damn if it doesn't feel like I'm being tortured. My lips actually hurt, and the sharp twinge drops straight into my heart.

"Oh honey, you look so sad." She extends one arm and drapes it around my shoulder. "It will be alright. Come on." With a gentle tug, she guides me out of the entry hall. "Let's get you something to eat. You know what they say—skinny people are the most unhappy, so you must be miserable." She gives my arm a loving pat. "You'll feel better once you've eaten."

I can't find a way to refuse without looking pathetic, so I follow along. I'm basically mute tagging along as she loads me up with snacks and goodies. She's sweetly blubbering about her husband, who's here with her, and their plans for a ski trip. My head bobs a few times, but besides a few "mmm's" of understanding, there's no other reply. When she's done, she gives me a beaming smile, full of white teeth, tells me to 'eat up,' and flits away.

Looking down at the food, I'm dead. Any appetite that should be here withers before caving away to repulsion. The food hits my gaze like pig slop, and I'm not hungry. I trash it and prepare to leave, only when I glance at the front exit…

Helena is blocking it with a group of ladies. They're chatting it up and having the time of their lives. After all she did, leaving in front of her nose would be awful, so I have to stay. But I can't remain in this room.

I'm trapped in a freight train, and it's roaring around me, razing my composure to the ground. The screaming, the lights, the people, the noise—

I close my eyes when the room erupts with an unanimous

shout, and I rub at my temples. Opening my eyes, there are tears in them, and one of them is about to slide down my cheek. Some kind of escape is needed, immediately.

I look to the right, and spotting the long abandoned hallway, I speed walk to it. I'd run, but that wouldn't be subtle.

Darting down the hall, I keep an eye out for any isolated place that's not a bedroom. The laundry room at the end is where I find my sanity.

My legs are weighted as I stumble over to the washer and plop my ass on the cold tile. Resting my spine against the appliances, my mind replays all the phone calls I made to Bentley, and I want to scream.

He's seen them. They rang for a while then went to voicemail, so I know he got them. And everything I've discovered tonight is adding to the festering wound lodged deep in my heart. He's gone.

Poof.

He disappeared and ran off to his hometown, all without the decency one should show to another human being.

Away from the noise, my heart wrings itself sick—twisting and knotting in all forms of agony while the truth shreds through me. I finger comb the roots of my hair and sniffle. Did I really mean that little to him?

The only answer is *yes* and that I'm a fucking fool. A fool who is no better than all the other sluts that have left parties with him. We are one and the same. I hit the precipice of my composure, and I'm on the verge of releasing a sob.

"Hello?"

I jump at the voice breaking through my bleakness. When I look up, my eyes trail over the long and broad body of Rich Prather. Bentley's friend.

I try to hide the tears blinding my vision and shift to move. "Sorry."

"No. Don't get up. Nora, right?" The toe of his high top Jordan drags against the floor with the step he takes.

Nodding, I ball my body in tight when he sinks down to sit across from me.

He tilts his head. "I saw you come in here."

"Through all that commotion?" I dab at my eyes, my brows coming together. "You saw me?"

His eyes widen. "You walked right past me. Didn't you see me?"

I shake my head. "No-no, I didn't. I'm sorry."

"No." He waves his hand in the air. "It's all good. I just noticed you looked upset, so I wanted to check on you." He nods up at me. "Everything cool with you?"

The question makes my heartbeat stop, and my brows raise. "Why are you checking on me? You don't even really know me."

Dark eyes flash with what looks like a mix between a smile and understanding as he smirks. "I know you hang out with Bentley, so we're not total strangers, right?"

Bentley. I can't even hear the name without it causing a massive sting in every available space of me. My fingers clasp together, and my head drops.

"You, uh, want to talk about it?"

My head bounds up, and I'm flooded with a dark gaze, naturally bronze skin, and jet black hair—the opposite of everything Bentley is, and right now, I desperately want that.

Chewing on the inside of my cheek, my shoulders curl inward. "Maybe there's not really anything I want to talk about, but more like forget."

"Really?" He casually extends one leg out, leaving his other leg up to prop his forearm on it. "I'm pretty good at helping with that." Something about the crooked smirk he gives me lessens the sting. "What do you want to forget?"

Breath snags in my throat. I can't mention Bentley, but maybe I don't have to. "Can I ask you a question?" I curl myself in tighter, heart drumming in my throat. "If it makes you uncomfortable, you don't have to answer it."

He laughs. The sound is dark and smooth, and I kind of like it ."First things first, nothing makes me uncomfortable." He grants me that crooked grin once more. "Try me and fire away."

It takes me a moment to summon the courage, but after what feels like too long, my brows furrow, and I dare to ask the question I've always been dying to ask Bentley. "Am I...attractive?"

His eyes droop like he's bored, and his broad shoulders lurch. "What kind of a question is that? You don't know?"

"Please." A tremor hits my vocal cords. "Just answer the question."

"Tell you what," a shiver runs up my spine when his dark eyes drag down to my mouth, and his voice goes dry, "Instead of hearing it from my mouth, why don't you come back to my place and find out my answer."

Those words—the sensual way he says them—it's a defibrillator to my heart and soul. My tears stop, and I lock eyes with him. A strange mixture of exhilaration and guilt passing through me as I sink into his darkness. I swallow past the knot in my throat and nod, giving him my answer that sounds just as dry as his. "Okay."

He smiles, extends his hand, helps me off the floor—and then we leave.

Fragments of You

Chapter 20

Bentley

I'm leaving the gym, freshly showered. For the first time, there's a lightness in my shoulders and more of a sharpness to my step. No, I haven't returned Nora's phone calls, but that's only because of my uncertainties. The debate of how to approach her and discuss what happened remains an unsettled one.

I don't know what to do, so I'm sleeping on it, a lot. I'm looking at the stars again too, hoping that they'll give me some kind of answer.

Stargazing is on my mind when I go into Tanka's Coffee Shop, a local place that I'm pretty sure my family has kept in business all this time. My family loves this place and its quiet downtown location. I'm not going to rag on their daily visits, because I love it too. This is the only coffee place I visit when I come home, and since it's late, I'll be getting a decaf.

The bell at the top catches against the white door and chimes, announcing me. The front is deserted. I look past the serving counter, toward the back, trying to spot the owner. "Tanka?"

"Yep!" Her voice travels from the back room. "I'll be right with you, Bentley."

"No problem."

I pace around for a moment, observing the odds and ends she keeps supplied here.

Aprons, spatulas, specialty pouches of soup mixes, coffee cups with quirky sayings. Her shop has a nice flair. The black and white checkerboard tiles, adding to the unique niche she's created.

I glance over my shoulder when the bell goes off.

A woman steps in, possibly close to my age, and boy, it looks like she's about to pop at any moment. I try not to make assumptions about the state of women, but she's obviously pregnant—like she could have her baby here, pregnant. She's also kind of unkept. Her hair is tossed up in the worst bun I've ever seen, and she's donning raccoon eyes that I doubt are from having a long night of getting laid—more than anything, they look like they're from crying.

Giving her a quick smile, I flick my eyes away. My attention returns to the various goods on the shelves. I tink my finger against a white ceramic bowl, wondering if Mom would like it.

"Oh my gosh. Bentley?"

My gaze snaps up.

She walks over and stands in front of me—her gaze blatantly roves my torso, and I'm not even going to lie—she looks mesmerized while taking me in. Her eyes are wide as she sucks in a breath. "You uh…" Pink climbs in her cheeks, and her mouth falls open. "You ummm. Wow. You look great."

"Why, thank you." The compliment is nice, but I have no fucking idea who this is. I feel bad for needing to be reminded, but playing along won't make this any better. I give her my softest smile. "I'm sorry. What was your name?"

The crimson that was in her cheeks drains. She goes pale. "You…you don't remember me?" She tilts her head, shifts her eyes to the side, and bites down on her lower lip.

Oh fu-

I'd know that motion anywhere. My eyes widen. Shock and horror unite in my blood then dump into my heart. The sensation forces me back a step. "Oh my God." My voice sounds stunned, but there's nothing I can do to change it.

When she locks eyes with me, I know I'm right. They're deep blue. Like I remember.

My throat constricts, and I struggle to swallow before saying her name. "Ivy?"

Fragments of You

Chapter 21

Nora

My fingers are tangled in Rich's midnight-colored locks, his lips are on mine, and his tongue is dipping into my mouth in soft strokes. He has my back pinned against the counter of his darkened kitchen. His tall frame looms over me, and from the moans he's making, I take it he's enjoying this.

He's doing everything right, so I should be enthralled.

But I'm not.

Every time his lips envelop mine, all I can think of is Bentley and how perfectly he commanded my mouth—how he left my lips on fire with every connection he made. Each taste of Rich's beer and tobacco leaves me wishing it was the heavenly combination of faint whiskey and strong mint, and the way my neck cranes back to accommodate Rich is wrong.

I squeeze my eyes closed harder, wishing the truth flooding through my mind would go away, but I know it's not going anywhere. I finally collapse into it.

I'm not made for this person.

After being fitted against Bentley, Rich grinds on me like a puzzle piece that's almost right, but not quite. There's a gap between us, and Rich can't close it. *Damn it.* The realization twists deep in my soul—I'll never spark for him, the way I did for Bentley—never meld or yield to this man after a simple touch or smile. The way my heart pounded when Bentley called me beautiful—so hard, I thought my ribcage would shatter—Rich will never be able to attain that.

I'm sick over the awareness. Bile climbs up my throat while trying to accept that I'll never experience Bentley again.

A new shard of my heart fragments off.

Why did he have to ruin me for other people? Why did he have to possess me? Was it not enough for Bentley to have my mind? He was always there, haunting me, even when I tried to forget him. Wasn't that enough? Did he have to take my heart too? Take it only to ribbon it to shreds?

Rich groans, disrupting my thoughts, and how wrong this man is make me flinch. My fingers clench into his shirt. He moans again, but it's not the sound I want. A chasm splits open in my chest, and tears spill out my eyes.

At first, Rich doesn't notice, he groans long and deep, but when my lips go lax against his, he slows the pace.

I try to hold back a sniffle and fail.

He goes still and pulls away. "Hey, sweet thing." A frown paints over his face. "Everything good?"

I try to look down. Crying over another man has embarrassment blooming through my body, but he won't give me the chance.

Rich cups my face in his hands and forces my attention. "Nora, if you're not comfortable doing this—"

"No, I'm enjoying it. Really." The lie releases a massive ache. It kneads into my heart, embedding itself before traveling up my throat. I clamp down on my mouth, desperate to bite back the sob trying to escape. I'm not successful—it still slips out.

Rich's brows wrinkle, and his eyes soften. "Oh, Nora…"

I jerk my head away, just in time to hide the onslaught of tears pouring out of my eyes, shame cutting through me head to toe as I cover my face with my hands. It shouldn't be like this. But it is. One more sob, and I clutch onto the countertop, bawling.

"Holy fucking shit." Rich comes up from behind. His two large hands rub up and down my arms. "You poor thing. Come here."

Shaking my head, I try to reach behind me, hoping to reassure him that there's no need to comfort me.

Either he's not taking the hint, or he doesn't understand, because his broad chest presses against my back, and his hands massage up and down my arms. "Nora, I mean it. It's alright to cry. Let me hold you."

Hold me. Not kiss me. The soft way he says it quells my tears, stopping the sensation that I'm drowning in my grief. I sniffle and wipe at my cheeks. "I... I'm so sorry. If you want, go on—"

"God, no." He spins me around and grabs onto my shoulders. "I mean, you're hot and I *do* want this, but..." Scanning intently over my face, he sighs. A calloused thumb smoothes over my cheek as he frowns. "I'm no white knight, so I don't know why I feel so protective right now, but taking advantage of you seems wrong." The corners of his eyes crinkle. "We don't have to kiss anymore. We don't have to do anything."

I put my hand over his and try to smile. "Thank you." My voice is weak.

"Man." He shakes his head. "I've never seen a girl so broken-hearted." His brows come together, his eyes tightening. "Can I ask what happened?"

Apprehension sets heavy in my stomach. I'm debating if I should mention Bentley or not. A huge voice tells me it's best to leave him unnamed, while a small one taps at the back of my head, warning me it's better not to say anything at all. I'm not sure what to do, so I look at the floor and frown.

The memory of Bentley—the wound that I thought was icing over, melts all over again and cuts me afresh, somehow deeper than before. My eyes wet, and a whimper escapes.

"Holy shit." Rich sweeps me in his arms, crushing me against him. "God, I wish I could help you. I don't know why I wish that—I just do."

Clinging to his shirt, my shoulders shake with each sob.

"Thank you, Rich." I pat gently at his stomach. "You're a good person."

He huffs, making his chest compress against my ear. "No. I'm not, Nora." His low voice rumbles deep in my ear. "I'm a rotten, awful bastard who doesn't give a fuck about female feelings. But this? Watching you sob while kissing me—holy fuck it's sad. I always said I'd never find a woman who had a heart, but I guess I was wrong. " Air compresses out of me when he holds me tighter. "This one time, let me help more than I hurt. Go ahead, sweet thing." His large hand smooths over the top of my head. "Go ahead and cry on me tonight. Use me."

So I do.

I cry in his arms.

I cry until I fall asleep.

Chapter 22

Bentley

My heart is in my stomach—thunking so fucking hard I feel the vibrations in my feet. I haven't said anything besides Ivy's name since I don't know exactly what I *should* say. And I'm also not reacting how I expected. Yes, I'm shocked to see her, and that word is the understatement of the year, but…

After all these years, I thought the sight of Ivy again would break me and crumble me into dust—reminding me that I failed in making her love me.

I was wrong.

The only failure I see is Ivy, with her bloodshot puffy eyes. She truly looks miserable.

"Uh—"

My spine stiffens at the sound of her voice.

Her eyes trail up and down my body once more, resting on my pecs for too long.

I grimace. *I should have worn a different shirt.* This one is skin-tight.

"It's really good to see you again."

"Is it?"

Her eyes go wide at the cold tone of my voice. It even surprises me, but I'm not going to apologize for it.

She ducks her head and nods. "After all these years—" Her voice fades off for a sec. Her lips screw up in a tight smile, and she tries to make eye contact again. "Seeing you makes me so happy. My wish must have come true."

All I do is raise my brows while a deadened stare glazes over my eyes. If this is her idea of complimenting or expressing regret, she's more shallow than I ever realized. I fold my arms across my chest and take a step back. "When are you due?"

Her breathing rattles, and she looks down at her stomach. "Three weeks."

"Yeah." I nod, ice forming around the edges of my heart. "It looks like it."

"Hey!" For the first time since she's seen me, fire sparks in her dark blue gaze. She scowls. "Don't be like that. You're ruining a good moment."

"A good moment? What are you expecting here, Ivy? " I hunch up my shoulders. "You're going to tell me I look good and think that will be enough to pacify everything that happened?" One of my brows arch. "Are you really expecting me to accept you with open arms while you stand here and try to bullshit your way around what you did?"

"It always worked before." She looks away—tearing her eyes away to the wall. "You were always easy to appease."

"Before you fucked the whole town, sure. I guess I was."

A wince pulls at her puffy features. "You're being mean."

"No. I'm acting exactly how I should." My blood heats the longer I stand here and watch Ivy try to sweep past the pain she put me through. "You're irrational. You're waltzing in here without even so much as an apology and trying to butter up to me with half-assed compliments. That won't work, Ivy."

"I'm happy to see you."

"What you did was wrong. If you were a decent human being, the first words out of your mouth would have been that you were sorry, not that I look good. I don't need you to tell me that." I smirk. "I *know* I look good."

Her eyes flick to the floor. "After all this time, I don't know how to address what happened, so I thought—"

"You thought sucking up to me would do the trick?" I scoff, disgust roiling in my blood.

"Why not?" she shrugs. "You always liked compliments. That's how I kept you around. Seems like you've changed."

A growl leaves my throat. "Thank God I did. If anything, just to resist your bullshit." Anger and fury boil away in my gut, getting hotter the more she spews out her twisted words. I move for the exit.

"When did you become so bitter?" Tears stream down her cheeks, but they look fake as hell. "Don't you care about how you made me feel?"

"How I made *you* feel?" I examine her face, and take note of the permeant sneer affixed to her features. It's so different from what it used to be.

Or is it?

Perhaps it was always this jaded and cruel looking, but I was blind. I step back, shaking my head. "You're seriously heartless. You know that?"

"Am I?" She eyes me up and down, coldness rippling in her baby blues. "Maybe you've just grown an ego because you think you look halfway hot, and you've forgotten how I can make you feel."

"Unbelievable." Repulsion swirls up my spine. "I can tell you how you made me feel—like trash that was kicked aside. Like I meant nothing. Like my heart was ripped out and hacked apart while it was still beating. And fuck you for that. Fuck you for making another human feel like he isn't enough."

"Weak," she mutters under breath.

It should slice through my existence, and knock down my pride a few notches—but I'm done letting Ivy drip an ounce more emotion from me.

I squint. "Thanks for proving what Lena told me the other night."

"What's that?"

"That you're an awful person." I slide past her and move for the exit. Screw getting coffee tonight.

"You'll never get over me, you know." Her voice rings out like a bull horn in the shop. "I was your first, and you don't get over that. You'll regret turning me down tonight."

The bell catches on the door as I yank it open. I pause long enough to look over my shoulder. "Sorry, sweetheart." A sneer twists across my mouth, and my painful past slams shut for good. Ivy doesn't know it, but all she's done tonight is heal me. The shackles she left me with have dropped off and fell into an abyss thanks to her ugliness. "I learned how to live without you a long time ago. You taught me how to do that."

I now see her for what she is. Ivy is venom, and I was a fool to ever give my heart to her.

Lena was right.

There was never anything wrong with me.

"Fuck you, Bentley Harris!"

Stepping outside, I ignore her screams. The air feels different—the breeze hugging around me like the winds of change, and while I don't have everything figured out, I know I have to go back, and soon.

I need to return to Colorado and forget the last several years even happened.

Actually....

I need to see Nora.

After two years of knowing her, I need to find that girl, sit her down, and have a long discussion—one I've been avoiding because it scares the shit out of me.

Do I mean anything to you?

Even now, it has me gulping past a lump in my throat as it loops through my head, but I'm not going to ignore it anymore. I'm going back to face the things that terrify me. I'm going to finally let myself bleed out to one person again and confess what I'm scared to even think.

It's time. I'm going to do it.

I'm going to tell Nora I'm in love with her.

Chapter 23

Nora

"Man." Rich pumps his fist in the air and smiles. "Look at that catch." He stands up. A loud *clap* hits the air as he smacks his thighs while laughing. "That ain't no hail Mary, but it's damn close. And that's the game right there." Sinking back down to his couch, he grabs his notebook and starts writing.

Sitting on the opposite end, I tuck my knees tighter into my chest and grin. "I think you were made to be a sports analyst."

"Oh God, yes." He doesn't even lift his head. There's a boyish charm plastered all over his face thanks to his crooked smile, and his eyes are bright as his pen flies across the paper. "Sports is life, sweet thing. Without it, I'd probably die."

Sweet thing. The way he says it makes my heart go warm and soft. My lips quirk up. Rich is nice, and I've thoroughly enjoyed his company over the last week and a half.

We haven't done a dang thing. No sex, kissing, hand holding, we haven't really even flirted, but he's been kind to me—and his company has bandaged over the hurt that continues to linger. Without him, I wouldn't even be smiling on most days.

I was quick to accept when he texted me at work earlier, inviting me over for pizza, beer, and a college game.

He hollers when the final quarter ends and booms out a big 'hell ya' before returning to his notebook, jotting more stuff.

Watching him, there's the biggest smile spanned across my mouth. I knew he reported on sports, but getting to know him better and seeing his passion is so enjoyable that I can't help but be caught up in his enthusiasm.

The grin fades when my phone buzzes in my pocket. It's a text, and I already know it's from Tessa since our time together has been nil.

I ended up getting a new job at a new pharmacy a few days ago, and between settling into my new position and Rich, I've been putting her off. Muffling a sigh, I pull out my phone and look at the screen. Sure enough.

If you don't get your ass over here by tonight, I'm getting a new friend.

Threats of dissolving our friendship are only used as the ultimate way to get my attention. Guilt pricks at my insides. She has every reason to be upset since I'm failing in the friend department.

My night with Rich is going to be a short one. I quickly text Tessa back.

Get the hot tub ready. I'll be there.

A smiling emoji is her immediate response—a good sign that I'll be forgiven.

Rising to my feet, I collect my paper plate and glance at his. "Are you done with that?"

"Oh, yeah, but you don't have to clean up." He extends his hand, asking for my plate. "I don't mind."

"Neither do I, and I'm already on my feet." Snagging the plate out of his hands, I stroll away and head for the kitchen.

Boards groan under his ample weight as he follows along.

"Are… uhh… are you heading out?"

His distinct scent swirls from behind—chewing tobacco and cedar. At first, I wasn't sure about the smell. It was so different, so not Bentley, but now I like it. Its warmth reminds me of a hug, and I find the ending notes comforting. My stomach flexes while placing the plates in the trash.

"Nora?"

It dawns on me I still haven't answered his question. Spinning on my heel, a flush hits my cheeks when I meet his dark gaze. "I am. I promised my other friend I'd meet her tonight."

"Oh." He pockets his hands, and his mouth flexes down. "Tessa, right? I always see you two together."

He's noticed so much more about me than I thought. More than Bentley ever did. Warmth blankets over me, and if Tessa wasn't so upset, I'd stay in a heartbeat. "I'm afraid I've been neglecting her."

"Is that my fault?"

"Maaaaybe." I purse my lips when he chuckles.

He shuffles a step closer, his heat entering into my bubble. "Should I apologize for monopolizing you?"

I shrug.

"Because I don't want to." The gentle tone lacing his words causes the room to swirl around me. Breathing is labored when he extends one hand out and rests his palm on the island, boxing me in on one side. His dark gaze sinks to my mouth. "I keep hoping you'll change your mind, Nora. I might be holding out for longer than I should be. I've tried to not spend time with you, but I can't help it."

I manage a dry swallow as desire pools into the lowest part of my stomach. "Rich—"

He waves his free hand in the air, signaling for me to stop. "I'm not the most patience person, Nora." His thick brows pinch together, eyes dropping to the floor. "But I'm pumping the brakes because I can tell you've been hurt." What sounds like an embarrassed laugh softly slips out. "Funny, I've spent my whole life watching all the men in my life get run over by women. Never thought I'd see a bruised up girl, and that it would put my dick in a chain." His throat bobs with a gulp, "Sorry if that's rude."

"It is and it's not." The urge to touch him coils down my arm and around my fingers. I reach my hand out, letting it float in the air, but stop. It seems so bold, but my heart isn't that, at least not right now. "I appreciate your honesty. Just don't forget that we all get hurt, Rich—women included."

His head bounds up, the corners of his eyes pinching. "I see that now. I can see... Shit, this sounds awful, but now I see not all women are bitches." He reaches his hand out and cups my face.

My pulse jumps like it's jolting back from the dead, and I'm finally aware of my beating heart once more. A blush creeps up my cheeks as I get lost in dark mahogany eyes.

Calloused fingers soothe over my skin as he sighs. "I've only done casual flings, so don't expect too much from me, but I'd like to think we could last more than a few weeks." Uncertainty flickers in his tightening gaze. "And who knows. Maybe causal is what you need for a change."

He's not promising me anything. Rich is putting all his cards up front, and is showing sheer honesty, and that's more than I got from Bentley. My hand that was floating wraps around his forearm, and the organ behind my ribs swells in my chest, telling me it's still there. Still alive. "Maybe. Let's see what happens first."

"Good." After patting the side of my face gently, he drops his hand and takes a step back. "You better get to Tessa."

"You're right." I lightly pat his stomach and slide past him.

I've crossed into the living and am collecting my purse when his voice catches my ear. "Oh, by the way. My birthday is next week." He stops short of the living room and leans his tall body against the frame of the entrance. "I've rented out part of O'Malley's Rec and Pub here in town. We'll have a pool table, a few bowling lanes, and a dance floor."

"Wow." My brows lift. "Going all out, I see."

"Always do." He grins. "Anyway, I'd like for you to come... As a matter of fact, I'd like for you to come as my date." He halfway shrugs, and it looks so unsure.

I kind of like it. After watching Bentley parade around, this uncertainty is a welcomed sight. I hike my strap higher on my shoulder and nod once—euphoria filling the cavity in my chest. "I'd love that."

"Awesome." His face lights up. "Thanks, Nora."

"My pleasure." I give him a smile and move for the door. "See ya later."

I step outside, and the door latches behind me. The air is crisp, working its way through the weaving of my sweater, bringing a delightful shiver to my skin. Touching my hand against my neck, my pulse zings through my skin, into my fingertips. I relish feeling it again. It seems like such a small thing, but it's something. My mouth quirks upward. I like him.

Then my heart drops, straight into the ground.

Tessa won't. She's going to hate this, and because I've been avoiding her for so long, she's going to demand answers. I stop a groan and head to my car. Might as well get it over with. The sooner, the better.

I hop into my car and head straight to Tessa's, hoping she won't wring my neck too hard, even though she probably will.

"So. Besides your new job, which has only been going on a few days…" Tessa's voice already has that edge to it—the nosey pushy one, and I haven't even been here for ten minutes. "You going to tell me where you've been for almost two weeks, or do I have to play twenty questions?"

I take a sip of wine, desperate to control my quickening heart, and slump deeper into the water. "You don't want to know."

"Oh, brother. That's the worst possible answer you could give." She exhales long and hard. "You know that means I have to find out now, right? "

"Don't. I'm telling you now not to prod."

"Nora Rae Davis, you better tell me what you're doing."

She moves to stand up in the hot tub, and despite the steam

circling in the air, my blood chills.

"Fine! Fine." My back presses into the hard plastic of the hot tub walls. "I've been with Richard Prather."

Her eyes widen, mouth hinging open. "Rich?" She drops her glass into the water. "Shit." A scowl flashes across her face, and as she fishes out the glass, crimson red wine mingles in the hot tub and spreads out like ink. "You really think that's wise, Nora? Fucking Bentley's friend just for the hell of it?"

"We haven't slept together."

"Really, Nora?" One of Tessa's brows arches high, disdain sharpening her features. "All that douche does is fuck around." She grimaces and jerks her head off to the side. "Hell, I think he's worse than Bentley."

My shoulders deflate. "Well, he's been nice to me."

"Oh, I am *sure* he has."

"I'm being serious, Tess." Irritation rattles my gut. I sigh, swirling my index finger through a trail of red. "Besides, Bentley has nothing to do with it."

"Uh-huh, she counters flat and cold. "Says the girl whose heart was shattered a few weeks ago."

"Exactly." I bite the inside of my lip. "So lay off and allow me some fun. I think I've earned that much. Besides, I really like his company."

"If it wasn't Rich, I'd say go for it. As it is—" She squints at me.

"What?" I toss back a quick sip of wine, intense heat boiling just beneath the surface of my skin. "You think this is a rebound or something?"

"Think, or know?" Her head tilts while her shoulders sink under the water. "Nor, this is a disastrous idea. When Bentley comes back he'll be so pissed."

"*If* he comes back." I snort hard through my nose, directing my attention to the snow-crusted mountains. "Rich doesn't know what happened between us, and he hasn't mentioned him. I don't think anyone knows if he's coming back."

"Unless his apartment is listed on the market and he's quit his job, I'm sure he'll be back."

"Doubt it," I mutter.

"Delusional much?" The water shifts around her, and even that motion simmers with her annoyance.

Glancing over, I scowl—the irritation grinding against my nerves makes the look deepen.

"Hey, it's your life." She puts two hands up in surrender. "But don't be so naive to think Bentley won't come back. Also, don't think he won't have something to say about you sleeping with his pal."

"I'm *not* sleeping with him." I ignore her eye roll. "Besides, this isn't Bentley's concern." I drain my glass and set it aside. "Rich is a grown-ass man—I'm a grown-ass woman." A chill hits my shoulders, and I tuck my arms tightly across my chest. "If I decide to have sex with Rich, then so be it. Bentley can shove it up his playboy ass for all I care."

Tess tilts her head and scrunches one side of her slim nose. "Sounds like revenge to me."

The accusation should make my heart bleed out with agony, but it doesn't. Simply because Bentley already did that. He exsanguinated me when he packed up and left me in his bedroom without even a goodbye.

Today was the first day I felt anything besides darkness, and that's because of Rich. He doesn't have my heart, but he does make me feel better, and at the moment, sleeping with him kind of sounds like fun, especially after how he made me feel this afternoon.

"Any other time, Tess, you'd be right, but as it is, you're wrong. This isn't revenge." I pinch my lips tight, shaking my head. "This is me just moving on from something that was never meant to be."

"Yeah, don't be so sure about that." Black hair tumbles everywhere after she releases it from the pony holder. "And I don't care what bull crap you're trying to spew my way. You being so defensive gives you away. You're totally fucking Rich Prather which is gross because he's gross."

"Whatever, Tessa. Suit yourself."

She grabs a towel, secures it around her body. "I'll see you inside. I have chili going in the crockpot." She escapes into the house.

Sitting alone, I let the red water slosh around my shoulders. It's probably the wrong attitude, but Tessa's words and accusations grate at the raw edges of my heart, making me aware of how desperately I want to forget Bentley. So far, Rich is proving to me that he might make me forget, even if it is just a fuck.

I let his words replay. *"And who knows. Maybe casual is what you need for a change."*

I've never done a casual *anything*, but maybe I should change that.

My fingers stroke up and down the stem of the wine glass, and I shrug. I shouldn't even be contemplating this. However, I'm beyond caring. I look to the mountainous horizon from the balcony and smirk. I want to make Tessa's accusations come true. So I'm going to do it. I'm going to sleep with Rich and see if I like him. I don't care if he can't commit.

Honestly, I don't want him to. Commitment. The word alone slices through my stomach like a double-edged knife—forget actual monogamy. Stable is the last thing I need.

I nod and push out a breath, letting my air trail in the frosty night, my mindset like steel in concrete. For once, I'm going to let loose and have fun because I deserve it. Good-girl Nora be damned.

Chapter 24

Bentley

"Wait, what?" Lena's voice blares in my ear while I undo the front lock to my house. "You saw Ivy last week and didn't tell me? Why the hell not?"

"Because I was scared you'd track her down and gouge out her eyes."

"You're damn right I would have."

I chuckle, step into my house and flick on the light.

It's been a month since I left, and there's a blanket of dust covering my black coffee table. When I look over my shoulder, I frown. My curtain and the rod for the front window are on the floor. "What happened here?"

"What happened where?" Lena asks.

"Oh, nothing big. My curtain rod fell off." I bend down and pick it up. Glancing at the brackets, I gather it's an easy fix since they're intact.

"Really? Weird. Anyway," she huffs over the phone. "Shame on you for not telling me about Ivy."

"I could say the same." Tossing the curtain rod onto the couch, I throw my duffle bag next to it. "You failed to tell me that she's pregnant."

She coughs. "I didn't know you'd be coming home so soon. I thought she'd be gone wherever. Also, I wasn't sure how you'd take the news of her being knocked up."

"It didn't bother me." I untuck the mail shoved under my armpit from earlier and skim through it. All junk, not a surprise. "A little shocking, but honestly, she looked so bad that it didn't hurt."

"It didn't bother me." I untuck the mail shoved under my armpit from earlier and skim through it. All junk, not a surprise. "A little shocking, but honestly, she looked so bad that it didn't hurt."

She sucks in a breath. "How was she? A total bitch?"

"Not a first, but when she couldn't bullshit me, yeah." My eyes widen, and I shake my head. "And not an ounce of remorse either."

"As expected."

"Glad I finally wisened up and discovered it wasn't me after all."

A light chuckle rings through the earpiece. "Told you I was right." Smugness lives in her tone.

I roll my eyes. "Shut up."

Silence dangles in the air. She's listening to me—for once.

My eyes close, and fatigue from the plane ride home finally catches up. I moan and rub one of my shoulders. Why can't they make those seats a little wider?

"And what are you going to do about Nora?"

Lena's voice makes my eyes fly open, and the question shoots anxiety straight to my gut. It grows when I look around the house. Everything is flooding back, and fast. Tension climbs in my neck.

It's taken me a month to decide what to do with this girl, but I finally found my answer on the plane ride home. I've decided *not* to confess my feelings. At least not yet. I round my shoulders. "I'm going to offer her an apology and an olive branch."

"That's it?" She doesn't sound impressed. "No confession, no—"

"No." My answer is firm. "After what I did, I don't think it's right to do that. Perhaps it would have been different if I knew she felt something for me, but I don't." My foot taps the floor in a nervous rhythm. "For now, an apology with a new offer of friendship and the hopes to one day date her. I want to make sure she has some space."

"Mmm," I can hear her smile over the phone, "I always knew you'd come out okay."

"Thanks," I say through a chuckle.

"You're welcome. Now rest up. I'm sure you're tired."

Taking a glance at my phone, I *tsk*. "No time. My friend Rich is having a birthday party tonight. I told him I'd be there, but I'm not staying for long."

"Oh yeah, Rich. I've heard you talk about him before. Tell him I said happy birthday."

I snort. "I won't because he's a dick, and I don't want him knowing about you."

She laughs. "Well then, thanks for protecting me. This is a no-dick zone." She pauses. "I mean, not no dicks, but just… ahhh… well you know what I mean."

"I do." My nose screws up. "And gross, by the way."

"Oh, shut up. You're one to talk."

Unbuttoning my shirt collar, I chuckle, all while desperately feeling in need of a shower and change before heading out.

"Anyway," she cuts out, "I'm going to let you go. Love you butt face."

"You too stupid."

After we hang up, I place my phone on the table, strip out of my shirt, and go down the hall.

My heart thunks with each step. Lena distracted me, but in the silence, all I can think about is Nora. I was putting it off while at home, but walking back in here has me wondering how she reacted. I swear I can still smell her.

I know that's impossible, I mean, it's been a whole damn month, but I still feel her. When I get to the bedroom and see the side she slept on, I can't breathe. Slowly, I approach the bed and tentatively sink down to sit on *her* side.

Hers.

God, how I want this to be her side forever. I graze my fingers over the pillow she laid her head on, and my pulse goes wild. That's the pillow I'm using tonight. It will be the only connection I have to her until I figure out how to set up a meeting. I'm sure she's pissed, but I plan to beg on my hands and knees if I have to, requesting her friendship once more. One more chance is all I need.

How I could be dumb enough to run out on her, I'll never know. But that mistake will never happen again. I clutch the blue fabric of the bedding in my hand and sigh. "Right."

First things first. Rich's party. I'll do that tonight, then figure out a way to see Nora again.

Taking a shower and redressing in fresh clothing, I comb my hair, splash on cologne, then head out the door.

If the parking lot is any indication, then O'Malley's is hopping for this party. Not a surprise, though. Rich is never one to slack off on invites, and I expect most of the cars are here for him.

I'm looking around the entrance, entering the private party area, when a girl stops me. One I kind of recognize.

"Bentley. Hi." Her hazel eyes light up, and she's just loud enough over the crowd. "Oh my gosh, it's so good to see you again. It's been what…?"

"Uhh." My eyes dart around the room. "A long time." Not remembering their names isn't always a good thing, especially when they seem as nice as this one. I try to brush over the fact that I have no idea who she is. "I went home for a bit, but I'm back now."

"Cool. Cool." She flashes her white teeth and glances around. "It's a nice turnout." That smile gets stolen away by a lopsided frown. "Too bad the birthday boy is too wrapped up with his new girlfriend. Guess I got interested in him at the wrong time."

"Girlfriend?" My brows knit tightly together. Looks like our girl doesn't know who Rich is. "You're mistaken. Rich doesn't have a girlfriend."

"Umm," she chuckles, and it sounds nervous. "I think he does. He's only had eyes for one since he's been here." She points through the crowd. "Take a look for yourself."

I duck my head, bouncing my eyes through the gathering. My eyes hit the table, and my heart plummets to the ground—my blood stops pulsing. Horror withers up and down my spine while playing the part of a cruel mistress, forcing my eyes to watch the sight before me. I want to look away, but I can't.

There's no fucking way.

I can't be seeing this. I just can't be.

It's Nora… with Rich.

He's seated, and she's standing over him, in between his legs. Her hands are running the course of his shoulders, and he has his arms wrapped around her legs. Both of his hands rub up and down the backs of her thighs, disappearing under the hem of her short skirt a few times.

"Fuck." My chest blows out, and I hunch over.

For a while, I can't do anything but stare—helplessly. The woman who's done nothing but take up my headspace for the past month is in the arms of my friend. I can't think of a way to stop it. However, when he grabs her wrist and yanks her down onto his lap, a growl leaves my throat, and my spine stiffens.

"See what I mean?"

My attention snaps back to the girl that was talking to me.

"Girlfriend," she says, jerking her head in their general direction.

My teeth grit. Over my fucking dead body.

The girl smiles. "Do you think—"

"Excuse me." I storm away, blood boiling in my veins. With each step, as I draw closer to their fucking table, my skin heats that much more. My fists ball and unclench, and I picture ramming a beer bottle up Rich's nose and watching him bleed.

Fuck, that would be so satisfying.

I shove past a few more people, ignoring their protests. I don't care who I have to fight to reach that table. I'm going to get there. Then I'm going yank Rich across it by his shirt collar and fuck him up.

Only, when I get there, my heart bottoms out.

Rich has his face buried in Nora's neck, and she's squealing, fluttering her legs in the air.

The sight of *my Nora* in his arms cuts through my ribs, but instead of tapping into that, I focus on how they shouldn't be together. Folding my arms over my chest, I glare and decide their party is over. "Happy Birthday, fucker."

Nora's body goes stiff. Rich's eyes widen. When Nora cranes her neck to look back at me, I see a sight I don't like.

Anger. It's evident in her heated squint. I'm pretty sure she hates me. I can't say I blame her. But if she hates me, I fucking loathe Rich.

And his stupidity remains intact. He eventually laughs and smiles, still holding onto Nora. "Thanks, dude. You made it."

Stupid, fucking, idiot.

He's always been clueless and has no idea when I'm truly pissed at him. I roll my eyes and look at Nora.

Even though I don't want it to, my voice softens. It's still corded thick with tension, but it is softer. "How are you?"

The glare drops off, and all I see is ice. "Fine." I can't read her. Her face and eyes say nothing.

For once, our easy-going give and take are derailed. I can sense her tension, and I'm sure she feels mine, but that's it. There's nothing else I can grasp onto. My fists bundle tight together once more as I watch her slide off Rich's lap. She pats him on the shoulder.

"I'm going to go dance."

He winks. "Sure thing, sweet thing."

Sweet thing. Bile hits my throat. I want to vomit.

Nora slinks past me, her mini dress showing off every fucking mouth-watering curve she's got—ones I wouldn't even know about unless I'd seen her naked. I'm fucking pissed at the free show she's giving to Richard. I bite down on my tongue till I taste blood, but the compulsion to speak to her still wins out. She's almost beyond me—I catch her gaze in time.

"It's good to see you again." The words nearly gurgle out of me. That's how damn thick they are.

She freezes, glances over her shoulder, and nods. "You

too." I notice her faster-than-usual pace once she breaks our gaze. Breezing away, she hurries off to the dance floor quicker than I can speak.

I avert my eyes back to Rich, and contempt spears through my core as my hatred seeps out like poison. I feel it rotting me from the inside out, starting in my chest, draining down to my limbs

Rich still doesn't notice and has a huge smile on his face, "Dude, it's so good—"

"Nora is off-limits, Rich."

His jovial face falls away. When he laughs, it sounds like shock. "Wh-what? Dude, what the hell are you—"

"I mean it, Rich." My clenched fists slam down on the table. "Don't touch her. Don't kiss her. Don't sleep with her. Do–
—"

"Whoa." He springs out of his seat and turns his hands up. "Bent, you're too late."

"No." Nerves send my shoulders into twisted knots. "You lie. I know Nora. She doesn't move that fast. I haven't been gone *that* long. There's no way—"

"Yeah, dick." It seems like he finally catches on as he sneers at me. "I'm not just saying that for fun. You're way too late." He falls back down in his seat and pours himself a shot. "And if you're going to act like a fuckwad, then go home. What? Did you not get any pussy the whole time you were away?" He takes the shot and slams the glass on the table. "I don't know what the fuck your problem is, but figure it out."

"My problem is you." I grit my teeth, fury pumping hot in my veins. "Also, I don't believe you. She'd never run with someone like you."

"Then ask her." Rich points to the dance floor. "If you won't believe me, then find out for yourself."

I glance over my shoulder—the sight of her, grinding away with a group of girls on the dance floor, needles away at the restraint of leaving Nora alone. I squint and growl. "I will."

If Rich says something while I rip myself away from the table, I don't hear it. All I'm aware of is Nora, and right now, it's in the worst way possible.

I'm several feet away from her, but I'm heading in that direction. Fury combusts and wraps down my entire body when she breaks away and struts off for one of the halls. I don't know if she's avoiding me, but I *won't* let her get away.

So I follow after her. I don't know where the hell she's going. I don't care. Wherever it is, I'm going to corner her and demand some fucking answers.

Envy rakes hard at my soul when I continue to stalk after her, and she doesn't notice, but I still follow—I still chase her. Partly because I love her—always—but mainly because she's driving me fucking crazy.

Chapter 25

Nora

I'm stalking for the bathroom furthest away from the gathering, feeling a bit wilted. My neck is damp and sweaty from a mixture of the dancing and the throng of people that have shuffled around all night. My skin is also roiling with flames as I fume about Bentley.

Douche. I'm determined to have a knock-out night with Rich regardless.

I promised Rich birthday sex tonight, and it will be our first time. Rich seems thrilled, and I won't let Bentley ruin this. He's ruined enough for me. I'm escaping to the bathroom now to put him out of my mind before I go to bed.

While Bentley was away, I spent this whole time thinking that whenever I saw him, I'd be reduced to tears. I wasn't. If anything, seeing him again stoked disdain low in my belly. Guess I'm not as broken-hearted as I thought.

"A-hole," I stumble through the door, feet throbbing, and go for the first mirror. Part of me still can't believe he showed up and *then* proceeded to ask how I was in a nonchalant manner.

He did it all as if nothing had happened. Like the sex that melted my heart was nothing.

Like *I* was nothing. Staring in the mirror, alone in the abandoned restroom, I scowl, hating his existence.

BANG

The metal thunk of the bathroom door being violently kicked open makes me leap. My shoulders recoil as I hold my breath to see what's happening.

"Rich?" Bentley emerges.

I clutch onto the porcelain sink, my knees swaying. "You followed me?" A stilted swallow runs down my throat.

"You and Rich?" He spews out. "Richard fucking Prather?"

"You shouldn't be in here." The words nearly choke up in my mouth.

"And you shouldn't be fucking him."

I try to form a rebuke, but it withers with Bentley drawing closer because I've never seen him so pissed.

A red tint shades his face, and harsh lines etch deep into his features creating a fearsome scowl. He pockets his hands, thumbs out, and slowly swaggers for me—his chest massive thanks to the tight flex of his lats and back. He's pulling himself up straight and puffing everything out. It makes him look two times his normal size. It's intimidating.

Sexy, but intimidating.

My mouth dries like it's stuffed with cotton, a touch of aggravation grating on my nerves. Regardless of how far I try to throw him from my mind, he pulls reactions out of me that I can't control, and I really hate that.

"You hear what I said, Nora?" He halts in front of me, his back to the stalls. "Stop sleeping with him." The words grit out from between his teeth.

Bastard. I rest my butt against the lip of the sink and tilt my head back. "That's not your call to make, Bentley."

"Oh, isn't it?" He glares at me. "Do you have any idea what he's like? Any clue as to how much he'll hurt you?"

A fury licks up and down my spine at the hypocritical words. "Trust me. I've been hurt plenty." I don't hide the snark in my tone. "I'm sure after all the shit I've dealt with, I can handle Rich."

"Don't deceive yourself." His nostrils flare. "He'll fuck you till you can't see straight, then chuck you. Like he always does."

"Oh." My back stiffens. "You mean like you?" Ignoring Bentley's dropped jaw, a sneer twists across my mouth. "You mean like how you did?" I push myself off the sink and stand up straight. "Because that's what happened. You banged me senseless and then left."

"Nor—"

"Oh my god! What's a man doing in here?"

We jolt at the shriek of another woman entering the bathroom.

Bentley's head snaps to the door, and he scowls. "Get the fuck out. Can't you see we're talking?"

Heels click-clack on the floor as she flees, nearly falling over herself before disappearing—poor thing.

Bentley's chest rises with a deep breath when we lock eyes again. I watch a pause occur. It looks like he's trying to piece together the words he wants to say, and I can't say I've seen it before. "I told you it was a friends-only thing." The tone of his voice levels out. "I said we weren't going to make it awkward."

"Only, you *did*." I eye him up and down, the urge to slap him coursing hard in my fist. "You want to fuck like an irresponsible adult? Fine. You want a no-strings-attached thing? Fine." I buckle one knee. "But what you *don't* do is say things won't be awkward and then split." I fold my arms across my chest. "The only person who made things weird was you, and now you don't even want to take responsibility for it."

"Nora. I had to go home."

"And you never thought to tell me?" The words burn in my throat. I bury the sensation, so I don't cry. "Never bothered to answer my texts or calls? I thought friends shared that sort of information."

"I uh. I found out..." He fades as his eyes dart around the space. They bounce everywhere but land nowhere, and that grinds away at my patience.

"Found out what, Bentley?"

"My-my—" He blinks a few times, a resolve settling in his eyes. "My Grandma was sick. She—"

"Oh, no, you don't." The words growl out as a wave of heat explodes through me. Rising to my toes, I close most of the distance between us and point my finger at his nose. "Don't you dare lie to me, Bentley Harris. Both of your Grandmothers are dead. They passed away years ago."

"I—" The color leeches from him, leaving his natural glow blanched underneath the fluorescent lighting. "I—told you that?"

"Yes. Yes, you did." I square up, getting right in his face. "You stupid, bullshitting, lying, no good fucking piece of sh—"

The rest of my insult muffles against his mouth, so does my shout as his lips crash onto mine.

His hands clasp around my face, and his frame—sleek yet powerful presses into me as he kisses with an unyielding force that sends my ass crashing into the sink. Our feet shuffle around on the floor in a frenzy, and I strike against his chest twice. He takes the blows, then nips my bottom lip hard, forcing a squeal out of me. I try to shove him away, he grunts, fingers squeezing around my head, refusing to let go. The connection is rough, animalistic, devoid of anything caring, until his pace slows and he releases my mouth from his teeth.

A sense of surrender coils around me, and I no longer want to hit him, even though I should because he deserves it. He deserves my hatred and so much more, but wrapped up in his arms, with his lips pressed to mine, sparks of what we were flicker against my skin and heart, and it ignites in me. I sink into his touch, going motionless.

He pauses. I feel his breath shudder against me, and his hold laxens. Soft lips envelop mine with a supple tenderness, and he soothes over the area he nipped with his tongue, whisking remnants of the pain away with each tender sweep. He uncups my face, moving his hands to slink up and down my body—a small moan escaping him each time he grazes the sides of my breasts and hips.

I become lightheaded, and the room darkens as my fingers rove him. I start with the swells and dips of his chest, slowly working to clutch my nails into the bulk of his shoulders. His shoe taps against my heels to nudge my ankles open, wider and wider until I'm nearly spread eagle. He moves forward, placing his frame between my legs. I'm secured by his hands, one dead center on my back and the other weaving into my hair. Bentley bows me backward over the sink, our lips never breaking.

My spine obeys the position Bentley commands, but my breathing staggers at the teasing of his cock brushing and growing against my body. We kiss at the most torturous pace—connecting then breaking away to gasp, our soft groans echoing off the walls before our lips find each other again. His frame tightens, and I think he's going to take me right here, but his kisses ebb into whispers. Then they stop.

He pulls me upright and connects our foreheads. I feel the deep furrow of his brow as we huff in unison, our breaths colliding and echoing heavily in the silent air of the restroom.

After what seems like an eternity, just when I think the wounded anger he left me with has soothed over, he breaks the quiet with a gentle murmur.

"I just don't want you getting hurt."

I freeze. *Hurt.* Suddenly, I can't breathe. I can't move or think as the sole word brands into me like a hot poker. My eyes snap open, and I glare at him. A fire roars behind my gaze as wicked heat seeps out my pores. "Hurt?"

"Nora?" Confusion blinks across his expression.

"Fuck you." I yank my head out of his caressing hold, shoving him away. "Get off me."

"What?"

"Hurt?" Squaring my shoulders, my skin flushes. "You have the nerve to talk about me getting hurt?" A bitter laugh slips out. "Do you have any idea how many times you've hurt me?"

"N-n-no." He slowly shakes his head. "Nora, don't say that. What happened with me leaving—"

My mouth falls open. "You think this *only* has to do with you going home?"

"No…" He shakes his head. "Don't tell me there's more. Don't tell me I've—"

Wetness clouds my vision as an ache craters through my ribs. "You've cut through my heart so many times that I've lost count." My chest lurches with a sharp intake of air that ends up feeling like shattered glass. The pain it brings slices its way down into my soul, resting in my belly. "It happens every time you promise to call and don't. Same for when I get all dressed up just to be forgotten by you."

I blink, and a steady stream floods down my cheeks, falling without permission. I know my heart is echoing the same pattern—bleeding out as I stare at the one thing that breaks me apart just when I've pieced myself back together.

"Do you have any idea how gutted I am when we're at a party, and you come over and flirt? When you make me think I'm something special, then I see a random girl hanging off your arm moments later? A girl I know you'll take home even though she means *nothing* to you?"

My lip quivers with every word uttered. Each admittance of what he does strips off another layer, and I feel myself seeping everywhere, but I don't stop.

"Do you have *any* fucking clue how many times I've watched you sneak out of gatherings with a girl whose name you can't remember while I'm left standing there, wondering why it isn't me?"

That Grecian gaze of his cracks and tears form. "Nora—"

"Tell me something, Bentley." My interruption is quick, simply because I don't want to hear his voice. Not at the moment.

My voice quivers while my stomach tumbles to my heels, and my heart shreds apart as if it's being clawed and ripped into fragments.

"All those girls you've been with… is it them you call at two in the morning when you can't sleep? While they're screaming your name, do they know ahead of time that you hate snuggling and will just want to sleep undisturbed afterward?" I'm forced to bow over some from the hollowness expanding inside of me. "When you want to see a new movie, is it them you contact first?"

A tear escapes, trickling down his face, then another with a slow, sad blink. "Sweetheart—"

"What about in public?" I toss my head back in a feeble attempt to ignore the dismembering agony rushing through every limb, blinking through the mass of tears clouding all my vision. "Can they look at you when someone's making a joke and decipher how you feel about it? Not because you've said anything," I shake my head, "But because you have a look in your eyes only I can read?"

Silence.

"Can they do that, Bentley?"

He takes a loud swallow. "N-Nor—"

"Because I fucking can!"

My fingers clutch into my palms until I bend a nail. "I can do that because I *see* you. I see everything about you, but," my chest and shoulders bounce back and forth while I sob, choking on a gurgle, "You can't see me. You *never* see me."

His eyes close, and he hangs his head.

That sight. The cowardly avoidance of my gaze…

Fuck, I hate him. And he's not worth my tears. I realize now that I've been crying over a fool.

Pushing it all back, I force my posture straight. "Shove your self-righteous protective speech up your ass. Because you've shattered me more than Rich ever will." I hear his sigh but ignore it. Instead I opt to give him a hate-filled once over and kill my regards once and for all. No matter what it takes, I'm leaving this restroom a different person. All those so-called 'feelings' will be slaughtered tonight—laid to rest here in this room.

I scoff, "I was so stupid to love you."

His head snaps up, and his eyes are wide.

It's a gratifying sight right before I hurry away with my heels clicking on the tiles.

"Nora."

It sounds like panic and alarm ringing through his voice, but I don't stop.

"Nora. Nora. Wait."

His hand grips around my forearm, halting my much-needed departure, the firm grip of his hand sears into my skin. I dare to look into his eyes. My stomach wants to lurch with a flash of surrender thanks to the tears welling up in his rounded gaze, but it dies quickly. Hair tumbles off my shoulders as I toss my head back.

"You—" His chest rattles with broken air, and his voice falls apart for a moment. "You-you love me?"

Disgusting. Is that hope I hear?

His lips pinch up in the most remorseful-looking smile I've ever seen. "You really love *me?*"

A blast of ice couldn't make my heart colder. *He's pathetic.* I rip my arm from his hold and take a step back. "Not anymore."

Then, I walk out.

The last thing I hear is him calling after me, and honestly, I don't give a single fuck.

Because he killed the last one I had to give.

He killed it, along with my heart.

Chapter 26

Bentley

"**F**uck. Fuck. Fuck." I'm in the bathroom, squatting—my elbows on my knees, my hands over my face. Tears fall out of my eyes and absorb into my palms.

She loved me.

Rawness scrapes down my insides, making me bleed with an agony so deep it hurts to breathe. The truth stabs away at me like the heartless bitch it is, laughing in my face while I come to the realization of everything that's slipped away.

Nora was in love with me. Holy shit.

She didn't have a crush, and she didn't just like me—she *loved* me.

And I was too fucking dumb to ever see it, and I've hurt her who knows how many times. The knowledge of that—learning I've been a source of her pain—sends repulsion avalanching down on me. I can't even think about all the times I've done the things she's mentioned. They're innumerable. My gut wrenches itself in a hard wring.

I'm nothing but an undeserving piece of filth.

I thought I tarnished Nora by having sex with her, but that wasn't the worst of it. All these years, I've been destroying her.

and I didn't even know it—breaking off pieces of her heart and discarding them because I didn't know I had them. To put it plainly, I've fucked her over too many times to count.

And how I handled our time in the bathroom just now? Yeah. I fucked that up too.

I shouldn't have lied to her.

My eyes squeeze tighter, knowing my confession was right fucking there. I was so close to saying I'm in love with her.

Instead, I got scared, thinking she'd refuse me, so I used my Grandmother's story, and it blew up in my face—that's my own damn fault. If I'd been honest with her, she'd probably be in my arms right now, and I'd be soothing over a small part of the colossal damage I've caused.

Right now, I'd be worshiping her—kissing up and down her body, confessing how sorry I am for leaving her, telling her how much she completes me and how I couldn't get her out of my mind the whole time I was away. That the left side of my bed is *her* side and only hers.

Now she's gone.

A groan slides out. I hunch over more when acute nausea cuts at my insides. Gripping my fingers in my hair, the tight twisting of my heart implodes, tearing all of me into shreds. I rock back and forth. "Fuuuuck."

"Um. Excuse me."

My head jerks up at the feminine voice.

A short brunette stands above me, a look of bewilderment on her round face. "I think you're in the wrong room."

Pulling to my feet, I scrub over my face. "More like in the wrong body." Me and women. Ivy, Nora... this shitty life can't be mine. "Excuse me." My shoulder brushes against her while pushing past.

I'm not sure where I'm going, but I do know I need to get the fuck out of here and figure my shit out.

Going out the swinging metal door, I hook around the tiled exit.

"What the fuck did you say?" It's Rich's voice.

Two hands clasp around my shoulders. I swing with my left and miss. My dress shoes scuff along the floor as I'm shuffled to the side, spun around, then slammed into the wall.

The wind knocks out of my lungs—the surroundings circling all around me. Finally, I catch my bearings, and I'm staring at Rich. He's right in front of me, his large hands clutching at my shirt collar.

His jaw clenches. "I'll only ask you once more, what the fuck did you say?"

I scoff. "Why do you care, Rich? When have you ever cared about what happened to a woman?" My palms connect with his chest, and I shove him away.

He loses his footing, sliding a few inches before catching himself. He wisely keeps his distance, scowling while tugging at his shirt. "She left crying, so what did you say?"

"Crying?" A heavy pause blankets over me. Awful as that sounds, hope flickers in my chest. There might be a chance, a chance she still feels something for me.

You only cry if you feel. That's what Mom always says. And if she feels something for me—Fuck. I can't give up just yet.

"Bentley," he growls, interrupting my thoughts. "What did you say?"

I cross my arms. "I told her to stop sleeping with you."

He grunts, closes our gap, and grabs me by the shirt collar. "What's it to you, Bent, huh?" His grip tightens, and he jostles me enough to make aggravation flare in my veins. "Why do you care if she sleeps with me? When have you ever, *ever* cared who I've been with?"

Weighing my options, my breathing catches. I don't want to tell Rich anything, but…

No more lies.

They've been fucking me over for the last two years. I steady my determination and spew out the truth, finally allowing my heart to be on display.

"I'm in love with her."

Horror splashes across his face, and his tan color drains away. "No." That sickened look only lasts a second. His face goes red, and he pins me harder into the tiled wall.

My teeth grit, my heart pounding like a jackhammer with a fresh shot of adrenaline. "I swear to God, Rich, touch me one more time, and I'll break your fucking nose."

His hands drop, likely because he knows my five-foot-seven ass can still beat him in a fight. The upper hand is mine every time we box.

"When did you fall in love with her?" I hear the snarl working deep in his voice.

Shoving off the wall, I stand tall and tug at my mussed shirt. "Probably longer than I think, but I finally realized it last month."

"Before you left?" A deep crease forms between his brows.

My vision drops to the floor. "Yeah." My admittance is quiet—shame shatters through me like a wrecking ball. "The same night I left, actually. I took her home and...," I sigh, "And hurt her."

"No-no way."

I look up, and his face has gone white. My head cocks, confusion washing over me.

He gulps, and his eyes widen. "You?" The spiking in his voice sounds like disgust—when he points at me, his finger is trembling. "You're the one she's been crying over." A snarl seizes over his dark features. "I've been holding her, letting her cry in my arms this whole time, and it's over you? Do you have any fucking idea..."

"Any idea of what?"

His breathing quickens. Breaking away, Rich walks down the hall and punches the wall. "Fuck!" The word rings off every damn corner of the wall, sticking around as he storms back to me. "What I've been fighting, is you?" He bumps against my chest. "I oughta strangle you."

I should punch him, but the realization of what I'm witnessing hits me like a lightning bolt.

"Holy shit." My heart stops in my throat. I struggle to swallow as I look into Rich's eyes, catching sight of a fury I've never seen before. I never thought it was possible, but it's happened. My breath goes hot, like the rest of my body. "You're falling for her, aren't you? You of all people."

"Well, why shouldn't I? For once, I've met someone who's not a bitch. Nora has a heart." He eyes me up and down. "Why shouldn't I feel something for her? Why can't I have someone like her?"

Wow.

The one person I vowed would never get close to anyone I cared about has been embracing the woman I'm in love with—all because I ducked out and left. One mistake has jeopardized the person I care about the most.

Fuck my life.

I chuckle, but it's low and unhinged. Rich doesn't like it and shuffles back a step. I rake through my hair, shaking my head as I mull over what's happening right now— us fighting over the same girl, but if Rich thinks the road to Nora will be easy, he's mistaken.

"You're the biggest dick on the face of the planet." My lip pulls up in a sneer. "If anyone doesn't deserve her, it's you."

"At least I didn't hurt her."

"At least she doesn't love you," I growl. "She loves me. She said so tonight, and I'm going to get her back."

At least, I still hope so.

I move, and his hand grips on my shoulder. Disdain, hatred, contempt… it all flashes in his tight searing glare. He lowers his head, meeting my eyes. "Like hell you are." His eyes narrow. "Before you talk out of your ass, you need to remember who's been loving away all her pain."

The words should send a whirlwind of fury down my spine, but they don't. Determination coats every fiber in my body, and my chest puffs out. "Then she won't be sleeping with you for long—not when she only ran to you because she didn't have me."

Heat quickly flashes in his dark eyes. "Fuck you—" His arm hurls back for a punch, but it's an easy read since Rich doesn't possess a poker face.

Sweeping my foot behind his, I throw my hip into his back and grip the back of his shirt. I haul him over my body and flip him, smashing him into the ground, onto his back. A simple defense move I've learned in Judo classes.

He groans and winces, looking hazy and confused as he tries to focus on me.

My neck tightens up, and I shove my finger down in his face. "I told you not to touch me." Brushing off my shirt, I step over him. "Happy Birthday."

O'Malley's is disappearing in my rear-view mirror as I race home to figure out how I'm getting my girl back.

Maybe I was beaten in the bathroom, but right now, all that's coursing through me is rock-solid determination. Rich made a mistake in running his mouth... Nora isn't over me. Nora will never be over me because she's mine. She's always been *my* Nora, and now it's my turn to be hers.

I just need to find a way to see her again, and while I know that's going to be a battle, I don't care. I won't let Nora get away. Not without a fight.

Chapter 27

Nora

I'm sitting alone in my apartment, in baggy sweats and a t-shirt. It's been a week since I've seen Bentley and stormed out on him. He's called, texted, left voicemails and flowers on my front porch. I haven't responded, and the only thing that stirs in me when he reaches out is aggravation.

He should have given up by now, but if anything, my dismissal seems to have made him more hellbent. A call or text once a day was the norm, now he's doing it twice, sometimes three times.

The first few were apologies, but it's changed. Now it's always the same, be it text or voicemail—the consistency seems like he's written it down.

I'm not giving up on us. I'm begging you, give me a chance to show you I can be more. Please, at the very least, call.

But I'm not going to—if anything to make him pay for what he's done—to let him experience the hurt I went through when he ditched me. A minor punishment for putting up with his shit for over two years.

I frown when my cell phone goes off and I see yet another text from Rich. He's been trying to get a hold of me too, and

I haven't responded to him either. When I read the message, shame claws at my heart.

Hey. Call. Just wanna make sure you're okay.

Rich has done nothing wrong, but after the party, I can't even stomach the thought of looking at him. I guess my words about Bentley *not* ruining us were a big fat lie, because he did.

I don't even know how he did it—he just did. In his own Bentley way, he screwed everything up for me once more. *Fuck him.* At this point, I'm afraid the remnants of him will haunt me forever.

I sigh, looking at my TV that's been on a shopping channel for far too long. *Maybe I should move to Florida.* I haven't been at my new job that long, and while it's a good pharmacy, it's proving to be a very mediocre experience. At the moment, there's nothing left here for me.

My eyes glaze over while I envision sugary beaches, salty water, and threatening hurricane seasons. I'm flipping my arm over, wondering what I'd look like with a tan, when my phone rings.

It's Tessa. I pick it up and put it on speaker. "Hello?"

"Still brooding?"

"Why not?" I chew on the inside of my cheek. "There's nothing better to do."

"You could come to my place for pizza."

"No," I grumble and lay down on my side. "I've seen you every day this week. I don't want to see anyone."

"But I want to see you. Besides, sulking alone never made anyone feel better."

My eyes roll. "Tessa—"

"The pizza is from Johnny's... and it's stuffed crust."

I'm already sliding off the couch. That place is my favorite, but Tessa doesn't like them, so we always get something else. Plus the stuffed crust... Yes. I'm drooling just thinking about it. There's enough cheese and grease to make your ass grow just by looking at a slice, and the flavor is an orgasm to the mouth.

"I'll be there in a minute."

"Good." She sighs, "Because I'm sick at the thought of having to eat this by myself. Their pizza is shit."

I smirk. "You mean it's *the* shit."

She laughs, but it sounds strained.

I'm slipping on my shoes when my eyebrows furrow. "Is everything okay?"

"What do you mean?" Her voice breaks up.

Okay, something is going on. Tessa only sounds shaky when she's guilty about something. I come to a stop and scowl. "What are you up to?"

"Nothing." She clears her throat. "Just get here. I got this pizza for you." She hangs up before I can say anything.

I pull the phone away from my ear, looking at it with narrowed eyes. She's plotting something, but I have no idea what that is. As it is, I decide to go with it because a pizza from Johnny's is involved, and I can forego just about any trespass for that.

Leaving the house, I make the ten-minute drive to her place.

When I get there, I don't knock. She and I abandoned the knocking formalities a long time ago.

"Tessa?" Pushing the door closed behind me, I kick off my shoes, glancing around quizzically at the silence greeting me. "Hello?"

"I'll be right there, Nor." I finally hear her from down the hall. "The pizza is in the kitchen."

"Alright." I wander through the sunken living room, heading towards the kitchen archway. I go up one step and stop dead in my tracks.

"Hello, Nora."

My heart drops into my heels.

Bentley is here, right next to the box of pizza.

Fragments of You

Chapter 28

Bentley

Nora's eyes are wide, swirling with horror. She's also frozen. Her fingers are clutching into the wooden frame of the arch. She has one foot in the kitchen, one still on the step.

I ball my fists and take a nervous shuffle back. Even in sweats, her eyes sad and shattered, seeing her a week later leaves my heart drumming in my throat. I know this is the last place she expected to see me, but I'm here.

This week has stripped me to a new all-time low. Each time Nora didn't get back to me, it solidified how much I actually hurt her. It helped me realize the severity of my abuse of her—the burden was eventually too heavy, stealing my appetite and sleep. I knew I needed to do something, if anything, to offer a sincere apology for what had happened.

The bathroom didn't count.

I ended up calling Tessa out of desperation.

Honestly, I'm shocked Tessa even allowed this. But I'm only here because of Tessa's blessing, and don't get me wrong, getting this set up was hard. I've groveled to Tessa for three days straight for this chance. Even when she finally said yes, she still threatened to chop my dick off if I fucked this up.

The thought of dying at the hands of Tessa makes a weak smile wash over my mouth.

It breaks whatever hold was on Nora, and she retreats. She shakes her head. "No."

Instinctively, I rush for her. "Nora, please—"

"No." She turns around and bumps right into Tessa, who's seemingly appeared out of thin air. I hear a breath loosen from Nora while she looks up at her friend. "How could you?" The tone is overloaded with hurt, and it makes my heart ache.

Maybe I shouldn't have come.

But Tessa doesn't seem to feel that way. She grabs Nora by the wrist and tugs her down a step. "Come here. We're going to talk."

Nora protests, but follows.

Tessa doesn't take her far, just around the wall, down the hall where I can still hear everything. I fold my arms and lean against the edge of the counter, hoping on every damn star in the sky that my chance isn't lost before even beginning.

"Look," Tessa says. Her point-blank tone makes my neck tighten. "He's stupid. He's an idiot, but what happened in that bathroom didn't do anyone a lick of good. You don't have closure, and neither does he. What that talk accomplished was bringing on a whole new set of problems."

Nora sighs.

"And I swear," Tessa grunts, "That if I hear one more sigh out of you, I'm going to lose my damn mind."

"But-but—"

My pulse beats hard against my chest, and I wring my hands together. Just her voice does me in, and it makes me pray harder.

"This whole week has been ridiculous, Nora. You've been rude, snappy and I can't take it. I also can't fix it, so go in there, suck it up, and talk to him. I don't care what the outcome is. Kill him, choke him, kiss him, just get some real fucking peace out of this, once and for all, and stop living your life like an emotional train wreck."

Silence lingers for a long time. My head lifts at the soft sound of Nora.

"Yeah," she sniffles, "Okay."

I lose my breath, my fingers biting into the countertop, while my heart races at the speed of sound.

She's going to talk to me.

Holy shit... she's going to talk to me.

I owe Tessa my life because this talk I'm about to have is worth that. Nora's worth everything. My body tenses when they step into the kitchen together.

Nora breaks away, stands in front of the sink, and crosses her arms.

Tessa moves to leave.

"Thank you," I call out to Tessa.

She glances over her shoulder, long black hair whipping all around her. It's pure fury and reminds me why I stay away from Tessa Stevenson. The crack in her silvery orbs could make the dead quake with fear. The girl is a force—a reclusive container full of fire. Poke at her, and she'll explode.

She gives me a once-over and squints. "Don't you dare expect me to do anything like this again. You have me convinced that you care, but I won't be betraying Nora's trust like this again." She arches her brow. "Make your one chance count."

I nod. "Understood."

Her lithe frame goes around the corner, disappearing for now, but I know she's not far, and she won't hesitate to throw me out on my ass if I botch this the way I did at Rich's party.

Right. Make it count.

One shot at convincing the girl I love that what I threw away isn't what I wanted. I take a hard gulp and slowly shuffle forward one step. My heart wants to shred apart at the seams when I see the hurt swirling in Nora's gaze. She won't look at me—her eyes are glued to the floor.

Examining her, I see how wounded and broken she is. I know I'm the source of it. My stomach lurches into my throat, and I blink back a tear.

Fuck. How could I have been so blind?

I was wrong when I told Rich he didn't deserve Nora. If anyone fits that category, it's me, but here I am just the same, hoping she'll see some sort of worth or potential in what we had.

"Nora."

She flinches, and sharp pains prickle up my skin.

My shoulders drop, and I try again. "Nora."

No flinch this time.

"Please. Please look at me."

She shakes her head and flicks her gaze to the wall. "I can't."

"Why?" I close more of our gap, my heart tromboning between my stomach and throat. "Because you hate me, or because it's too painful?"

She scoffs. "What difference does it make?"

"All the difference." I shrug and pocket my hands. "One means everything we had between us is dead—the other is…" I sigh. "Hope. Hope that maybe we can start again."

She hugs herself tightly, sealing herself away.

"Pain can heal, Nora. Fractures can be mended. But hate?" I shake my head, my heart weighted in my chest. "Hate only turns into bitterness. So…," my throat goes dry, "Do you hate me? Honestly, I wouldn't blame you if you did, but I'm hoping you don't."

"I…" she pauses, collecting a deep breath, "I don't know what I feel." Finally, she looks at me. Those sugary brown eyes I love getting lost in are marred with sorrow, and I don't recognize them as her brows furrow. "God. Do you have any idea how you've made me feel all this time?"

"No." I'm not going to bullshit her. I want to say I understand, but I really haven't a fucking clue, so I don't say it. "I don't, Nora. I really don't. And I'm not going to stand here and pretend like I do. All I can tell you is that I'm so incredibly sorry."

Brown eyes become wet with tears, and it drives me deeper into my penance, whipping down my back in vicious strokes until my hands shake.

"I'm sorry for everything, Nora." Sorrow weaves through my body and voice. I want to hold her, but I can't—to show her how much I regret my actions, but I don't know how. The only thing I can offer is the apology that should have been hers in the first place. My words pour out on their own, my usual filter disintegrating the longer I look at her.

"I'm sorry for running out on you. Sorry for not noticing your worth. Sorry for being a fool and thinking I had so little when in reality, I had it all. Sorry for not telling you sooner how much you mean to me. You're so important to me, Nora. I'm sorry I failed to see that, and I'm sorry I failed to show you when I discovered it."

She coils away from me, and her lip quivers.

My voice breaks, a weight bearing down on my shoulders that could drag me into the ground. "If I could go back and do it over, I'd change so many things… but the only thing I would change is myself. Not you. Never you." A tear spills out my eye and trickles down my face.

She sniffles and studies me. At first, I don't think she's going to say anything, but then she speaks at last, "Why did you leave me? After we had sex, why did you leave?"

I can't look at her when I say it. The truth of my actions brings so much shame on my head, I wish I could cover it up—but unlike my time in the bathroom, I'm not going to lie.

"I was scared. I discovered how much you mean to me, and I couldn't tell you." My voice waivers, and I have to grit my teeth together to continue, "I had my fucking heart ripped out by a girl I was with. All these years it made me think I wasn't enough. I know that was a lie now, but I never should have ran out—I hate thinking I might have made you feel the same way."

Her mouth falls open. "Oh my God." She sounds like she wants to cry. "You really think this is going to fix everything?"

"It was a mistake, Nora." I step up as close as I'll allow myself as my heart twists painfully behind my ribs. "A stupid, cowardly mistake, and I'll live the rest of my life regretting it—regretting how I misused and hurt you. I'm not going to kid myself, I'll never be able to erase that moment, but I'm going to try."

She wipes tears away from her face. "How? How can you do that?"

"By doing whatever it takes to care for you. I mean it, Nora. If you give me another chance, I'll prove it to you. Prove that I'm more than just the mess you saw. I used to be more. I can be that again—I know I can."

The words knead themselves deep into my being while I speak them, binding in me a new strength. The Bentley who lived in fear and selfishness is dying and resurrecting—I'm returning to what I once was. The protector Dad raised me to be, I can only hope I'm not too late.

Her eyes narrow in a look of disdain. "That's a lot of big talk for someone who's never done anything good for me."

"It's not talk," I add vigor to my voice. "I mean it, Nora. Every damn word. All I need is one more chance."

She lets out a bitter laugh. "You really think you deserve that?"

"No." I shake my head, agony running a wicked course through my body. I hate admitting this, but it's the truth. "I don't deserve anything, especially not you."

No more lies.

Not now. Not ever.

"Wow." She looks away from me. Her gaze goes glassy, and she scoffs.

Shit. I'm losing her. I'm watching my moment crumble apart, and I'm fracturing along with it. I hate this. Even if it's what I deserve. I squeeze my eyes closed, fighting the blackness scratching at the edges of me. If this fails, what will I do?

How do I live?

How do I live without my heart? Because that's what she's holding... all of it, and it's hers to shatter or to nurture. Either way, I don't want it back, even if she won't have me. It will mean that I'll die lonely, but I'll die belonging only to one person, and I can't think of a sweeter way to go out—her prisoner forever.

My eyes fly open at her huff. When I look at her, I see coldness and disconnection.

A jolt of panic shocks my core.

Her mouth snarls up. "You know, I don't think I've ever met a more stup—"

"Go out with me." I throw the words out—a desperate last chance attempt to keep a connection I'm not worthy of. My pulse hammers against my neck while I speak.

She goes quiet, blinks a few times, then tilts her head. "Why on earth should I go out with you?'"

I hunch my shoulders. "I can't think of a single reason why you should." That's the pathetic truth, but there it is. If I'm going to stick to bearing my heart out and showing Nora all of me, this is the start.

I take advantage of the silence when she doesn't say anything and gives me a baffled look instead.

"I'm not saying I deserve you, Nora." I frown, letting my soul bleed truths that I've tucked away. "God." Tears blur my sight of her. "After everything I've done, I'm the person that deserves you the least." I brush the moisture away with the heel of my palm. "But when I look at you," I give her a once over, loving how fast my heart beats when I look at her and sigh, "The way my heart feels convinces me I'm the person that wants you the most."

Something new breaks in her gaze—I don't recognize it. She shakes her head and presses her back against the countertop. "Don-don't say things like that."

"I can't help it, Nora. I want to show you who I am, and I won't apologize for it." I rake through my hair, the desire to hold her consuming me like a flame. Instead, I force my distance and press my ass against the ledge of the counter. "I'll apologize for all the ways I hurt you. I'll do that for as long as I live, but I won't say I'm sorry for showing you how much I care."

Her shoulders bunch up, and her eyes widen.

The urge to ask her again forces the second request out of my mouth. "Please, Nora. Go out with me. Three dates."

"Three?" She looks disgusted as her nose pulls up.

I nod, the resolution setting me on a challenging course that I can't stop. "Three. Three dates so I can treat you the way I should have all along. Please." My voice is a plea. "I'm begging you. Please."

The disgust is quickly replaced. Something that looks like borderline anger smooths over her face. She tosses her head back and nods. "Fine."

My spine straightens.

Did she really just say yes?

I freeze and arch my brow, waiting for her to change her

mind. She doesn't.

Instead, Nora shoves off the back of the sink and stands up straight. "You have three dates, Bentley." Her voice isn't warm, but it isn't cruel either—disconnected would be the word I'd choose.

"Thank you." I don't care what this is on her part, but I'm going to accept it. I smile softly. "How about this Friday?"

"Sure." She's already moving for the exit of the kitchen.

"Dress nice."

"Yeah, okay."

That's the last thing I get her to acknowledge before she leaves. There's not a glance back as she leaves the house, firmly shutting the door behind her.

And after she's left, emptiness settles in the room and my heart. All I can hear is a faint buzzing of the fridge as the hollowness expands, eating up the air around me.

Tessa doesn't come out right away, so I stand there and huff out a large breath. "Shit." I rumple through my hair.

Three dates. That's all I have to make someone whom I've broken see that I can be better.

Fuck, that's not a lot of time.

Chapter 29

Nora

"Shit, Nor." Tessa places my tea next to me and sits in the adjacent chair. "If you're hating the idea of going out with him this much, then why did you agree?"

"Honestly?" I drag the mug closer but leave it on the table. "It felt good. After all this time, it felt good to watch him beg." I pucker my lips, looking over at the sink, replaying the experience.

The satisfaction that hummed through me when he said the word 'beg' was the most gratifying experience ever. The word on my ears was amazing. Like music, really. After all these years, he's begging *me* for attention, and knowing I can shut him off whenever I want, is a serious reason to rejoice.

I pick up the drink. "I'll go out with him these three times, use his money, then dump his simpering ass." A smirk lifts my mouth. "It will be fun."

"Good grief." Tessa scowls and tucks her legs under her. "Nora, what the hell is wrong with you lately? Do you hear yourself?"

"I certainly do." Her tone bristles my feelings the wrong

way, causing aggravation to spike. I return her scowl. "I fail to see what I'm doing wrong."

"How about everything." She waggles her finger. "The Nora Davis I knew, never would have done something like this. Damn." She slumps into her chair. "I feel sorry for Bentley."

"What?" My nose scrunches up. "Are you and Bentley buddy-buddy now? I thought you hated him."

Her face dulls. "I hate everyone—you know that. Although, I disliked him more than most. However…" She yanks up the slipping shoulder of her top. "I could see it when I talked to him, Nor, he feels awful for what he did. I used to think he was hurting you intentionally. Now I'm certain he's just an idiot."

My head jerks back. "But he ran out on me—"

"And he regrets it." She gives me a lopsided frown. "I think you should give him a chance."

My mouth dangles open. "Give him a chance? Why I nev––"

"Nora, he cried." She sits her tea down with an authoritative thunk and looks dead into my eyes.

The air deadens around me. "What-what do you mean 'he cried'?"

"How many ways can you interpret that?" She looks down and traces her finger along the tabletop. "When he came by my work to talk to me about you, he legit cried. If you had told me eight months ago that Bentley Harris would cry over losing you, I would have laughed. But I saw it for myself." She half frowns, and her voice softens. "He cares about you, Nora. This isn't an act."

Something about the way she says it wraps around my heart, daring me to tenderize the hardness I've built up for him. I freeze that feeling away. I can't let that happen. My fingers grip tightly around the mug. "You're wrong. You'll see that you are."

Pfft. She shakes her head. "Whatever."

I'm about to retort when my phone goes off. It's a text from Bentley. Our date is in about two hours. Looking at the text, a groan bubbles up in my throat.

Just a reminder. Make sure you dress nice.

My face sours. Why is he so intent on making me dress nice? I'm calling it now—all we're going to do is grab some sushi and sit in strained silence. Bentley's a playboy, not a dater, and I guarantee that unless it involves planning how to dick someone down, that he'll fail miserably at anything romantic. I doubt he has an ounce of romance coursing through his veins. Tonight is going to suck.

However, I also won't miss the opportunity to make him hurt when he sees me. If he wants me dolled up, so be it. It's not like he's getting anything from me.

"Thanks for the tea." Looking at Tessa, I scoop my phone off the table and stand. "I'm going to leave so I can get ready."

"Okay." She stands and collects the mugs.

I'm halfway out of the kitchen when her voice catches my ear. "Hey, Nor."

"Yeah?" I crane over my shoulder, freezing when catching sight of her stare. It's stone-cold stoic, and intimidating. A gulp gets stuck in my throat, and my voice is weak. "What is it?"

"Don't be a bitch tonight. You're better than that."

Am I though? I don't feel like I am anymore. But I don't dare voice that. All I do is nod, then I leave.

When six o'clock hits, I'm wearing a black dress that's snug fitting with a daring neckline—one that tempts but doesn't show. Perfect for what I'm planning tonight.

I'm also nervous, with each pump of blood racing faster than expected, and my palms are clammy. When the doorbell goes off, my pulse thumps even quicker, and I freaking hate it. Going for the door, my lips pinch in disgust.

Why do I still react to him? God knows he doesn't deserve any reactions from me. But while I can't control it, maybe I can stop him from noticing. I plaster on a wooden expression and yank open the door.

My outward countenance is challenged at the sight of Bentley. My fingers clutch into the door handle.

He looks hotter than ever in a white button-up with a black blazer, and I can already smell him—the airy fragrance that always feels so right makes my stomach flutter.

No. I won't descend this quickly. Three dates. Then I'm done. I trap the butterflies, sealing them away, dooming them to a dark pit—but they release and pound in thunderous flaps when he gives me a once over and sighs.

"God, Nora." I swear he sounds breathless. I hate it. "You're so incredibly beautiful."

There's so much candor in his voice. It zings through my body, electrifying my shoulders and limbs. I go slack-jawed, staring at him.

He cocks his head, meeting my gaze. "Haven't I ever told you that before?"

All I do is shake my head. I'm afraid to speak, scared I'll say *thank you* and open my heart to him in the process. That's not what I'm here for.

"Then I'm sorry this is my first time to tell you that." He almost smiles. "I'll make sure it's not my last."

I don't respond. With my lingering silence, he looks down at his shoes and bounces off his toes. An awkward silence descends like a low brewing cloud, and I welcome it.

"Oh—" it shatters when he clears his throat, and a rustle occurs. I didn't notice it until now, but he's had one hand pinned behind him this entire time. "Here." He sweeps his arm around and sticks it out. "These are for you."

I gasp at the dozen red long-stemmed roses—complete with baby's breath poking out. I'm smacked in the face by the gesture. Fuck-boys don't bring flowers. They bring condoms—but I mustn't think about that. Squeezing that thought of surrender away, my trembling fingers graze the plastic surrounding the bouquet.

I gulp, "Th-thank you." My line of vision falls to the ground, and a flush climbs in my cheeks. *Shit.* A stupid bundle of flowers is undoing me. I regather my senses and try to strengthen my voice. "Let me put these in some water."

With them in hand, I dart further into the house and find a vase under the sink. I can't ignore the fact that Bentley has stepped inside and is walking around. He's been in my apartment a few times, but tonight, I wish he wasn't. He doesn't belong in my safe place anymore.

I chuck the flowers in water as quickly as possible then head for the front door.

What follows is a dance so awkward it could put a circus to shame.

We move, dodge, and shift around while he tries to get the front door for me, then it's the same outside while we figure who should lead the way. The car isn't any better as he escorts me and lets me in. Our whole exchange is full of throat clearing, shuffles, and mumbled apologies. When I finally sit down in the leather seat, I steal a loud exhale and try to dispel the blush overtaking my body.

The effort is short-lived.

He climbs into the driver's side, and my senses go mad. His clean scent fills the car and, with it, my nostrils. My knees involuntarily weaken, and I don't know why because bitterness sweeps through my veins—the twisted damage of everything he's done—nettles my blood, and I know that's the only thing I should be aware of.

Not him. I shouldn't be noticing him and the fact he's recently had a haircut. I also shouldn't be noticing that he's nicked himself while shaving. It's a small spot near the collar, but I see the red mark and can't help but wonder if it hurt. I seal my eyes shut. *No. No.*

"Thank you for joining me tonight."

My spine stiffens, and my eyes fly open. When I look over, those his eyes are warm pools of tenderness, and the look in them is like a key, scratching and fiddling at the locked entrance of my heart.

I respond by throwing on another deadbolt. "We said three dates, but you know I may not do another one." I force the coolness of my voice.

"Oh… oh." A tight smile pulls at his mouth, it looks like it's desperately masking hurt and rejection, but I never hear it in his voice. "I know." He breaks my gaze and starts the car. "I'm just glad that I have one chance. It's not enough…" His voice softens. "A million dates would never be enough to show you how important you are, but at least I have one chance." He drives out of my parking lot.

Damn. That wasn't the answer I expected. Guilt jumbles my insides. I avert my head to stare out the window. My attention is forced to him again when his soft sigh catches my ear. Glancing over, there's a small smile tugging at the corner of his mouth.

My brows furrow. "What?" The question comes out more cordial than I want.

He touches the top button of his shirt, "I'm nervous." His voice is so gentle, yet it sounds so happy.

"Nervous?" I scoff, but it lacks harshness—he's depleting me of that right now. "I didn't think you ever got nervous."

He chuckles. "Then I've done a good job faking it." His index finger tugs at his collar, and he squirms. "I'm always nervous around you, Nora."

"No way." My shoulders bunch up, and my pulse throttles against my neck. "You," I force a deep breath, "You always made *me* nervous." The confession stumbles out, even though I'm trying to strangle it away.

"*Hmp,*" he laughs. "Then I'm sorry. Sorry I was too blind to see that there was always a possibility of *us.*"

What should be a gentle statement ends up threading a strand of contempt through my soul. I open my mouth to give a snappish reply, but it dies on my tongue when I notice Bentley turning the opposite way of the sushi house.

I grip at the seat belt, clenching my fingers into it. "We aren't going for sushi?"

"Sushi?" His face bunches up. "Hell no. Sushi is… well…," his shoulders lift then drop, "…it's just sushi. That won't do for tonight. I promised you a date." His voice purrs at the end, and my thighs almost want to squeeze together like they used to when he'd use that tone.

Chewing on the inside of my mouth, apprehension threatens to corrode through my composure. "I didn't think you'd know how to date."

His head jerks to me, and one of his brows is raised. "There's a lot you don't know about me, Nora." He shifts around in the seat, repositioning. "I've been on a lot of dates."

A lot. The word kneads hurt into my sternum. I stare at the floor. *Why does it bother me to hear that?* I conceal a frown.

"But it was with the wrong person."

My response is a side-eye glance since I'm afraid of what I'll feel if I look at him head-on.

"Nora," his voice croaks. "I hope you'll give me a chance." I notice his white-knuckled grip on the wheel. "I've made so many mistakes—give me a chance to fix one of them."

A huff leaves my mouth. "And what mistake would that be?"

Lines form deep between his brows, but his eyes never leave the road. "Not cherishing you sooner."

Shit. Those words are like Cupid's arrow to my soul. I don't say anything. It's the only way to keep the padlocks that are guarding me intact.

Bentley falls silent too.

The quiet that settles between us is thick—so thick it's choking me. It's awkward, but I'm doing all I can to use it to my advantage. *Three dates.* I keep repeating it. *Three dates, then hang him high and dry.* It won't be hard—it will be what he deserves. The occasional softness I feel for him will fade. I just need to keep my focus intact.

Some time passes, and soon, I think the disdain I'm trying hard to infuse is finally taking hold. He goes down a quiet street that's lit with soft streetlights.

Then he turns the corner.

My throat drops into my feet, and I can't tell if it's horror or shock mixing in me. A knot forms in my stomach, and I fold my arms across my middle. "Flambé's?" I barely get the word out.

He's taken me to Flambé's—a restaurant so expensive, prices aren't on the menu. I've never been because reservations are booked out months in advance, and my pocketbook cries at the thought of eating here. My fingers creep down my skirt, and

I clutch the hem. "Bent…" A breath rattles loose when he parks. We are definitely eating here. "Bentley, you shouldn't have—"

"Nonsense." He switches off the engine and turns in his seat to look at me. "I should have brought you here a long time ago." I swear his eyes glow in the light.

My heart hammers against my ribs. He undoes his seat belt, and the sound fills the car.

"Come on." He winks. "Let's go on a date." Sliding out, he comes around to my side and opens the door.

I can tell Bentley wants to offer me his arm, and I'm almost tempted to accept it. My knees sway and threaten to buckle with each step after I've exited the vehicle, but I don't cave in to the temptation. Wringing my hands around my clutch, I use that for support instead.

Stepping inside, I stifle a gasp as my mouth hangs open.

It's everything you'd expect. Dim lighting, chandeliers everywhere, and a dark floor with a sheen so intense I can see myself in the reflection. I opt to stand back while Bentley strolls up the front and gives his name for the reservation.

My inward composure isn't any stronger when we're promptly escorted to our table. The restaurant is quiet, and our booth is perfect—isolated, located at the end of the line, and it's something I would have picked. He could only pick this if he remembered things about me—an idea that I'm loathing.

Sitting across from him, heat spikes in my blood. I've been avoiding his gaze as much as possible so far, but it's going to be harder to do now—especially after we're done ordering. That process goes by way too fast, thanks to the limited items. This place specializes in imported wagyu beef, bacon-wrapped medallions, and filet mignon, so the selection is small.

We both order the steak, and Bentley places an order for a vintage red. I can't even begin to ballpark the price tag without being nauseous.

With no food and only water and olives to pass the time, waiting becomes strained, at least for me. Bentley seems to be far more composed than me as I struggle not to wiggle like a mad woman in my seat. I find myself pressing my spine into the black and gold jacquard seat back when he places his forearms on the table and interlocks his fingers.

"Nora, if there's anything you want to ask me, I'm an open book." His posture rounds. "I'm sorry it's taken me this long, but I'm not going to keep secrets from you anymore." A softness rolls across his gaze. "Whatever you want of me, Nora, you can have it."

I steady my breath, my blood racing a million miles an hour. He can't see it, but my nails are digging into my thighs. Hearing him talk like this is stamping down the deadness I'm so desperately fighting to conjure up. Right now, he's everything I ever wanted. I've envisioned this in the last two years, and while I know it's for the best, throwing it away is so damn hard to do. But I have to. Because we aren't worth anything together. Not anymore.

"Nora?"

My thoughts derail at Bentley's voice.

"Do you have anything you want to ask?"

My eyes scan the room, and at first, I don't think I do, but that turns out to be a lie. I look at him through my lashes. "What did you do while you were away?" I barely hear my own question while I drag my finger across the table-top in small circles.

"I thought about you." His admittance is soft, and his head drops. When he looks at me again, a ghost of a smile presses on his mouth. "I think I thought about you the entire time."

Why does he keep talking to me like this? The tenderness brings heat to the ice caging around me, and I work hard to strengthen my resolve. I grit down on my teeth, recalling the way he fucked and dashed. Honestly, it helps. I feel the coolness of disdain returning once again.

"What did you do?"

"Spent a lot of time with Rich." I shoot the name out because I think it's going to feel good.

It doesn't.

I can't win tonight. Regret brews in my stomach when I watch him trying to hide a wince while looking away.

He doesn't make eye contact, but his voice is gentle and low. "Was he uh…," he clears his throat, "Was he good to you?" He looks up at me, tentativeness pulling across his features. "He can be…" Air collects in his cheeks. It looks like he's thinking hard, trying to decide on what to say.

The whole time, I'm sick. I don't know why I decided to say anything when I didn't even sleep with Rich. I'm regretting the dig. "He can be what?" My voice is quiet.

"Well… let me put it this way." He makes an uncomfortable-looking shift in his seat. "I'm stupid. I do and say a lot of things without putting a lot of thought into it. But, him?" He shakes his head. "Rich can be insensitive, on purpose." At last, his gaze meets mine, and I see streaks of sadness tearing through his eyes. "So, was he nice to you?"

The question is the saddest sounding thing I've ever heard. Remorse floods up, swallowing around my heart. I bob my head twice. "He was." My voice is unstable.

"Good."

Oh, God. I swear it looks like he's about to cry.

I watch moisture climb up in his eyes. Then he clears his throat and looks towards the general direction of the restaurant.

Shame washes down my body like an unholy bath. It starts at my roots and ends at my feet. Suddenly I desperately want to confess that I never slept with Rich and that I compared him to Bentley almost every chance I got, but I can't. I can't tell if it's from the pain of Bentley's betrayal or an inner working of my own fears, but the words fade before they hit my mouth.

I attempt to change the subject. "How were your sister and your parents?"

"Mmm." I still notice the sadness, but some of it retreats with a small grin. "They were good. Me and Lena had a lot of good talks."

"About… uh… us?" Once the question is out, I feel stupid. Curiosity shouldn't be here for me. I reach out for my water glass and take a sip.

"Some of it." His line of vision falls to the tabletop. "One night, we talked about something that happened a long time ago. Something that…" He takes a breath, shifting his shoulders from side to side. "Well, it happened and left an impact on how I deal with relationships."

My mind flits back to the kitchen at Tessa's. I recall him

saying he was in a relationship and that she cheated on him. *Is that why he cycled through women so fast?* Perhaps the occurrence left a mark on his heart, and he didn't feel safe with anyone. Suddenly my judgment changes. I try to stop it, but pity for him wraps down my soul, and I want to understand him more.

Rhythmically I tap my finger on the stem of my water glass. "Was it about that girl you mentioned at Tessa's?"

His head bounds up. I see uncertainty pinching at the corners of his eyes. His throat bobs with a swallow, and he nods. "Yes." He takes a deep breath. "Her name was Ivy and—"

"Your wine, Sir." The Sommelier appears at the table, with our red.

It silences our conversation during his presentation as Bentley tastes the wine and approves it. Soon the only sound that occurs is the trickling of the liquid as my glass is filled.

When he leaves, he takes the momentum of our discussion with him. I don't know how to circle back to our original discussion, so I hope Bentley does. My shoulders tense while we take our sip.

"Take a sip," Bentley observes the wine in his glass and smiles. "It's a good Cabernet."

He doesn't, and I can't find a way to ask him about what happened without feeling weird.

The rest of our dinner seems more subdued, and we talk about small things like his family and my new job. All the banter we once had is non-existent, but in its place, something more profound is sweeping in.

I still see fragments of the old him, pieces that made me notice him in the first place—his good humor, love for his family, the drive he has for his job and to be successful, his consideration of ensuring my comfort when we're together. Those areas are the same, but I see more.

Tonight, mixing in with the old version, I notice a warmth and attention for me that wasn't there before, one that's more than kindness and teeters towards devotion. It's tenderly soothing over the ache he left me with.

His regard tendrils around my heart with each gentle look he gives me—it begins choking out the thorns of hate I've planted. Every soft compliment he feeds me encapsulates around my hardened soul, melting at the raw edges he placed there. And I'm trying to ignore it, but I see uncertainty, shyness, and hesitation for the first time since knowing him. It comes through with each stutter or pause he takes, and it bends the stiffness I've resurrected in me.

His words loop in my brain. *"I'm always nervous around you."* Now I'm left wondering if this "new" side I'm seeing is new at all…and if it's not, then I have a lot more to contend with than I initially thought.

By the time dinner is over, and he's escorted me home, questions riddle me, forcing me to ask myself how far I'm willing to take this—how calloused I'm willing to make myself. The truth is, I'm not sure. When I undo the lock to my front door and face him, my fingers are biting into my clutch.

Moonlight spills over half his face, allowing me a final look at the eyes that have been too soft and understanding tonight, the ones that have been silently challenging me to give him one more chance. He smiles and goosebumps pucker on my arms.

"Goodnight, Nora." He pockets his hands and takes a step back. "I had a good time with you tonight." He gives me a once-over and sighs. "I don't know if you're still up for it, but I'd like to take you out again."

I nod before I even realize I'm doing it, "Sure." I try to infuse detachment in my voice, but it doesn't sound as convincing as before.

The smile reaches his eyes, and my head swims. "Great." His tone is so, so gentle— my limbs can't help but wilt. "Does Tuesday night work?"

I nod again but don't say anything.

The keys chime as he slides them out his pocket and gestures for me to go inside. "Wonderful. I'll pick you up at the same time."

My lips stay sealed. I step inside, shut the door, and listen to his retreating footsteps.

After I hear his car pulling out the parking lot, I rest my back against the door and slide my spine down until I'm sitting.

All I can hear is the thudding of my heart. I place my hand

over my chest, hoping to steady it. Looking up at the ceiling, I push out a deep breath. "Two more dates." My eyes close at the reminder. That's all I have left. Two more dates until I can wash my hands forever and be done with what we are... and thank God for that—because if this is the real Bentley Harris, and I think it is, then my heart wants him more than I ever thought was possible.

Chapter 30

Bentley

I'm smoothing down my shirt one last time while exiting the car to pick up Nora. Excited as I am for another opportunity, my nerves are strung high.

Saying our first date had rough patches would be the understatement of the year—and while her comments about Rich didn't help, I can't blame her for saying them. Rich was there for her when I wasn't. It sounds like he spent the whole damn month with just her, and I have to give him some credit. That's an eternity for him. So while having him rubbed in my face hurt, it wasn't the worst part.

The hardest thing was putting myself out there with Nora. Razing down the walls of protection and revealing my true inner self required a lot of willpower, and it scared the shit out of me. I haven't been vulnerable with someone in years, so it was difficult—especially since I know her heart isn't in it.

However, I also observed conflict. I know Nora, and it was there. Try as she may, she can't hide from me, and I know she remembers who we were. That makes hope spark that I can make her feel us again. Even with that hope, however, my hands shake as I go up to the front door. I opt for a knock instead of ringing the doorbell, and it's timid as hell.

A second passes, and I hear a light creaking. My pulse takes flight when the door cracks open, and she pokes her head out.

One look, and she's already calling to me. The urge to hold her, kiss her, shower her with my burning affection racks through my arms. Instead, I force myself a step back, my fists clenching. "Hello."

She ducks her head in a small nod of acknowledgment and steps outside.

My eyes can't stop roving her. She's picked jeans and a soft-looking sweater. The jeans hug at her hips just right, and the sweater is so her. Loose, elegant, dangling around her shoulders just enough to have me hoping it slips. It's perfect since we're not doing anything formal tonight.

A wide smile breaks across my mouth. "You look beautiful." I don't say it loud. Soft is how I've been with her, and it's not totally by choice. Anytime I'm addressing her, my tongue and tone overpower me, picking their own path of sentiment. A wicked lash of want strikes down my spine when a faint pink hits her cheeks.

"Thank you." Her voice is small while accepting the compliment, but she still acknowledged it, unlike the last time. She slinks past me, and my pulse hums with contentment while I tag behind.

She's different.

I already feel it. The frigidness that slammed me off from her the last time isn't as concrete tonight. Maybe that means we can discuss what happened.

It's the root of our hurt, and it needs to be addressed before we can move forward. I pocket my hands and silently exhale. I'm prepared to do anything to win Nora back, but it can't happen if I don't try to work through the scars I left her with. I'm hoping that when she sees her present, it will help that much more.

When I open her side of the door, I hold my breath.

"Oh." She stills, looking at the small box wrapped in gold paper on the seat. Two wary eyes look at me, but there's a minute smile pressing on her sugary mouth. "What... uh... what is it?"

I jerk my head for the car. "Get inside and open it."

She slides into the vehicle.

I shut the door and walk around. The whole time, I'm tapping my knuckle against my thighs. I bought Nora perfume––I'm just hoping I bought the right one. We went Christmas shopping together for our families over a year ago, and she raved over a particular scent while picking something out for her sister. The way she gushed over it was adorable, but she didn't buy it. I ended up remembering the smell because it left me wondering what it'd be like to lose myself in that fragrance. I'm still curious about it to this day. However, that's not why I'm buying it for her now. Now I just want to treat her like I should have been doing all along.

My eyes squeeze close.

Please. Please, let me have gotten this right.

A mistake isn't what I need. I climb in, shut the door, and look over––nervous energy raising up the hairs on my arms. Thankfully relief floods in when I see the look on her face.

She's clutching the bottle in her hand, and her eyes are wide staring at it. "You remembered me liking this?"

I nod while my throat dries up. "I did. *I do.*"

Her brows furrow, and she shakes her head. "But that was over a year ago." Looking at me, she seems baffled. "Bentley––"

"I remember how happy it made you. I remember––" My eyes briefly flick to the steering column, "––thinking how beautiful your smile was and how you couldn't stop smelling it." When I wrap my fingers around the gear shift, my grip is tight. The same occurrence happens in my heart––it wrings itself tight.

A sigh slips out of her. "I still don't––"

"I just remember, Nora." My secrets break open to her, falling at her feet. I hope she picks them up. "Even when I'm not trying, I always remember *you.* I wish I would have noticed it sooner."

She says nothing, but I see something working hard in those eyes of hers.

I hope it's good.

I don't have the courage to ask. Her refusal will break me,

and I don't know how she's lived the last two years watching me act like a fool. Reproach for my actions smears down my body, making me feel filthy, and wetness hits my vision.

I stop it by putting the car into drive since I'm sure the last thing she wants right now is my display of emotions. She has enough of her own to process right now. "Let's go on our date."

She nods, clutching the bottle, and it could be my imagination, but it looks closer to her heart than it did a moment ago.

Silence creeps while driving. Nervous anticipation climbs higher in me with each passing mile as we leave the city lights. She's not asking questions, and I can't tell if that's good or bad because she has to notice that we're not going to a restaurant. I've decided to take her to the field. The one I always go to when I want to stargaze—a spot I consider sacred.

I don't even know if she'll like it, but if I want her to understand me better, I have to be willing to show her who I am, no matter how small it is.

We still haven't spoken a word when I whip up to the electric fence near the entrance of the field several moments later. It's only after I kill the engine that Nora speaks.

"What is this place?" She ducks her head around, looking out the windows.

I reach for the seat behind me, "Our date."

Her face dulls. "Really?"

Pulling a basket from the back seat, I place it on the console between us. "Fine." I flip open one side of the basket. "If you don't like to call it our date, call it therapy."

"Therapy?" Her echo is confused.

"More specifically, my therapy." I reach inside and fish out a plate. Then, I pull out the first item of food... spinach dip. "I come here when I need to sort things out, but nobody knows that." After digging out her preferred style of crackers and a few slices of garlic bread, I pass the plate on.

Accepting it, she looks down at it and blinks, "My favorites?" She sounds stunned.

"That's not all of them—I have more." Reaching in further, I pull out grapes, sharp cheddar cheese, apricot jam, and a fig and goat cheese crumble I know she likes. I place them on one side of the basket one by one.

Her mouth is agape as she takes it all in.

Closing the lid, I point to the back. "There's cheesecake and chilled Moscato too. They're in a cooler."

Two brown eyes dart around the car, and I know it's shock I'm witnessing. I nailed every favorite she has, and it wasn't that hard to do—more proof that I've noticed everything about her for far longer than I've realized.

Finally, she slinks back into her seat and takes a bite of her cracker and spinach dip. She keeps eating, but it's in total silence, and each bite seems timid. Eventually, I end up eating a few grapes, just so I can hear myself chew since the silence is deafening, and it's not going anywhere.

I didn't expect an evening full of jokes, but I thought there'd at least be some talking—we need to have some sort of talk, but I don't know if I should be the one bringing things up. I don't want to push her away even more.

Trying to kill the lull that has anxiety poking at me, I look in the back and extend my hand towards the cooler. "Would you like some wine?"

"Not really."

My blood freezes at the tone. It's cold—colder than our first date.

Fuck.

I jerk my head up and look across.

Double fuck.

She's squinting, staring at me so hard my heart recoils inside my rib cage. I take a breath, and it's so fucking loud I know she hears it. The unyielding look plastered across her feminine features doesn't soften. In fact, her eyes narrow even more.

My shoulders tense. "What?"

She examines me for a flash—then, serious lines deepen on her face. "This is nice, Bentley. Obviously, you've proven me wrong." She gestures at the food. "You know how to plan dates, you know how to say sweet things, but I need more. Sweeping things aside won't work for me."

I exhale, bunched-up muscles releasing from their torrid knot. "I'm not looking to brush things away." She doesn't know it, but I've been waiting for this. Repositioning myself, I angle to face her better. "I didn't want to force you into a conversation. I know I've hurt you, so I want to go at your pace."

The coldness falls away to what looks like resignation as she slumps into the seat back.

My pulse breaks into a wild frenzy. "I mean it, Nora. I'll keep no secrets from you. Ask whatever you want. Yell, curse at me if you need to." The thought of bleeding my essence out to her cracks across me like a whip of terror, and my chest aches— but I'm going to keep my word. "I just want to make us work again."

Her gaze breaks. Shatters really. What looks like sorrow swirls in the dark edges of her eyes. It makes me want to cry.

I watch her chest heave with a broken breath, and a frown mars her beautiful mouth. "Why?" she asks.

The one word is loaded with hurt. I feel it radiate off her. It spears right into my chest, splintering apart in me and my shoulders sag.

"Why?" she repeats it, and her eyes water. "Why did you just leave me?" Her lip trembles and she breaks my gaze. "Did you not think of how badly it would hurt?"

"I didn't." The admittance is a whisper. I look down at my lap, and my pants blur. "I'll say it again, Nora. I'm so terribly sorry."

"I looked for you." Her voice is a whimper, making the remorseful ache in me grow. "I tore that house apart, hoping that you were there...," she sniffles, "Hoping that you finally wanted me."

"I did." I dare to look up. When I do, my heart crumbles apart. Her gorgeous face is streaked with tears and knowing I'm the cause of them releases a wake of pain down my body. "Nora." I pound my fist on my thigh, "I still want you." My teeth grit, and tears fall down my cheeks. "Damn it. I wish I hadn't fucked this up because I *do* want you."

She covers her eyes with her hand, and her forehead pinches together.

The sight has my soul straining for her even more. "I really, really do. I want to give you everything. All of me."

Her hands join the trembling. "I want to believe you." She dabs at her eyes. "But how can I trust you again after everything that's happened?"

Shrugging, my frown matches her. "I don't know," I say softly, as her head jerks up. That couldn't be the answer she was expecting. "I'm not going to bullshit you, Nora. I've done that enough already."

She nods, picks up one of the napkins I packed, and wipes at her nose.

When she doesn't speak, I take it as a blessing to continue. Rubbing my hands down my thighs, I wipe away the sweat that's formed and present the only offer I have since I've majorly fucked up the one that mattered most. "I'm not asking for your love or trust, Nora. I had them and lost it." My voice croaks. "I'm asking for an opportunity to gain it back."

Her head lowers.

I do the same, hoping to catch her gaze. "Can you do that? Can you give me a chance?"

"I—" She pauses. Her eyes dart around the car. "I'm not sure."

It's not a no.

That's what I tell myself while my heart plunks away. I ball my fists and wet my lips. "I'm not going to make promises. Trust me, I'm overflowing with them, but they won't mean anything to you. But I will say this. Have we ever done this before?" I wave my hand at the space between us. "Have we ever once had a heart-to-heart about how we feel about each other?"

She shrinks into the seat and shakes her head.

"Well, we're doing it now, and that has to mean something."

At least, I hope it does.

"Maybe," she sighs. "I guess we have one more date to find out." Her voice is timid, but what it releases in me is a well of optimism.

One more date.

At first, she was unsure she was going to do all of them, but she is now. I count my blessings. It even makes me want to smile.

"Now," I lean forward some, "How about that wine?"

"Oh." She puts her hand up and shakes it. "Bentley…"

"What?" I cock my head.

"I'm... uh... I'm not really hungry anymore."

"Honestly," I sigh. "I'm not either. Here, give me your plate."

She hands the paper plate back. I slowly pack up our items one by one. After that's done, I replace the basket, then move to my second part of the date by opening the door and sliding out the car.

"What are you doing?" She dips her head to lock eyes with me.

"Stepping outside." Moving to the back door, I open it, pull out a blanket, then close it. With the plush blanket draped over my arm, I hunker down and look at her. "Come with me?"

She scowls. "Why?"

I hold back an eye roll. "Just come on."

"But it's cold." Her arms fold across her chest. "I'm not dressed warm enough."

"You can have my jacket if it gets too chilly. Besides, I thought you liked the cold."

Her lips pucker, then she gets out of the car.

The nip in the air circles around me as I pace to the front of the car and sprawl the blanket over the hood.

Nora, seeming hesitant, looks at the blanket then looks at me. "What's that for?"

"To protect the paint." I point, softening my voice. "Don't be scared, have a seat."

A second passes but after that, she slowly climbs on. Her arms hug around her legs as she balls herself up.

I sit sideways, spin myself around, then give her a closed-mouth smile.

"So?" she shrugs. "What do we do?"

"Look at the stars." I point to the glittering sky as I look up. "Out here, there's no light, and we can see everything."

Looking up high, a soft gasp escapes her, and I know she's instantly as mesmerized by the sight as I am.

Scanning the inky blanket above us, I search. "The little dipper, right? That's the one you look for, isn't it?" I lower my frame and point it out to her after I find it.

"Oh… oh, yeah." Her voice perks up. "It is." She pauses, and her head plays a game of bob and weave, then she points. "You like the bright ones, correct?"

Resting my arms on my knees, a grin breaks across my mouth. "Yeah."

We lock eyes and almost… almost… laugh. Her smile, however, is short-lived. One of her brows wrinkles. "Bentley, a small part of me wants to believe I can trust you again. I just don't think I can."

I rock back further on my tailbone. "Then let's try to start with tonight." Moving closer to her, I close some of the gap, but make sure not to touch her. "Talk to me, Nora. Ask me anything."

She takes a deep inhale before pushing it out. "Break down the real reasons why you left."

The answer is so clear, and contempt runs down my spine as I say it. "Because I'm fucking stupid."

For the first time since we fell apart, she giggles, and my pulse quickens. "I'm figuring that out, but go on."

I take a deep breath and wring my hands together. "Because I didn't think I was good enough."

"You were for me." I can barely hear her voice, but the sadness running through it is strong. "You were always good enough for me. Every time I saw you, you were the only thing I wanted."

"Fuck." I scrub over my face, my chest swelling then blowing out from the unbridled confession. Tears well up my eyes. "Why was I so blind?" I look up at the sky. "I swear to God, Nora, after I got done being with you, I knew you were the only one I wanted for the rest of my life, but I… I felt like I ruined you. Tarnished you. I've spent so many years fucking meaningless people, and you were always on a pedestal. I didn't want you caught up in my filth." An ache spans across my sternum as I hang my head. "Not when you deserve so much more. I couldn't live with that thought. That's why I left."

"Because I meant *too* much?" I look over, and she's crying.

I shake my head, my heart melting at the sight of her. "No. Not too much… everything. You're everything, baby." Her soft gasp breaks more of my soul open. "I mean, damn. Kissing you was my wildest dream. I meant it when I said you're my fantasy come to life."

Her eyes widen, "I thought it was a spur of the moment thing?"

"Ha! No, far from. You made all my dreams come true that night. The only difference was, up until that evening, I was too hesitant to reach for you." Heat grows underneath my clothing as I rub at the nape of my neck. "Just about every time I didn't call you back, was because I didn't trust myself around you… I wanted to protect you, Nora."

She sighs, fire awakening in her gaze for the first time since tonight. "I don't need protection, Bentley. All I wanted was you. I can't tell you how many times I cried when you didn't call me back." Closing her eyes, she pinches the bridge of her nose. "I always assumed you forgot about me and spent the night with someone else."

"Sometimes, I did spend it with other people." My shoulders knot with the confession.

No bullshit.

I won't go into details, obviously, but I won't pretend I wasn't a major asshole several months back. I try to soften the gross admittance. "But you were always there. I was always thinking about you."

"I thought I never even entered your mind half of the time we were apart." Her lips pinch together, and she shakes her head. "I had no clue."

So many misunderstandings.

My shoulders sag. "Looks like we didn't know each other as well as we thought," I smirk, but it's competing with a frown. "Now, I had no idea you cried over me."

Her spine slouches. "Too much, even when I tried to move on." She clasps her fingers together. "I did so many things to try and forget you. I actually went out with Trevor because of you."

"Wh-what?" My heart plummets to my feet.

She nods. "It was at Rich's party."

"I remember that night."

"I thought you were going to kiss me."

I swallow past the lump in my throat, vividly recalling how

hard my pulse throttled in my neck while I dipped towards her mouth. "I almost did." My head drops. "I chickened out and needed some liquid courage."

"When you didn't come back, I went to find you." There's sadness coursing through her voice, and it's shredding my heart into pieces. "When I did, you were…" She looks away. "Kissing someone else."

"Oh fuck." I barely hear my own words. Shame slashes down my body in quick strokes. "You saw us?"

She nods and sniffles.

"Oh, Nora…" My chest deflates with a sharp exhale. "I was coming for you, but she stopped me. When it happened, I figured it was a sign that I should leave you alone, so I did. When I saw you left anyway, I didn't think you wanted me."

"I did want you. I thought *you* didn't want me." She looks at the field dead ahead, and her voice is quiet. "I left crying."

"God." Sickness strikes at my stomach. I have to slouch over for a breath. "I'm so sorry."

"That was the night I told Tessa to set me up with Trevor."

I sigh hard. "Fuck. Nora, I…" My frame rocks a few times, seeking comfort.

If I hadn't been such a fool, she never would have been hurt by him.

The hurt I saw in her eyes the night I picked her up at the diner was because of me. I rumple through the top of my hair, remorse hacking away at my composure.

My voice is unsteady. "I'm so sorry for my carelessness and lack of courage." I resist the urge to hold her, because that's what I want to do. I want to kiss her into oblivion while begging for forgiveness—to mumble my apologies against her sweet mouth. Instead, I pound my fist on my knee. "If I'd been braver, you wouldn't be going through this now."

She hugs herself tightly. "I could have said something too. Tessa told me over and over again. Instead, I just sat in sadness. I was a coward too."

"No. You're brave." I lean closer to her. "Showing me kindness after all the times I hurt you is the bravest thing I've ever seen." Lowering my head, I stare deep into her eyes. "I'm sorry for abusing your heart, Nora."

My words garner a reaction. Tears trickle down her cheeks, but I swear there's a small smile on her face. It's barely there, but I see it. She nods and wipes at her cheeks. "Thank you."

"Don't thank me. Don't thank me for giving you the apology that will never be enough."

"Wow." When she looks at me, her eyes are soft and rounded. "You really know how to say something in just the right way." This time, a broad smile pulls up her mouth. "Say more things the right way to me."

Looking down at her, I return the smile. "As you wish."

I utter every utterance that tugs at my heart... and they are numerous. Each time I'm granted a smile, I fall deeper into her, and our conversation flows more easily.

Time stops, but we don't. We continue to talk. We discuss it all. All the times we held back, our confusing flirtations and maddening attraction, how we kept each other up at night, and more importantly, all the times I hurt her. We fill each other in on the missing pieces to form a complete picture.

When I see it, our portrait is misshapen and marred, but we finally have something—understanding—and it begins to settle in for us both. Despite the flaws I've added to our masterpiece, I feel a peace pulse between us. The sensation only grows as we continue to trudge on.

There are tears along the way and innumerable apologies tumbling from my lips, but we keep going.

We talk until, at last, she's laying down, curling up on her side with droopy eyes.

In the crisp October air, we reacquaint ourselves better than ever before. We do it until the sun begins waking up from behind the earth—and while I know we still have a long road ahead of us, I can't help but feel that for once, I might have a shot at this. I might have a real chance of making Nora Davis fall in love with me all over again. Only this time, it won't be unrequited. I'm going to love her back, and I'm never going to let her go.

Chapter 31

Nora

Tonight, my heart is thumping in manic pulses, and for the first time since Bentley and I fell apart, I'm not fighting it. I'm enjoying the sensation.

It's our last date—but inwardly, I'm hoping it's not. After our talk last week, I couldn't help but change my perspective, and I even accept some partial blame.

Yes, the fuck and dash was wrong, and the hurt it left still twists deep in me, sending out a reminder it won't go away soon. But everything leading up prior to that? I'm wondering if things would have been different if I'd been more honest with him—if I'd actually told him he was hurting me instead of acting like I was fine every time we met up.

I'll never know the answer to that, but I'd like to think we would have avoided so much confusion and hurt if I had. Moving forward now, I can tell he's different.

The Bentley that's been taking me out seems so unsure at times, full of penance, even a little sad. Nothing like the fast, brash playboy I've associated him with being the last two years. Bentley was right when he said we didn't know each other as well as we thought. Seeing this side of him tangles up my heart, threatening to make it his captive more than ever before—but I'm not ready to tell him that. There's just enough hurt mingling through me to kill any sort of confession.

Maintaining the secret of these topsy turvy feelings remains my one goal when the doorbell rings. I can do this. I just have to maintain control of my headspace. After smoothing out my ponytail one last time, I take the deepest breath of my life and open the door.

He looks like the man who has always driven me wild, only a little bit better.

I'm greeted by dark wash jeans, and a gray sweater with a black collared shirt poking out the top and bottom. The cut of the shirt shows off defined pecs and a tapering waist.

When he smiles, warm and wide, my knees weaken. "Hi, cutie."

Breath sticks in my lungs. It's the first time he's used that endearment in a while, and the way he's saying it tonight—soft and sweet—warms my heart.

A blush creeps up my body. Tucking a loose strand behind my ear, I duck my head, desperately trying to conceal my heated face and pleasured smile. "Hey. Are you ready?" I slide outside and shut the door, thankful the moon won't expose my pink cheeks.

"Yeah." He bobs his head and steps aside, his sign he's ready to escort me to the car.

As we walk, part of me feels terrible at the expectancy flooding through me. He's been spoiling me the last two dates, and now I'm waiting to see if he's gotten me anything. *Maybe chocolate.* There's a brand of chocolate I spoil myself with every now and again. He's obviously been observing my preferences over the years more than I realized, and I'm wondering if he's gotten me another 'favorite' food.

Those thoughts flit away when Bentley comes up to the passenger door. He wraps his fingers around the handle and freezes. I know something's up when he gives me an odd look, almost like he's in pain. His eyes are tight, and his throat bobs with a swallow.

My fingertips bite into my thin purse strap as I look at him.

"What is it?"

His lips tuck inward, his chest rising with a huge breath. "I'm just hoping you like it."

"Like what?" My head cocks.

He pulls open the door, then dashes around to his side, not giving me a chance to question him further.

My brows knit together at his strange reaction. With caution, I make my approach to the car and peer inside. "Oh my—" My legs shake. I clutch one hand to my heart, the other on the door frame. "Bentley...no." The words are weak.

Sitting in my seat is a Gucci handbag. It's small, with the two bold metal G's displaying on the accessory. All I can do is stare at it, my jaw dangling open.

It's not until Bentley closes his side of the door that I jolt back to reality.

"Is it going to keep you from getting in the car?" I hear the tease in his voice. "If so, I'll take it back."

With shock coursing through my veins, I reach out but stop short. I keep my hand suspended in the air for a moment, unsure of what to do.

"You can touch it, you know. I bought it so you could use it."

The words pull a reaction from me. "Oh, I know, I just—" Admiring its short rectangular shape and the gold link chain for a strap, I pick it up and cradle it. A sigh slips out. "Bentley." I duck, entering the car. "You really didn't have to—"

He waves his hand at me. "I wanted to buy you something nice. A thank you for being an amazing person and for putting up with my stupidity for over two years. Do you like it?"

I gasp. "Like it?" The question is ridiculous. Looking down at the item in question, my fingers brush over the threading that creates a Chevron pattern. Warmth floods through my chest. "I love it." The words sound more like a gentle breath.

"Good." His response is tender. It causes more warmth to radiate through me and quickens my pulse.

He doesn't say another word. Starting the car, he drives out the parking lot with a light smile spanning across his face.

Tonight the silence doesn't feel right. We're not even a

block from home before I have to break it.

"Where are we going?" I ask it while running my index finger across the top of the handbag, relishing in its buttery softness.

"Guess it's a night for Italy. There's an Italian place I like to eat at, called Roma's. Have you ever been there?"

I shake my head, and I can't stop smiling.

"Well, that's where we're going. I've made a reservation. They have good wine, make a mean veal Piccata, and have the best bread in town."

"Oh." A thrill travels up my spine. I was so wrong about the dates. He knows how to plan them and never fails to impress. "That sounds wonderful."

"Great." His white teeth gleam in the darkness, and I can tell that tonight, we're going to be acting more like our old selves—I like that.

I'm snuggling into the seat back, delighted by that fact when he slows the car.

"Well, look at that." His voice rings with curiosity. "Someone's set up a little carnival at the lot." He points to a lot that was supposed to be a mall before the project failed. Now it's just a huge space in the middle of town. "Check it out."

Neon lights contrast with the night sky, bright and bold as I look over. The lines of the Ferris wheel call for the biggest center of attention—various flashing of blues, yellows, and reds acting like a beacon in the darkness. It widens the grin on my face.

"I spot some food trucks. Hmm." The car slows even more. A few cars zoom past as he pulls closer to a curb.

Glancing at him, my pulse taps hard against my neck when he gazes deep into my eyes. Mischief and humor are swirling in them tonight.

I swear he flicks his eyes down to my mouth, but I'm not certain because it's so fast. He leans forward, and I catch a hint of that scent I love. "How set are you on Italian?"

"I mean…" I flip both palms up and shrug.

His eyes snap to the field, then back to me. "Would you be willing to switch it up for some fun and a funnel cake?"

"Do you even *know* what a funnel cake is?" I point to his

ripped torso.

He tilts his head back and laughs. "Please." One eyebrow wrinkles. "With regards to junk food, I could put you to shame any day." He leans closer, and there's peppermint on his breath. "I just don't do it often."

He smells delicious. The struggle to not close my eyes, inhale, and get lost in his scent becomes very real. I fight against the impulse and win, yet my head draws closer to his. "Bull crap." I'm staring at his mouth. "I could eat so much junk food it would fold you under the table."

"You're on, sunshine." A smirk stays affixed to his face as he whips the car into the lot and finds a spot to park. "I know a fancy Italian dinner is quite the sacrifice to make, but maybe loosening up is better for us, huh? Besides, we can go there on our next date." His eyes flash wide in a look of embarrassment after he says it, and I know he's caught his blunder.

That sweet, innocent presumption makes me smile as I slide out of the car and into the chill biting through the air. The weather is changing fast, and we'll probably have our first snow soon. It's way too evident when a breeze crawls through the knitting of my shirt. I shiver, wrapping my arms around me.

"Here." The car beeps while Bentley locks it, and he passes a fleece jacket my way. "This ought to help."

Shrugging into the coat, I'm thankful for its warmth and for the way it smells—I'll be in heaven all night, but I frown when I notice there's only one. "What about you?"

He waves his hand in dismissal, "I'll be fine." Propping his hand on the top of his head, he starts off our brisk pace. "I'll warm up once I win all the stuffed plushies for you."

"Okay, sure." My eyes roll. "You won't be winning any because they're all rigged."

"Hmm..." His brows waggle, and a confident swagger takes over his stride. "Wanna bet? They call me the Carnie Breaker."

"The what?" A giggle slips out.

"The Carnie Breaker. You should know that." His walking slows, and his lips part. "Actually... we've never been to the fair together, have we?"

I shake my head, bundling the coat around me. "That's when you usually go home to see your parents."

He chuckles. "I guess I forgot. Anyway, they call me the Carnie Breaker because I can win at any game." There's a light in his eyes as he talks. "My sister loves me. Every year I win all the games for her. We leave with a car full of plushies, and I mean the big ones!" He holds his arms out, demonstrating the size of the larger ones, the ones nobody wins.

I pucker out my lips and walk in silence.

"Still don't believe me, huh?" He fishes out his wallet and pays for our entrance. After we step further in, he gestures for us to go to the games area. "Pick any one out."

He's so confident it should be painful because I know these games are going to crush his dreams. I fold my arms across my chest, shooting him a look of doubt. "Any of them?"

"Any." His eyes go wide, and a smile tugs at his mouth, then it falls. "Well, except the basketball. They bend the rims in. It's impossible to win those."

"Oooh, okay." I sigh, shake my head, and rake over the area. The first thing I spot is the bottle toss game. There's a giant hot pink zebra pinned to the net above that's calling my name. "The bottles." Then I point to the plushie. "I want that one."

"It's already yours, sweetheart."

He's not even looking my way when he says it. His head is down while peeling out a few coins, but I can see the confident smile plastered all over his face. He's so sure of his victory while he says it, and it's so damn sexy. "Let's go."

I'm trying not to laugh as he barrels his way through the small crowd, charging to the game that's going to be his demise. Growing up, my dad always tried to win this game for me. His strongest throw at most would topple over maybe two or three, and there's six.

I bite back another giggle and press my lips together, creating a hard line. "You're wasting your money." The words leave me while coming up beside him. He's just finished paying and is holding one of the balls in his hands, tossing it from palm to palm.

"Ha." Humor dances in his gaze, and I'm loving his mood

tonight—it's putting the dazzling lights around us to shame. "You just watch, cutie."

"Sure." I fold my arms across my chest and briefly look skyward.

He winds back his hand and...

POP

A metallic clatter echoes in the air, then each bottle falls on its side. Every damn one.

I jump into the air, tossing my arms overhead. "Oh my God. Oh my—" I laugh. He does too. "But how?"

"See? What did I say?" Looking at the person running the game, he points to my prized zebra. "That one for the beautiful lady, please."

Beautiful... A hoard of butterflies takes flight at the base of my heart. I almost don't need the jacket, thanks to the heat flooding my body. The word is so simple, but when it comes from Bentley, it decimates more walls, making bricks of protection fall off from me. At this rate, I'll be falling in love with him all over again.

A giggle slips out while wrapping my arms around the hot pink animal. "It's even cuter up close." My fingers stroke the fluffy mane, admiring the oversized cartoon eyes. I look up at Bentley through my lashes, awe for his skill stirring a touch of lust in my veins. Anger made me forget how effortlessly sexy he is, but tonight it's on full display, and it's reeling me in—the hook attaching deep into my soul. "You really can win any of these?"

"Mmm-hmm." He widens his stance and cinches his arms across his chest. "Pick another animal. I'll make sure you leave with it."

His smugness uncages my hormones, allowing them to feast on my dirtiest fantasies—watching him knock down those bottles was the start. The windup, his muscles flexing... Bentley is wrecking me tonight. I try to downplay the need for him by scanning the booths.

Ring Toss is just down the way. A multi-colored pastel alpaca sways in the breeze, and I point, "That one."

Pocketing his hands, he gives me a smirk that could make my panties catch fire and jerks his head. "Let's go get it."

I follow after and watch as he wins it. Then he snags the monkey I want at the shooting game, then the teddy bear at the darts, and the puppy dog at the water gun booth.

Each time he succeeds, he grins at me in that boyish way, and each time, my heart sways toward him. The sweet looks he gives me bends my soul, melting the ice surrounding it until I'm aching to know all of him—because I'm starting to see it now.

Bentley is beautiful.

A beautiful, sweet mess that I want to keep close to my heart. I think Tessa is right. He never meant to hurt me, and there's comfort in that.

I hum in contemplation while alone.. He's gone to the car to drop off my animals and get us more junk food. I'm uncertain how I'll stomach anything else.

Between the games, we've feasted on candy apples, hot dogs, ice cream, fried Twinkies, pizza, and cheese sticks.

When he rounds the corner with a funnel cake, I groan. "Are you serious?"

He tips his head back and laughs. "Giving up?" He digs his fork in and takes a bite. "I told you I could eat more than you."

"I think so." My stomach rolls with sickness overload when he takes another big bite.

A spark catches in his eyes, and he points. "Let's go on the Ferris wheel."

Ferris wheels. Known for secret handholds and stolen kisses. I'm so not ready to kiss him, but the thought of being near him—smelling that fresh scent and brushing against his natural body heat accelerates my pulse.

I nod. We walk that way while he polishes off the funnel cake.

Loading in, I wonder if he will sit close or drape his arm along the seat back. He does neither. He maintains a respectful distance, resting his wrists on his thighs. The consideration stokes desire in my veins.

Tonight, Bentley Harris is hitting nothing but high notes for me.

My fingers clutch to the plastic siding with the wheel's slow ascent. I do like this ride, but the sway of the seat does make me a little nervous. Blood whooshes in my head with another rock, but it dies with a new distraction. The sound of Bentley sighing. It sounds contented, and the expression on his face is amusement.

"What is it?"

He leans back, propping one ankle over the other. "I was thinking that this is full circle for me. The last time I was on the Ferris wheel—" His voice fades away as he looks out to the skyline.

Ivy? He mentioned her once at Flambé's, but we never got to talk about what happened. My finger trails over my jeans. "Her name was Ivy?"

"It was." The acknowledgment isn't laced with pain. It comes across as tepid and distant.

Intrigue prods me along as I lower my voice and tilt my head. "Do you mind telling me what happened?"

"Not at all, but actually," a short pause ensues as the wheel finishes its first lap. His gaze snaps over to mine, a light smile playing on his mouth, "You already know what happened."

I blink in shock. "I do?"

A pensive look pinches at his eyes. "Do you remember that high school 'friend' I told you about months back? The one I said who'd been cheated on?" His line of vision falls after I nod. "That wasn't a friend. It was me."

"*Oh, Bentley.*" Dismay shoots through my heart, and the jacket no longer blocks the chill in the air. I shiver and frown as I recall him mentioning the name of the girl who cheated on his friend—I hadn't realized it until now. "I can't imagine how that made you feel."

"I'm fine now, really." He chuckles, shaking his head. "It took way too long, but I finally got over it and realized I allowed her lies to fuck me over for no reason. There was never anything wrong with me, and thinking I could hurt her by being with meaningless people was stupid because she never cared. It never affected her—the only person I was hurting was myself."

My brief time with Rich floods my mind, and I only sought his comfort after one time with Bentley. I imagine what it would be like to spend years with someone only to have it thrown back in your face. And from what I remember, Bentley told me the circumstances were extreme.

Who knows what I would have done. All the times I saw Bentley with different women flashes in front of me, and now I don't see it as him having a good time. I see him chasing—pursuing away the temporary to forget what was possibly an ever festering source of pain.

How can you spend so much time with one person and know so little? A deflated sigh trails out of me as the wheel slowly reaches the top. "No," I finally reply softly. "Not stupid, Bentley. Just human."

"Thanks, Nora."

The way he speaks my name is light, and there's a slight twinkle in his eyes as I glance over. It competes with the skyline behind him. My breath is lost when his eyes sink to my mouth, and the tone of his voice lowers. I can hear the love in it, and my knees squeeze tight.

"And just for the record, screw ups and all, you were always different, Nora." His forehead nearly connects with mine. "Always. I didn't know it at first, but from the first day I met you, you were always... right here. " He pats his hand against his heart and smiles.

My chest expands, taking in the sweet words, and the key he's been using so desperately to open up my locked heart slides in and turns, unlocking me. It's decided right then and there—I want to date Bentley, and I want to fall in love with him all over again.

But I don't want to tell him. He has me, but I need more time. Unlocked does not mean healed—there are still a few bandages that aren't ready to come off yet.

Scooping a piece of hair behind my ear, I turn my head away, not trusting myself with the look he's giving—the tenderness in it teases at my secrets. A breeze encapsulates me while we sit at the top, watching the city lights dot the dark horizon. With a smile curling up my mouth, a minuscule piece of my hurt falls away, and a small confession leaves my lips.

"You were always different for me too, Bentley." My eyes stay locked on the city while the thumping of my heart betrays my calm outward appearance. When I hear him hum with happiness, I still can't look because he's always been my Achilles, and right now, I'd surrender at his feet.

We finish our ride in gentle quiet, and then he takes me home.

Walking up to my front door, my pulse remains wild, quickening and skipping every time we swagger too close to each other. The breezes that bothered me earlier fail to draw out a shiver as tender heat runs through my body.

I doubt I'm the only one feeling the pull between us. While undoing the lock, I sense the same heat radiating off him, hitting my back. It's causing a weakness in my knees—one I wasn't sure he'd be able to resurrect.

When I spin around to face him, I hug the Gucci bag to my chest and hope it conceals the fact that I'm struggling to breathe.

One side of his mouth tugs up, and his gaze flies to the plushies creating a small pile outside my door. "Are you sure you don't need help getting them inside?"

"No." I sound breathless, but I can't hide it. "I'll manage, no problem."

He doesn't say anything, and we stare awkwardly at each other—small smiles working on our faces—minute shuffles occurring here and there. I have so much I want to say, but I can't think of a way to form them, so I say nothing.

More time passes. At last, Bentley pockets his hands and blows out a huge puff of air. "So that was our third date."

"It… it was." My line of sight drops to the concrete, and my neck tightens. *Please. Please ask me out.* Part of me feels like I should be giving him the green light, but after all the tatteredness I've been through, I no longer know how to put myself out there. All I do is pray, my palms clammy and hot.

"So… uh…." He takes an audible swallow. When I stare at him, his body looks tense. "May I pick you up next Friday?" He shuffles side to side, and his eyes tighten. "That might be presumptuous. I mean…, if you don't want to—"

"I do." The words burst out before I can even think about stopping them. One of my shoulders pulls up, and I say it again—much calmer, "I do. I'd really like that, Bentley."

His body relaxes, and those Grecian eyes look like a dream with the twinkle emitting from them. I swear they glow. "Good," the word breathes out. "I'll pick you up at the same time."

"Okay." My reply is a near whisper, and my eyes slide down to the keys in my hand. *I'm happy*. Then I look up and shriek, stumbling back.

Bentley is right in front of me—his eyes half-closed—his lips puckering out while his head strains forward. It has all the signs of a goodnight kiss.

"What-what are you doing?" One of my hands shoots out, blocking him from me. Dating this man and kissing him are two different things, and there's no way in Hades I'm ready for a kiss. My cheeks light on fire. "Bentley—"

He holds his hands up, and he's laughing. There's no sound, but his smile is ear to ear, and his shoulders shake. He takes a step back. "It was just going to be on the cheek, I swear it."

"But still…" My arms fold across my middle while my stomach somersaults. "I—"

"It's okay, Nora." One more laugh slips out. He unpockets his keys and walks backward for several paces. He comes to a stop and stares at me for a moment. His eyes travel up and down my body—his admiration far too evident when he speaks. "Good night, Nora." The way he utters my name is love in itself. He turns on his heel and walks away.

I watch him until he disappears into the darkness. I do so because I'm his captive… bound to him and everything he does, and I always will be. He'll always command my attention, even if I don't want him to, but I'm done trying to fight it.

I listen to the motor start, then the crunch of tires as they roll through gravel, and finally the engine's rev as it takes off on the main road.

With blood roaring in my ears and weak knees, I rest my spine against the front door. Moonlight beams high and bright tonight, and as leaves rustle, I bring my fingertips to my mouth and sigh.

"Yeah…" I whisper it into the cold air, witnessing a battered leaf break loose from a tree and flutter away into the distance. My heart is doing the same—breaking off even though it's bruised. It's rushing to a new experience, and my destination is Bentley.

Forgiveness for the wrong he's done over the years sweeps over—drawing me deeper into its currents, trapping me in its riptide. I'll never make it back to shore, back to the contempt I had for him. And I don't want to. I can't think of anything better than owning this man all to myself.

But make out sessions…?

Let's just say he has a little way to go.

Fragments of You

Chapter 32

Bentley

I'm leaving the grocery store with all my meal-prep necessities. All the calorie-heavy foods I've been throwing Nora's way are starting to show. That carnival night didn't help. When I woke up, the first thing I did was decide to jump back on the bandwagon for health. Letting myself go and getting a gut won't do me any favors in wooing Nora.

The sliding doors for the exit pull open, and I come to a halt.

Fuck.

It's Rich. We lock eye to eye, and he stills too. It's the first time we've seen one another since his birthday. Looking back on it now, I realize I was a total dick to him, even body slamming the guy to the floor. Safe to say, I owe him a big kiss to the ass.

I release a big exhale and move outside. My nod is stiff while I make a slow approach. "Hey."

He pockets one hand and nods back. "Hey." His tone is flat. I don't blame him, but he doesn't walk off. He remains staring at me like he knows I have something to say.

A few people maneuver around us. We shuffle to the side,

removing us from the line of traffic. Once we're in a corner, I clear my throat and look up. If I'm going to cut the bullshit and lies out of my life, this includes Rich. Life changes must be an all-encompassing act, not a compartmentalized one—but that doesn't mean it's going to be easy.

My fists tighten around the loops of the plastic sacks. "I owe you an apology." Even my voice crackles while I say it, but I don't stop. "I was... upset that night." My gaze flicks to the ground. "I said and did a lot of things I shouldn't have. I'm sorry."

"Eh." He halfway shrugs. "It was a heated moment. Body slamming you into the wall probably didn't help. Maybe our conversation would have been better if I hadn't done that first."

"Maybe. Anyway, sorry I was a fuckwad. I wasn't thinking straight."

"It wasn't that big of a deal." He rubs at the nape of his neck. "I ended up leaving with some trick anyway." A soft chuckle escapes him. "She was all excited. I guess she thought Nora was my girlfriend and was put out when she saw us together."

The girl.

I vividly remember the girl who was upset about them being together.

He moved on fast. Still, though, there was no denying what I saw in his eyes that night. Rich was falling for Nora. My shoulders sag, and I frown. "Well, maybe Nora would have been your girlfriend if I hadn't interfered."

"Ha!" He smiles. "Probably not." Folding his arms, he leans against one side of the brick enclosure. "Nora never felt like she was mine. Besides, can't have my dick in one place too long."

There's a look in his eyes when he says it. It seems like a wince he tries to shield from. While I know he does like his freedom, I'm wondering if he's hiding his emotions even now. I say a prayer he'll be alright and won't hate me forever.

I lurch when he pats me on the arm, and his features darken.

"I don't know what you did, but know this—"

My heart races when his gaze narrows, and he leans forward.

"Fuck her over and hurt her like that again, and I'll kill you. She's a nice girl."

Yeah… he liked her. A lot. My swallow is hard, and my pulse refuses to calm down. I nod. "Understood."

"Alright." He brushes past me. "Cool. See ya, Bent."

"Yeah." My grip finally loosens around the grocery bags, and I begin the trek to my car. "See ya."

I'm just about to step onto the paved parking lot when his voice catches my ear.

"Football party. My house. Next Friday. Food and drinks."

I look over my shoulder, and he's the Rich I know—loud.

"Bring a side. And bring Nora, as your date, of course."

A smile tugs at my mouth. "Thanks. I will."

"I was right, you know." He points at me. "I always said you were the one who was going to get castrated." He smirks. "You're too fucking soft."

Replacing my sunglasses, I laugh and nod. "Yeah, I guess I am."

And I wouldn't want it any other way.

Fragments of You

Chapter 33

Nora

"How's it going, Ladies?" Bentley asks, coming out of Tessa's house.

A few weeks have whizzed by since our 'last date.' He's been around more and more—slowly infiltrating and integrating into my life in the best way possible. Gone are the occasional dinners and movies. We've seen each other every night this week at his request, and when I told him I planned to meet with Tessa this evening, he asked to come along, even offering to make dinner for us.

He strolls over to the hot tub, resting his hands on the plastic siding. "Everything alright out here?"

"It was." Tessa says, skimming the base of her wine glass on the water. "Then you came out." The tone is dry, but mischief cracks in her silver gaze.

Bentley chuckles. "Then I'll make it a point to come out and check on you more often." He cocks a grin. "It's the least I can do after you wouldn't let me get in the hot tub."

I slink back into the water, relishing in the excellent wine and easy banter. Tessa and Bentley have been getting better acquainted by spewing off light-hearted insults and quick remarks.

"Don't come at me," Tessa raises her hand, pushing it towards his face. "I told you this is a girl-only zone."

"Ha." He tips his head back. "If anything, my abs would bless these waters. Consider it a loss."

"Man," Tessa's lips pucker and she snuggles down in the water, "I knew you were bad, but I didn't know you were this full of bullshit. I feel sorry for Nora."

Mirth sparks in his eyes. "Just dishing out what you're serving."

"Well, I didn't ask for shit." She points to the house. "Go back in there and finish your baked chicken or whatever it is you're making us."

"Baked chicken?" Bentley's face scrunches up. "That sounds nasty as hell." He takes a step back and nods his head upward. "I grill thank you, and I'm damn good at it."

"Doubt that." She gives him a lackluster once-over. "With your physique, I can't imagine you eat anything fun."

"You're gonna eat those words, Tessa. Just wait." He turns his head towards me, and his eyes change. They soften around the edges, and I don't miss the long gaze he gives my mouth. When he speaks, his voice is just as tender. "You need anything, sweetheart?"

I shake my head. "Only dinner, whenever it's ready."

"It will be done soon. The chicken is resting. I'll come back out when the asparagus is cooked." His mouth pulls up one more time, and he leaves.

I settle into the water, paying attention to the line of his shoulders and the sexy swing that occurs with each step. My fingers tighten around my wine stem after catching a peek of his ass—his black jeans fitting tight enough so I see its lifted shape and the twitch it makes while walking.

My legs squeeze together, and I squirm in the water even after he disappears.

"You're happy." Tessa's voice shatters my diversion.

Taking a sip of wine, I use it to fuel the warmth already running through me. "I am." My mouth lifts up. "You like him too."

"Eh." She shrugs in that fake dismissive way. "I do, but

don't tell him that." A small tug works at her mouth. "I'm glad it's working out. I thought you two were going to kill me." She turns her attention to the mountain view and rests her head back.

My smile fades, and looking at my friend, guilt needles away. I haven't been the person she's needed these past few months, but Tessa's stuck around and hasn't complained much. My shoulders rise then fall with a sigh. "Hey, Tess."

Her eyes whip in my direction. "What?"

"I'm really sorry." My throat goes dry, uttering the words. "You've done a lot for me these past months. Paying back my bonus, saying I could live with you, and trying to give me advice with Rich and Bentley." I wiggle my toes under the water, breaking eye contact. "I've been pretty bratty, and you didn't deserve that." A weak, apologetic smile finds my lips. "I'm sorry for the way I've acted."

Waving her hand in a nonchalant way, her lips pucker. "Don't worry about it. That's life, Nor. One of these days, I'm going to go through something, and I'll be a less than ideal friend." A lightness finds her gaze. "But you'll stick around because that's what we do for each other. We'll always have each other's backs… won't we?"

I nod once and look deep into her eyes. "Always."

She clicks her tongue. "That's my girl." Her head tilts, and she examines me, setting her wine glass down. "Speaking of Rich, are you sure going to his house tomorrow is a good idea?"

My brows knit together. "Why wouldn't it be? From what I know, there's no bad blood between any of us."

"Nor…" Her slim shoulders lift. "You slept with him, and that can't be—"

"I didn't." I think she finally believes me when her lips part open in what looks like shock. After taking one more sip, I set my glass aside. "I know it looked like we did, but we really didn't. We made out, once." My voice deflates. "But I couldn't get over Bentley. I honestly never slept with Rich—he was a friend."

She sighs. "Wow. I'm sorry I didn't believe you."

"Don't feel bad." I chuckle through my nose. "It's not like I gave you a good reason to. I was being stupid."

"Well…" Her brow arches. "You *are* stupid." She smiles after she says it. "I'm glad, though, that you had enough sense not to sleep with that douche."

I lean back in the water. "Me too."

"And I bet Bentley feels better knowing that. He talked to me about it and told me what Rich said. Something about it being too late. Poor dude was crushed by the idea that you'd been with Rich."

"About that." My shoulders tighten, and shame pounds away at my tummy. "I… uh… I haven't told him that I never slept with Rich."

"What?" The water disturbs and ripples with her upright jerk. "Nora, why not?"

I clasp my fingers tightly under the water, feeling my pruny skin. "I've wanted to. I just don't know how to approach it. It feels weird to bring it up."

"It's weirder *not* to." Her eyes widen. "Nora, you have to tell him. Bentley will take you, either way, I don't doubt it, but it has to bother him. And now you're going to Rich's house—I can't imagine how he feels about that." She blows out a big puff of air. "For him to go and bring you says a lot about him. He deserves to be told."

The mere idea makes my gut flood with nausea and anxiety. My body tenses. "But–but—"

"Do it, Nora. If you care about Bentley, and I know you do, tell him."

My head drops, and I stare at the water. "Okay."

Tessa's right. After all these years, I'm admitting she knows more about life than I do. *I need to tell him.* And I am going to.

But how?

Bentley shuffles in behind me and closes the door to Rich's house, surveying the area. "Wow." A low whistle rings through his teeth.

It's balls to the walls packed, which isn't a surprise given the person who's hosting it—all his parties are wild.

Tonight, my awareness of Bentley is high. Every breath and shuffle he makes wrap down my core, making my attention his prisoner. When his shoulder brushes against my back, goosebumps prick along my skin. The contact makes me yearn for more. I almost wish he'd wrap his arm around my waist and fit me against him, but I'm still unsure if I'm ready for it.

"Hey, there's Rich." Bentley raises his hand and waves.

My pulse unravels more, beating at a nervous pace when I spot our host across the room. He's got a beer in one hand and a blonde hanging off the other. I haven't seen or talked to him since his birthday. I'm sure that hasn't left the best impression on Rich. If he decides to give me the cold shoulder, I'll take it with a smile, or at least try to.

His dark gaze meets mine. When a faint smile presses on his mouth and he waves, my shoulders loosen.

My neck tenses when Bentley's muscled torso glides against my back.

"Maybe we should scrounge up some food, huh? Talk to a few folks?"

I nod, desperately trying to swallow past the lump in my throat and follow after him.

We load up our plates, which includes way too much spinach dip for me and raw broccoli and carrots for him. Making the rounds, we chat with a few people, together, like an actual couple—both of us interjecting our opinions, including and referencing each other regardless of whether the subject matter is large or small. Our presence is unified. In a public setting, it feels strange, but also like my missing piece that's finally been found. Bentley's companionship is a fragment in my life, but one of completion—he just makes life sweeter.

I'm relishing in our growing oneness sometime later when Bentley elbows at my arm.

"Would you like a drink? I know we don't have a DD, but one whiskey won't hurt us." The look in his eyes strike at my chest, calling my name, asking for surrender. "How about we share one?"

I stroke at my neck and say yes, butterflies soaring high in my stomach.

He taps me on the nose and heads off.

My eyes rake up and down his body as he walks through the crowd. He smiles and says hi to people along the way. Everything he does quickens my pulse.

Yep. I smile, watching him disappear around the corner, into the kitchen. *My Achilles, for sure.* A serene sigh leaves me, and my eyes close. Tessa is right, beyond right—to be honest... I *am* happy. So damn happy I have to stop myself from crying every time he picks me up or offers to come around.

I sink into it all, finally allowing myself to wonder if this is it. If Bentley Harris is the one that I'll share all my dreams with. My head dizzies at the thought, but something overtakes it all. I open my eyes and focus across the room... my throat chokes itself. *Shit.* A blonde is strutting toward the kitchen. She vanishes into the room and doesn't come out.

Neither does Bentley—for a long while.

I count to ten for the third time, and nothing happens.

Nervous tension floods through my limbs. It erases the feel-goods that have been climbing in my body. Pressing my back into the wall, a sick tickling of my gut tells me something's wrong. *He's ditched me again.* Drinks don't take that long to pour. My emotions are flooded with the sinking reminder of every time he's ever left me in the lurch.

Flashbacks hammer away at my serenity, busting apart our new foundation. All I can remember is how he ditched me the last time for a blonde, and the way it shredded me apart. I fear it's happening again, that he's forgetting me for someone else.

But there's a difference.

This time, I won't be destroyed. If he's decided to flounder around, I'm done. And I'll tell him that right here, right now. I'm done being a fucking doormat.

I push off the wall and swim through the crowd. Each beat my heart makes slams at my ribs because I'm scared. Even with the determination rushing through my veins, letting go for good won't be easy—not when I've enjoyed everything we've been.

When I reach the wall dividing the kitchen, my fingers bite into my palms. I suck in a deep breath and hold it, grounding myself for an awful sight, one of him jamming his tongue down someone else's throat.

I round the corner and—

"Hey, thanks." Bentley is standing in the kitchen, our drinks in his hand. The blonde is here, but the space between them is a great divide. They're on opposite sides of the room, and from the looks of it, Bentley is making a wide circle away from her and saying goodbye.

My limbs go limp, relief and shame cutting through me at once. Hot tears hit the back of my eyes as I watch him. *I was wrong.* So terribly wrong.

"Hey, there you are." Bentley's voice catches my ear. "I was just about to come get you. Sorry it took so long. He ran out of solo cups, and all the glasses were dirty."

I have to look away as a stronger wave of shame ripples down my body, bathing my conscience and distrust in a shade of sinful crimson. Before I know it, tears are streaming down my face.

"Nora?"

I pat them away in hopes he won't catch on to how awful my thought process was. My shoulder flinches when he pats my arms.

"Sweetheart, are you alright?"

The sweet way he asks it makes joy catch in my heart. It combines with the guilt swirling in my body until I'm smiling, yet crying. "Yeah." I wave a hand in the air, still not able to look at him. "I'm fine, I just... I just..." I can't finish. The words choke up in my throat, and I sob—part happiness, part grief.

"Hey." He ditches our whiskeys, placing them on a short bookshelf, and grabs hold of my hands. "Something's upset you." Hooking an index finger under my chin, he forces my attention. "Is it this place? Do you want to get out of here?"

I shake my head, stopping my tears, joy flooding out the guilt. "It's okay. We can stay. I just thought—"

"Nora, I don't want to stay. Not anymore." Scanning his face, I notice tightness swirling in his gaze as he glances to one corner of the room. Sadness pricks at the corners of his eyes right before he tears them away.

I look over. It's Rich, and he's slowly migrating in our general direction. My heart plummets to the floor, and Tessa's words replay in my head.

You need to tell him.

In the last few moments, I think Bentley and I are both having wicked memories of the past. I squeeze his hand back, pulsing it in my grip, and nod. "Why don't we go?"

"Alright." He ushers us for the door, and we move together, united, like we've been all night.

When we step outside, most of the chains of our ugly past fall off, but there are still some things that need resolving. I feel remnants of it while Bentley walks with his head hanging lower than usual.

A lump lodges in my throat, but I know what needs to be done. I slow our pace by grabbing onto his arm. "Bentley."

His head bounds up. "Yeah?"

"I uh…" My voice gives out, and I try again. "I have something I want to tell you." I can hardly hear myself, thanks to my pulse thudding in my ears, but I keep going. "It's about, Rich."

"Oh." It sounds like pain lacing through his voice. "You know what, Nora. I don't think—"

"No, Bentley, I'd really like to tell you. I—"

"No!" His lips press down, and he shakes his head, refusing to make eye contact. "I don't want—"

"I never slept with him." The words blurt out.

His vision jerks over to me, and he stops walking. His eyes are wide while he takes a few blinks. "What?" The question is so quiet, I hardly hear it.

I take a hard swallow and repeat it. "Rich and I, we never slept together. I made out with him once, but that was it."

His chest shakes with a breath. "But he said—"

"I don't know what he told you, Bentley." My brows furrow. "But we never slept together." I go quiet, and my line of vision falls to the road for a second. "I couldn't forget about you."

There is no time to think. He scoops me into his arms, pressing me tightly against his chest, so tight I hear his racing heart. "Fuck." The word breathes out.

My pulse taps hard against my neck as he runs his hands up and down my back. I take the moment to breathe in his scent—my favorite smell in the world.

"God, Nora." He sniffles, and I know he's holding back tears. "I wasn't going to mention it. After what I did, I had no right. But—"

My ear presses into his chest with the deep breath he takes. I lift my eyes, even though the only thing I can see is his chin. "But?"

"Knowing he hasn't had you. That what you and I had still meant something to you, even after all the stupid shit I did. I just…" He sobs, and my heart breaks with the sound. "Fuck. I don't deserve you."

The words knead their way into my soul. I nuzzle against him, losing the battle with my own tears.

"Nora." He says my name so gently it could put a soft breeze to shame.

My eyes close at the soothing pitch. "Hmm?"

"I have something I've wanted to talk about."

"What is it?" I whisper.

"Be my girlfriend." He tightens his arms around me, and my blood hums in my ears. "Please, baby. Be mine. I know that's a lot to ask of you, but I can't live another day not having you."

I crane my head back, a smile lifting my mouth, the full sight of him blurring thanks to my happy tears. "I was always yours. Now, will you be mine?"

"Already am." His fingers stroke the back of my hair, and he lowers his head.

My eyes close—lips meeting in a gentle, heartwarming kiss. The pressure is faint, but the undercurrents of love infused in it send my body melting against his hard planes. The light groan he tries to hide at the back of his throat unbinds my reservations. I try to deepen the kiss, only to have him frustratingly pull away.

"Bentley," I say in a near plea, "Please. Don't stop."

"Slow, huh?" The gentleness in his eyes and voice steals my words as he tucks a loose tendril behind my ear. "Trust me, I'm dying to go faster, but let me show you how different I am now.

You're mine, but allow me to fully earn the rest of your heart with my actions, and let's go slow for your heart's sake."

The first sprout of love blossoms in my heart, and I'm amazed at how perfect he's becoming. He believed himself to be broken for so long, but the end result is a soul more tender than I could have ever asked for.

And for that? Yes. He's more than welcome to stop our kiss... this time anyway.

Chapter 34

Bentley

"Did you put enough butter on the popcorn?" Nora's voice carries through my house and into the kitchen.

Flicking off a light, I return to the living room, shaking the bowl as I go. "Just enough for my taste." I wink.

Her nose wrinkles. "That means it's going to be gross."

"Oh, be quiet." I plop down on the opposite side of the couch, placing the bowl between us.

"Humph." She tentatively tries one piece and sticks out her tongue. "Gross. Put more butter on it."

"No way." I grab a handful and point to the TV. "Stop griping about my health decisions and start the movie."

She grabs one of my couch pillows, rests into my arms, and presses play.

We're watching an action flick, but my focus isn't geared for that. Tonight, each fiber in my body thrums hard for her—straight down to my heartbeat which is following her rhythm. We've been dating for four months, and our time together has been slow but phenomenal. This sensation, however, is different. I'm so in tune, it's like I'm holding her for the first time.

Any shift she makes robs me of breath. Her slight twitches elevate my pulse, and the scent of her shampoo has my head floating. There's a heavy temptation to start massaging her shoulders and initiate something more, but I opt not to.

My main focus has been relenting control to Nora and acting only when I think she's ready. At present, she's far from doing anything intimate, so that's out right now. The wait is torture, but I'm fucking hand-over-fist in love with Nora Davis, and I'll wait two lifetimes if that's the time for her.

Bearing my focus to the screen, I stamp down the fever crawling up my body. After a bit more struggle, I manage to focus on the movie, and we enjoy the flick in comfortable silence.

Later, I look at the bowl, and the popcorn hasn't been touched. It seems like Nora didn't like it at all. I decide to hog it and bring it to my lap.

"Oh no!" Nora's voice shrills out.

My handful of popcorn falls to the floor with a jerk. "What is it?" I sit upright, juggling the bowl, struggling not to drop it while resting it on the coffee table.

Frantically tugging at her ear, she looks down at the sofa. "My earring. It's gone. I know I had it on when I got here."

Oh shit. It sounds like she's about to cry, and I can't handle that.

"It was a gift from Granny."

"Oh, God." I plunge my hand down into the cushions, my heart accelerating. If she's talking about her mom's mom, Granny Norrie, then it's a big deal. Nora was named after her and loved her even more than her own parents. She saved everything she got from her, straight down to the envelopes that Norrie sent to her on birthdays. We have to find that earring.

"It's alright." I force my hand deeper, hitting the wooden frame. "We'll find it. I'm sure it's in the couch."

She scrambles to her hands and knees, searching with me.

We're both digging, poking, and prodding, sweeping our hands back and forth. Anything to find that piece of jewelry. No luck, but the lack of it doesn't seem to discourage us. If anything, our panic increases. I'm sitting sideways on the couch, elbow deep, praying to find this item when Nora gasps.

I look up.

Fuck.

We're nose to nose, eye to eye. We both still.

In the midst of our search, we've navigated toward one another again, and the adrenaline is heavy. My arm is extending past her body, and my eyes have a clear view of her luscious lips as they pant.

That sight is testing every ounce of willpower I have. I glue myself in place and hide how turned on I am from being so near to her. I don't want to push Nora away by being forward because from now on, we're going at her pace. We went at mine once, and I fucked it up.

I keep my eyes locked on hers, but when hers dip to my mouth and her chest strains for a breath, I know she feels it too. She feels what's been chasing down my blood all fucking night. That sets my heart ablaze and sends my head humming.

We're both huffing for the smallest amounts of air. When her lower lip trembles, she steals the rest of my willpower, causing it to shatter.

My throat goes arid. "Nora…" I gasp, and I'm almost whispering. "Nora, I-I…I'm going to kiss you. I'm going to kiss you so fucking hard you're going to forget whose air you're breathing."

She takes a broken breath, and her voice is a whisper too. "Do it."

My mouth collides over hers. I moan, cupping her face, gripping my fingers in her hair. The connection isn't gentle, it's greedy, but God, how I love it—love her. But tonight, even with my long agonizing wait… even with the impulse pounding through my blood begging me to strip her bare and lay her beneath me, I make the choice to only kiss. This is all about Nora.

But that doesn't mean it's easy.

Another moan leaves me, and my fingers tighten in her locks. I battle away the thought of tugging her onto my lap. It's hard, but I'm winning, just barely. Thank God, I don't have to fight long.

She moves, and I find out I'm not the only one wanting more.

In one fluid motion, she pushes me till I'm seated on my

ass, with my back against the cushions. She climbs on top of me, straddling my thighs, throwing her arms on either side of my shoulders. My eyes squeeze shut while I relinquish control and focus on her.

She's wild—grinding me, moaning against my mouth, her hair cascading around me. Her chest rubs against mine. I feel every curve of her. Her build molds against me perfectly, and I want to explode. Long fingers dig into my neck, and she breaks our kiss to nip at my ear lobe. Gripping my hands around either of her thighs, I dig my fingers into Nora's jeans. It's small, but I'm at least taking the liberty of caressing her beautiful legs. She peppers supple lips up my neck, and my heart pounds between my collar bone. I moan, wanting to pop off in my jeans. Instead, I praise her.

"God. Nora. Yes. Your mouth feels so good, baby. Kiss me just like that." My words spur her on, and she whimpers, clenching her legs around my hips. "Sweet Jesus, you know what makes me feel good."

Her fingers grip into my shirt. She pulls my shoulders off the cushions and turns my torso, angling me so I'm nearly lengthwise with the couch. Her palms press against my chest, and I know she wants me to lay down. I comply.

Her hair curtains around us in our descent. I see the dark passion flooding her gaze, dilating her pupils, burning out the nutty color, making it pure hickory. She looks so lost and consumed, but I still don't want to push her—I want to be different this time. Better.

I shift my head back, exposing my neck, and she rubs against me. When her hands snake under my shirt and connect with my abs, I grit my teeth, searching for restraint. Her soft lips kiss, nip, and lick, making a delicious trail from my collar bone to my ear. She repeats the pattern, ice-picking away at my control. I grip her middle harder and groan.

My cock hardens, and my breath is labored as I fight not to feel her up. Then... she grinds on me—grinds on my cock and fucking moans. Her beautiful body rocks against me, and she creates the most gorgeous pressure that has me singing her name.

It's also battering my sanity, ravaging it to Hell. Much more of this, and I'll be flipping her underneath me and stripping her down, and that's not what tonight is about.

"Nora," I say her name just before I'm pushed off the cliff of control.

She doesn't stop at first. She bucks against me, creating more pressure. I cup her face and force her attention.

"Hey." I smile, loving the way she nuzzles our noses together. My thumb strokes over her cheek, and I sigh. This moment is heaven, but I won't go fast with her. Never again. "Let's find that earring, huh?"

Long delicate fingers trace along my jawline, and she licks her lips. "Forget the earring." Her lips overtake mine before I can refuse.

At first, I give in, clawing at the control I almost lost. But then she bites my ear lobe, and I want to buck and thrust against her. I reclaim myself with a grunt, then slow her down. This time my voice isn't as soft. "Nora, if we don't stop now, I won't want to stop at all."

Her chest raises, and her eyes search mine, but only for a moment. Two dark eyes trail down to my mouth, and she leans in. "Who said anything about stopping?"

If that isn't a green light, then I don't know what is. This time when she kisses me, I give in. I kiss her back desperately, allowing my tongue to dip in, tasting her exclusive sweetness. My fingers skim up and down her body, burning me as I feel her. I catch the hem of her top and slide my hand under it. I stroke the skin around her hips. Each brush against her elicits a moan out of me and makes my cock jerk.

She tugs at my hair, sucks my lower lip between her teeth, pressing her chest into mine. The way we fit against each other completes my soul, and I shiver. She nips my lip one more time, then undoes the first two buttons on my shirt. Her tongue glides over the exposed area, and my cock overloads. I become rock hard and yank her down by her hips, moving her over the bulge in my jeans, overloaded with the need for her to ride it any way she likes.

Our kiss breaks, and we're panting. When our gazes meet,

they're both fire. I can see hers—feel mine. Brushing fallen hair away from her face, we stare motionless. It's like we know we're about to plunge into the waters of no return together, and our anticipation is going to drown us.

My chest struggles for a breath, and my question is a whisper. "Bedroom?"

She nods, sliding off me.

I stand up, cradling her in my arms as I walk the length of the hall. Her laboring breaths trail down my neck as she tucks her head under my jaw.

Her soft lips trail kisses along my heated skin, hardening my cock some more. I think what follows is going to be easy— that when I place her down on the bed, we're going to fuse into each other with zero reservations.

Until I cross the threshold of my room.

Her frame stiffens, and all breathing has stopped. I know she's afraid of what happened last time. The silent fear is practically seeping out of her skin.

I place her down gently, knowing that if I place her down on the bed, replicating our last time together, her fears will deepen.

After her feet hit the floor, her breathing kicks up again. It's choppy, with each ragged intake cutting at my heart. Fuck, I messed things up the last time.

Standing in front of her, I put one hand on either side of her shoulders and meet her gaze. "Nora," I draw her in close. "I promise you. I'll still be here in the morning." Her head drops, but I hook my index finger under her chin and tilt it up. "I'm not going anywhere." The resolution coursing in me works itself in my voice. "Not ever again. The first thing you see when you open your eyes tomorrow will be me."

She rests a hand on one of my biceps and nods. "Okay." I can hardly hear it, but there's a smile on her lips when she accepts my hand and follows me to the bed.

I reverse our circumstances by laying on my back first. She makes a slow approach, and I widen my legs apart, letting her straddle me. My blood rushes when she yanks my shirt up and rakes her nails down my stomach. I lurch halfway off the bed, hissing at the glorious marriage of pleasure and pain.

I murmur her name, sinking into the way it sounds. "That's it, Nora." I grasp around her waist, bearing more of her weight down on me. "Pin me down. Take whatever you want, baby."

A sigh leaves her, and she places her hands over mine, guiding them down to her shirt, like she's asking me to take it off. I help peel it over her head then toss it to the side.

Moonlight shadows over her body, and my pulse accelerates. I haven't forgotten how beautiful she is during this time of not having her, but seeing it all over again obliterates my restraints. I coast my fingers down her midsection and curse. "Holy fuck. You're so damn gorgeous."

A paled-out crimson hits her cheeks, but my excitement falters when she jerks her head to the side and frowns.

My brows pinch together, fresh worry bubbling in my chest. "What is it?"

"Bentley..." Her voice trembles. She doesn't look at me, and her head hangs forward. "I'm scared."

Her words shoot right through me like I'm made of paper. *I made her feel this way.*

If I hadn't been a coward, she wouldn't be here, preparing to give herself away while scared shitless. I reach up, tangling my fingers in her hair.

"That's my fault, Nora." She finally locks eyes with me. I can see the sadness even in the muted pale light. "I'll never be able to apologize for that enough. But..."

Gently grabbing her hand, I unclench her fingers and place her palm on my chest, over my heart.

Her eyes widen.

"Feel that?" I ask her. "Do you feel how fast my heart is racing?" I smile when she nods.

I secure my hand over hers. "I'm scared too. I'm opening up in a way I haven't done in so long, and that scares me." This isn't a one-night stand. What we're about to do is a commitment... one I plan on keeping for life. Reaching up, I soothe my thumb over her cheek. "Let's be scared together, huh?"

Her shoulders loosen, and a smirk paints across her mouth as the fear rubs out. When she speaks, it's the voice of a vixen and not my sweet Nora's. "Undo your pants, pretty boy. Let me see that cock."

Whatever I said, I said it right, and thank fuck, because I like this version of Nora. My heart hammers hard against my ribcage. When she yanks down my jeans and boxers, I hold my breath. The sheets fist in my grip when she frees my cock, and glides down, positioning between my legs. With sin lighting up her eyes, she holds my dick in her palms and gives it a few pumps. I hiss in anticipation.

Those sugary lips I love so much wrap around my cock, and her tongue hugs the underside. It feels like a dream. My head falls back as she slides down the entire shaft, and I feel my tip touch the back of her throat. I twitch underneath her, sealing my eyes shut.

Her head bobs up and down, drawing me up more and more with each pass. She sucks up to the tip and swirls her tongue around the head, and moans.

"Shit, Nora. Fuck yes." My body tenses as she repeats the whole sequence—bobbing for a moment, then slowly coming to the top to savor me. Each time she does it, more of me unhinges, and she doesn't stop.

I feel like I'm her damn instrument, and she's playing me, drawing out the sounds she wants to hear while I grunt and sing back to her, telling her how amazing she is.

My spine arches when her mouth sinks down, and she takes in all of me again, her nose hitting my skin. With gentle hands, she cups my balls and flares out her mouth, somehow taking me in a little bit more while she massages my nuts.

A groan spills out, and my fingers thread through her hair to hold her in place. "God, baby, you suck so good."

My voice gradually raises until my shouts echo in the room when she deep-throats me at a rapid pace, making it grow until that familiar tingle takes hold of my balls.

"Nora." I apply some pressure to her head with my one hand slowing her pace. "Nora." It's all I can do to say her name as that tingle churns to a hardening that's begging for release. "I'm about to cum."

She releases me from her mouth, wrapping her hand

around my length. "And? What's wrong with that?" The fear I heard moments ago is gone. Now, all I hear is a mistress who's in control.

I fucking love it.

My chest tightens with affection as I pass my fingers across her cheek. "I don't want to go off in your mouth, sweetheart. I *want you.*"

I can barely comprehend what happens. She moves so fast, it could be a blur, but she's up on me in a second.

"Fuck!" I shout when she slams down on me, taking every inch available. My cry nearly drowns out her own squeal of pleasure. However, the twinkle of a lust dancing in her eyes grips itself around my heart.

"Then have me, pretty boy." Her reply is throaty and hot as fuck. "Go off in me."

"Damn," I smirk, enjoying the hum in my ears and the way my cock feels inside her. "You're dirty." My hips buck up once, and she bites down on her lower lip, her eyes rolling back for a second. "Ride me, Nora." When she rocks, I pant. "Ride me hard."

She does. This love of mine rides me harder and faster than I've ever been taken in my life. Her tits bounce with each slam she serves, the headboard hitting against the wall with each thrust. Her hair follows the rhythm of our sex as it swings around her. We curse, hiss, scratch at each other, and scream until I'm sure the neighbors hear us.

Her pace quickens to manic and lost. My fingers bite into her hips as I relish in the feel of her riding me—of her sliding up and down. It steals my soul, making my body hers and only hers. Her love erases the memories of anything I used to be. The longer she glides the length of my cock, the more I want to cry at how much I fucking love this woman.

Nora. She's truly perfect.

The thought shatters me, pushing me to an earth-bending release. "Fuck, Nora." That sweet name chants off my lips as she clenches around me in her own release. Each pulse of her milks me dry.

My body relaxes after the long-awaited release, and I revel

in how satisfied I feel right now. "Nora…" I'm huffing. "Oh my God."

She rolls off me, and I can tell she's just as spent as I am. "Was it okay?"

"Okay?" My voice spikes. "Babe." I turn into her, capturing her mouth for a long kiss. "Holy shit. I've never…" I stop. I don't want to compare her to anyone else because she isn't like anyone else. Instead, I soothe over her hair, loving the way it's tousled itself. "That was incredible."

"Good."

I laugh when her cheeks pinken.

"Really?" I ask, running my hand up her back. "You'll ride me like that but blush afterward?"

My kind of woman.

Dirty, but only for me and only in the moment.

I go to take off my condom.

"Shit." I don't have one on. "Nora, we didn't use a condom." I haven't made that mistake in years, but that's what Nora does to me. She makes me lose control.

She rests her hands on my chest and yawns. "Good. They ruin the moment." She winks. "Besides, I'm on the pill."

"But—"

"Don't spoil this by making it complicated. It will be fine." She gives me a quick kiss. "Also, I enjoyed it too. Can we please… uh… do it again in the morning?"

I sigh, dropping the condom issue, smoothing over the crown of her head. "Absolutely, yes."

"Good." A smile tugs at her mouth.

I stop her when she tries to roll away by catching her elbow. "What are you doing?"

"Going to sleep." She sounds confused.

"So we are, but you're not going anywhere." I snuggle up next to her, keeping her head on my pillow, throwing the sheets over us both. My eyes become heavy.

"Um," her body tenses when I put my arm around her. "I thought you didn't snuggle."

"I do, with the right person. And you're that person." I hitch my leg over hers, making us flush against each other. "I want to hold you, Nora. I want to fall asleep with you in my arms, and I want to wake up seeing your face and then watch you wake from my kisses."

She nuzzles her face against my chest, flinging her arm across my body. "Seriously?"

"Seriously." I sigh. "Go to sleep. I promise to be here, and we'll wake up in each other's arms."

"I can't think of anything better."

It's the last thing she says before falling asleep. And for the first time in years, I hold someone with meaning in my arms, stroking over her long locks—a smile stuck on my face as I fall asleep after peppering her forehead with kisses and drowning in contentment.

I was wrong.

Love isn't a big, fat lie. Love is incredible, and I'm a lucky bastard to have Nora's affection. Dozing off, I'm convinced I'm the luckiest guy on the planet.

Fragments of You

Chapter 35

Nora

Birds chirp this morning while I stir. Not only that, there's a pair of warm lips, gently sucking on my left nipple, and a hand expertly massaging my right breast. Turns out Bentley wasn't kidding when he mentioned waking me up with kisses. I keep my eyes closed, not wanting to spoil this because, dang... it's amazing, and the best wake-up call ever.

I fake heavy breathing, pretending to be asleep so he'll continue. His index finger swirls around my nipple. It pebbles under his touch, and my legs clench together, unable to deny the reactions he pulls from me. Still, I keep my eyes closed.

He chuckles, and it's deep and sleep-ridden. "I know you're awake, Nora." The grog in his voice is heavy and a further turn-on. He bites at my nipple and moans. "Your thighs tightened. Twice now."

A small laugh slips out. "I didn't want to disturb you." My fingers find his hair, and I comb through it, admiring how the gel has softened.

"Mmm." His sound of contentment rumbles, and his tongue flicks my breast.

A shudder releases up my spine.

"I have no intention of slowing down." He slowly travels kisses up my body, pecking and sucking away at my shoulders, collar bone, neck, and jaw. I groan and squirm each time he lavishes me with his affection.

His lips find mine, and the connecting kiss is supple, igniting a slow flame that wraps up my body. It makes me melt, calming yet quickening my heart all at once. My eyes flutter open. My pulse fails when his heavy eyes, full of sleep and sex, lock on mine.

He smiles. "Good morning."

"Hmm." Raising my head off the pillow, I return his light kiss. "Good morning."

"Did you sleep well?" The question is mumbled against my mouth while he kisses me in between the words.

"I did." I nip at his lower lip. "Did you?"

"Oh, God, yes." He brushes his nose against mine before kissing me once more. "Too good. If this is how I sleep after having you, then you're mine every night."

"Well," I smirk. "Then I'm yours."

"Damn straight."

His lips overtake mine and what ensues is a make-out session—a gentle, half-awake one that makes me wetter than our hard and fast crash last night. I feel his cock grow against my inner thigh, and my body rolls, pressing into him as much as I can, loving the way his tight abs grind against my stomach. He pulls away, and I'm panting. His light eyes brim over with a carnal gleam.

"My turn." The corner of his mouth raises. My breath stalls as his hand coasts down my body, gripping into my waist. "Spread your legs, sweetheart."

"Bentley."

He's already halfway down my body, lapping at me occasionally with his tongue. The objections die on my lips, and my legs open for him on their own.

He expels a heated breath onto my clit, and a heaviness settles in my sex. I'm already throbbing with need for him, and he hasn't even touched me. I whimper as a finger pushes in and curls upward.

"So fucking wet for me," he purrs. "Always making me feel good, baby."

My eyes close, and I moan. I would never have guessed it, but Bentley is full of compliments during sex. His vocal adoration fills me with abandoned lust, fueling our sessions, making me feel like the most incredible woman alive. He revs my engines in all the right ways. I'm groaning his name as two more fingers cram inside. Then his mouth connects with my clit, and he sucks.

"Oh. Shit! Shit, Bentley." The world blacks out. I squirm and buck. My back arches when he pins one of my legs down to the mattress, keeping me open to him.

He works me with his tongue, his fingers pumping me like a sex god, in a way that renders me his captive. I'm begging him to go harder and faster, even though my lower half fights to stay open.

He doesn't disappoint.

The performance he gives to my body makes my nerves short circuit and go haywire. I scream his name, my climax coming into view. In seconds, he's built me up and is now going to unravel me—and I'm going to let him. I'm going to let the man I once thought so out of reach capture my soul in ways I could never foresee. I start to pant.

I hear a dark chuckle when his mouth leaves me. "That's it, baby. Come for me." He dances his fingers inside, and the sensation is pure unlawful pleasure. "Come on my fingers. Squeeze me hard, draw me in."

My body obeys his words, and my legs tremble as I come— sweat dews on my skin.

He moans, no doubt loving the effect he's had. I hear approval in his voice. "Fuck yes. Amazing. You're perfect, Nora, and you're mine. All mine." His mouth returns, and he alternates between licks and sucks.

I want to kick my legs, but they're too weak. My body shakes instead, and I mewl.

The hand that was pinning my leg down leaves, and he finds mine. He brings it to his hair, threading my fingers through it. "Pull on my hair, baby," he orders it, still pumping me. "Show me how good I can make you feel."

Again, I obey, tugging at it harder than I should, but he seems to like it. The moans leaving him fill my ears, making me dizzy. I'm building up again, and it's incredible, but I need more. My pussy aches for *him* to fill me. "Bentley." I can barely utter his name. "Please." It's a plea. "I…I need you."

"I'm yours." His fingers pull out, and he flies off the bed, going to his side drawer.

I frown when he rolls a condom on, but I don't say anything. Experiencing him without it was beautiful, and I will make it happen again.

I'm huffing in expectancy as he lays over me. My legs are shot, so wrapping around his back isn't an option, but I know it won't matter. He lines up, and I stop breathing, preparing to take in his fullness—one that's almost too much thanks to his size but also just right, but nothing happens. He doesn't move, and my blood stops.

"Bentley?" My brows knit together, and I wonder if something is wrong.

Two soulful eyes search mine, and his knuckles brush over my cheek. "I don't want you saying anything in return. You understand? Not a damn word."

"Wh…" Something of anxiety tingles in my veins. I find my voice and prod him on. "What? What do you mean?"

A fire sparks and ignites in his gaze. He takes a deep breath and pushes it out. "I love you, Nora."

He slams into me before I can reply, and I scream. He slams in and out. His pace is fast. The thrusts so hard and quick all I can say is his name, but his words have found their mark, and I let them absorb. I spread myself wider and tilt myself up, accepting everything I can. My heart thuds in my throat when I hear it again.

"I love you," he says in rhythm to his slams. "I love you," he repeats it, and his voice cracks. "I love you," he cries.

The phrase doesn't stop, and his pace doesn't slow. Bentley keeps saying those three words even with his head slumped forward and his lips pressing to my neck. When he finally releases, he shouts it, despite that it's muffled against my skin. Then as he relaxes, falling into me, it's spoken one last time… softly.

"I love you."

Spent, exhausted, and sweat-drenched, I do as I'm told. I don't say a word. But stroking my hands up and down his back, I can't help but smile—because even though I'm not allowed to speak it, I already know how I feel about him, and I know what I would tell him.

That I love him too.

Chapter 36

Bentley

"**B**entley, are you ready?" Nora's voice floats into the bedroom of the cabin we're renting. "I'm starving."

"Yeah." Exhaling, I struggle to breathe out all the nervous energy sitting in my lungs. I look at the oval solitaire ring encased in the navy velvet box. "Shit." It's a good thing I can hardly hear the word—I don't need Nora catching on to anything. I've been planning this for months, and it needs to go off without a hitch.

Pocketing the ring in my thick wool dress pants, I make one more wish that she likes my plans. We're high up in the mountains but are still dressing up a little for tonight. All I've told her is that I've made reservations at the high-class french restaurant here in the ski village. We plan to walk there at Nora's request. My sweet love adores the snow, and I'll do anything to make her happy—especially on the night I plan to propose.

When I step out into the living room, I'm shocked she can't hear my thunking heart. It's beating so hard the pulse reverberates in my fingertips. My smile is tight, and I hope she doesn't notice. "Let's go."

"Great." She springs off the couch and grabs her purse.

"I'm famished." Feeling her ear, she pauses. "Crap. My earrings." Crossing the room, she pats my chest on the way. "Go wait outside. I'll be right there."

"Alright." Just as well, I'm nervous as fuck, and some fresh air would serve me well.

Pleasant brisk air brushes around me when I step out. The chill it causes on my neck forces me to breathe deeply, which calms me a little.

Right.

I pat the ring in my pocket, then take a big stretch, hoping to prepare for the night. I know she'll say yes. Our weekend here has been insanely awesome. This trip was booked with the intention of skiing and a proposal... skiing hasn't happened. It's been nothing but long sessions in bed.

Yesterday we even had our ski gear on. We were almost out the door when she gave me *that* look. The one where she bites her lip, cocks her brow, and trails her eyes up my body.

Her clothes were off in seconds, and we made love against the door of our cabin. Honestly, I didn't mind. The ski rentals were expensive, but I'd rather have Nora chanting my name any day, repeating that she loves me. Tessa told Nora that we sex it up too often, but I said we're only making up for lost time.

I'm walking away from the house, smiling about that fact... the one about me having her forever when the front door opens.

"Okay." There's a brightness in her voice. "Now I'm ready. I can't..." Her voice drops off, "Oh!" Now I hear surprise. "What's this?"

I look back, and Nora is bent down, lifting something out of the snow. My head tilts, and I close some of our distance, then squint to get a better look.

"Fuck!" I smack my forehead. The fucking engagement box has fallen out of my pocket and into the snow. A hard sigh leaves me as I stand across from her. "Are you fucking kidding me?"

When she looks at me, there are tears in her eyes. "Bentley...this-this is..."

"It is." I muster a smile and gently take the box out of her hands. "I'd planned to do this at the restaurant. That's the real reason we're going."

She covers her mouth with her hands, and they're shaking.

I love seeing her this way, even with the botched plans. In the end, plans be damned. All that matters is her. "Well..." I stroke my thumb over her cheek, pop the box open and take a knee. "Let's not allow the moment to be wasted."

Her eyes widen as I extend the ring up.

"Nora Davis—"

"Yes." Her enthusiasm echoes in the atmosphere, and she hops. "Yes!"

I laugh. "Now, wait." I hold a hand out in the air and wave at her to stop. "You have to at least let me finish."

"Okay. Okay." A large grin tugs at her mouth. She interweaves her fingers and bites her lip, looking down at me.

Everything she is, all the love that runs in my being for her, pours out. My body becomes hot, and I'm surprised the snow-encrusted ground beneath me doesn't melt. I speak, and my voice is dry but soft.

"Nora Davis, I love you. We've had a long road, and it hasn't been easy, but I love you. And I can't help but think that I always have." Her figure blurs as tears fill my eyes. "I'm your captive, baby, and I don't know how to live without you. Please. Make me the happiest man on earth. Be my wife. Marry me?"

"Yes." She grabs my hand and pulls me to a stand. "Yes, Bentley, yes."

"Thank God." Our noses nuzzle, and we kiss. It's long and tender, and I don't notice the nip that should be here in the air.

She pulls away, and there's that gleam in her eyes. They take in my frame, and then she shimmies against me. "How important is this dinner to you?"

I shrug. "I mean, I did make the reservation, but we could break it." A smirk paints across my lips, and I ask an obvious question. "Why?"

"Mmm." She bites down on that sugary mouth and arches her brow. "I'm in a mood to taste something else." With one hand, she grips her fingers around my cock.

It stands at her attention, already prepared to please her. I yank her into my arms. "Oooh," I growl. "Fuck yes. You're speaking my language, sweetheart."

She giggles. It grows when I sling her over my shoulder and walk. Her laughs and shrills fill the air, and her legs flutter.

My chest swells at the sounds of her joy, and I laugh too.

I carry her back into the cabin, preparing to become her servant for the night.

And I do.

I make love to my sweet Nora, praising and obeying her every demand until the sun comes up.

I do it all with pleasure, rejoicing in the fact that while I messed up so many times and stumbled in my journey towards her, that she somehow loved me—saw my worth even when I didn't see it in myself. This woman is the second half of my soul, and she's restored me from shattered fragments, making me whole. She's given me hope and shown me that love is real and not a lie. She's stuck it out with me, fuck ups and all, and I don't deserve her. I never have, and never will, but I don't care.

I love her, and I'll spend the rest of my life losing myself to her and her alone.

My heart will always belong to Nora Davis—soon to be Harris, and nothing can ever change that.

The End

Acknowledgments

To my love, R:
Once again, thank you for everything you do. From taking care of life, making sure I eat, or get writing time in, even forcing me to catch up on sleep when you see I'm exhausted. Thank you for allowing me to chase after my author dreams, and for sacrificing so much to make it happen. I couldn't do this without you.

Lee: AV: Sammie: Melanie:
You ladies are my rocks. From cheering me on, pointing out details, big or small that need to be changed, and laughing with me, thank you to each of you beautiful souls. My author journey shines brighter because of you. Thank you, a million times over. These books only exist because you inspire me to be better, and tell me I can do it.

My cover designer: Cat
Babe you killed it with this cover. I cried and squealed when I laid eyes on it—I'm still staring at it to be honest. Thank you for your beautiful work and passion. I just adore you.

My editor: Brian.
Thank you so much for making my words pretty, and for helping me craft a better story. I came to you with book that I loved, and not only did you nurture it, you made it bloom into something more beautiful than before. Thank you so much.

To my readers:

Thank you from the bottom of my soul. Writing is sweeter because all of you read my words, and love them. I can't tell you how much it means to have people out there reading my stories, and telling me how much they loved them. All of you make my dreams come true, so thank you.

More books by

Garnet Christie

About The Author

Garnet Christie is a romance author who loves serving up hot Alpha males who are searching for a true connection and looking to fall in love. When she's not writing, she's spending too much money on K-pop merchandise, drinking tea, eating chocolate, and avoiding falling asleep at a normal human hour.

Website: www.garnetchristie.com
Instagram www.instagram.com/authorgarnetchristie/
TikTok https://vm.tiktok.com/ZMeP1Ko9w/

Join my Facebook group: Garnet's Societea and catch all the tea to stay up to date.